Out of the ashes of the past
rose a haunting mystery...
and a love that could destroy a family

"Before You Go: One Dance."

He stood before her and she thought, *How could anyone have let this man go?*

One dance. It was a fair trade.

They strolled into the tent, transformed into a fairyland of ferns and white flowers, and walked onto the floor to the strains of "I've Got You Under My Skin."

After weeks of stealing glances and cherishing the simple sight of him, Meg felt overwhelmed by the intimacy of actual contact. This was it, her one moment of pure, permitted ecstasy. In a trance she swayed with him to the delicious, sensuous strains of the Cole Porter tune, played in a slow and sultry tempo.

I tried so . . . hard to resist . . .

The line hung in the air after the lyric moved on. No one was trying harder to resist than Meg. But it was a hopeless struggle; she was beaten down from the effort. She felt his cheek against her hair and his heart beating against hers, and she thought, *How can this be wrong when it feels so right?*

EMILY'S GHOST

"HIGHLY ORIGINAL AND EMOTIONALLY RICH READING . . . *Emily's Ghost* is pure and unadulterated reading pleasure . . . this outstanding contemporary novel is a veritable feast for the senses."   —*Romantic Times*

"I LOVED *Emily's Ghost*. It's an exciting story with a surprise plot twist."   —Jude Deveraux

"A WITTY, ENTERTAINING ROMANTIC READ THAT HAS EVERYTHING—a lively ghost, an old murder mystery and a charming romance."   —Jayne Ann Krentz

"An engaging heroine, a sexy senator, and a rapscallion ghost make *Emily's Ghost* an irresistible read."

—Susan Elizabeth Phillips

"Mystery . . . romance . . . intrigue . . . suspense . . . a ghost . . . *Emily's Ghost* has it all . . . a gripping novel of love and triumph. The paranormal events will give you chills and the beautifully expressed emotions will stir your heart."   —*Inside Romance*

"THIS IS A NOT-TO-BE-MISSED STORY OF LOVE, friendship and joy that transcends time and death."

—*Heartland*

ANTOINETTE STOCKENBERG

Embers

A DELL BOOK

Published by
Dell Publishing
a division of
Bantam Doubleday Dell Publishing Group, Inc.
1540 Broadway
New York, New York 10036

The trademark Dell® is registered in the U.S. Patent and Trademark Office.

ISBN: 0-440-21673-7

Printed in the United States of America

Published simultaneously in Canada

August 1994

10 9 8 7 6 5 4 3 2 1

RAD

For Mom S.

ACKNOWLEDGMENTS

My thanks to all those who helped me in the research of this book: To Dr. Howard Browne, a continuing source of medical data; to June Swan, Carol Reiff, and Police Chief Richard Blaisdell, all of Bar Harbor, for the local nitty-grit; to Fred Aleguas for his pharmaceutical input; to Barbara Schenck, a fellow writer, for her metaphysical expertise; to Martha Milot—*merci*!—and especially, to my brother-in-law, Chicago Homicide Lieutenant Richard Stevens, the *real* thing.

Readers who are interested in the 1947 fires that ravaged Maine will find Joyce Butler's book on the subject an excellent source.

Damaris, Steve, and John—where would I be without you?

CHAPTER *1*

Meg Hazard, shivering in the predawn chill, pulled the blanket up around her shoulders and said, "Money isn't everything, Allie."

Her sister laughed derisively. "Oh, *come* on." She threw her head back in a way that profiled her long neck and thick black hair to perfection. "The only ones who say that are those who have it and those who don't. And *I* say, both sides are lying through their teeth." She pulled her knees up closer to her chest. *"God,* it's cold up here. Was it this cold when we were kids?"

"Of course. We're on top of a mountain. In Maine. In June. You know the saying: In Maine there are two seasons—"

"—winter and August. Mmm. I do know. Which is another reason I'll take a job anywhere but here. You can't make any real money in Maine, and meanwhile you freeze your buns off trying."

Meg smiled and held one end of her blanket open. "Park your buns under the blanket with me, then. I *told* you to bring something warm."

She glanced around at the dozens of tourists sharing the rocky summit with them. Some were murmuring; some were silent. All were waiting. "The sun will be up in precisely— four minutes," Meg said, peering at her watch.

The two sisters huddled together under the pale pink sky, their breaths mingling, their minds in tune.

"Tell me *why*, exactly, I let you talk me into this again?" Allie asked.

Meg laughed softly and said, "I was just thinking about that. You were five and I was seventeen when I brought you up here the first time. You were so excited, you forgot your Thermos of hot chocolate. I had to drive us back for it—"

"—and Dad woke up and said we were crazy and if Mom were alive she'd give us what for—"

"—and then, when we finally got up here, you were mad because we weren't the only ones on Cadillac Mountain, so how could we possibly be the first ones in the whole U.S. to see the sun that day?"

"You told me we would be, Meg. I distinctly remember."

"So you stood up and told all the other tourists to please close their eyes because *you* wanted to be first."

Allegra Atwells looked away with the same roguish smile that had melted every single male heart that had ever come within fifty feet of it.

And then she threw off her blanket, stood up, and shouted at the top of her lungs: "Would everyone please close their eyes so that I can *finally* be the first one to see the sun rise in the United States? I'm from Bar Harbor, folks. I *live* here."

Virtually every tourist there turned in surprise to gape at her. Meg groaned and buried her face in her hands, and when she looked up again, a thin sliver of bright gold had popped up into the now bloodred sky, casting the first of its rays across Frenchman's Bay below.

Allie Atwells had probably got her wish.

"Twenty-five, and still the same," Meg said, leaning back on the palms of her hands and looking up at her sister with a kind of rueful admiration.

Allie stood defiantly on the rocky outcrop with her hands on her hips. The rising wind whipped her long black hair across her face and pressed the white shirt she wore against her shapely breasts. Her face—even in the early morning sun, even without makeup, even after an all-nighter spent deep in gossip—was cover-girl gorgeous, the kind that modeling agencies would kill to represent.

"Of course I'm still the same! How can I be anything else?" Allie said, throwing her arms up melodramatically. "I've been stuck in this godforsaken corner of the country all my life. I haven't *been* anywhere, *done* anything, *met* anyone. . . . Thanks to your nagging, I've done nothing but work and study, work and study, work and study."

Meg laughed. "And now here you are, six years, four apartments, two majors, and eleven part-time—"

"Twelve," Allie said with a wry look. "You forget I worked for a week at the front desk of the Budgetel before you talked me into coming home for the summer."

"I did that because finding a full-time job is a full-time job. Anyway, *twelve* part-time jobs later—and you have a degree. Think of it, Allie," Meg said, motioning to her to sit back down beside her. "A *degree*." She threw one arm around her sister and pressed her forehead to Allie's temple. "The first one in the family; we're all so proud of you."

"Oh, Meg," the younger girl said modestly. "It's not as if it's from *Cornell's* hotel school. It's no big deal. I still have to start at a pathetic wage in an entry-level job. A degree doesn't make me any better than you or Lloyd. It only means I didn't marry young the way you two did."

"Yeah, and I know why," Meg said with an ironic smile. "Because the minute you say yes to someone, ninety-nine other men are sure to cut their throats, and you can't bear the thought of all that blood on your hands."

Allie's violet eyes turned a deeper shade of perfection. "That isn't why I've never married, Meg, you know that," she said in a soft voice. "I just haven't found the right one."

Meg sighed heavily and said, "Whereas I, on the other hand, married my one and only suitor—and then lost him."

Allie shook her head. "Paul wasn't the right one for you, Meg. You know he wasn't."

Meg's brow twitched in a frown, but then suddenly she smiled and said: "Was too."

"Was not."

"Was too!"

"Dammit, Meg!" Allie grabbed a short brown curl of her sister's hair and yanked it hard, then said in a voice endearingly wistful, "It's good to be back, Margaret Mary Atwells Hazard. I've missed you."

"And I," said Meg softly, "have missed you too, Allie-cat."

They sat there for a long moment without speaking, content to watch the kaleidoscope of reds and pinks that streaked across the morning sky. On a good morning—and this was one of them—the view of the sea from Cadillac Mountain went on forever.

"Maybe you're right, Meg," Allie murmured at last. "Maybe money *isn't* everything."

Meg nodded thoughtfully, then stood up and stretched. "Let's go home, kiddo. We've got work to do."

Homicide Lieutenant Tom Wyler was stuck in a traffic jam as thick and wide as any he'd ever had to cut through back in Chicago. But at least *there* he had resources: a siren, a strobe, a hailer to warn people to get the hell out of his way. Here, creeping along the main drag through Ellsworth, Maine, he was just another tourist, without authority and without respect.

And without air conditioning. In a burst of economic caution he'd decided on Rent-a-Wreck instead of Hertz or Avis at the airport. The three-year-old Cutlass they gave him ran perfectly fine; if it were, say, January, he'd have no complaint. But he was dressed for the Arctic, which is roughly where he thought Maine was, and with the midday sun beating down on a dark gray roof on a hot June day, he felt like complaining plenty.

"Go heal somewhere else," his surgeon had advised him. *"Away from the bloodshed. Somewhere cool, somewhere quiet, somewhere where every citizen isn't armed up to his goddamned teeth."*

Wyler was shell-shocked, and he knew it. He needed time to think, time to heal, time to decide whether he even wanted to go back to the bloody fray. So he'd chosen a small, very small, resort town with a reputation for quiet evenings and grand scenery. He didn't need theme parks, topless beaches, casino gambling, or all-night discos. All he needed, all he wanted, was a little peace and quiet.

So why, having fled to this supposedly remote chunk of granite coast, was he feeling his blood pressure soar and his temples ache?

Because this isn't what it was supposed to be, he realized, disappointed. Because he'd pictured the route to Bar Harbor as a quiet country road lined with gabled houses with big front porches, and laundry billowing from clotheslines out back. Instead, he found himself inching past a more familiar kind of Americana: Pizza Hut, Holiday Inn, Dairy Queen, Kentucky Fried Chicken, and McDonald's, all vying with one another for his tourist dollars—that is, if the fella on the curb selling Elvis-on-velvet paintings didn't get them first.

Shit. He'd picked a tourist trap after all.

His disappointment lasted right through Ellsworth and over the causeway onto Mount Desert Island. The island, too, was pretty developed. The road that fed into Bar Harbor was lined with campgrounds and cabin rentals and, eventually, big motels perched high on a ridge to his right, presumably with views of the ocean he knew was somewhere to his left. The motels must be what had replaced the string of Bar Harbor summer mansions that he'd read were lost in the Great Maine Fire of 1947.

All in all, he wasn't impressed. Shifting his wounded, aching leg into a more comfortable position, he reflected on how thoroughly he'd failed to follow his surgeon's advice: He'd plunked down good money to spend at least half a summer in a place that wasn't cool, wasn't quiet, and as far as he could tell—judging from the number of gun shops he'd passed along the way—where every hunter-citizen was armed up to his goddamned teeth.

"Unseasonable, ain't it, de-ah?" The mailman handed Meg a bundle of mail, pulled out a handkerchief from his hip pocket, and mopped his beaded brow.

Meg put down her watering can and took the packet. "I don't mind," she said, stepping back to admire her new flower boxes. "Did you ever see a more charming geranium? Allie brought them up with her from Portland."

"Awful pretty," agreed the mail carrier. "Pink do sit well with Dusty Miller. The blue lobelia's a nice touch. Flesh out a bit, them boxes be right as rain."

The flower boxes, painted a dusty rose to match the shutters, were sitting on the veranda—after they began renting rooms, Meg made everyone stop calling it a porch—ready to be mounted under the big bay window of the Inn Between. The job was waiting for Everett Atwells, but as Meg poked through the mail packet she realized that it would have to wait a little longer.

"Dad! Mail's here!"

Everett Atwells ambled out from the side of the house, paint scraper in one hand, a hopeful smile on his craggy face. "You're right around this mornin', Desmond. Hot enough for ya?"

The mailman lifted his chin in an upward nod of greeting.

"Corn weather, without a doubt" he said, and went back to his rounds.

Everett eased *Fly Fishing Magazine* out from among the bills in his daughter's hand. "Two minutes," he said with an apologetic wrinkle to his nose. "Then it's right back to the grindstone."

Meg responded with a resigned sigh.

Her father took that sigh personally. "Jeez-zus, you're a driver, woman."

"*Some*one around here has to be," she said, running her hands distractedly through the straggles of her overlong hair. She reached in the pocket of her khakis and pulled out a rubber band. "High season is right around the corner, and look at this place," she said, yanking her hair back in a short and all-too-functional ponytail. "Between painting and papering, we have twice as much work as we have weeks."

"The guests'll fall asleep just as easy starin' at stripes as they will at florals."

"You *know* what I'm talking about, Dad." She pointed to the inn on the left. "Look at the Elm Tree Inn." She pointed to the inn on the right. "Look at the Calico Cat. They're perfect. Perfect! And then look at *us*," she said with a despairing sweep of her arm across the front of their big, rambling Victorian. The pale gray clapboards of the Inn Between were holding on to their paint, more or less, but the white trim—and there was white trim everywhere—was a sad and peely mess.

"We ain't perfect," Everett allowed, squinting at the high, pointed turret that dominated the front of the house.

"Yep," he said with a yank on his cap. "Definitely needs paint."

"Oh, take your magazine and beat it," Meg said, shaking her head and resolving not to smile. "I'll pick on Lloyd instead."

"Don't I know it?" Everett said with a wink.

He ambled off without a care in the world toward a chair under the huge oak in the back of the yard. Meg sighed and flipped through the mail, plucking out the "Final Notice" the way she would some evil-looking weed from her garden. When she looked up again, her sister was standing on the front lawn next to the Inn Between's sign and hanging a NO in front of the VACANCY.

"No kidding? On a Wednesday?" Meg broke into a big, relieved grin. "Maybe we're finally turning the corner on this bed-and-breakfast thing," she added as she bounded up the porch—the veranda—steps. "Who was it? A couple? A family?"

Allie shrugged and yawned at the same time. "Comfort took the call. All I know is they're due in an hour."

"Damn. Room five isn't made up. But I've got to get over to the Shop 'n Save or there'll be nothing for afternoon tea today. Allie, would you—"

Allie looked at her older sister incredulously. "Meg, I'm exhausted; we were up all night. I was just going back to bed—why can't Comfort do it?" she demanded in the perfect pitch of a whiny twelve-year-old.

Meg lowered her voice: "Because we only have an hour, and Comfort will take an hour and a half."

"What about Lloyd, then?"

"Lloyd's working on the furnace. Possibly you don't know how upscale we've become. We're actually promising hot water in our ads nowadays."

"Well, if I'd known you wanted me back in Bar Harbor just because you were one slave short, I might've thought twice—"

"Yoo-hoo, Meg? And oh, my goodness, *Allie!*"

Both sisters turned to see Julia Talmadge, the well-groomed owner of the well-groomed Elm Tree Inn, approaching them with a cheerful wave and a man in tow. It was the man who caught their attention. Tall, trim, good-looking, and thoroughly overdressed in corduroys and a heavy flannel shirt, he possessed something else that set him apart from the men of Bar Harbor: a cane.

"So you're *back*, Allie. How *are* you, dear? You look *fabulous*—but then! Listen, dears, I want you to meet someone. This is Tom Wyler, all the way from Chicago. He'll be staying at the Elm Tree for the next month; how*ever*, there's been a dreadful mixup in the booking date. I don't have Mr. Wyler down until tomorrow."

Eyeing the newly hung NO sign with obvious skepticism, she said, "You *can* do something for Mr. Wyler, can't you, dears? Just for tonight?"

"Definitely!"

"I'm sorry."

The two sisters exchanged surprised and hostile glances. Julia stared at them both with dismay. Wyler indulged himself in a silent oath and readjusted his weight on the cane.

"Meg, for Pete's sake! He can have room five."

"Room five is taken, Allie. You know that."

"But the callers wouldn't even give Comfort a Visa number!"

"We promised them."

"What about first come, first served?"

"Now—dears—I didn't mean to make this awkward for you—"

"This *isn't* awkward, Julia. Meg is just being Meg. Can't you see, Meg, that this man is *injured*?" Allie asked, turning to him with a look that suggested she'd just made him a knight.

Suddenly she did a double take. "Wait a minute—I've seen you recently."

"Oh, I doubt it," Wyler said quickly.

"Yes, I have. Wait, *I* know—the cover of *Newsweek*! You're on the cover of the *Newsweek* that's in my room!'' she cried. ''The one about violence in the streets!''

Hell. Just his luck. ''That's an old, old issue,'' he said irrelevantly.

''Violence in the streets, or *Newsweek*?'' the older sister asked dryly.

Wyler lifted one eyebrow at her and said, ''Both. But in any event—''

The younger sister interrupted. ''The cover was a collage of a murdered victim, some cops, and a gang. You were one of the good guys, weren't you? I *never* forget a face,'' she cried, pleased. ''My God. What an amazing coincidence!''

''That story was done four years ago,'' Wyler insisted, as if she had no right to dredge up ancient history. He'd been a sergeant then, and hungrier for recognition than he was now. ''Anyway, maybe I'll just try the inn on the other side of you,'' he murmured.

Allie was scandalized. *''What*! The Calico *Cat*? *You* can't stay at a place called the Calico Cat! It's just not . . . appropriate,'' she decided instinctively.

''Not to mention, there's a NO VACANCY sign hanging there, too, Mr. Wyler,'' Meg added.

Julia was becoming impatient. ''I'll call The Waves. Presumably *they'll* know whether they have a room or not.''

Wyler smiled thinly and said, ''That's very kind; I—''

''He will have my *room*,'' said Allegra Atwells. She had the look, the tone, the absolute command of a high priestess at the altar. Everyone was impressed.

Almost.

''No. He won't.''

''Meg!'' Allie said sharply. ''I can do what I want. This is all about control, and you know it.'' She turned to Wyler, who by now was weaving from the pain, and said, ''I'll bunk down with my sister. Are you allergic to dogs? Oh, God, and cats, of course: I hope you don't mind sleeping with cats. We keep them out of the guest-side of the house, but they pretty much have the run of everything else. Just give me five minutes—''

''Mr. Wyler, I'm sure you can appreciate the spirit in which my sister has made her offer, but it won't be possible. Her room is nothing more than a dressing closet; it has no private bath—''

''Neither do our guest rooms!''

''—and I'm sure you'll be more comfortable at the Waves or somewhere else.''

''There won't *be* anywhere else. If we're full, everyone's full,'' said Allie with embarrassing candor.

''Please forgive my sister, Mr. Wyler,'' Meg said through set teeth. ''She hasn't had her nap.''

''Meg,'' murmured Allie in a voice soft and hurt and low. ''Is this how it's going to be all summer?''

Meg opened her mouth to say something, and then stopped. She turned to Wyler with a grim look. Apparently she thought it was all *his* fault. ''If you could give us half an hour,'' she said stiffly.

Wyler looked at Allegra for *her* reaction. She was beaming. He took that to mean he had a room . . . her room . . . *some* room. ''Thanks,'' he said, sweeping both sisters up in the same grateful glance. ''I'll keep out of everyone's way.''

Flushed with victory, Allie turned suddenly shy and dropped her look from his. ''It will be our pleasure,'' she said in a devastatingly old-fashioned way. She slipped her arm around her older sister and squeezed her affectionately as they walked toward their house, leaving the detective feeling like a loose ball that had been fumbled, recovered, and run into the end zone for a touchdown.

He pivoted awkwardly on his cane and began heading back to the Elm Tree Inn with Julia Talmadge.

''There. You see? All's well that ends well, Mr. Wyler.''

Wyler murmured something polite in agreement.

In the meantime he was thinking that he'd never seen anyone so beautiful in his life. Allegra Atwells was drop-dead, knock-down, stop-traffic gorgeous.

Her face was so disturbingly beautiful that he'd scarcely paid attention to her body. Her body, he remembered only vaguely—that it was tall and sexy and that she carried herself like a queen.

Too bad she was a spoiled brat.

"How did you hurt your leg, Mr. Wyler?" asked Julia Talmadge without a trace of nosiness in her voice. She might have been asking him how he took his morning coffee.

"Gunshot," he said curtly, hoping by his tone to nip further inquiries in the bud.

"Oh, yes; a hunting accident. We see a fair amount of that up here," she said pleasantly. Obviously she made no connection between him and the old *Newsweek* article. If only Allie Atwells were so dense.

"Do you remember Orel Tremblay, Allie?"

Meg, back from the Shop 'n Save, was scrubbing a guest bath with Ajax while her sister was changing bedding in room 5 across the hall. Meg's voice, cheerfully puzzled, rang out above the flush of the toilet. "Remember? The old recluse in the little cottage up the hill behind Pete's Bike Rentals? We used to see him grocery shopping sometimes. He always wore that red-and-black-checked deerstalker's hat, even in summer."

"I guess," her sister answered vaguely. "What about him?"

Meg came out of the bath with an armload of used towels. "He wrote me the strangest letter. Here. Read it." She turned and cocked one hip so that Allie could lift the envelope that jutted from the pocket of her khakis.

Allie looked at the address, written in a shaky hand, and extracted the letter. Aloud she read,

Dear Mrs. Hazard,

It's real urgent I see you right away. Wednesday would be good but not before eleven nor after six. You could say it's a matter of life and death. The nurse will let you in. Please make the time. I used to hear you were an upright woman.

Yours,
Orel V. Tremblay

"For goodness' sake," Allie said, frowning. "Are you going?"

Meg dumped the linen into a plastic hamper and shrugged. "He claims it's a matter of life and death," she said ironically. "Do I have a choice?"

At that moment Tom Wyler showed up in the doorway with a hopeful look on his face. Both sisters greeted him in the same breath, one with less enthusiasm than the other.

"I hope I'm not too early," he said, glancing around the still unmade room. Your handyman sent me up here."

"That was our brother Lloyd. *Your* room—my room, that is —is all set," Allie said warmly. "It's upstairs and to your left. Come on. I'll help you with your bags."

"Hold on, I hear Terry," said Meg, sticking her head out the hall and flagging down an eleven-year-old boy in full trot. She steered him into the room. "Take Mr. Wyler's things into Allie's room, will you, honey?"

The boy, dressed in torn jeans and Keds, fastened two piercing blue eyes on Wyler, looked him up and looked him down, and said, "Why? You sleepin' with my aunt Allie, mister?"

Everyone rushed to say no at the same time. The boy gave an indifferent shrug and ran downstairs for Wyler's bag.

"They grow up so fast nowadays," Meg said wryly to the detective.

"I know; I have one of my own," Wyler remarked in the

same wry tone. He began the painful journey up one more flight.

Allie fell back on the half-made bed and threw her arms out wide. *"Married!"* she wailed. "How *could* he?"

"For Pete's sake, Allie," her sister said. "What's the big deal? You've just met the man."

Allie rolled her head toward her sister. "So? Can't I be attracted to him?"

"You're attracted to him because he's hurt," Meg said flatly. "He can't chase after you the way the rest of them do—not yet, anyway."

"Not true. I'm attracted to him because of the look in his eyes, so sad and tired and fed up with the world. And because —don't you laugh—because he was on the cover of *Newsweek*. I mean, don't you think that's fate? What are the odds that a four-year-old magazine would be lying around in my room with him on the cover?"

"What are the odds that you've actually read the article inside?" Meg said, grabbing her sister by the ankle and half pulling her off the bed.

"I scanned it. There's not much about him; just an angry quote of his about children doing violence to children. Don't you think he's good-looking?"

Meg scowled at a new water ring on the mahogany dresser. "Yeah, I guess," she said, distressed by the ugly stain.

"I'll just go see if he needs anything," Allie said, bounding up from the bed.

Meg held on to her sister's shirt. *"Not* until you're done here. Why do you always make me play the evil stepsister?"

"Because," said Allie, wriggling out of her grasp with a grin, "you were born to the role."

CHAPTER 2

Orel Tremblay's house looked a little like Meg remembered the old man himself: tired, withdrawn, and frayed around the edges. The cottage was vinyl sided, like many Maine houses, but the gutters were rusted through and the top panel of the aluminum storm door was missing. The wood window boxes, sprouting weeds, were split and rotted. The front lawn had taken on the spontaneous look of a meadow; small swarms of insects hovered over it in the afternoon sun. The property looked dispirited, as if it had tried and tried again to brave the relentless onslaught of time and nature, and now it just didn't care anymore.

Meg knocked on the door. It was opened by a nurse who was clearly expecting her. The nurse led Meg past a living room filled with surprisingly good furniture and into a rugless bedroom fitted out with a hospital bed, a small bureau, a wood chair, a La-Z-Boy recliner, an aluminum walker, and a nightstand buried under bottles of medication.

Meg moved closer to the sleeping form on the bed. She hadn't seen Orel Tremblay in a year; it might have been ten. He was quite emaciated. His hair was thinner; whiter; longer. He hadn't shaved, or been shaved, in several days, which made him look homeless somehow. And yet his nightshirt was clean, and the bedding crisp and well turned down. He had a good nurse.

"Mr. Tremblay," whispered the nurse in a hovering voice. "Look: Here's that Mrs. Hazard you wanted so much to see."

The old man's eyes fluttered open. He made a querulous sound in his throat and turned to Meg, fixing her with a listless stare.

At last he spoke.

"My God," he said, shaking his head. *"You're the spittin' image of her."*

"I'm Meg Hazard, Mr. Tremblay. I've seen you in town—although we've never officially met," she added. She spoke loudly, assuming that his senses were as frail as his body.

The nurse gave her a sharp look and whispered, "He can hear just fine, and he knows perfectly well who you are."

She ordered Meg to take the rush-seated chair, and then she left the room. Meg sat with a Raggedy Ann smile stitched to her face, waiting to hear what Orel Tremblay could possibly have to say that was a "matter of life and death."

But he only stared, as if her face, with its hazel eyes, full lips, and wreath of chestnut-brown hair, was not her face at all but something borrowed for the occasion.

"Who am I the spitting image of?" Meg finally blurted out.

Orel Tremblay didn't answer the question directly. Instead he said in a slow, mournful ramble, "I seen you so many times . . . in the market . . . gassin' up your car . . . window-shoppin' on Cottage Street . . . and every time, every time . . . it give me such a start, I figured my heart would go, right then and there."

He lifted one of his hands—big, misshapen, arthritic hands —and rubbed his brow with the tips of his fingers, as if he were stroking a lamp of memories, calling forth the genie of time past.

"Even now," he said with a bitter sigh, "I have to pinch

myself that you're not her. How could you be? She's dead; has been, this half a century.''

He continued to speak with an effort; every word seemed to cost him. ''The thing is, when I met your grandmother, she was your age—that would be, what, thirty-some?'' In the same mournful voice he added, ''She was the most beautiful woman I ever saw.''

Meg smiled in disbelief, but the old man seemed not to notice. ''I never loved another woman after your grandmother,'' he went on. ''I never loved a single, other woman.''

Loved her? Since when? Who was he, and what in God's name did he have to do with her grandmother?

''I never knew my grandmother,'' she told him. ''I guess you know she died in the Great Fire of '47.''

''Of course I know it, gahdammit!'' Orel Tremblay snapped. ''Why d'you think I asked you here?''

Meg said testily, ''I don't have any idea, Mr. Tremblay.''

''True, true. How could you?'' he muttered, fumbling with a control button on the side of his hospital-style bed. Slowly he raised himself into a semi-sitting position. After a deep breath or two, he reached over for a glass of water that stood on the bed table. The drink seemed to revive him: He was able to continue in a more civil tone, and his words flowed more easily.

''I'm old, and I'm dying, and I know it,'' he said, dismissing her sympathetic protest with a fluttery wave of his hand. ''I don't own much,'' he went on. ''Just a few sticks of furniture that I made—I was a cabinetmaker—and the equity in this house. And the chipper-shredder. And the dollhouse.''

It was an odd list, but Meg let it pass; she was waiting, still, to see why she'd been summoned.

''I have a niece somewhere who's bound to show up the day the will gets read,'' Tremblay said, snorting with derision, ''and that's about it. Now. Help me out of bed.''

''Oh! Shouldn't I get the—''

"*Daow*," he said, shaking his head impatiently. "No need. Just muckle onto that walker and set it alongside. The other bedroom's within hailin' distance. I'll make it," he said grimly.

Meg helped the old man out of bed and into his slip-ons, and walked slowly alongside him as he shuffled behind his walker into the hall. The nurse popped her head through a doorway to see what her charge was up to, gave him a brisk, friendly smile, and retreated to another room. Meg and her host continued on their slow journey into the second bedroom.

At the doorway, Orel Tremblay paused and jerked his head toward the room within. "I'll go first," he said, suddenly eager. His voice was shaking with anticipation.

Meg waited as he preceded her, marveling that the frail, bent-over figure with the skinny calves and liver-spotted brow had once been passionately in love with her own grandmother.

She stepped through the doorway after him. The room was dark; its shades were drawn, and the venetian blinds were closed. Then Orel Tremblay turned on a lamp.

It threw dim, golden light over the most beautiful, the most exquisite, the biggest dollhouse Meg had ever seen, a masterpiece of gables, balconies, turrets, and chimneys, with many diamond-paned windows and exquisite French doors, the entire, wonderful structure sitting serenely atop a cherrywood table shaped to match its elaborate footprint. Orel Tremblay reached behind the dollhouse and threw another switch, and the whole brown-shingled fantasy lit up from within like a Christmas tree.

Meg was breathless with pleasure. A low, awed sound escaped her throat, and nothing more; the words simply weren't there.

Orel Tremblay nodded his head vigorously. "Ain't it just?" he kept saying, his voice dancing for joy. "Ain't it?" He was watching her intently, savoring it again through her eyes.

Meg approached the superb miniature and peered through a

tiny lattice-paned casement. Inside she saw a dining room furnished in stunning detail. The Chippendale-style table, the focal point of the room, was elaborately set for a formal dinner that would never be eaten. Everything, from the impossibly tiny gold flatware and crystal stemware to the thumbnail-size hand-painted platters—everything was incredibly complete and perfectly rendered to scale.

The silver chandelier with its half-inch candles; the sideboard covered with silver salvers; the Oriental rug, twelve inches long and nine inches wide, knotted from silken threads into a pattern of stunning complexity; the mauve brocade drapes, held back by tiny gold braid; even the bits of wood in the marble-manteled fireplace, kindling and log sized . . .

"This . . . is *magic*," Meg whispered, finding her voice at last.

She peeped through another window: the library. Another fireplace, this one with a mantel of burnished mahogany, held a porcelain-faced clock and charming examples of chinoiserie: tiny twin red vases and a pair of lamps with bases of blue-patterned porcelain. A brassbound bellows less than two inches long looked as if it might actually be workable. Portraits the size of postage stamps hung from moldings on two of the walls; they were original oils. Two armchairs, covered in kid leather, filled up much of the room, which was cozy more than majestic. One wall was lined with books; it wouldn't have surprised Meg to learn that they had pages that turned and stories inside, written by best-selling authors of the day.

She peeked through a gabled window on the top floor. Inside was a maid's room, starkly plain, with an iron-frame bed, a small bureau, a commode, a mirror—and a maid. The maid, a porcelain-faced doll wearing a white cap and an apron over a black dress, was one of several in the garret rooms.

"When was the house built?" Meg asked. She had a tremendous sense that she'd seen it before, but whether in a newspaper or on television, she had no idea.

"The estate house—the real house that this is modeled after —was built in the 1880's. This miniature of it was built during the Great Depression," Orel said. "To give the help something to do, y'see. I myself did some repairs on it later. *In 1947*," he added in an oddly meaningful tone.

He began lowering himself from his walker into a small armchair placed nearby. Meg broke out of her gaping reverie and hurried to assist him. After he was settled, she turned and stared at the dollhouse. It was so incredibly beautiful, and yet it was so incredibly . . . something else. Forlorn, maybe; and sad. It would never really be lived in, after all.

"I know this house," she said, puzzled. She turned to Orel Tremblay. Her face, usually friendly and confidant, was troubled. "How would I know this house?"

The old man was nodding triumphantly. "Your grandmother!" he cried, pointing a gnarled finger at the lovely house. "That's how you know! She was a sleep-out nursemaid there! This is a replica of the Eagle's Nest—the old Camplin estate house!"

"Ah. That's how I know," Meg said, not really reassured. She had heard the name many times, but she couldn't recall having seen any photos of the place. If they existed. How *did* she know the house?

"Your grandmother took the job in the spring of '47. She was merely fillin' in for the children's regular nursemaid, who took a fit to elope with the chauffeur after the boy got fired. Then in October come the fire."

Meg peeked through the casement window of another top-floor room. It was the nursery itself, with two little brass beds and a rocking chair, and impossibly small toys scattered on the floor. A boy doll lay in one bed. A girl doll was sitting on the floor with a set of minuscule play-blocks. A nursemaid doll— her grandmother, presumably—stood looking out the gabled window at some imaginary vista beyond. She was the only doll in a shorter length dress.

"I never knew the job was only a temporary placement," Meg said, filled with a sudden sense of loss. "How sad."

"For God's sake! Didn't your people tell you *nothin'* about her?"

"Yes, of course. I know that my grandmother was very devoted to her two sons," Meg said defensively. "My father still talks about the blueberry tarts she wheedled from the cook at Eagle's Nest for him and his brother—they were just boys when she died in the fire, of course. I guess the cook was from Paris and homesick, and my grandmother's Quebec French was very good. She used to listen to his stories."

"Oh, yeah; the cook," the old man said, nodding. "Jean-Louis. Short fat guy with brown beady eyes. Couldn't speak a word of English. Personally I have no use for a man who can't be bothered to learn our mother tongue.

"But that was your grandmother all over," he mused, rubbing the stubble of his beard. "Everyone loved her. She had this glow about her . . . this wonderful warmth. . . . You couldn't help but be drawed to her. Everyone was. Everyone—"

His expression suddenly turned dark and angry, surprising Meg once more; he seemed too fragile for such wrenching shifts of mood.

"You have Margaret's smile," he said suddenly, veering away from his anger. "Not *exactly* the same: You're less open. More guarded. Well, that's no surprise," he said with a thin shrug of cynicism. "Times are different."

But Meg *was* surprised, because she truly didn't believe that times were that different—at least, not in Bar Harbor. She didn't lock her door and she'd never been robbed and she always felt safe on the town's streets. She knew and liked everyone, and everyone knew and liked her. That was the whole point of living in a small town, even one as visited as Bar Harbor. That was why, like her grandmother, she'd never leave Bar Harbor.

"Times aren't so very different, Mr. Tremblay," she argued, convinced that her smile was as open and unguarded as her grandmother's.

He gave her a long, searching, and utterly dispirited look. "Maybe not," he said wearily. "Maybe not."

There was a pause, and then he said, "She never did want to be more than my friend."

"My grandmother, you mean," Meg said, shifting gears with him.

Orel Tremblay nodded. "Oh, I'd of stole her away from her old man in a shot, if she'd of let me. Your granddaddy was a drunken lout," he said contemptuously. "He didn't deserve Margaret. But she was just . . . so . . . *loyal*, don't you know. To him, and to their two boys. And damn it to hell—it cost her her life. It was criminal."

"What?"

"You heard me."

Meg was well aware that her grandmother had become trapped in Eagle's Nest during the Great Fire and had burned to death. Naturally her family had never dwelled on it, even though the fire itself was a major event in Bar Harbor's history.

Meg began edging away from the dollhouse. It seemed no longer charmed but sinister, a painful reminder of a family tragedy. As for her grandfather: Yes, it was true; he drank. That was nobody's business, least of all Orel Tremblay's. Suddenly she was sorry she'd come.

"*Mis*ter Tremblay. I don't understand what you're driving at. As far as I know, my grandfather and grandmother were a happily married couple—average happy, anyway. But even if they weren't, I don't see what the point is in your dragging up the fact. They're both dead now. I think the decent thing would be to let them rest in peace."

"Aaagh, you're right," Orel Tremblay said, more annoyed than embarrassed. "Whyever did I bother? Never mind,

What's done is done. *Mrs. Billings*!'' he shouted, with astonishing vigor.

The nurse came in, and Meg went out. That was the end of
her visit with Orel Tremblay, unrequited lover of Margaret
Mary Atwells.

At the family supper that night, Meg's strange and wildly
unsatisfying visit with Orel Tremblay was *the* hot topic. Nothing else could touch it—not young Terry's second black eye of
the month; not his mother's honorable mention at the pie ba-
zaar; not even the '82 pickup Meg's older brother Lloyd had
just got for a song. Everyone wanted a word-by-word blow,
and they did everything but bang on the table with their
spoons to get Meg to tell her story.

Meg wasn't inclined to go into detail. For one thing, they
had an outsider at the table tonight—Tom Wyler, sitting
smack-dab in the middle of the Wednesday chaos they called
Chicken Pie Night. She stole glances at him, perfectly aware
that he was watching her watch him. He made her uncomfortable, although nobody else in the family seemed to feel funny
about having him there. Allie was still enchanted by the man,
and their nephew Timmy seemed to be thrilled to know someone so tall and smart with almost the same first name. His
twin brother Terry was ignoring Tom Wyler, but that was
nothing new; Terry wasn't on speaking terms with anyone except Coughdrop, the family part-Golden Retriever.

Meg looked to her father, Everett Atwells, head of their
extended household, for *his* reaction to the newcomer. No
problem; to him Tom Wyler was apparently just another
mouth to feed. Of her relatives, only her brother Lloyd looked
unhappy to have him here. That was probably because Tom
Wyler clearly had money and a job, and at the moment Lloyd
had neither.

The real test, of course, was Uncle Bill, her father's older
brother. Uncle Bill was outspoken, outrageous, and unman-

ageable. He was a kind of litmus strip for the family. If Uncle Bill liked someone, everyone else was allowed to like him too. If he didn't, he made life such hell for the newcomer that the family, out of pity, usually ended up taking the poor wretch back to where they'd found him.

They had no choice in the matter, because Uncle Bill, not the marrying kind, wasn't the cooking kind, either; he ate with the family as often as he could and *always* on Wednesday, when Comfort served her Chicken Pie with Secret Seasonings.

So it was Bill Atwells's voice, as usual, that elbowed its way through all the rest.

"Are you gonna tell us what happened or not, Meg? In the meantime, pass them pertitters. And I don't mind another dollop of chicken pie while I'm at it, Comfort; it's wicked good tonight. Well, Meg? Don't just sit there poundin' sand. You went to the man's house and the nurse let you in and what?"

Meg cast a wary eye at her irrepressible uncle. She was treading over tricky ground here. Bill Atwells might find it fascinating that someone had had a crush on his mother, but he wouldn't think much of the "drunken-lout" description of his father. And what about Allie? Did Allie really need to be reminded that drinking ran in the family?

Meg tried simple evasion. "We don't want to bore Mr. Wyler with our little small-town dramas, Uncle Bill."

"Don't be silly, Meg. Tom *wants* to hear," Allie said with a confident, beguiling look at her invited guest.

Meg had seen her sister—who could look seductive reciting the alphabet—use that look before. It was very effective, almost a form of hypnosis.

Tom Wyler gave Meg a good-humored smile and said, "I like a good mystery."

"C'mon, tell!" said Timmy.

"What're you afraid of?" asked his twin brother Terry.

"Okay," Meg said with a sigh. "As I said, Mr. Tremblay's not in great shape physically. But he's very sharp mentally. It turns out that he's noticed me around town. In fact he says I look exactly like Grandmother.''

"Don't be silly," Everett Atwells said. "You look exactly like you."

"Well, all right; but here's the part he seemed determined for me to know: He was wildly in love with Grandmother."

"That son of a bitch!" Bill Atwells said through a mouthful of chicken pie.

"It never went anywhere, Uncle Bill; you won't have to challenge Mr. Tremblay to a duel," Meg said ironically.

"When was *this*?" Everett demanded. Plainly it was all news to him.

Meg explained that Orel Tremblay and Margaret Mary Atwells had both worked at the Eagle's Nest at the same time, and that Tremblay, like the rest of the staff, was smitten with her grandmother's great natural warmth.

"Which, by the way, he told me I didn't have," Meg added wryly.

"He said that to you? That he had a thing for Grandmother, and that he thinks you're cold?" Allie was agape with indignation. "What nerve!"

"He didn't exactly say *cold*," Meg said, coloring. "I think he said I was 'guarded.' ''

"Well, that *has* been true since Paul killed himself," said Comfort naïvely. "He knew about Paul?"

"No . . . I don't know. Paul did not kill himself, Comfort. Anyway, cold or hot was not the *point*," Meg said, exasperated. "Orel Tremblay wanted to show me the dollhouse; it was because of the dollhouse that he summoned me."

She went on to describe in great detail the exquisite miniature of the Eagle's Nest that was hidden away in Orel Tremblay's unassuming home. She avoided dwelling on the obvious —that the dollhouse was a replica of the tomb of Margaret Mary Atwells—and she made no mention at all of Orel Tremblay's scathing opinion of her grandfather.

She limped to the end of her story, which clearly had no conclusion, and waited, knowing that her family would jump all over her to provide one.

Uncle Bill weighed in first. "That's it? He had you over there to look at a dollhouse? What for?"

"I don't know."

"It must be worth a pile," said Lloyd. "How much, do you think?"

"I don't know."

"How come *he* has the dollhouse?" asked Terry suspiciously.

"I don't know."

"Probably he *stole* it," his twin brother said. "After he fixed it up he kept it for hisself. Brother. What a dumb thing to steal."

"It must be worth a *pile*," said Lloyd again. "How much did you say it was worth?"

"I don't know."

"This dollhouse—" Meg's father began.

"I never understood what they were doing at the Eagle's Nest in October, anyway," Allie said, interrupting him. "Okay, we know Gordon Camplin was staying on through the hunting season. Fine. But why keep his wife and two children and the whole staff there? Why not send them back to New York or Boston like everyone else? Did you ask Mr. Tremblay?"

Meg shook her head. "He threw me out."

Her family began hooting her off the stage with cries of "So you don't know *beans*!"

Meg wouldn't have cared, except for Tom Wyler. He was sitting there as calm as a clock while her family took turns beating her up. It bothered her that he was neither embarrassed *nor* amused by their antics. She had the sense that he was watching them the way a psychologist might watch a play group through a one-way mirror.

No doubt it was part of his job. She was struck by the way he held himself, so casually alert, so ready to spring. If a fire alarm went off, he'd be the first one into action. But whether it would be to help the women and children, or to step over them on his way out the door—that, she couldn't know.

"Uncle Bill? A piece of my roobub pie?"

Without waiting for an answer, Comfort cut a wedge the size of an Egyptian pyramid, eased it onto a dinner plate, and passed it down the table to her husband's uncle. Comfort began dividing what was left of dessert among the rest of the family, and the talk settled down into pleasing, pie-filled murmurs about everyone else's day.

Uncle Bill, however, wasn't interested in everyone else's day; he was interested in the new man at the table. Uncle Bill had money—he'd sold his hardware store at the peak of the boom in '87—and as a result he tended to respect other people who had money. He wanted to know how much respect Tom Wyler deserved.

"*So*. Whatsit you do for a living, Mr. Wyler?"

CHAPTER 3

Tom Wyler disliked being asked that question so much that he usually did what most cops do: hung around people who already knew the answer to it—other cops.

But he wasn't among his own kind now. He was at the table of an odd bunch who seemed to enjoy picking on one another almost as much as they enjoyed eating. The Waltons, they were not. And yet they weren't mean. He'd experienced mean, up close and personal, like the time his third foster father threw a coffee cup across the table, opening an inch-long gash on his forehead. Wyler still had the scar to remind him of his nightmare youth.

"I work on the Chicago police force," Wyler said as vaguely as he could.

Allie chimed in with, "He was even on the cover of *Newsweek*!"

"Well, now, that sounds interestin'. What exactly do you do?"

"I'm in . . . ah . . . homicide." *Dammit.*

"Homicide!"

The usual electric current rippled through his audience.

"A homicide officer in Chicago. *Well*, now," mused Bill Atwells. " 'Course, the idea of needin' a man—much less a team—just for trackin' down murderers is a little hard to fathom. Worst thing *we've* had lately was a break-in at the day-care center; stole three hundred fifty dollars in bake-sale proceeds. Shocked us all. But *homicide;* well, now. That's different.'' He sat back in his chair with his arms folded across his beefy chest and nodded. "Ayuh."

Terry gave Wyler a skeptical look from under half-lowered lids. "You don't look like a homicide cop," he said as he pulled absently on Coughdrop's ear. "What's your rank?"

"Lieutenant."

"Let's see your badge."

"Whist!" warned his mother. "You're far too bold, child."

"Comfort, don't scold him," said Allie, laughing. "This is the most the boy's said since I've been home. Anyway, Terry's right," she said, turning to Wyler with a smile that kicked his hormones into overdrive. "You *don't* look like a detective. Tell us something really scary. Tell us about a serial killer."

"Allie, there is a time, and there is a place."

It came from her older sister. Wyler had noticed during dinner that Meg Hazard was acting more like a mother than a sister to Allie. But it was obvious, at least to him, that Allegra Atwells had no interest whatever in being mothered anymore. *That* ship clearly had sailed.

"Something really scary . . ." Wyler repeated, stalling for time.

He could tell them that the severed head they'd found in the sixth district did end up matching the body they'd found in the fourth. Or he could tell them about the minister raking the leaves of his front lawn who was gunned down in a drive-by shooting intended for his neighbor. Or, he could tell them about the little girl's face, little Cindy's face, with a bullet hole in it. . . .

"I'm afraid *all* homicides are scary," he said tersely.

But Timmy, for one, seemed eager to show how up-to-date he was. "Mostly shootings, right? Nowadays everything's guns," he said sagely, pressing his fork into the last of his crumbs.

"Is that how you got hurt?" asked his twin brother Terry, narrowing his steel-blue eyes. "You were shot?"

"That's a long story," Wyler said, deliberately laying his napkin on the table and pushing his chair back. "But it's not tonight's story."

Christ, he thought. *They're like a bunch of trial lawyers.*

"Okay, boys, now that you've guaranteed we'll never have Mr. Wyler as a paying guest . . ." Meg said, throwing him a wry, sympathetic smile. "How about you clean up these—"

"I *remember* that dollhouse!" Everett Atwells shouted as he emerged from a very private trance.

He'd said little during the meal; Wyler had a hunch that Everett Atwells liked having his older, louder brother there, taking charge. But now Everett's mild manner and vague expression were transformed: He was like a kid who'd remembered, finally, where he left his slingshot.

"Ma used to tell us about a dollhouse when she came home at night, that it was a magical place where sprites and fairies lived. Bill? You remember?"

His older brother shook his head. "Nope. But then, I wasn't the one pinin' away for Ma every day like an abandoned puppy. And you not a kid, either. What were you, fifteen, when Ma—?"

Everett hardly heard him. He was somewhere else, another time, another place. The sudden flashback to the summer of '47 was clearly a gift, and he was overjoyed to have it.

"I remember now!" he said with rising excitement. "Ma said the dollhouse had a nursery just like the real one in Eagle's Nest. And there was a nursemaid doll just like her, only the doll's uniform was longer than the fashion then, and Ma said—yes, I remember this!—she said the fella who was repairing the dollhouse actually shortened the dress to match the hemlines of '47."

A beatific smile lit up his face, as though he'd made a quick stop in heaven. "God, Bill! How can you not remember?"

The twins exchanged looks, and then Terry snorted and said, "A grown man, playing with doll clothes? What is he, a pervert or somethin'?"

Comfort Atwells sucked in her breath. *"Not* another word, Terrence Atwells. Leave the table this instant. The rest of your pie can stay right where it is. *What* kind of talk!"

Timmy got shooed away next and screamed bloody murder over it. "What'd *I* do? I didn't do *any*thing! Can I at least have the rest of his pie? *Ma-an* . . ."

That left the grownups, if you counted Allie as a grownup.

And Wyler was doing exactly that. The whole Atwells family was interesting to him, the way any cohesive group was interesting, whether they were cops on a squad or kids in preschool.

But Allegra Atwells! She was mesmerizing. No question, she was every man's fantasy. Violet eyes; full lips; hair the color of a gleaming clarinet . . . no matter how hard he tried, he couldn't take his eyes off her.

From across the table, Meg Hazard watched Tom Wyler with a mix of amusement and pity. Lieutenant Wyler had fallen into The Trance. She knew it, and everyone else at the table knew it. Like everyone else, Meg could just be nice and ignore it.

Or not.

"Well, Mr. Wyler," she said, following the direction of his gaze. "You look like you're ready for bed."

The detective flushed and said with obvious irony, "You seem to've read me like a book, Mrs. Hazard."

Like that was so hard. "We don't stand much on ceremony around here, Mr. Wyler," she said, letting him off the hook. "So if you want to pack it in for the evening—feel free."

She added a wry smile. "I think you'll find most everything

you want in your room, except an extra blanket. Don't let this heat wave fool you; our nights get cool. I'll bring you a spare.''

"Don't bother, Meg; I'll get the blanket," Allie volunteered, jumping up from the table.

"No, you won't, Allie-cat," Everett Atwells said with a benign and fatherly smile. "Meg's been running you ragged ever since you got here. You're having a nice cup of tea with me in the parlor; you can catch me up on all your news. Trouble with our Meg is, she forgets there's more to life than work.''

"Silly me," said Meg, rolling her eyes at Allie. "Whatever was I thinking? Comfort—great meal, as usual.''

Everyone agreed and then everyone took off: Everett Atwells, with his newfound daughter; Lloyd, for a rendezvous with the furnace; Comfort, with a stack of dirty dishes; and Meg, with the limping detective at her side. Only Uncle Bill stayed behind, with his Dutch Master cigar and his bottle of Canadian Club, ruminating. They let him be; it was his way.

"I seem to have made myself pretty obvious back there," Wyler said when he and Meg were alone in the upstairs hall.

"Everybody does; we're used to it.''

"She's very beautiful.''

"Yes.''

"How old is she, anyway?" the detective ventured as they stopped to pull a blanket from a linen closet in the hall.

"Allie? Oh, she looks twenty-five, but don't let that fool you; she's really seventy-two.''

He laughed—a musing, pleasant laugh.

It was nothing new, this relentless cross-examination about her younger sister. Even so, Meg was a little disappointed in Tom Wyler. She'd have thought a Chicago homicide detective would be less . . . impressionable, somehow.

"And she's still not married?''

"Nope. No one wants her.''

"What?"

"That's another joke." Meg looked him in the eye and smiled. Really, men could be so pathetic. "Actually, Allie does have fewer boyfriends than you'd think; a lot of them are intimidated by her looks. Well, here's your blanket, and here's your room—holler if there's anything your heart desires."

Again, the suggestion was innocent enough; but it brought the telltale flush back to his neck.

My, oh, my, he really did *take a hit*, Meg thought, oddly dismayed.

"Look, ah . . . Meg . . . I want you to know I'm grateful for the room. I know it's an intrusion."

"Not at all," she lied. "What's another body, more or less?"

His mouth curved upward in a dark smile. "Funny—I hear that line all the time in my work."

Suddenly Meg remembered what he did for a living and wanted him out of the house. It was instinctive with her, like turning off the television if the twins were watching and the news was violent.

"Good night, then," she said abruptly.

Meg spent the rest of the evening answering inquiries and working up the numbers for the Inn Between's quarterly tax return. She kept one ear cocked to the hall, listening for strange footsteps, but the only sounds were the clicks and whirs of the calculator on her battered oak desk. The family was on its best behavior; the halls were unnaturally quiet. It was a school night, so the chances were good that Timmy was doing homework, and excellent that Terry was playing Nintendo. Comfort had retired to her room with her needlework; through the plaster walls Meg could hear the soft strains of a Barry Manilow tape.

There was no sign of Lloyd, which probably meant that the furnace was resisting his amateur's efforts to make it hum. Meg would've liked to go down and see what was what, but she didn't want to give Allie, trapped in a tête-à-tête with their father, the chance to escape. Allie was best off where she was.

Bleary-eyed by eleven, Meg changed into cotton pajamas and was brushing her teeth with cold water in the bathroom down the hall when she heard Allie say softly, "No, no, go back to sleep."

Meg popped her head into the hall. "Go back to sleep *who*?" she asked her sister.

Allie, smiling, shook her head and held an index finger to her lips, then continued on to Meg's bedroom. By the time Meg caught up to her, Allie was peeling away her blue jeans and tossing them on a wicker chair alongside the iron bed that Meg had brought back with her after her husband's death.

"Tom was out like a light," Allie explained, pulling a man's white T-shirt over her head to sleep in. She blew a kiss to the cover of *Newsweek* that she'd tacked on the wall facing the bed. "Poor thing."

"For Pete's sake, what were you doing in there anyway?" Meg could not keep the annoyance out of her voice.

"*Meg*," her sister said, picking up on it at once. "I was just checking on him. He *is* hurt."

"Hurt, schmurt. You can't go barging into a stranger's room. He's a cop. He might've had a gun."

"He does have a gun. Hanging in a holster on the bedpost."

"Oh, *great*."

"What's the big deal? It's not as though we haven't all seen guns."

Meg was fuming. "It's one thing to have a hunting gun stored under lock and key, and another to have a pistol hanging fifteen feet away from where a potential juvenile delinquent is sleeping. Have you ever heard the term 'attractive nuisance'?"

Allie, stretching her locked arms in front of her, let out an enormous yawn. "You're making way too much of this, Meg," she said, pulling back the quilt and getting tiredly into

bed. "God, I'm exhausted. This dollhouse thing has really set
Dad off. We just went all through The Formative Years: 1942–
1947. *You* should've been there, not me; you care so much
more about ancient history. Who gets the wall?"

"You do," Meg said, crawling in beside her sister. "At
least that way I can keep an eye on you."

"What if I have to get up to pee?"

"Pee in your pants."

"Oh, like the old days, when I was three and you were
fifteen. Is this the same mattress?"

"Very funny. I thought you were tired."

Allie threw an arm around her sister and squeezed her affectionately. "I am, I am. But I'm just so . . . *up.*"

Meg, lying on her back, stared at the cracked ceiling and
sighed. Allie was always "up" when she was falling for
someone.

"Night, Allie-cat," Meg said, turning off the little clay
lamp on the nightstand. "Don't let the bedbugs bite."

They lay alongside each other in the dark, each with her
own thoughts, for a moment or two.

"Meg?"

"Hmm?"

"This one's different."

"Hmm."

When Tom Wyler opened his eyes, the first thing he saw
was Allegra Atwells, enchanting in a white sundress with a
low square neckline, standing in a pool of sunshine in front of
his bed. The sides of her black hair were pulled back in
combs, leaving her flushed face in plain view for him to adore.
In her left hand she held a big straw hat with a yellow band.

"Up and at 'em, sleepyhead!" she said in a voice as lilting
as her getup. "I have a full day planned for us!"

He lifted himself as far as his elbows. His first thought was
that he'd died of his wounds and gone to heaven. His second

thought was that divorced fathers didn't get to go to heaven. "What time is it?" he said groggily, still disoriented. A big striped cat with tufted ears and a white throat appeared from nowhere, walked over him, and jumped to the floor.

Allie held out a slender wrist for his examination. "Nine. How you slept through the twins' morning *toilette*, I'll never know. But now they're off to school; there's plenty of hot water; and the bathroom's available. It doesn't get any better than this—almost."

It was that "almost," delivered with that half smile, that set his heart to turning over at a brisker pace. Oh, yes; he was awake now.

But confused. "Did I sleepwalk into your room and beg you for a date last night?"

She laughed—which made him suddenly want to take her in his arms—and said, "Your manners are *much* better than that. No, I planned your day all on my own, as I tossed and turned in bed. It starts with a quick tour of Cadillac Mountain, so c'mon," she said, giving his blanket a bold yank. *"Up."* She turned and, with a graceful sweep of her hat, floated out of his room.

Since he wasn't wearing pajama tops (the room had an enormous, unstoppable radiator), he wondered how she could be so sure he was wearing bottoms. He was, but a fat lot of good they did: He looked down and groaned.

Ready. Willing. Able.

Damn it. This was *not* what he had in mind. A woman—any woman, but especially this woman—was an unnecessary complication. Who could rest around a beautiful woman? A man had a—well, the only real word for it was an *obligation*—to pay strict, constant attention to a beautiful woman. Just in case. Because you never knew. You could get lucky. She said herself she'd tossed and turned.

Damn it. This was not what he had in mind. A box of books and a stack of CDs was what—

"Lieutenant Wyler. *Do* you mind?"

It was Meg Hazard. She'd pushed the door the rest of the way open and was standing in Allie's pool of sunlight with a clutch of new towels in her arms and an ironic, infuriating smile on her face.

He yanked the blanket up to cover himself and instantly felt like an ass for doing it.

"We don't leave our guns draped over the furniture around here," she went on to explain. "Would you mind putting that away?"

"It isn't loaded," he said shortly.

"I'm glad to hear it. Terry shoots at things all day long on his video screen; no one wants him graduating to the real thing."

"I understand completely," Wyler said. What he *didn't* understand was why a closed door meant nothing to these people. "I'll move my things next door as soon as I can," he added to reassure her.

"No hurry," she said offhandedly. He couldn't tell if she meant it or not. "Allie tells me you two are doing Bar Harbor," she added.

Allie. White dress. Big hat. Red lips. The vision returned, pushing out the reality of Meg in her workaday khakis, blue shirt, and mercilessly ironic smile.

"You have a nice day, then."

"Yeah," he muttered. "You too."

She left with her towels and he thought, *She thinks I'm too old for Allie*. Naturally; a woman her age *always* thought a man his age should keep his hands off someone Allie's age.

He got up and went to shower. The towels he'd seen in Meg's arms were laid out for him, and a new bar of soap, all for free: She'd refused his offer of payment at dinner the night before. She had no kids, apparently; he wondered why. God knows the nurturing instincts were there.

She was a funny blend of kindness and drill sergeant. Personally, he found it a little off-putting. It was easier to like an angel, easier to fear a dragon. You knew where you were with either one; you could take predictable action. But the combination types—and Meg Hazard was a combination type— seemed to enjoy keeping you off-balance and making you feel like a fool. It rankled. He felt his cheeks burn just thinking about the pitying looks she'd given him at the dinner table.

Well, Meg had nothing to fear. He had no intention of getting involved, temporarily or otherwise, with her beautiful child-sister. He was in Maine to put himself back together, physically and psychologically. For that he needed peace and quiet, and lots of rest.

"See down there? That's Eagle Lake."

They were twisting their way up a corkscrew road, part of the Acadia Park Loop, that led to the summit of Cadillac Mountain. For some reason unknown to Wyler, Allie Atwells didn't like to use her seat belt, rearview mirror, or brakes. She drove like a madwoman. Wyler, who had been in a police chase once or twice in his career, clung to the door handle and craned his neck.

"Where? I missed it."

"Never mind; there's an overlook coming up."

The overlook came and the overlook went; a sharp right, a drive-through, and they were back on the Loop Road without Wyler, at least, having overlooked a damn thing. He was much more concerned about pitching over the edge into instant oblivion.

"Pretty, huh? In the winter my dad and Lloyd ice-fish on it. I tried it once, but—not for me. I like my water without a foot of ice on top. How about you? Winter sports, or summer?"

"My idea of winter sport is heaving another log on the fire," he said, trying with every ounce of his will power not to shout JESUS CHRIST, SLOW DOWN!

"Ah, see that? You and I *are* alike," said Allie, flashing

him a thousand-kilowatt grin. "We don't go out of our way to suffer pain and torture."

Traffic ahead of them on the two-lane road slowed, then stopped; they were near the summit. Allie kept the car from rolling back by balancing the clutch. But the engine died, forcing her—at last—to place one foot on the brake. She turned the key and started the engine again, casually lifting her foot from the brake to the gas while the car rolled back at about a thousand miles an hour into the Taurus behind them.

The driver of the Taurus leaned furiously on his horn; and that was when Wyler got an inkling, first hand, of Allegra Atwells's casual power over the opposite sex. She turned around and waved apologetically and that was that; the man was putty. He waved back with an utterly moronic grin.

The same grin, Wyler assumed, that he himself had worn through most of dinner the night before.

"The Escort's crying for a tune-up," Allie said gaily, "but that's got to wait for my first paycheck."

"You have a job lined up, then?" he asked as they pulled into the summit parking lot.

"No, but I'm not really worried. The hospitality industry is one of today's hot fields. And I have a lot of related experience. I even managed a Pizza Hut. Besides, I've put together a really professional résumé, and I'm including a videotape of myself, to show I'm right on top of current technology."

"Oh, yeah. The videotape should do it," he said with off-hand irony.

But Allie wasn't like Meg; she didn't look for meaning behind the meaning. Allie didn't have *time* for irony; she took what you said at face value and moved on.

He liked that in her. A lot.

She was out of the car before he could get her door. From the parking lot it was a few steps onto the summit, a grassy knoll with rocky outcroppings.

Allie, charging ahead, suddenly turned to him and said, "Oh! I'm not going too fast, am I?"

"Not at all," he said. His vanity had made him leave his cane in the car, and now he was in a sweat keeping up with her. "March on."

A gust of wind tore the straw hat from her head and sent it cartwheeling across the mountaintop.

Shit, he thought. "I'll get it," he said cheerfully.

He began a painful hip-hop after the hat over her objections and was saved from out-and-out fainting by a younger, faster tourist who scooped up the hat and brought it back to Allie with a flourish.

"Damn puppy," Wyler muttered as he trekked painfully back to the two of them.

The puppy said, "She tells me you have a cane in the car; would you like me to get it for you, sir?"

"I can get my own cane," he said with a thin smile. "Thank you."

For God's sake, he thought. *I'm forty. I'm not a sir yet.*

The fellow reluctantly rejoined his own group, and Wyler and Allie were left to enjoy what was a pretty spectacular view, even through the haze.

"Acadia is the second most visited of the national parks, even though it's one of the smallest ones," she said as they strolled over to the view of the east. "Way down there, nestled on the shore—that's Bar Harbor. It started out as a summer colony for artists and literati, then became a rich man's playground during the Gilded Age. That's who donated a lot of the land for the park, you know: the Vanderbilts and Rockefellers. The woman who owned the Hope Diamond lived in Bar Harbor, and God knows who else; people like the ones my grandmother worked for. The idle rich. Meg knows the history better than I do."

"What's that longish island on the left?"

"Bar Island," she answered, relieved to know the answer.

"Only it's not always an island. At low tide a sandbar to it gets exposed; people walk out to the island all the time then. It's the tourist thing to do. Want to go? We'll have to check the tides—"

"Let's hold a turn on that one," he said with a shrug. "I'm not as keen on the ocean as most of the tourists here."

"Why'd you come, then?" she asked, puzzled. "Obviously not for the hiking."

She didn't mean it the way it sounded, but his manhood was feeling a little beat-up. He smiled in grim agreement. "The truth is, I was told to go someplace the opposite of Chicago to convalesce. I chose Bar Harbor."

"How *did* you get hurt?" she asked, clearly dying to know.

"I, ah, got caught in a crossfire," Wyler said. It was the most reckless thing he'd ever done—even more reckless, he thought dryly, than getting into a car driven by Allie Atwells.

"How awful," Allie said, wide-eyed. "Was it one of those drive-by things?"

"Not exactly. It was in the hallway of a housing project. . . . Look, you don't mind if we talk about something else, do you? It all seems long ago and far away."

"You said you chose Bar Harbor, but I don't think choice had anything to do with it," she said, toying with the ribbons of her hat. "*I* think it was fate."

When she looked up at him her cheeks were high with color. She was unbelievably lovely. It was all he could do not to touch her face, the way a blind man affirms the reality of someone precious.

At that exact moment an image of her older sister, mocking and ironic, flashed in front of him. It put things instantly in perspective. What the hell was he *doing*, traipsing around a mountaintop with a twenty-five-year-old? He wanted to sit down. His leg hurt. He began a drift back to the car.

"So," he said to change the subject, "Meg thinks you're coming into the family business?" Such as it was.

"Not right away. She knows I need to spread my wings and make some real money first. I've told her that later when I'm rich I'll come back to Bar Harbor and buy her the biggest hotel in town. C'mon. You can take me to lunch. If we don't eat now, we won't have room for high tea at the Jordan Pond House. No one comes to Bar Harbor without having high tea there; it's the oldest tradition in town."

Wyler had kept his eyes wide open on the road to the summit; on the way down, he kept them closed. They reached the foot of the mountain in thirty-two seconds. Allie delivered him in one piece, which made him feel the same affection for her that, say, a bungee jumper feels for the guy who runs the crane.

Whatever the reason, he was enjoying the rush. When Allie dragged him into a restaurant with great seats and a view of the harbor, he was delighted. This was more like it.

The fact was, he *had* become something of a fart since Lydia walked out on him. During the first whole year after she left with their son for the West Coast, he did nothing but lick his wounds. During the second year he buried himself—even more than before the divorce—in his work. Third year: ditto.

He'd convinced himself that he was honing his skills to be razor-sharp. What he'd really done was blunt his judgment with overwork until that star-crossed night in the hallway of the housing project, when all of it—his resentment, his hurt, his guilt, his fatigue—got blown apart with four shots of a nine-millimeter. Three for him. One for little Cindy.

Wyler's euphoria evaporated. He sat smiling at Allie, who was bubbling over the menu and the size of her appetite; but he was feeling as flat as an uncapped bottle of seltzer. He wanted it back, that high; it felt good. Right now he'd take it any way he could get it. He thought of wine.

"How about a bottle of Chardonnay to celebrate the taking of Cadillac Mountain?" he said as the waiter stood by.

The cheerful look on Allie's face disappeared; she became a mirror image of his own faltering mood. "Oh? Do you think so?" she asked vaguely. She glanced at her watch. "Oh—too early," she said, tapping on the crystal.

He looked at his own. "Ten to twelve? Is it critical? We can let the bottle breathe for ten minutes. Or move our watches ahead," he said, smiling.

But she wasn't smiling along with him. They ordered lunch and no wine. It was no big thing. And yet it was obvious to him that he wasn't going to be happy either with or without the Chardonnay, and neither was she.

It was a quiet lunch.

CHAPTER 4

"**H**e's getting in his *car*," wailed Allie, spying on Wyler through a curtain of polyester lace.

She was in the parlor with Meg, who was cleaning up the remnants of the cocktail hour at the Inn Between. The crackers and cheese were gone, and so were the guests, off to dine at Bar Harbor's restaurants, probably the cheaper ones.

"*Now* what do I do?" Allie wanted to know.

Meg was gathering up the sample menus, returning them to the wicker basket that lay on the carved drum table.

"What do you mean, what do you do? You wash up and then you help Comfort set the table for supper."

"Not that," Allie said distractedly. She turned away from the window. Her face was pale. "I couldn't tell him about the drinking, Meg. It came up at lunch, and I couldn't tell him."

Meg had a tray of empty wineglasses in her hands. She put the tray back down and said, "Come sit. Tell me."

Meg took the Windsor chair, and Allie took the wing chair. Meg remembered how tiny and lost her sister had looked the first time she climbed up into it on her own. She still looked tiny and lost.

"He wanted to order wine for us and I panicked. Usually I'm pretty good about saying I'm in AA. But not today."

"Well, that's no sin, Allie. No one says you have to tell everyone you meet."

"But I *want* him to know. I want him to know that I had a problem in high school—okay, a big problem—but that I'm in recovery. Meg, I'm not kidding about him. We had a wonderful time. He's so . . . so droll. He's more mature than anyone else I know."

"Because he's older than anyone else you know."

"More than that. I felt . . . I felt *good* around him. I felt right. Kind of the way I feel around you, only with a lot more sizzle."

She slid her hands between her blue-jeaned thighs and hunched her shoulders together with a waifish smile. "It was a wonderful morning—until the wine. What will I do, Meg? I can't just go to breakfast with him for the rest of my life."

"Aren't you getting a little ahead of yourself?" Meg asked. Which of course was absurd. *Ordinary* human beings got ahead of themselves. Women like Allie merely had to whisper, "Jump," and the men around her asked how high.

Allie gave her sister a look of one part sadness, one part longing. *"You* tell him."

"What? Me? Why?"

"Only this one time. Tell him that I ran around with a wild bunch—Bobby Beaufort and the rest of them—because I was young and didn't know any better. Tell him what it's like in Bar Harbor in the off-season, how dull, how boring it is. Tell him . . . tell him about what an awful time it was for us, about Mom dying young and Paul being killed. Tell him about your miscarriages."

"What do *my* problems have to do with Tom Wyler?"

"You were depressed," Allie said simply. "First one miscarriage, and then—right after Paul died—another. Well, actually, I thought you held up amazingly well," she admitted. "But don't tell Tom that. Tell him you were too depressed to watch over me. Without you or Mom, well, drinking is what happened to me.''

''Allie! You're supposed to take responsibility for your own actions.''

''I know. I *do*. But just this once,'' she pleaded. ''It won't sound like whining and excuses if you do it for me. Meg—I'm so ashamed of it all. But he has to know.''

Meg started to object, stopped, waited, shook her head. Allie was dearer to her than anyone else on earth. Ten years earlier, after Allie had begun to behave erratically, after her grades had begun to plummet—but most of all, after Meg had found a pint of vodka in Allie's clothes hamper—Meg had been forced to pull out of a downward spiral of her own, caused by Paul's death and, after that, her second miscarriage.

Allie hadn't wanted Meg's help. The sisters had fought, cried, talked, and fought some more. The road to Allie's recovery had been filled with a thousand potholes and detours; but it became Meg's deepest desire to see her sister safely down it. As far as Meg was concerned, it was Allie who'd saved *her*.

''You really don't want to tell him on your own?''

''I can't,'' Allie said in a whisper. ''I just can't.''

''All right, then, tell you what. I'll do it for you, *if* you agree to send your résumé to the White Horse Hotel here in town.''

Allie looked up sharply. ''Meg, I don't *want* to work at—'' She sighed melodramatically. ''Okay. But it's a waste of time.''

Allie returned to her stakeout of the Elm Tree Inn. But when Tom Wyler didn't come back until very late, she devised an alternate plan: She'd visit friends in Ellsworth the next day, leaving Meg plenty of time to hoe the field for her.

The next morning it was foggy and damp, which fit right in with Allie's scheme.

"He'll be socked in all day," Allie said. "Make an excuse; take him something."

She began rummaging through the kitchen cupboards. "Here! Blueberry chutney. Take him this. He can't possibly have any. Ask him how he's doing. See if he needs anything. Tell him about my drinking, but try to get a feel for how he feels about me first. Tell him what a great time I had and tell him not to go seeing anything without me, only don't say it like that. Ask him back over to dinner—no, don't do that, I'll do that—but try to find out his favorite food. I think they make something out there called goowumpkee; maybe Comfort has a recipe. He's been divorced for three or four years, you know, so he's not on a rebound or anything. He has a son, Mike, who's twelve. And he wasn't raised by his parents. And his name really is Wyler; I saw it on his Visa card. And, Meg?"

"God in heaven, *what*. What else?"

"No one else would do this for me, I know that. I do love you."

A breathless kiss, a scented hug, and Allie was off, leaving Meg in the novel position of having to sell her sister door to door.

How hard could it be?

All morning Meg kept an eye on Tom Wyler's Cutlass behind the Elm Tree Inn, telling herself that she'd go over there first thing with the blueberry chutney. But one crisis (a mouse in the toilet in room 4) led to another (three people showed up for a room with one bed), and by the time Meg looked up again, the sun was out and Tom Wyler was walking toward his car.

In a panic Meg ran next door, gripping the jar of chutney as if it were the key to the city, hoping to intercept the lieutenant. As it turned out, Wyler wasn't going anywhere except back to his room with the map of Mount Desert Island that he'd retrieved from his glove compartment.

"Oh. Well. I happened to see you, and I wanted to give you this. Before you left for the day," Meg added illogically, thrusting the jar at him.

He stared at it blankly. "What a treat. Thank you."

She laughed, despite herself. "You'll never eat it. It's an excuse. I wanted to talk to you about my sister."

A careful look settled on Wyler's brow, the kind of look she was sure he got when some stoolie offered to turn in his mother. Meg didn't like it, but it was too late to back out now.

"Why don't we have coffee in my room?" he suggested pleasantly. "You'll be my first guest."

His room was actually a small efficiency apartment that Meg found depressingly updated and charming. Everything, from the pine shutters and floors to the needlepoint rugs, was warm and cozy without being precious, just the thing for a convalescent. Behind a folding screen she saw part of a bed neatly made up with a log-cabin quilt. A small sofa, a natural-finish wicker chair, and an oak library table that doubled as desk and dining table took up the rest of the room. There were shelves for books that he was in the process of filling.

"Julia has a wonderful knack," Meg admitted ruefully, looking around her with an innkeeper's eye.

"It's very nice here," he agreed. "Very quiet."

"As opposed to us, or to Chicago?" she demanded.

He flashed her a grin. "Definitely both."

Coffee had been freshly made. Wyler filled two mugs while they chatted about fog, a new event for him, and then they got down to the business of Allie. Meg took the chair, which left him the sofa.

By now she thoroughly resented the errand she was on. She said, "It was Allie's idea that I come here, Mr. Wyler. My sister thinks you misinterpreted her behavior at lunch yesterday. She had a wonderful time, but she's afraid that when the subject of alcohol came up, she didn't handle it very well. There's a reason for that."

"Ah."

"When she was in high school, Allie had a problem with alcohol; but she got counseling, and she's been in recovery since then. Personally, I think she's put it completely behind her, but I guess they don't like you to say that. Everything with them is one day at a time."

"Sure."

"She's *very* up-front about it. Usually. But you seem to have thrown her off her stride."

He stroked the handle of his mug thoughtfully. "I didn't mean to."

Meg hid behind a sip of coffee, trying to assess his reaction. Tom Wyler had a heck of a poker face when he wasn't around Allie. "Anyway," she continued dutifully, "Allie is anxious to finish the grand tour with you whenever you feel up to it."

"Great," he said easily. "I'll look forward to it."

"And your favorite food?"

He blinked. "Pardon me?"

"Allie wants to know that, too," Meg said lightly. *And then I'll be done with this mission, thank God.*

"Junk food, I suppose," he said with a startled laugh. "It's an occupational hazard."

He really *did* have a nice laugh; too bad it took an act of Congress to wring one out of him. Allie was right: He *was* good-looking. Tall and square-jawed, with a good head of hair . . . that take-it-or-leave-it smile . . . okay, so maybe Meg *was* able to see why Allie was so taken with him.

But she still had to wonder what kind of man it was who felt obliged to hang a gun on his bedpost in a town like Bar Harbor.

"Lieutenant," she said—because that was how she thought of him since the gun business. "I know you think I mother my sister too much. But in some ways she's young for her age, whereas—"

"—I'm old for mine?" he suggested cheerfully. "More war-weary? More cynical?"

"Yes. All of those things," Meg said, annoyed by his flippancy.

She stood up and tried again. "We're a very close-knit family. My mother died when Allie was three. I took care of Allie until I married, and then, after my husband died, I came back and Allie and I went through some really rough seas together. She doesn't understand this, but she saved my life. She means *everything* to me."

"I can see that," he said, giving her a level look.

His eyes were blue—not a deep, Yankee blue, but a softer shade, tinged with gray. Meg returned his look in silence; two could play the quiet game.

"This is all wildly flattering," he said at last. "But . . . hell, *I* don't know what's going to happen. I'm assuming, nothing. It's obvious that Allie feels sorry for me," he added with a good-natured, rueful smile. "I doubt if it's anything more than that. Is that the reassurance you came for?"

"That's *not* why I came," Meg said instantly. "I came because Allie asked me to. I came because . . . because you *matter* to her," she forced herself to say.

He put aside his mug. "Look, do you mind if I say something? I think you and the rest of your family fuss too much over Allie. I suppose that's because she's so ridiculously beautiful; she's like some Ming vase you're afraid will break. But give her some credit. She's stronger than she looks."

"You're an expert, I take it, on pottery and the human psyche?"

"I've learned a thing or two about people along the way," he allowed, ignoring Meg's sarcasm.

What *nerve*. He was talking about someone he hardly knew; someone Meg knew and loved more than anyone else in the world. "Let me be more specific, Lieutenant," she said, indignant. "When Allie was a baby, she hated to take naps. One afternoon when she was three, she was being especially contrary. My mother lay down with her, hoping to lull her to sleep. But my mother never—''

Meg took a deep breath, held it, and let it out. "My mother never woke up. She had a heart attack—a silent attack, they call it. Allie had no idea, of course. She tried everything to wake her mother. She shook her, kissed her . . .''

Meg looked away from Wyler. "Finally Allie climbed over my mother and toddled out to the yard where I was hanging laundry. She began pulling me by my skirt. She said, 'Mommy's sick. She keeps sleeping and sleeping.' I didn't know what she meant. . . .''

Meg couldn't go on. *This is all none of your business*, she thought, turning to face him at last. Her eyes were glistening, her heart constricting from the memory. But she had to make him understand how vulnerable Allie was.

"So you see, Lieutenant," she said, "it's not my sister's *beauty* that makes her so fragile.''

Wyler was leaning forward, his forearms resting on his thighs, his hands locked loosely as he watched her intently.

This is how he must be when a man admits that he's stabbed his wife, Meg realized in a flash of intuition. The thought offended her deeply. How could he sit there so impassively, as if this were all in a day's work?

"Well," Meg said briskly. "I guess that about wraps up my speech. Thank you for the coffee." She began heading for the door.

Behind her she heard him struggle to his feet. It must have hurt; there was a wince in his voice as he said, "I'm sorry about your mother, Meg.''

Mollified, she turned and conceded, "It was a long time ago.''

"But not to you. And not to Allie. I see that now.''

"It's just that she's not the kind of girl to be trifled with,'' Meg said doggedly.

"Trifled?" he said with a hint of a smile. "People still use that word?"

"Around here we do."

"I should have guessed." He reached out his hand to Meg's hair, startling her as he untangled something there.

"A burr," he said gravely. "It looked so out of place."

The effect of his touch on Meg was electric. She blushed and stumbled over an explanation. "Oh . . . I . . . it . . . weeding. Thank you."

He took the thorny little ball and set it gently on one of the ruffled daisies that sat in a ginger jar on the library table. "I'll keep it to remind me what I'm in for if I'm ever tempted to play fast and loose with your sister," he said without irony.

"Yes," Meg said in a faltering voice. "Just . . . just remember that."

By the time Allie came home, Meg was asleep, so the replay of Meg's mission had to wait until Allie came down to breakfast. By ten o'clock Meg, who liked to rise at dawn, had already answered half a dozen mail inquiries, served breakfast to the guests, talked to a town councillor about a proposed parent-built playground, outlined a piece for the *B & B News-letter*, and listened, with her brother Lloyd, to a *real* plumber pitch the merits of installing a new furnace at the Inn Between.

Allie, still in pajamas, headed straight for the coffee machine. "Dad says to stay out of your way because you're in a heck of a mood," she said. "What's wrong?"

Meg had the kitchen table buried under wallpaper books and paint chips. "Nothing's wrong. Eat your cereal at the counter," she said, holding a paint chip next to a pattern swatch for Allie's inspection. "What d'you think? Too much contrast?"

"Cut it out, Meg," Allie warned, glancing out the window.

"Damn," she muttered. "Gone again." She pulled out a chair for herself. "What did he say?"

"He? Who?" Meg asked, coloring.

Allie's violet eyes narrowed like a cat's. *"Meg!"*

"Oh, all right. But I wish you'd get a life. The whole point of your coming home for the summer was to concentrate on getting a real job. You need *this* distraction like—"

"—I need oxygen. That's all there is to it, Meg," Allie said, nipping her sister's nagging in the bud. "So tell me everything. He knows about the drinking?"

"Yes."

"And why I started?"

"Some of the reasons. *Not* about my miscarriages."

"And that I've fallen like a ton of bricks?"

"I didn't put it that way," Meg said dryly.

"You should have; it's true. Who would've believed it?" Allie said with a faraway look. "Love at first sight."

"It's *not* love at first sight," Meg said sharply. "There's no such thing." But she was thinking of Tom's touch on her hair, how completely electrifying it was, and becoming frightened.

"What else? What else did you find out?" demanded Allie.

Meg was forced to answer a nonstop barrage of questions from her sister: what Tom was wearing (clothes), how he looked (good), how he sounded (fine), how he *really* sounded (fine).

Exasperated, Meg finally said, "I don't know anything else *about* him! I didn't get into his life story. I did what you told me to do. You want to know more about him, ask him yourself. Now *please*. Get dressed. You have to pick up Comfort from the Shop 'n Save."

"Me? Why can't Lloyd do it?"

"He's working on the pickup again. I guess it's an oil leak this time."

Allie rolled her eyes. "Well, what do you expect for five

hundred bucks? God. Will we ever have enough money? *Ever?*''

"Get dressed.''

Allie was still off on her errand when a knock came at the screen door. Tom Wyler, waving a white bakery bag, grinned and said, "Danish. Still warm. Finest kind.''

"Oh! Allie's not here—''

The phone rang and Meg answered it, holding the door open for the detective and motioning him inside.

The caller, sounding urgent, was Orel Tremblay's nurse. Would Meg please come around at once? Mr. Tremblay was in a dangerous state of agitation and refusing medication. Apparently he wanted to finish some business he'd begun with Meg a few days earlier. Could she come? At once?

"I can't, right now,'' Meg said, distressed. "I don't have a car. Can it wait another—''

"I'll drive you,'' Tom volunteered, without knowing whether it was to the corner or to Alaska.

Meg whispered to him, "It isn't far. Thanks.''

She hung up, and not many minutes later they were pulling into the drive of Orel Tremblay's neglected house. The weather was gray and still and cool, a twilight time between sun and rain. Meg was struck anew by the forlornness of the place; Tom, too, seemed oppressed by the scene.

"Shall I wait in the car?'' he asked.

"Yes—no. I'd rather you came in, if he lets you,'' she said. "After all, you're used to this sort of thing.''

Tom cocked his head at her. "What sort of thing?''

"Well—disorderly conduct. What if he has to be subdued?''

"Heck, and me without my baseball bat,'' Tom said dryly.

"I didn't mean anything by that,'' Meg said apologetically as they walked up the steps. "I had no idea city cops were so thin-skinned.''

"We get that way after we've been spit on a thousand times."

She looked at him, shocked.

"Forget it," he said. "Probably you babysat for the police chief's kids."

"How did you know that?"

"Call it a hunch."

They were at the door, which was opened instantly. A different, younger nurse than the one Meg had seen on her first visit stood before them, looking relieved that they had come. Behind her was Orel Tremblay, crouched over his aluminum walker like an angry gray squirrel. The nurse was right; he was very upset.

He stared at Tom in surprise. "Gahdammit, who the hell are *you*?" he demanded.

Meg introduced him. "He's my ride, Mr. Tremblay," she explained.

"Ah, never mind," said the old man impatiently. "Get in here, both of you. I don't have time to be sorting you out."

He turned and began working his walker toward the room that held the dollhouse. He moved in a kind of frantic slow motion; Meg sensed that he was using up a precious last hoard of energy, something he'd been saving under his mattress for a day like this. The young nurse stayed behind him, all the while mugging incomprehensible warnings to Meg and Tom.

At the door to the dollhouse room, Orel Tremblay dismissed the nurse, flipped on the light, and shuffled inside, with Meg and Tom bringing up the rear. When Tremblay threw the switch that lit the dollhouse from inside, Tom permitted himself to look impressed.

He lifted one of the dolls, beautifully dressed in a velvet gown of hunter green, for a closer look.

"Don't *touch*!" the old man said, scandalized.

Tom smiled an apology and put the doll back gently.

As for Meg, she was deliberately keeping away from the

dollhouse, reluctant to be caught in its spell again. Since her first visit she'd thought many times about the house. But her fascination kept rolling into a brick wall of unease, and each time, she would turn her thoughts in some other direction.

The dollhouse was an exact replica of the house in which her grandmother had burned to death. That was an undeniable fact, and it spoiled the charming plaything for Meg. So she studied the dusty venetian blinds instead as she waited for the old man to tell her why she'd come.

Tremblay had settled into an armchair placed strategically for the best view of the dollhouse. He was calmer now, but whether that was because he was gazing at his beloved miniature or because Meg had finally come to see him, Meg didn't know.

Tremblay held up a palsied hand to his visitors, warning them not to say a word. A stillness as thick and heavy as a Maine fog fell over the room as Meg and Tom waited to hear what he had to say.

"Margaret Mary Atwells!" Tremblay said abruptly.

Meg jumped in her chair.

"This is your story, long overdue."

CHAPTER 5

"**M**argaret Atwells used to bring the two Camplin kids over to the carpenter's shop whenever the weather was wet," Tremblay began. "The boy—James was five at the time—took it on himself to oversee my repairs to the dollhouse. I can see him still, strutting around it like some pint-sized lord of the manor.

"Sometimes I'd let his younger sister play with a few of the less valuable pieces—the maid dolls and their beds and bureaus and such. She was too young to play with such finely made things, of course, but Margaret was very fond of the girl, and I hated to put myself in the way of her pleasure.

"But never mind. The point is, because of them Margaret spent many a soggy afternoon in the carpenter's shop, and I got to know her some. Or so I thought."

"But—"

"But what?" Tremblay said, turning to Meg in annoyance.

"That was in '47. Everyone knows we had a drought in '47."

"Not in spring," Tremblay snapped. "Spring was one long gully washer."

Chastised, Meg sat back and let Orel Tremblay resume his tale.

"It was in *July* that the weather turned bone-dry," he said, "which is the way it stayed right into the fall. So I didn't see much of Margaret anymore, except in passing. One day in August I was doing some carpentry on the south piazza of the main house. The children were napping in a hammock nearby, and Margaret wandered over to chat. I remember thinking she had something she wanted to say, only she couldn't quite make the plunge. She kept bringing the talk around to Gordon Camplin, the children's father.

"What did I think of him? she asked. Was he a good man at heart? Did the rest of the staff ever speak ill of him? Being sleep-out help the way she was, she had little contact with the others, except for the cook. I found her manner queer. Here she's working for the man for four months . . .

" 'You ought to know,' I says. And she answers—I'll never forget this—she says, 'I *do* know' in the saddest, most downtrodden way. Like someone told her she had cancer.

"That's when I began to wonder. Whenever I saw her after that, she looked sad . . . distressed. The next time Margaret brought up the subject of Gordon Camplin, it was late September. Most of the big houses were closed down, except for the ones that were being kept open through huntin' season. It was shaping up to be the best Indian Summer anyone could remember. Wonderful color and warm days—but eerie, like it was *too* good. Everyone was worried about a fire, y'see.

"All the Camplins were staying on, for different reasons. Old Mrs. Camplin, she stayed almost year round. She was fierce about the big house, bein' as it was a wedding present from her husband.

"Her son Gordon, he liked nothing more than to hunt—unless it was to gamble. Gordon was a keen bettin' man. That didn't sit well with his wife Dorothea; she was a very proper Christian. *Very* proper.

"*Old* Mrs. Camplin didn't approve of her son's gamblin', either. It was common talk that the two women—the mother and the wife—stayed on just to make sure Gordon didn't bet away the farm, so to speak.

"Anyway, when Margaret come to me the *second* time about Gordon Camplin, she was in a state of deep agitation. She told me that Gordon Camplin had fallen madly in love with her, and she didn't know what to do. She couldn't tell her own husband, and she was afraid to tell Camplin's wife Dorothea."

This was news to Meg. "Camplin! But you said *you* were the one in love with my grandmother!" she blurted.

Tremblay gave her a biting look. "That ain't the point. Margaret couldn't afford to give up her job as nursemaid—I believe your grandfather was unemployed yet again—and she wanted my advice."

"What did you tell her?" Meg asked.

"That she was mistaken. God help me, that's what I told her," Tremblay admitted in a low voice.

He tried to defend himself. "You have to understand: Gordon Camplin was a very wealthy, very powerful man, a force in Bar Harbor. He still is," he added bitterly. "What good, I asked Margaret, would be gained by her going into a pink stink? There'd never been any talk of him bein' a canoodler; no one would've believed her. There was only the gambling weakness, and as you know, Gordon Camplin could —and can—cover his debts."

He turned away from Meg's troubled face and appealed to Tom. "You're a man; *you* understand. Some have power; some are powerless. It's the way of the world."

Tom neither agreed nor disagreed, which was about par for the course. But Meg saw a flicker of anger in his blue-gray eyes. *He* wouldn't have let Meg's grandmother stay on, she decided. If *he* had loved her, he would've defended her.

Tremblay resumed. "I told Margaret she was imagining things . . . that it was my fault, confessin' my own devotion to her; that now she was seein' an admirer behind every potted palm. I told her not to jeopardize her career by saying or doing nothin' foolish. I told her . . . to stay put." He sucked in a long, shuddering breath. "And she did."

"Was my grandmother at all specific?" Meg asked, more gently than before. "About how Gordon Camplin was coming on to her?"

Tremblay shook his head. "She did say that at first it was done more by way of innuendo. She said a woman knows these things, knows when a man is . . . pressing."

"And then what happened?" asked Meg, because she knew that the story did not end there.

"For a while, not much. Life went on as before, except that Margaret cooled considerable toward me. Once, I got up the nerve to ask how things was between Camplin and her. She gimme a hard look and said, 'I'm still here, aren't I?' But I didn't mind. She *was* still there. That's what counted.

"In the meantime the drought worsened. I never saw nothin' like it, not in thirty years. The woods was mere tinder; the leaves still on the trees crumbled in your hands. Wells were going dry one after th'other.

"Day after day we had hot, dry, hateful weather. By the middle of October there was a dozen Maine fires burnin'. Two days later, there was fifty. It was terrible, terrible. I remember when I first heard the news of Bar Harbor's fire. When news got out that a fire in Dolliver's Dump had carried over into the cranberry bog alongside it, I felt kind of . . . queasy. Never mind that it wa'n't burning in the timber yet. They could not put it out in the bog. That said it all.

"For three days, we waited and we watched. Everybody knew there were hotspots burning in the bog underground, that the fire wasn't really out. It was, how can I explain it, like watching a living thing, creeping and slithering and bubbling, a monster just biding its time.

"And then, like *that*, it leaped from the bog into a growth of spruce and pine . . . and with the wind northwest and brisk . . . that monster burst into a roaring fireball, crowning forty, fifty feet above the trees. They rushed in two hundred reinforcements, but the men couldn't do a damn thing. They tried to make a stand in the open pastures of Hugh Kelly's farm. No luck. The barn caught fire, and then some dry slash left over from a logging operation. Right there is where they lost the war. They couldn't stop the fire; they couldn't direct it. All they could do was hope and pray that it'd fetch up against Eagle Lake.

"But it didn't, and after that it was anyone's guess where the fire would head next: Somesville, Hull's Cove, Northeast Harbor; Bar Harbor itself. No one knew. It all depended on the wind. It was a terrible, terrible time, like a grievous punishment was about to be visited on someone, only no one knew who."

Tremblay paused long enough to ask for a glass of water. Meg rushed out to get some, but the old man wouldn't wait. On her way back into the room she heard him say to Tom, "Some claimed later that Bar Harbor was doomed to suffer God's wrath because Bar Harbor was where the greed and money was—the bankers, the railroad men, the rubber tycoons. That's where the unseemly excess was; the selfish, money-grubbing arrogance."

Tremblay looked up, his eyes burning bright with cynicism. "Don't you believe it," he said to them both in a croaking voice. "Rich man or poor, most of us behaved in the exact, same way: we all tried to save our precious things. You've heard the stories—the millionaire New Yorkers who chartered planes back to Bar Harbor to save their artwork; the common folk who covered the airport fields with fridges and couches and mattresses; the minister's wife who packed up her wedding pots—her wedding pots!—for a granddaughter not yet born. Things! That's all any of us thought about, me included.

He threw a complex look at the brightly lit dollhouse, sitting in inscrutable splendor in front of him, and shook his head. "That was *my* thing," he murmured with a lift of his chin toward it. "That was all *I* could think about."

Meg handed him the glass of water and he drank it thirstily, as if he'd been fighting on a fire line. A bit of water dribbled down his whiskery chin; he wiped it with his sleeve.

"I ain't sayin' this town didn't pull together, don't get me wrong. Why, there was acts of heroism that even now bring tears to my eyes. Neighbor helpin' neighbor, mistress helpin' servant, stranger helpin' stranger. It was wonderful. Well, you both are too young to know."

"That's not true!" Meg said with spirit. "My father and his brother were among the early evacuees; they were in the caravan that went on for hundreds of cars. They've told us how they crept along on unlit roads with sparks and ash falling all around, and how they were afraid they were going to burn to death, and how all the while they didn't know where . . . where . . ."

"—their mother was," Tremblay finished with grim resolve. Well, *I* know, and this is *her* story."

Having silenced Meg, he continued. "As I say, my concern was with the dollhouse. I'd worked on it on and off the better part of a year. My heart, my soul was in it, much more than anything I ever done on the big house. I don't know why. There was somethin' about it . . . still is. Anyhow, I wanted to move it out of harm's way, but I couldn't, not by myself."

Tremblay paused and studied their faces, as if he was having second thoughts about continuing. He clamped his jaw tight; but when he opened it again, the words came pouring out in a torrent of present tense.

"So just after two," he said, "I go into Eagle's Nest for the last time. Things look as under control as they're gonna get, considerin' the circumstances. Old Mrs. Camplin is orderin' everyone about, including her daughter-in-law Dorothea. The old woman's two pugs are runnin' around yappin' and snappin' at the servants. I never do see Gordon Camplin. Margaret

—she's dressed in deep lavender, and her hair is tied back in a loose and shining bundle—Margaret passes through the commotion with the two Camplin kids. The little girl is draggin' a blanket behind her on the floor. Margaret and me don't say nothin' to each other.

"No one's free to give me a hand, so I go back, determined to move the dollhouse to safety myself, even if I break it tipping it on its side to get it through the door. Then come the seven blasts at four ten—the signal for Bar Harbor to evacuate. It sends me into a panic. For the first time, I really believe it's all up for Eagle's Nest and the outbuildings, including the carpenter shop. I gotta move fast.

"So I take a two-by-four and smash out the windows of the shop with it, and then I take a sledge to the window frames. That opens a hole big enough to slide the dollhouse through, and onto the bed of the open truck that I've backed up to the window ledge.

"My heart's poundin'. There's glass everywhere, and I can smell smoke through the knocked-out windows. The wind is howlin'; leaves are whistlin' right through the shop. I don't have much time. Nobody does. I've got the dollhouse half on, half off the worktable as I shimmy the thing back and forth, trying to slide it towards the truck; it was a gut buster, I can tell you. It's almost dark and the electric's out, of course; I'm doing everything by lamplight. That's when I see Margaret on the other side of the window.

"She frightens me half to death. Her hair's undone, lifting and falling wildly in the wind. She has a look on her face of terror. I assume it's of the oncoming fire. I run to get the door for her. She comes in and throws herself in my arms and I am in a state of shock.

" 'He's tried to rape me,' she says. 'Please, you have to help me. I need to get away, to get to the police.'

" 'What!' says I. 'He's attacked you *now?*' It's plain I don't believe her. The timing seems downright comical. And she don't look what you call disheveled; except for her hair undone and the look in her eyes, she looks the way she did earlier in the day.

"She pushes me away, she's furious at me. She reaches in her pocket and waves a letter in my face. 'You *still* don't believe me!' she says. 'Read *this*, then, read *this*! It's a letter from Gordon. He's obsessed with me,' she says, 'that's what he is. He claims he's risked everything for me. And now he's threatening me: if he can't have me, he won't let anyone else have me, either! See for yourself!'

"She tries to force the letter on me, but all I can think to say is, 'Where did he try this?'

" 'In the nursery, where else?' she says, as if the attacks were a regular thing.

" *'What?'* says I. 'With the *children* there?' It all seems so incredible to me. I don't know what to think, what to believe. And all the while I'm aware that the dollhouse is teetering, because she's leaning on it for support. I don't know what to do—save her, save the house, I don't know what.

"While I'm standing there like a fool, there's a loud banging on the door. I run to open it: it's Gordon Camplin. He looks grim but steadylike. He's looking for Margaret Atwells, he tells me. Then he spies her, hanging back by the dollhouse.

" 'Mrs. Atwells!' he cries. 'We've been looking all over for you! The household is packed up; everyone's ready to go. The last escape route off the island's been cut off by fire. We've been told to assemble in the Athletic Field. We may have to evacuate by boat. For God's sake, will you come? The children are hysterical without you.'

"Meanwhile, *I* don't know *who* to believe. I look at him: calm, concerned, acting reasonable, trying to keep his large household together. And I look at Margaret: crying, angry, near incoherent. She don't come forward, but hangs back like a cornered thing.

"I begin to—I think I'm going to—intervene. But Gordon

speaks first. 'Whatever else has happened, they need you now,' he says quietly to her. 'You're imperiling us all when you delay. Please. Come.'

"He holds out his hand to her. She stands there, for a short lifetime. I can see that she's agonizing whether to believe him. Finally, she gives a long sigh . . . and comes out from behind the dollhouse . . . and goes away with him."

Tremblay stared into indeterminate space, his jaw a little slack, his eyes dull and unseeing. "It was the last time," he said at last, "I ever saw her."

This is her story? Meg thought, crushed with disappointment. She glanced at Tom. *There is no more*? But of course there was. Tom, at least, knew it. And he was waiting for it.

And in the meantime Orel Tremblay was looking at Meg with a sad and considering gaze. "You're right," he said in a shaky, surprised voice. "You're not at all her spitting image."

"She was telling the truth, wasn't she," Meg whispered.

Tremblay dropped his gaze from her and nodded. "When she walked past me with her head so high, that's when I saw the marks, black-and-blue and crystal-clear: the imprints of four fingers on her arm. I don't know how I missed 'em when she come in. Her cape must've covered them."

"And you let her go," Meg said. "You let *him* go."

"Something you must not do," Tremblay said with a penetrating look at Meg.

"But how was it possible?" asked Meg. "Everyone was evacuating. When would he—how could he—? No, I really don't see it," she said firmly, picturing the chaos of that night. "Besides, it would be a tremendous risk. My grandmother certainly would've reported him to you or the police or *some*one."

"No risk at all," Tremblay said with a black look.

"That's a very serious charge," Tom said quickly.

Meg, puzzled, stared at the two of them.

"Well, think about it," Tremblay retorted. "The big estates was fallin' like dominoes . . . everyone was half hysterical . . . confusion all around . . ."

It dawned on Meg at last. "Excuse me, wait a minute. . . . You're not talking about rape anymore, are you? You're talking about . . . *murder*? You're saying that Gordon Camplin raped my grandmother and then murdered her?" Meg asked, breathless with shock.

"Make him pay," Tremblay said grimly.

"But—but what *proof* do you have?" Meg wanted to know. Her hazel eyes were wide with emotion. "You weren't even there! You were *here*, with this . . . this *dollhouse*," she said, regarding it with sudden loathing.

"That's right," Tremblay said, wincing, as if her words were a slap in the face. "I loaded the dollhouse onto the truck, threw a tarp over it and the furnishings, and left it as near as I could to the Field. Then I joined the rest of the town. By then there were a couple thousand people milling on the waterfront, waiting to be carried off by boat. In all the confusion I never did hook up with the Camplins and the others. Everyone'd got scattered."

Tremblay didn't have to recount that last, legendary scene, which had since passed into history. All the world, and certainly Meg and Allie, knew of it: knew of the huge line of fire that enveloped the townspeople to the north and to the west, and the wild, gale-driven sea that offered their only refuge, to the east. Knew of the bright, moonlit sky that hovered over the black, billowing smoke, and the thundering roar of the wind that drowned out their anxious, awestruck chatter.

Twenty-five hundred people survived a night of almost biblical terror. The devil had licked at their heels, and then— when the road to Hull's Cove suddenly opened—angels had led them to safety. The twenty-five hundred were members of a very exclusive club—but her grandmother was not.

Tremblay's strength was fading fast. "In the investigation," he said in a dry whisper, "Gordon Camplin told the police that the last he saw of Margaret was when they were on the way to the main house. Supposedly she changed her mind and decided to return to the carpenter's cottage, to evacuate with me."

He shook his head. "What could I say? It sounded plausible. Even *I* wanted to believe it."

Meg's mind was working clearly now. "How did they account for my grandmother's ending up in the main house?"

"Anybody's guess. The Camplin family had already gone on to the Field. Gordon's version is he made a quick pass alone through the house and left. *My* version is he saw the chance of a lifetime and took it."

"No witnesses," murmured Tom. "No crime scene . . . nothing left at all. I take it you didn't offer your version of events to the police," he said to Tremblay in that dry tone Meg knew so well.

Again Tremblay shook his head. "Who woulda believed me? Gordon was one of the heroes of the evening. He was all places at once, helping the early ones onto the boats and then later, after the road opened back up, helping the firefighters make a stand at Eden and West Streets, even though his own Eagle's Nest was gone by then."

"No, I'm sorry, I can't accept this, Mr. Tremblay," said Meg. "It's too crazy."

"Don't call me crazy," the old man said in a croaking roar.

Tom silenced Meg with a single look and said, "What you've told us needs to be thought over very carefully, Mr. Tremblay. It's a very serious charge."

"Make him pay," Tremblay repeated doggedly. And then, with sudden, unarguable fatigue, he said, "I'm done."

On the other side of Tremblay's front door Tom gave Meg a sharp look and said, "Are you okay?"

Meg took a deep draught of fresh air and let it out in a rush

that left her weaving. "I . . . don't know. I'm pretty overwhelmed."

"You're white as a sheet," Tom said, alarmed. He slipped
his arm around Meg to steady her. "Let's get you home," he
said.

He led her to the car and they drove in silence for a few
minutes until Meg's light-headedness passed.

"Well?" she asked in a voice still faint. "What do you
think?"

"I think your Mr. Tremblay makes a convincing witness,"
Tom said carefully.

"Do you believe him?" she asked, rejecting Tom's evasive
answer.

"I haven't decided."

"You don't *decide* about believing someone. You either believe or you don't."

"Okay; I believe I haven't decided."

"Damn it, Tom! Why are you being this way?"

"I'm just your ride, remember? That's all."

"It's not all. You came in. You heard him. You can't just
pretend—" She sighed and started over. "Let's just *assume*
that a witness came to you who you thought was reliable.
Wouldn't you have an obligation to investigate his story?"

Tom said, *"If* I believed Tremblay's story, the only obligation I'd have would be to pass it on to the proper authorities,
in this case, Chief Dobney."

"Chief Dobney! Oh, but you can't do that! Not yet!" Meg
said, aghast. "This is still a family affair!"

"Look, Meg—this isn't *The Rockford Files.* I'm not a private eye. . . . Ah, there's Allie," Tom said, obviously relieved.

Allie was sitting dejectedly on the bottom step of the front
porch, her chin resting on one fist, her other fist clutching the
forgotten white bakery bag.

Wyler parked the car on the street, wondering how he'd let himself get sucked into this latest turn of events. God. If it wasn't one sister, it was the other.

He slipped from the front seat to get Meg's door. No question about it, Tremblay's story had grabbed them both by the throats. But Wyler had managed to shake off the old man's grip. Meg, he could see, was having a harder time of it. She was still sitting in the front seat, upset and completely caught up in the tale.

As for Wyler, he'd told Meg the truth: he didn't know whether to believe the old man or not. But even if he *had* believed Tremblay's story, he wouldn't have admitted it to Meg. He knew instinctively that she was the kind of woman who'd want him to investigate immediately and solve the crime in a day or two, just like on TV.

He had his own unsolved mysteries, a drawerful of them: They were bloody, they were recent, and there was nothing speculative about them. He wanted to explain that to Meg—although he had no idea why it mattered—but right now Allie made that impossible. She'd taken one look at her sister's face and, dropping the abandoned-waif routine, had come running.

"What's happened? Where *were* you?" she demanded to know.

"Tremblay's," said Meg. "I'll tell you all about it." She turned to Wyler, her eyes bright and hard. "Thanks for the *ride*, Lieutenant," she said, clearly dismissing him.

"Wait, Tom; you're not leaving?" cried Allie.

Wyler turned from Allie's violet, don't-go gaze to Meg's get-the-hell-out-of-here look. One sister seemed to cancel out the other.

"Will I see you later tonight?" Allie asked, breaking the deadlock.

Wyler glanced at Meg. It seemed like a good time to make her understand that his interest in the Atwells family was social and not professional. "Love to," he said. "How about seven?"

As he walked away, he felt the hair on the back of his neck rise. Whether it was from Allie's smoldering look, or Meg's, he wasn't too sure.

After he left, Meg sat down on the bottom step with Allie and told her all she'd learned from Tremblay.

When she finished, Allie, agape, said, "He *must* be senile."

"I don't think so, Allie. If what he's saying is true—"

"You're crazy, Meg! Camplin comes back here every summer. Even divorce hasn't stopped him. And it's not like the guy has turned into a guilty recluse or anything. He's just as active in society as his ex-wife. Why would he come back to the scene of the crime year after year?"

"What scene?" Meg asked. "There *is* no scene, not after the fire." She plucked a dandelion that was growing in a crack in the sidewalk. "If there really was a crime, we're going to have to tread carefully. I want you to promise me—*promise* me—that you won't breathe a word of this morning's visit with Mr. Tremblay to anyone. I need time to think."

"Fine with me," Allie said, shaking her head skeptically. "I think the whole thing's a fantasy, anyway."

CHAPTER 6

Dusk, and the mosquitoes, had come and gone, and Meg was still on the porch swing, alone. No one came out to sit with her, and she couldn't blame them. She'd been scary to be around ever since the day Orel Tremblay had first summoned her. Jumpy, irritable, all her senses heightened—she'd never felt such edginess, as if something momentous or horrible or shocking or joyful—or all of the above, for all she knew—was about to happen. She thought of animals in the field, jittery before a storm: that was how she felt.

She pulled her shawl more closely around her and gave the worn gray floor of the porch a shove with her foot, sending the wooden seat swinging and squeaking on its chains.

It was Orel Tremblay's fault. He'd summoned her from a very busy, very useful, very ordinary life and handed her a dilemma she couldn't possibly resolve.

If she went after Gordon Camplin, a prominent member of Bar Harbor society, she ran the very real risk of being sued for slander. Like all business people who dealt with the public, Meg had a healthy fear of liability. The ceilings of the Inn Between might need a new coat of paint, but all the smoke detectors worked, and the fire exits were clearly marked.

On the other hand, if Meg ignored Orel Tremblay's story, then Gordon Camplin would go free. Well, obviously he'd *been* free, for all of his—what? Seventy-five years? Was it worth it to deny one old man a few years of freedom just to satisfy another old man's dying wish to avenge a woman whom Meg had never even known?

She wasn't sure. Maybe that was where the jitteriness came from. Indecisiveness wasn't Meg's thing. She sighed, aware that the decision, when it did come, would be hers alone. The rest of the family had too many concerns on their minds than to go rummaging in the past looking for more: Comfort had the twins to worry about, and Lloyd had Comfort, and Everett Atwells had his advancing age. Allie had Tom Wyler. And Meg? Meg had *all* of them to worry about.

And now Margaret Mary Atwells as well. That might make one too many generations for Meg to handle. She shook her head, laughing under her breath. Where had all this mother-hen-ness come from, anyway? She told herself that she'd merely stepped into the void left by her mother's death. She told herself that if her mother hadn't died so young, Meg Hazard would be living on a houseboat on the Intracoastal Waterway and earning her living as a wildlife photographer.

Meg gazed out at the moon, silver and solitary and somehow cruel, that hung in the late-evening sky. *Trouble is*, she thought, *I'm too young to be matriarch of this clan. On a night like this, with a moon like that, I'm definitely too young*.

The sound of a man's voice, and laughter, low and melodious, drifted through the darkness to mock her thoughts. It was Allie's laugh, with something new in it, something . . . surprised and delighted. Allie didn't surprise easily. She'd had too many men cut open their veins and spill their desire at her feet. What could Tom Wyler possibly be saying that surprised and delighted her?

Meg gave herself another push on the porch swing. *Creak, creak. Creak, creak.*

"Whoops . . . occupied," she heard Allie say.

And then the voices turned and faded, hers and the lieutenant's, and Meg sat alone for a long while, wondering how it was that Allie could feel so convinced that he was the one.

Allie had risen before dawn for the long drive down to Boston to interview at a Days Inn there. She was trying to save on travel expenses whenever she could, and Meg appreciated that. She just hoped Allie didn't get an offer to interview at the Maui Prince Hotel. They'd have to take out a third mortgage on the Inn Between.

Meg was helping Comfort put out a continental breakfast of cranberry muffins and poppy-seed cake for their guests when Lieutenant Wyler showed up at the kitchen door. Meg let him in and was surprised to see that the cane was back.

"I overdid it last night," he admitted. "Your sister is convinced that I can walk away my wounds."

"Her degree's in hospitality, not hospitals," Meg reminded him. "In any case, you're safe for now. She's in Boston. As you know," she added, just in case he didn't.

"Sure," he said easily. He handed Meg a windbreaker that Allie had left behind. "Actually, I plan to hobble across the sandbar to Bar Island at low tide," he said, glancing at his watch.

"Why?"

He shrugged. "Allie says it's the tourist thing to do." He looked at Meg thoughtfully and said softly, "How're you doing today?"

"Oh . . . better than yesterday. Although I have to admit, this thing about my grandmother is obsessing me." She shrugged helplessly. "I could use some advice," she said with a beseeching look.

"Yeah, well—I'd better be off," he said in a tone that struck her as practically rude. "You know what they say: time and tide wait for no one." He started backpedaling out of the kitchen.

Meg felt like a patient who'd tried to get her dentist to look at a tooth in the middle of Main Street. She gave him a *be-that-way* look and said, "Lieutenant? Don't forget: After the tide rolls out—it rolls back in."

"Elemental physics," he agreed, looking back at her with a dry half smile.

The walk down to Bridge Street was shorter and easier than Wyler had anticipated. Allie was right: walking helped.

He was surprised at how quiet the town was, even allowing that it was a weekday. How *did* Bar Harbor manage to survive on a tourist economy? Give him a big city like Chicago with its broad shoulders anytime; at least it was diverse. Still, there was a certain tattered charm about Bar Harbor that he found appealing. It didn't pretend to be anything more than it was: a once-grand watering hole humbled by a war, a Depression, a fire, and the income tax, not necessarily in that order.

He was aware that old—very old—money still summered here. But they were being mighty discreet about it; Bar Harbor was no South Beach. He liked that too. Why rub everyone else's face in it? It only led to class warfare. He daydreamed in a general way about the gap between rich and poor, between master and servant, and that led him, inevitably, to Meg's grandmother.

The way he saw it, Margaret Mary Atwells's case had two parts to it: (1) was she murdered, and (2) did it matter. The knee-jerk answers were: no and no. But even if someone were looking for trouble, even if someone were determined to find some irregularity in the victim's death, it still came down to this: it made no real difference. The course of history would not be changed, the flow of money would not be altered.

But, of course, Meg Hazard could do what she wanted. Just so long as she didn't drag *him* into it. He had no intention of spending a busman's holiday here. He swept aside all thoughts of Margaret Mary Atwells as he made his way to the damp and pebbly sandbar that was now fully exposed between the town and Bar Island.

He'd imagined a treacherous, narrow slit of sand cutting a swath through crashing seas. What he found was a sandbar the size of a highway, strewn about with rocks, with a calm and gentle sea receding from both sides of it.

He found that vastly reassuring. The plain fact was, Lieutenant Thomas Wyler, who'd seen more dead bodies than he'd ever care to count, bodies that had been run down, gunned down, cut up, burned, and strangled—this same fearless officer of homicide investigations was afraid—*God*, how he hated to have to admit it—of water.

He snorted out loud at the thought. He knew exactly where the phobia had come from, of course. It happened when he was seven and playing hooky from school. He'd headed straight for Humboldt Park, a green and peaceful Chicago oasis that nowadays was a haven for rival gangs—where before long he got hot and decided to take a dip in the pond. He'd stripped down to his underwear and struck out boldly. But the muddy bottom was so squishy and disgusting that he had no choice but to swim for deeper water.

Which would've worked out swell if he'd known how to swim. Instead, his feet had got bound up in seaweed, and he very nearly drowned before a passerby leapt in, fully clothed, and hauled him out, then rolled him over and gave him what used to be called artificial respiration. When he came to, the first thing he saw were leeches clinging to his ankles. To this day, the sight of seaweed swaying just beneath a water's surface made him nauseous.

Right now he felt almost brave, picking his way around the exposed, rank, half-dried seaweed. When he got to Bar Island, Wyler breathed an irrational sigh of relief. Here he was. Now what?

He'd brought a book in his backpack, a history of Bar Harbor that included an account of the fire. He didn't dare admit it to Meg or Allie, but he'd been fascinated by Orel Tremblay's story of the evacuation from the town dock, and that was part of the reason he was here now. He found a comfortable spot on the west side of Bar Island, across the water from the town pier where everyone had assembled in fear that long-ago night.

Today, at least, the setting was idyllic: warm and sunny and still. Wyler took off his shirt, then his shoes and socks, and rolled up his khakis. The ticktock of time flattened into a monotonous hum, the drone of buzzing insects. For the first time since he'd arrived, Wyler felt totally relaxed. He decided to begin his history at the beginning, on page 1.

He read for a while, turning the pages lazily, stopping now and then to gaze at the huge old shorefront "cottages" across the way that had been spared by the fire, or to listen to the ear-splitting din of a passing lobster boat, its unmuffled engines piercing the pristine silence of the morning.

Sometime after chapter 3, he fell asleep.

The crowd that had gathered was big, the first sign that the hostage crisis had gone on too long. He got out of the squad car and went up to the containment officers. "So what have we got?" he said.

"Everyone in the building's out, except for the hostage taker and the little girl. We've got the girl's mother—the guy's girlfriend—in custody; she's zonked out of her mind. Useless. The guy swears he went to school with you. St. Teresa's on Campbell Street? That right?"

"Yeah. For a year."

"He said you got whacked on the knuckles more than he did. That you wanted to be an airline pilot. That he wanted to be a priest."

"Who remembers?"

"Apparently the girlfriend said she's leaving him. He freaked. The kid's not his, by the way. Anyway, he won't send her out until he talks to you. He's thrown out a gun. One gun. The kid's name is Cindy.''

''Everyone in place?''

''Oh, yeah.''

''Okay, where's the hookup?''

But there was no response to his ''Eddy, this is Tom Wyler.'' Only blubbering. He could make out the words ''not my fault.'' Then more blubbering.

''Eddy, listen to me. Send out the little girl. Send out Cindy. And then you and I will talk.''

''Can't . . . do that . . . you . . . come in . . .'' Wracking sobs. ''Nothing ever . . . turns out right.''

Drugs, booze. But did Eddy have another gun?

He handed the phone back to the negotiator. Their approach was by the book. Backup in place. The hall was lit; no problem there. The apartment door was open, a good sign. Only one little thing, the filthy quilt bundled on the floor in the hall. Wyler pushed it with his foot. It resisted. He bent down . . . lifted one corner.

A four-year-old, blue eyes open, blue eyes blank. Thick black lashes. Pretty. Cindy. Dead. Jesus.

Then a shot, two shots, three shots, all in slow motion. An answering hail of shots from behind him, thunderous.

He was down, his leg on fire, the seaweed wrapping itself around him, pulling him down, pulling him under, on fire.

Wyler jolted awake from his island nap in time to hear the explosive rat-a-tat of a lobster boat's unmuffled engine as it passed nearby. He was sweating profusely; his hair was drenched.

Not again.

He thought he'd put the dream behind him; he hadn't relived the episode since his arrival at Bar Harbor. *Dammit.* He was back at square one.

Wyler stood up, stiff all over, and was struck by an instant, bone-piercing chill: the sea breeze had filled in, dropping the temperature ten degrees. He looked at his watch: almost noon. Noon! Noon was not when low tide was. He dressed slowly—he was sunburned, of course—and limped back to the sandbar without much hope.

He'd read about swift Maine tides, but this was ridiculous: The highway of sand was gone, rolled over by whitecapped seas. Forget walking, wading, or swimming. In a helicopter, maybe. He jammed his cane into the sand in disgust. Two hours until high tide, six more after that before he saw the sandbar again.

Elemental physics, he'd told her.

He tried signaling a runabout, but the boat was too busy running about. A sailboat glided into sight, but its sails blocked him from its owner's view. Eventually a lobster boat showed up nearby, but it went deliberately on its way despite Wyler's yells and whistles.

Finally another boat, a slow-moving skiff with an outboard, began heading his way from the Bar Harbor side. Clearly he'd been spotted. Throwing his dignity to the wind, Wyler began waving his cane and his backpack in wide arcs above his head. As the skiff drew nearer the shore, it became obvious that the person on the helm was a woman, and one he knew.

He swore under his breath as Meg Hazard hove into view. *Any*one but her. The only thing worse than being a fool was having announced it beforehand. *Time and tide wait for no one*. Shit.

"Hey, there," he said in a loud, utterly false voice as the skiff drew near. "Fancy meeting you here."

"Small world," Meg shouted, doing her best, he thought, to suppress a snotty smile.

She cut the outboard, turned, and released the engine to lift its prop out of the water, all in one fluid motion, as the nose of the skiff anchored itself on the small strip of beach that was still exposed. Clearly she knew her way around the water.

"Hop in."

Wyler climbed over the bow and dropped into the skiff with a thunk. He swallowed the jolt of pain that shot through his leg and smiled briskly. "Go ahead," he said, inviting her razzing. "I deserve it."

"Hey," Meg said with a shrug. She took a weathered oar from the bottom of the skiff and shoved off with it, then lowered the prop back into the water and started up the engine, backing down from the shore.

"Probably this kind of thing happens all the time, tourists getting stranded," he said hopefully.

"Not usually."

She sat down on the aft seat; he followed her example amidships. "So how did you find me?" he asked, although a voice inside told him to never mind.

"A boater must've seen you and passed it on; I heard it on the police scanner."

"Super." He sighed in disgust and looked away. When he turned back to her, he was surprised to see that she was studying him intently. Caught in the act, she blushed and said, "You got burned today."

"I nodded off. Blame it on Bar Harbor."

She didn't answer.

"Still mad?" he asked playfully.

Again he'd caught her by surprise; her blush deepened, giving her cheeks a healthy, rosy glow. The wind whipped her chestnut hair across her face and he noticed for the first time how sun streaked it was. Angry or embarrassed, Meg looked very attractive just then. *She's in her element*, he decided. *Being outdoors suits her*. Her sister was made for candlelight and dancing. Meg was made for—well, for this.

"*Yeah*, I'm mad," she said calmly, squinting in the sun. "I don't see why you can't help me out on this. You're here. You know the ropes. You could at least tell me how to get started."

"On—?"

"Oh, come on, Lieutenant; don't play dumb. I'm talking about Gordon Camplin. If you don't want to advise me, just say so."

"Okay. I'm saying so."

"How can you *say* that? What if he's guilty?"

"What if he isn't?"

"He could easily have gotten carried away by my grandmother! He could easily have become obsessed! Men do that!"

"All too often."

"Then what's the problem?"

"Men are doing that *now;* that's the problem. Everyday, everywhere. *They're* the ones I have to—"

"Oh, like you have to ration your energy to track down murderers."

"That's right. I'm rationing."

"But you're not doing *any*thing. You *have* the time!"

"I *am* doing something!" he said, out of patience with her at last. "I'm putting myself back together again. Call it the Humpty Dumpty syndrome."

"I can't believe this; where's your sense of outrage?"

"I'm fresh out of outrage just now," he shot back. "I left all I had with a four-year-old named Cindy. You want outrage? Check her coffin," he said viciously.

"Well—" She faltered, then rallied. "Well, excuse *me*," she said, grabbing a stern line. "Around here we keep going till the job's done. We don't have the luxury of taking timeouts to renew our *spirits*," she said, spitting out the last word with contempt.

"Around here you don't *need* the luxury of time-outs. Every *day* is a time-out."

"Really? Wait until August," she said, throwing the outboard into neutral. She played the wind perfectly; the skiff glided to a perfect stop alongside a small floating dock. Above them a grizzled old-timer sat fishing on the edge of the fixed pier, a drop line dangling between the legs of his trousers down into the water.

"Afternoon, Daniel," Meg said, nailing the boat with a quick hitch over a rusty cleat. "How they actin'?"

"Ain't," he answered.

Meg gave Wyler an out-of-the-boat-*now* look. He scrambled onto the dock, too annoyed with her to care that he was doing it awkwardly.

"I was right about you after all," Meg said, turning her back on him. "Your heart is hardened."

Pushy, controlling, relentless. . . .

She undid her hitch and took off in the skiff, ignoring his shouted, parting remark: "Thanks so much! Are you sure I can't take you to lunch?"

Wyler stood there for a while, mulling over her anger. One thought, more than any other, kept scurrying to the front of his mind: There was no better cover-up for a murder than a fire of biblical proportions.

CHAPTER 7

Meg knew something was up when she overheard Terry saying to Timmy, "Did we pull the heads off *all* our G.I. Joes?"

A minute later the twins were in their room, overturning a plastic laundry basket filled to the brim with discarded and broken toys. Coughdrop was with them, tail wagging, tongue heaving expectantly at the thought of buried edibles long forgotten.

Meg paused in their doorway, holding a stack of *Country Living* magazines destined for the guest rooms. "I thought you two decided G.I. Joe was kid stuff," she said, curious. "What's up?"

Two pairs of piercing blue eyes looked up at the same time. "We need 'em for the dollhouse," Timmy said. "They're gonna be the national guard."

"Yeah; we're gonna play L.A. riots," said Terry. "Hey, Tim, maybe we can make, like, a smoke bomb or something. To look like fire."

"*What?*"

"Cool. Or what about if we painted all the inside bulbs with red nail polish, to make it look like the house was on fire."

"Or even better—"

"Hold it! L.A. riots? *What* dollhouse?"

"The one they're unloading outside," Terry said, rummaging through the pile intently. "Here's one! No, wait, the legs are gone, too," he said with real regret. "I remember now."

Meg stepped over the mound of debris and marched over to the boys' window. Far below, she saw two men in the process of muscling a dollhouse—*the* dollhouse—from the back of a Ford pickup parked in front of the Inn Between. A third man was stepping down from the veranda and walking back to the truck.

"Don't bring it up on the porch," she heard him tell the other two. "She says it won't fit through the front door. They have double doors leading to the garden; we'll go in that way."

Meg threw the sash all the way up. "Hey, down there! What're you doing?"

The third man turned and looked up at her from under the rim of his baseball cap. "Deliverin' the dollhouse. The furniture is still being boxed up; we'll bring it soon's it's done."

"Waitaminnit, hold the phone! Wait till I get down there—"

"Meg! For heaven's sake, whatever is going *on*?"

Comfort, winded and panting, was standing behind her sons with a look of absolute bewilderment on her face. She held out a business-size envelope to Meg. "He gave me this. From Orel Tremblay, he said."

Meg took it and tore it open.

Dear Mrs. Hazard [it said in a wobbly hand]: *This is yours, free and clear. You're the only one can see the connection and do what's right by Margaret Mary. I don't pass on this burden lightly.*

The letter was accompanied by a formal-looking document, signed and witnessed, bequeathing the dollhouse and all its contents to Meg.

Meg handed the letter to Comfort, who read it, collapsed on the lower bunkbed, and read it again.

"But you're not even related," she said blankly. "And Mr. Tremblay's not even dead!"

"Those aren't always requirements," Meg said, distracted.

They were to Comfort. "Won't someone else want it? The niece you talked about?"

"Probably," Meg admitted. She turned to the twins. "Don't even *look* at a box of matches. Ever!" she warned. She rushed downstairs, with Comfort and Coughdrop close on her heels.

Working through a rising tide of excitement, Meg cleared away a brass lamp and some gardening books from a gateleg table in the sitting room. In the meantime Comfort filched a blanket from the nearest guest room and threw it over the dark pine tabletop, then swung open the old French doors that led to a patio surrounded by rhododendrons and mountain laurel, some of it in bloom.

"In here," Meg said breathlessly to the three struggling workmen. It was beginning to dawn on her that the dollhouse was coming to *her*, Margaret Mary Atwells Hazard, direct descendant of Margaret Mary Atwells, and that both their fates were bound up in the fate of the little house itself. She didn't know why, she didn't know how. But Orel Tremblay believed she would see the connection; right now, that was good enough for her.

But first they had to get the dollhouse inside, and Coughdrop wasn't making that easy. The dog was on the threshold of the sitting room, barking noisily and pacing back and forth across the width of the French doors, determined to keep the intruders out.

"Pay him no mind," said Comfort to the deliverymen. "He wouldn't bite a biscuit."

She called the dog back and he came, but he wasn't happy about it. Two seconds later he lunged back toward the dollhouse. In trying to hop out of his way, one of the men ended up stepping on the dog's paw, sending Coughdrop into a yelping fury and scaring the dickens out of one of the others, who promptly let go of his end of the dollhouse, upsetting the balance. The unsupported end dropped to the floor, popping two of the pillars on one of the roofed verandas.

Aghast, Meg cried, "Oh, *no*," and grabbed the dog by his collar and tried to separate him, still barking furiously, from the house and its movers. At the last minute Coughdrop remembered that he was part retriever and lunged for one of the fallen pillars, then broke free of Meg and took off for the garden with the stick between his teeth. Comfort chased after him, screaming his name in a tremulous, shrill voice that brought the twins downstairs instantly to see what the ruction was all about.

In the meantime Meg was refusing to let any of the workmen move an inch until she had a chance to look the patient over, as it were, for other, more serious broken bones. Into the middle of all the chaos strolled Allie with her new and fairly constant companion, Tom Wyler. And since it was Wednesday, Chicken Pie Night, Uncle Billy was right behind them.

"Good Lord," said Bill Atwells, stopped cold by the sight. "Eagle's Nest! Damned if I don't remember it after all!"

Allie knew at once what was going on. "Meg, he's giving it to you, how *wonderful*. Well, he *should*, when you think about it; he owes us. Why is it half on the floor? Oh, God, it's broken already! Oh, for Pete's sake—"

"What happened?" asked Uncle Bill.

Meg was on her hands and knees, still checking for damage. "Oh, Coughdrop went crazy."

"I said it before and I'll say it again: that dog's dumb as a bucket of fish manure." With a muffled "oof," Bill Atwells lowered his ample weight to the floor. "It don't look too bad. Them pillars'll stick right back in."

"I've never seen Coughdrop behave like that," Meg said,

wondering. "Listen to him out there." She stood up and directed the dollhouse onto the table, then gave the men a little something for their trouble and saw them to the door.

Everyone was gathered around the empty house, marveling at its craftsmanship. Allie wanted to know if the furniture came with it, and when Meg explained that it was being packed up for delivery, her sister said, "Great! We'll have a house-decorating party. It'll be like a tree-trimming party, only with tables and cradles instead."

Meg's first impulse was to say, "Not on your *life*," but her uncle made that unnecessary.

"Don't be silly, Allie," he said. "You can't go risking breakage that way. These ain't Barbie doll accessories. This kind of stuff's for the collector." He turned to Meg with a broad grin, obviously pleased at the turn in the family's fortunes. "It's a fairy tale, Meggie," he said, "and you're our crown princess."

"I don't think crowns are my style," Meg said thoughtfully. She ran her finger along a delicately wrought banister of the dollhouse. For all its power to please and enchant, the house seemed to have an equal and opposite power to disturb and repel. She thought of haunted houses and witches behind cobwebby curtains and suppressed a shudder.

Was she alone in feeling that way about the house? Everyone else seemed pretty delighted by it, including Tom Wyler.

"Well, Lieutenant?" she couldn't resist asking. "Don't you think this proves how serious Orel Tremblay is?"

Uncle Billy looked up from the dollhouse. "What d'you mean, 'serious'?"

Damn. Meg had forgotten her uncle was there. She'd forgotten *anyone* was there besides Tom Wyler. It was becoming awkward, the way she kept picking fights with Tom. If only he'd bend a little and get involved.

"I only meant, how seriously Mr. Tremblay feels about the

history of Bar Harbor," Meg said quickly. "He wants to make sure the dollhouse stays right here."

Uncle Billy grunted. "You're the right owner for it, then. *You'll* never leave Bar Harbor."

Tom, hands in his pockets, had been watching Meg lie her way out of her jam. Out of the blue he said to her, "How about joining Allie and me for dinner in town?"

Allie's head shot up in amazement.

Meg saw the warning look her sister was firing across her bow. "Gee . . . no, I'd better not. I have to get the dollhouse settled in."

Allie slipped her arm through Tom's and chirped, "See you all later, then."

Wyler extended his hand to Uncle Billy and said, "Nice to see you again, sir."

Uncle Billy, surprised no doubt that Allie was seeing someone with old-fashioned manners, said, "You betcha. And by the way," he said to his niece, "how'd that interview go in Boston?"

"They want me," Allie said with an elegant shrug of her off-shoulder top. "But it's too far away from . . . where I want to be," she added, giving Wyler the kind of look that made men leap over tall buildings.

They left, with Allie carefully avoiding Meg's wide-eyed look of surprise, and Meg was left to control her rage as best she could. She'd brain Allie when she got back. *She* hadn't known that they wanted Allie. So Allie'd thumbed her nose at *Boston*. Boston! The best possible choice! Not too far for the family, not too close for Allie. They'd talked about Boston constantly during the last year. Boston was *it*, as far as Meg was concerned. Maybe a job as guest representative *wasn't* the moon and the stars. Maybe the pay *was* piddling. In fact, Allie *had* come back unenthusiastic. But to turn it down because of the *location*. Boston was *perfect*.

Boston was as far from Chicago as you could *get*.

* * *

"Well, it can't stay in the sitting room, that's for durn sure." Everett Atwells didn't know much about decorating, but he did know that normal knickknacks didn't run four-by-five by two-and-a-half feet.

"I know, Dad," Meg said, smiling at her father's consternation. The house could've been a horse, as far as he was concerned. "I've been cleaning out the back shed to keep it in."

"And a filthy mess you've made of yourself, girl," he said, surveying his smudgy offspring. "So, what're your plans? You gonna run an ad, or just bring in someone to auction it?"

"Dad! I'm not *selling* it!" Meg said, scandalized.

"Well, what the heck else can you do with it? Give tours?"

"I don't know. But it stays. At least for now."

"Okay, noodle." He leaned over and kissed the top of his daughter's head. "You know the situation best."

The situation. That would be their financial situation, of course. Precarious at best, terrifying at worst. This year was better than some but worse than most. It was interesting, the way her father assumed that the proceeds from any sale of the dollhouse would go into the general pot. In his mind it was one for all and all for one. But then, anyone who'd ever been there on Chicken Pie Night would know that.

She tapped the deck of cards sticking out from his shirt pocket. "How'd you do tonight?"

Instantly he reached behind for his wallet. "Ten bucks. Are you short—?"

She laughed and shook her head and sent him on his way. It was late, eleven thirty, but Meg was too tired to shower, so she brewed herself a cup of tea and went out to the sitting room to just . . . look, for a while, at her inheritance. Comfort had managed to recover the purloined pillar; Meg rolled it between her fingers, clucking softly over Coughdrop's teeth marks in it, and fitted it gently into place on the miniature veranda.

It was designed to slip in easily, a nice little feat of engineering. The whole thing was so beautifully, enchantingly constructed. Meg would've liked to turn on its lights, but apparently she needed a transformer, and that was arriving with the furnishings. Tomorrow. She felt as impatient as a new homeowner waiting for moving day.

She and Paul had never quite managed the down payment on a home of their own, of course. At one point they were almost there, and they had gone to Uncle Billy for the rest of the money. But he'd just shaken his head and said, "Don't like the house; don't like to lend."

Well, everyone knew Uncle Billy was tight as the bark to a tree. But Meg had embarrassed Paul by convincing him that they had a chance, and he never quite forgave her for it. She smiled, remembering Paul's fierce pride. How he'd hated working in Uncle Billy's hardware store. And yet she'd never have met him otherwise. When they moved to Trenton, she hoped Paul might be happy with his new job as a contractor, but the recession had nipped those hopes in the bud.

Finally, when he landed the job at the boatyard in Southwest Harbor, his life turned around. He loved working on boats, loved everything about them: their exactness, their beauty, the wonderful freedom they promised. "Better than the bike," he decided, which astonished her. The Harley-Davidson had been bought with down-payment money. It was a dumb thing to do, but he'd been so unhappy.

The ad to sell the Harley was still running, and Meg was still pregnant, the weekend Paul lost control of the bike on the Park Loop Road.

After that: no bike, no boat, no house, no baby, no Paul. Meg went numb, and then she went home, because—as Comfort had so simply put it—"home is where they have to take you in." When she got there, she found Allie in a mess and Comfort overwhelmed with the job of caring for twins. Somehow the three of them managed to survive. Nowadays Meg, at least, was content. Maybe not joyful, but content.

And now, at last, she was a homeowner. The irony was that the dollhouse was probably worth as much as some starter home outside of town. She'd told her father that she wasn't going to sell the dollhouse, and she meant it. Maybe what she needed was a piece of Alice's mushroom, to shrink herself down to fit inside.

Meg stood up and stretched wearily, then circled the exquisite shingled structure, still holding her half-drunk cup of tea. The house wasn't the same without its interior lights lit, no doubt about it. It was like a jack-o'-lantern with no candle, a Christmas tree with the plug pulled out. And yet even now—she could feel it; it wasn't her imagination—the dollhouse had an undeniable *presence*. Something, somehow, was beckoning to her from within. Call it magic, call it soul; the house had it.

She just didn't know what to do about it.

The dollhouse was still in the sitting room and Meg was still in the back shed preparing the site when Allie came in to invite her sister to, of all things, a séance.

"Gee, I'm afraid you're too late," Meg said dryly. "I just signed up for AT&T's Reach Out program."

Allie picked up a broom and poked her sister in the behind with it. "I'm serious. Julia's having a séance at the Elm Tree Inn. Actually, they don't call it a séance; it's a 'darkroom session.' It turns out Julia Talmadge has a friend, some college pal from Wellesley, who channels—you know, who has one of those spirit guides helping her get in touch with the beyond? The friend lives in Philadelphia, and every Tuesday night she and a dozen friends get together to peek on the other side of the veil."

"*Roseanne* must be too down-to-earth for them," Meg quipped good-naturedly.

"Meg! We're really lucky to be asked. Normally the group is closed to outsiders."

"What's this channeler person doing so far from Philadelphia?"

Allie held the dustpan while her sister swept a mound of dirt onto it and said, "Julia told me one of the group happened to visit Acadia last summer and got strong psychic vibrations in the park, especially near Thunder Hole. So the group's taken over most of the Elm Tree Inn through the weekend. And tonight they're going to test the spiritual waters around here."

"I see. Kind of a New Age group tour. Well, I hope a spirit or two obliges them," Meg said. "Maybe they should just stick to whale watching." She shook her head thoughtfully. "I wonder how they can afford this junket? I mean, it's definitely cheaper to go to church."

"Different strokes for different folks, Meg. Julia says three or four of them are wealthy widows looking for their husbands."

"Gee. Why settle for old when you can afford new?"

"Meg!"

"I know, I know," Meg said without contrition. "Sour grapes." She sighed and took another sweep with her broom into Allie's dustpan. "But some of these women make wealth look so . . . *natural*. It's like magic money just falls from the sky on them."

Allie cocked her head up at her sister. "What about the dollhouse, Mrs. Hazard? Didn't that fall from the sky?"

Meg sucked in her breath and blushed to the neck of her dark blue T-shirt. "God, you're right. I keep forgetting I'm an heiress."

"Don't worry; no one around here will ever let you do that. So what about it? Wanna come?"

Meg wrinkled her nose. "I don't think so. I'm due to visit Orel Tremblay in an hour, and the taxpayers' committee is having a meeting this afternoon. So I won't be able to move in until tonight—move the furniture in, I mean," she said quickly.

"Okay, then. I'll drag Tom. He's never been to a séance."

"You're just looking for an excuse to hold hands," Meg teased, but there was a brittle edge in her own voice that surprised her.

"You laugh," Allie said with a woeful look, "but a séance is about what it will take. I've never seen anyone look so interested and do so little about it. I thought he was going to kiss me, that night we had the full moon. Everything seemed so right. And yet—nothing."

"I remember that night," Meg said quietly.

"He absolutely fascinates me, Meg. I've never met anyone else who's had the willpower to—"

"—resist you?"

"—to resist me before. I feel like a piece of candy during Lent. I don't know what he's waiting for. He seems to've drawn some line for himself that he just won't cross. He wines me and dines me—well, he seltzers me and dines me—and seems up for anything I want to do. He laughs at my jokes. He tells plenty of his own. He'll stroke my cheek or caress my shoulder, but that's as far as it goes. Do you think maybe his wound's a little higher than he's told us?"

Meg laughed out loud. "Now, *you* have what I call a healthy ego," she said, hanging up the broom. "Did it ever occur to you that there might be other reasons for him not to be throwing himself on you?"

Allie emptied the dustpan into a waste basket. "He's *not* still in love with his ex-wife, if that's what you're thinking," she said quickly. "That I know. She's remarried and lives in California and he seems okay about it. He said she always wanted to live in the suburbs anyway, and they don't let you do that if you're a city cop."

"There are other possibilities, Allie. Maybe there's a girlfriend. Maybe you're too young. Maybe he doesn't like flings. Maybe he's gun-shy. Maybe you're too pretty. Maybe he's afraid to come near.''

Of all the reasons that Meg rattled off, the last was the one that, wouldn't you know it, managed to sink in.

"Afraid? Of what? It's not like we're Mafia. Who would scare him off, anyway? Dad? Not in a million—*you*! Meg! How *could* you?" Allie cried, flinging the dustpan to the floor. It bounced with a jarring, metallic clang, a call to arms.

Meg sighed and bit her lip. All their lives they'd fought this battle of Meg-knows-best.

"Allie, listen to me; I did *not* scare him away," she said, taking her sister by her arm. But Allie yanked it free and turned away from her.

"Okay," said Meg. "Be that way. All I told him was . . . all I said was . . . oh, hell, I don't remember exactly. But basically it was to go slow because you were dear to us. Is that so awful?" She held her arms up in a gesture of frustration, then let them flop to her sides.

Allie ran her hands through her long black hair, apparently toying with the thought of tearing it out. She turned to her sister in a blaze of violet-eyed fury. "You don't get it, do you, Ms. Corleone! This is *serious*. Tom Wyler *matters*. No one else *does*. No one! And right now that includes—"

Allie bit off the finish, turned, and marched out of the shed, slamming the door on her sister.

Meg stood there, shocked. This was new, this fierceness. Meg and Allie had arm wrestled over many things in her life, from curfews to colleges. But Meg had never seen such hostility in her sister's eyes before. It sickened her to think that they were being driven apart by someone who didn't even exist for them two weeks ago.

This one's different, she remembered Allie's saying on the night he arrived. God, how could she have known so fast? How could anyone know? Obviously Tom Wyler wasn't rush-

ing into anything. Whether it was because he wasn't interested
—ha!—or whether it was because Meg had scared him off, he
was definitely taking his time.

And that was fanning Allie's interest into a blaze the size of
the Bar Harbor Fire.

When Meg finally got the call from Orel Tremblay's nurse
that he was alert enough to see her, it was late in the afternoon. In ten minutes she was standing on his front steps, a pot
of red geraniums in her arms, knocking gently on his door.
The nurse let her in; immediately Meg knew that something
had changed. She could see it in the sad smile on the nurse's
face, hear it in her muted footfalls as she led Meg into the
darkened room where the old man lay dying.

That he was dying, she had no doubt. He'd lost more
weight: his cheeks were pale and sunken under the white
straggle of beard that had been allowed, like his front lawn, to
grow unchecked. His hospital gown hung loosely on his
wasted body. It seemed hard to believe that his collarbone, so
clearly outlined, would not pierce his skin. There was so little
left to him. If she had wanted to, Meg could've counted every
bone in his hand.

And his eyes: they seemed to see her, and yet they didn't.
He was focused on something else now, something that he
alone could see hovering at the foot of his bed.

"Mr. Tremblay," she said with infinite tenderness, "I've
come to thank you. For your gift. I . . . I know what it means
to you. I understand."

He didn't turn to look at her, but only moved his head in a
whisper of a nod.

"I believe your story, Mr. Tremblay. I won't stop until I
prove it's true."

He closed his eyes; they stayed closed. She had a moment
of sinking panic, until a tear slipped away from under his
eyelid and trickled across his cheek, along his ear. And then

he opened his eyes again, and turned his head to look at her, and tried to say something through another glaze of tears. But the words wouldn't come. He turned back to stare at whatever it was that Meg was still too alive to see.

She lifted a chair as if it were made of spun glass and placed it gingerly next to his bed. Then she took his bony, silken hand in both of hers, and held it until the sun went down, and a little beyond. Only once during that time did she speak. After the nurse looked in and took his pulse and left, Meg whispered to him, "It's safe with me. I promise."

She felt a pressure under her hand as if a tiny bird, a finch, perhaps, had fluttered its wings there. And when he died, she thought she heard the soft, quick flutter of that same bird pass close.

CHAPTER 8

Tom Wyler didn't have the faintest idea what to wear to a séance. Dark and formal? Light and casual? He settled on a tie and blazer, but then he took off the tie. And then the blazer.

If word got back to the precinct that he'd sat around a table holding hands with a bunch of flakes, he was dead meat for sure; the guys would never let him hear the end of it. Not that he had any great grudge against psychics. The Boston P.D. had used them in their hunt for the Strangler, and so had L.A., when they'd run out of leads in the Hillside case.

He thought of Meg Hazard and her burning need to know the truth about her grandmother. Too bad she'd decided not to come tonight. Granted, the séance route was a little serendipitous, but it was one way for Meg to get her answer: summon the lady and ask her herself.

He came out of his room wearing chinos and a polo shirt and whistling a half tune, only to find that everyone was already gathered in the grandly furnished parlor of the Elm Tree Inn. The Sunset Room, as Julia Talmadge liked to call it, had a different look now that its three bay windows were walled in by drapes; tonight it seemed more claustrophobic than cozy. The side buffet, normally covered with an array of wines and cheeses before dinner each evening, was covered instead with lighted candles, some in brass holders, some in silver, some in crystal.

A dozen candles burning, and not a bite to eat. Already he was disappointed.

He smelled a smoky something that at first he thought was pot, and wondered whether he was going to have to bust them all right then and there. But it turned out to be some pungent herbal incense. *Terrific*, he thought. *A bunch of Indian wanna-bes*. It was going to be a long night.

Still, there was Allie, beautiful and somehow appropriate in a simple blouse of diaphanous white that she wore over a long black skirt. Her hair was pulled back in a twist, leaving a halo of ebony around the pale perfection of her face. She wore surprisingly red lipstick.

"Hey there," he murmured when she came up to him with an amusing, vampy smile. "How did I ever let you talk me into this?"

"Oh, we'll have fun," she whispered. "You'll see."

Wyler had no doubt that she was right. Everything Allegra Atwells chose to do had a fun quotient built into it. Her energy was as boundless as her imagination. It was incredibly flatter-ing that she expected him to keep up with her on either front.

He was introduced to the company. Besides Allie and Julia, there were a dozen others scattered around the room. Their leader was named Zenobia and was the innkeeper Julia's age, about sixty. The rest of the group, mostly women, ranged in age from twenty to seventy. Everyone was relaxed and com-fortable with one another; obviously they were old hands at this.

The oldest guests were in the softest seats. The middle-aged ones were standing or sitting in rush-seated chairs, while sev-eral of the limber ones had plopped down on the red Persian rug that dominated the room. Zenobia suggested that Allie pull out the bench from under the grand piano and sit there. Wyler was told to take up a position between her and a potted palm. He noticed that the others formed a vaguely circular pattern, and that he and Allie were positioned outside it. Well, whatever worked.

"I can't believe your sister is skipping such a quick and easy way to find out if you-know-who is guilty of you-know-what," he murmured in Allie's ear.

Allie didn't think much of his irreverence; a sharp elbow in his thigh made that clear to him. *"Don't* make fun; you remind me of Meg. Be more open to things, why don't you," she said in a scandalized mutter.

Okay, so he was acting like a high-school dufus. It was a defensive reaction, of course; he was embarrassed to be here. Chastened, he settled down and decided to give Zenobia—first name, last name, he hadn't a clue—his undivided attention.

Zenobia was not only Julia's age but, he felt sure, of similar background. Her silk paisley tunic was a little more fey than Julia's button-front skirt and linen blouse, and her hair, gray and permed into long frizzles, gave her a touch of the aging hippie. New Age or old, Zenobia had the ease and poise of a woman who'd never had to ride a bus in her life and who still paid the dues at her country club. Oh, yeah. He'd seen the type.

Zenobia and Julia finished up a conversation they were having about how much peanut butter to put in chili, which gave the moment a kind of hopelessly surreal quality, and then the innkeeper turned off the lights and the psychic got down to business.

Zenobia had a wonderful voice, that was the first thing Wyler noticed: warm and relaxed and completely reassuring. She had a way of making all of them, including him, feel as if they were puppies in an animal shelter and she was looking to adopt. You wanted her just to pack you up and take you home.

"I want to thank our hostess Julia Talmadge," Zenobia began, "for making our first day here so delightful. Really, it's been *so* nice. Bar Harbor is a charming seaside town, and we look forward to exploring Acadia Park tomorrow. But . . . for now, for tonight, I'd like us to just take a moment and think: why is it that we are all here?

"Why is it," she continued in that wonderfully kind voice, "that each of us is here, in the Sunset Room of the Elm Tree Inn, on this particular evening of our lives? What events have led us to be here? Is there some significance to them? Do we exist in some particular alignment to one another, like the stars in the universe? Or are we merely specks in random collisions, glancing off one another like dry leaves on a windy day?"

She let the questions sink in, and then she said, "I for one believe that we are here because each of us has behaved in a particular way up until this moment. We've made a series of decisions, some big, some small, motivated by either reason or emotion, which have led us to be sitting right here, right now.

"We know, for example, that last summer Sylvie had a life-altering experience in Thunder Hole. Since then, she's managed to convince us all to take the time and spend the money to see for ourselves what greater force may hover there. We all know that as a result of her experience in Thunder Hole, Sylvie left a job she hated as comptroller in a ceramics import company, and opened her own pottery shop. We all know how happy she's been since she took control of her fate.

"Let's think about that for a few moments. Let's think about the events that have led us to be at this place, at this time."

Zenobia smiled on them all, a smile that even Wyler had to admit was positively radiant.

Yeah, he thought. *Charisma. Aura. Bedside manner*. Call it what you like, all group leaders had it, from preachers to presidents.

He glanced around the room. Everyone was following Zenobia's advice in his or her own way. One of the squatters had folded herself into the classic lotus position and sat with her eyes closed, thumbs and middle fingers touching. The guy standing at the mantel was staring at a pattern in the Persian rug. The elderly woman with the knitting in her lap, the one he'd dubbed Miss Marple, was busy clicking her needles in what he supposed was the rhythm of meditation. Some of the others simply looked blank, each in his own little trance.

And Allie? Head bowed, absolutely earnest. It surprised Wyler when she reached for his hand, probably in violation of the rules, and held it. Was it a plea for him to get more involved? Or simply a gentle reminder that a series of decisions, rational and emotional, had indeed led him to be at this place, at this time?

He didn't want to think about that. He shoved the thought aside. No gunfire allowed; this was a bullet-free zone. But the image persisted: sweet, dead little Cindy with the bright blue eyes. Four years old. Shot dead. Her killer dead. Wyler wounded. And all for what? For nothing. It depressed him unutterably. If he was here for any reason at all, it was because he was burned out, emotionally and intellectually. If he was here, it was because he was trying to hide. He stared at Zenobia, resenting her gentle prodding, resenting her kindness.

Dammit, he thought. *I won't let her bring Cindy back.*

He'd learned a trick of his own for clearing his mind of negative thoughts. A sergeant had taught him, when he was new to homicide, that a negative attitude was the kiss of death to an ongoing investigation. It closed you off from avenues of possibilities. The sergeant had shown him how to clear his mind by meditating on a single syllable, any syllable. Clancy's own choice was the classic "ohm." Wyler had laughed when Clancy first said it; but you only got to laugh once at a two-hundred-twenty-pound cop who could toss back a quart of Jameson's and still beat you at arm wrestling.

As it happened, tonight Wyler didn't need "ohm." The memory of Clancy was good enough to banish negative thoughts.

He glanced at Zenobia. Her eyes were closed. She looked as if she might be asleep. He was wondering how rude it would be if he just slipped away, when suddenly Zenobia tensed up. The next words out of her mouth—high-pitched and feisty and nothing at all like her normal voice—jolted him.

"Hey! Sylvie! About this Thunder Hole business!"

A shudder of awareness seemed to ripple through the group. They were expecting this, that was obvious. It seemed to bother them not at all that Zenobia was slumped over with her eyes closed and speaking to them in another dialect. Sylvie, in fact, seemed downright pleased to be the first one addressed.

"Yes, Arnold?" she said in a thrilled, hushed voice.

Sylvie was a thirtyish woman with the face of an artist, pale and ethereal, with wispy reddish hair roped into a long braid that hung down the back of her flowery, flowing dress.

"Tell us again about Thunder Hole. For those who don't know."

Wyler looked around. Who didn't know about Thunder Hole besides him?

"Oh!" said Sylvie. "Well, it's a place on the west shore of Acadia where the waves crash against the rocks into a small cavern near the path. On the day I was there, the wind must've been just the right direction, because the waves were huge. Crashing, and just huge. There was a group of schoolkids with their teacher there before me, and they were so noisy I thought about moving on.

"But for some reason, I stayed. Eventually they left, and I was alone. The waves just kept on crashing and crashing, and each time, I felt this spray of salt, like they were slaps, you know, across my face?

"And every wave, every slap, screamed the same thing to me: 'Wake up! You're sleepwalking through life! Wake up!' So I did. I went home, quit my job, and rented a little studio."

She was sitting alongside the buffet, and in the flickering glow of the candles Wyler could see her hands as she gestured through her little story. They were the hands of an artist, graceful and expressive; the hands of a potter, dry and cracked and with the nails trimmed short.

"You think you couldn't have figured this out without the waves?"

"Oh, no, Arnold. I'm sure I couldn't."

"You think the waves have some mystical power?"

"To communicate? Yes, of course. That's why we're all here."

"I beg to disagree."

A collective gasp of shock echoed around the room. Wyler began to perk up.

"How do you mean?" asked Sylvie in a faint voice.

"I mean, you're from Cincinnati! What do you know about salt spray? No more than me, a dust-bowl farmer from Kansas. Is there any doubt you'd be impressed by pounding seas? Sure you would. And you should. But that don't make it mystical, not in the way you *mean."*

"I don't understand . . . I don't even agree, Arnold. Why would you let us come, in that case? Why are we all here?"

"For pity's sake—to have a good time. To relax and hike and take in the salt air. To let yourself go. But don't expect the sea to hold no conversations with you. It ain't gonna happen."

Wyler tried very hard not to laugh and failed. It came out in one short whoop, just loud enough for Allie—still holding his hand—to yank his arm nearly out of its socket. He made a wincing face of apology to the scandalized company, afraid that he'd offended Arnold too deeply for the session to go on.

No such luck. After a moment Sylvie said, "I'll try to take your words to heart," and the conversation moved on to other, less provocative ground.

Arnold had lots of advice for everyone; Wyler found him an opinionated but likable son of a bitch. The farmer wasn't the least bit shy about telling an elderly widow to place an ad in the personals; about warning a couple to pull out their money from a financial planner they disliked; and about urging Julia to seek a zoning variance to build an addition to the Elm Tree Inn.

It was surprisingly specific and mundane stuff. Wyler had always had the impression that séances were more cosmic than this. Obviously the "metaphysical" in this meeting didn't refer to the subject matter.

After it was over—after Zenobia groaned softly and opened her eyes and began speaking in that reassuringly warm voice of hers—Julia turned on the lights, and the group dissolved into spontaneous pockets of conversation.

Wyler turned to Allie and said, "Arnold seems pretty savvy for a dust-bowl farmer. Although, personally, I think he gave the retired couple bum advice; they should stick with bonds and utilities."

"You're *horrible*," Allie said, exasperated. "Meg is right about you."

"Oh? And what does our Meg have to say about me?" he asked all too quickly. The fact was, he didn't give a tinker's damn what Meg Atwells had to say about him, because he already knew: She thought his heart was hardened. He remembered quite well their exchange on the town dock. The memory made his cheeks burn.

"My sister said—" Allie bit her lip and looked away, then looked back to him and took a deep breath. Wyler had the sense that this time she wasn't playing up to him, wasn't acting.

"You really want to know?" she asked, lowering her voice. "My sister said you're the worst of all worlds: You're from a big city, and you're a homicide cop. She said you've seen too much violence, too much evil in men, to be able to care about anything any—"

"Well, Mr. Wyler. What did you think? I found it all quite fascinating."

It was Julia Talmadge, smiling and diplomatic, ever the perfect hostess.

Wyler was mad enough just then to tell Julia the truth, that he thought it was a scream. Where else would you get a voice from beyond warning people not to listen to voices from beyond?

"As a matter of fact," he said, "I, too, found it fascinating. Where else would you get a voice from beyond warning people—ow!"

"Oh, dear; it's your leg again, Tom, isn't it?" Allie asked with a concerned look, taking his arm.

"It's more my foot," he said with a thin smile. The spot where she'd jammed her little spike heel was throbbing in pain.

"We'll just say our thank-yous, and then you can give me that novel, Tom, and I'll get out of your hair," said Allie with the smile of an angel and the grip of a steelworker.

In lockstep, they said good-night to everyone. Zenobia turned away from her admiring circle and gave Wyler a look unlike anything he'd ever seen before. Irritation, amusement, condescension—you could find anything you wanted to find in those gorgeous green eyes. The look stayed with Wyler as he and Allie strolled back to his rooms. He shivered, then shook it off. He took down the novel from his well-stocked bookshelf and handed it to Allie with a look of contrition. "Stay for coffee?" he asked. He wanted to apologize more thoroughly for being such an ass.

He'd been careful so far not to linger in his rooms with Allie, mostly out of deference to Julia and Meg and Uncle Billy and the twins and God knew who all else; but enough was enough. It wasn't his fault that Bar Harbor was such a fishbowl.

He was amazed when Allie said no.

"How could you *do* that?" she said, flinging the novel on the couch. "How could you embarrass me like that? Didn't you get *any* sense that something special was happening in that room? Is it possible that you're so . . . so—''

''Hardened?''

''*Hardened*, that you saw nothing but a bunch of flaky people grasping at mystical straws? Well, *I* felt something. How could you not? There were such wonderful *vibrations* in that room. But you! You could've ruined everything! God, Meg was right. Meg *was* right.''

''Meg is always right,'' he said laconically. ''That goes without saying. But I'm curious. Just how much time do the two of you spend picking apart my neuroses?''

''Don't flatter yourself, mister,'' Allie said, folding her arms across her chest and firing a scathing look at him. ''It's not all that much.''

But her cheeks darkened as she made the claim, which interested him very much.

''My sister said that homicide for you is nothing more than a game of chess. She said you're involved in the cases, but you're not *really* involved. You know? You can't let yourself care. You could lose that cool detachment that probably makes you very good at what you do. But—''

Now there were *two* of them pounding his heartlessness into him. He couldn't stand it; without thinking, he took Allie by her shoulders and kissed her, hard, to prove something, he didn't know what. It caught her completely by surprise. He felt her yield beneath his kiss and return it with a small moaning sound, felt her slide her hands up along his arms, to his shoulders.

He felt her push him away.

''No!'' she said sharply. ''This isn't what I want!''

She was standing there, breathless, her lips parted and a little swollen, her eyes wide with emotion.

''I'm sorry,'' he said quickly. ''Truly. I . . . well, I thought you were sending signals . . . have *been* sending signals. Well!'' he said, plunging his hands into his pockets. He let out a short, ironic laugh. ''I see now that I was a fool.''

''That's another thing,'' said Allie with a reproachful, glistening look. ''The first day we laid eyes on you, Meg warned me not to get excited about you. And what d'you know? She was right about *that*, too!''

When Meg came home that night Allie was waiting, red-eyed and woeful, in Meg's big iron bed.

''Where *were* you?'' the younger woman wailed. ''I looked everywhere.'' She blew noisily into a big white handkerchief.

''I was out walking. Why? What's wrong?'' Meg asked, sitting on the side of the bed. Obviously it couldn't be *too* tragic; Allie would've had the whole family out searching for Meg. It wouldn't have been the first time.

*''Every*thing's wrong!''

''What's he done?'' said Meg, absolutely certain who ''everything'' was.

''He *kissed* me!''

Three words; they were like three quick blows to the throat. Meg didn't know what to say. ''Ah,'' she finally remarked. ''Then you got your wish.''

''That's just it,'' Allie said, dropping her head to her chest. ''I didn't just *wish*.''

She sighed and lifted her head back up; a tear rolled down her face, reminding Meg of another tear, another face. Her time with Orel Tremblay had left her bereft of emotion. She had nothing left to give her lovesick sister.

She had to force herself to continue the conversation. ''You mean you kissed him first?''

''Worse. I practically forced him to kiss me. I threw everything you said about him being cold and remote in his face. Naturally he had to kiss me then. To prove he wasn't.''

''Allie! For God's sake—can't you at least make up your own insults?''

Allie moaned and twisted the top sheet around her fists, then began rocking from the waist up, like a child who feels she's been punished by mistake. Her hair was half up, half down, adding to her forlorn appearance.

"I don't know why I did it," she said in a singsong wail. "He was just so *irritating*, at the séance. You were right. He *is* irritating. He had the most wonderful chance to reflect on the turn of fate that brought him to me, and instead he just blew it! So now we have to start all over." She closed her eyes. "Oh, God . . . I can still taste his kiss, Meg," she whispered. "How I hate this."

"Yes. Well." Meg stood up and began unbuttoning her blouse, still damp from her own tears. "Orel Tremblay died tonight," she said abruptly. She threw the blouse on a nearby chair.

Stunned, Allie stopped mid-rock. "Oh, no. Oh, Meg." She climbed out of her sister's bed and put her arms around her. "I'm *so* sorry. Here I'm . . . oh, Meg. I'm such a selfish pig."

"Sometimes." Meg disengaged herself and stepped out of her skirt and tossed it on top of her blouse, then stripped off her underthings. She slipped a cotton nightgown over her head. "I'm tired, Allie," she said to her sister, who was hovering solicitously. "I just want to go to bed."

"No! Not alone. I'll sleep here tonight."

Allie ignored her sister's protests and climbed into the side by the wall. Meg turned off the light and the two women lay side by side in the darkness without speaking.

Allie broke the silence first. "Did he suffer?" she asked in a hesitant, sad voice.

"I don't see how someone can *not* suffer when he knows he's dying," Meg said with a shuddering sigh. "He was leaving so much behind. Not just the dollhouse, not just his unfinished business. But everything. Family . . . friends . . .

music . . . babies . . . the sea . . . books . . . trees. The stars, the moon. Everything.''

After a moment, Allie said, ''He didn't really care about most of that, though, did he.''

''But *I* do,'' Meg answered with a catch in her throat. ''I do.''

They were quiet again, until Allie asked, ''Did he say anything more about Grandmother?''

Meg shook her head in the darkness. ''It was too late for that.''

''What will you do now?''

''I think I'll go see Gordon Camplin,'' Meg said, voicing a decision she'd made earlier.

She sighed, and then Allie sighed, and Meg felt her sister's pain over Tom Wyler, as well as her own sadness. ''He's a jerk,'' Meg said, reassuringly. ''They all are, sooner or later. They really can't help it.''

''I guess.''

''I'll go see *him*, too.''

''Would you, Meg? I have no right to ask.''

''And I have no right to meddle.'' Meg rolled over on her sleeping side. ''So what else is new?'' she said with a weary sigh.

Morning came, and with it, bright sunshine. After a night of troubled dreams, Meg was happy to be awake, happy simply to be alive. She was quite determined to move forward on her plan to pursue Gordon Camplin. There was something about a deathbed promise that simplified everything. A deathbed promise left no room for caution, or even common sense. A deathbed promise had to be kept.

As they cleaned up after breakfast, Meg and Allie discussed strategies with wild abandon, because for a change they had the house to themselves. Comfort was in the principal's office (again), Lloyd was out tracking down used parts for the pickup (again), and their father was out fishing with his poker pals. No self-respecting visitor to Acadia would stay inside on a day so glorious: The half-dozen guests staying at the Inn Between were long gone.

Wyler apparently had taken his cue from the weather as well; his car wasn't in its usual space. Allie was disappointed, Meg relieved. In the meantime, Allie was being wonderfully cooperative about joining forces to nail Gordon Camplin. After all, a deal was a deal.

"If only it weren't so long ago," Allie said, folding the checked towel over the stove handle the way Comfort liked it. "What possible evidence can there be? Everything burned to the ground in '47. All that survived of the houses were the chimneys. Look at the photo."

Meg, sitting on a high stool at the Formica-topped work island that Lloyd had proudly built, was doing just that. She had an old, photo album open in front of her, an album that her father had put together at the age of fifteen to deal with his grief at losing his mother to the fire. Meg had taken it out after her second visit to Orel Tremblay and paged through it, looking for obvious clues. She hadn't found them then, and she wasn't finding them now.

The small black-and-white photograph of the ruins of Eagle's Nest, for example, offered little to see: a rambling granite foundation and seven naked, standing chimneys of granite and brick with gaping fireplaces in them. Everything else was flattened into burned-out rubble. It was hard to believe that so much grandeur could be reduced to so few ashes.

It was hard to believe that somewhere in the black-and-white rubble were Margaret Atwells's bones.

Meg took up a magnifying lens and pored over the photograph again. All it magnified was the fact that there was nothing left to see.

Allie said, "We at *least* have to go through the local papers that covered the fire—Bar Harbor, Bangor, Portland. I can do that.''

"Mmm, no, I think I should do that," Meg said absently, leafing backward through the album's pages.

"Oh, here we go: I'd-rather-do-it-myself. I should've known," Allie said, annoyed. "Are you going to let me help, or not?"

Meg had focused the magnifying glass over a family photo of her father, uncle, and grandparents. "Sure," she said without looking up. "You can find out what charitable committees and events Camplin's signed on to this year."

"What're we going to do? Go to some society affair disguised as waitresses?"

"No, we're going to *be* waitresses," said Meg calmly, looking up from the photo. "Everyone knows how hard up we are; and God knows we're experienced at serving cheese and crackers. We'll hire on as temps."

Allie gave her sister a skeptical look. "And then what? We trap him in the kitchen and hold a toothpick to his throat until he confesses?"

Meg shrugged. "Who knows? But I'd like to catch him in his element. His guard will be down then."

Allie warmed to the idea. "If that's true, maybe I should just get a job with the staff at his summer house. Maybe he'd suffer some kind of flashback episode when he saw me."

"I doubt it. You're not the one who looks like Grandmother. Here, take a look," Meg said, handing her sister the magnifying glass. "Do I really look like her?"

Allie zoomed the lens in and out on the small photograph. "Not really . . . yeah, maybe . . . especially the eyes, except your eyebrows are thinner. Your hair is lighter, but then, you're outside every chance you get. I don't suppose a nursemaid had that luxury. Look how small her waist is; smaller than mine, even."

"Corsets," said Meg instantly, feeling self-conscious that

her waist was bigger than either. "I like this photo. Obviously the family's dressed to go out. They look so normal. Look at that little peplum jacket with the fur collar she's wearing, and that gored skirt of giant plaid—and look, the hat she's holding is made of the same plaid." Meg plucked at the shoulder of her own vee-necked T-shirt. "Margaret Mary Atwells was more of a clotheshorse than *I'll* ever be."

"We live in a more casual era," said Allie generously, even though she herself liked to dress to the nines when the mood hit. She laughed and added, "Look at the grip she has on Dad's shoulder. And we wonder why he's so meek around women."

"Don't sell Dad short. Maybe she's holding on to him so he doesn't yank out the photographer's tripod. Terry would."

The sisters exchanged one of their ironic looks.

"Dad? I don't *think* so," Allie said, stealing a sip of her sister's cold coffee. She held the lens over the photo again. "One thing that's the same, although it's hard to tell in a person that's only an inch high—look at her smile. That's just the way you smile when some guest with a baby comes through, or when you arrange flowers for the sitting room. When you like something a lot."

"Really?" Meg took the magnifying lens and stared at the woman in plaid. It *was* a friendly smile, very natural, very appealing—but was it a smile to make a man besotted enough to kill?

Suddenly she didn't relish being connected to the photo, even if by the shadow of a smile. She turned the fragile black paper in search of other photographs of her grandmother, but she knew, and Allie knew, that there were none. The plaid-skirt photo was dated September 1947, a month before the fire.

"Okay," Meg said, closing the album with a resolute sigh. "I'll start with the historical society. Then the library. You start with the social calendar "

"Right now, today?" her sister asked eagerly.

"You don't have to run out the door," Meg said, smiling. "Whenever you have time. There's no huge rush."

"But there *is*," Allie answered, surprised by her sister's whenever-attitude. "Gordon Camplin could *die* if we're not quick."

"I don't see why," Meg said laconically. "I've seen him speed walking. He looks pretty damn fit."

Allie, hands on her hips, stared at Meg as if she'd just climbed down from a potato truck. "Don't be dumb, Meg; fitness has *nothing* to do with it."

"Oh. Right. What was I thinking. Obviously there's no connection between fitness and long life." Meg stuck her Bennington mug in the microwave for sixty seconds of coffee warm-up.

"That's not what I mean," Allie said impatiently. "What I'm trying to say is, if Gordon Camplin *is* guilty, he could very well be connected on some psychic plane to Orel Tremblay. With Mr. Tremblay dead, well—you know how sometimes an elderly husband will die within hours of his wife, or vice versa? It happens. All the time."

"Because they're *close*," Meg argued. "Gordon Camplin probably didn't even know Orel Tremblay was alive."

"Well, he knows Mr. Tremblay's dead, or will know, as soon as he sces the obituaries."

"Meaning what? We have to rush him off to the electric chair before he dies of natural—excuse me, supernatural—causes? This isn't about vengeance, Allie-cat," Meg said quietly.

Allie snorted incredulously. "What else, then?"

Meg gathered her golden-streaked hair and held it off her neck the way she did when she was working something through. "It's about . . . I don't know . . . it's about doing the right thing." She smiled self-consciously. "Doesn't that sound corny? Don't I sound old?"

Allie, twelve full years younger than her sister, laughed and leaned across the work island with an affectionate look. "You *are* old. Nyah, nyah."

"Yeah, brat? Then what's *this*," Meg said, reaching to pluck a hair from her sister's scalp. She dangled the strand between them like a contest prize: Long. Wavy. Gray.

Allie's eyes widened in horror. "Oh, *no*." She grabbed the hair from her sister's grasp. "This can't *be*. I'm only twenty-five years old." She stretched it between her fingers as if it were a kind of ruler, a fine-spun measure of her mortality. "Oh, no," she whispered.

Meg felt sorry that she'd pointed it out. Her sister's identity was completely bound up in her youth and beauty. What good could come of snatching it away from her? "Probably it's a one-shot," she said apologetically.

"I'm old," said Allie, entirely serious. "This is proof. I'm old. Gray, and unmarried, and old. I can't believe it. A gray hair before a husband." She walked over to the kitchen trash basket and dropped the strand into it. She was like a ship's captain, burying her shrouded youth at sea.

"Allie, get a grip," Meg said, becoming impatient with her sister's penchant for melodrama. "Buy a box of L'Oreal. You're worth it."

"Yeah," said Allie, staring into the trash can. "I'm worth it."

"Well, it's not as if you couldn't have married half a dozen different men," Meg said, amazed at the depth of her sister's distress. "What about Bob? Has he reproposed yet since you've been back?"

Although, come to think of it, Meg hadn't heard the roar of his Harley-Davidson rattling the cut-glass chandelier in the front hall.

Allie looked up blankly at her sister. "Bobby? Beaufort? Can you possibly be serious?"

"All right, not Bob. But someone, somewhere. You *will* be

married, obviously. For Pete's sake, if I have to, I'll go next door and drag your detective friend back to you, even if it's kicking and scre—''

''That's not necessary, Meg; here I am,'' said a voice from behind her, a voice that she hoped belonged to anyone in the world besides Lieutenant Thomas Wyler.

CHAPTER 9

Smiling, Wyler handed Allie a hardback book. "Here's your novel; you forgot it yesterday."

Allie's cheeks went crimson. She took the novel, lifted her chin, said, "Thank you very much; I think I'll go in the garden and read," and walked by him like a tennis star past a ball boy at Wimbledon.

Meg waited until her sister was outside, then nodded toward the hedge of mountain laurel that obscured Allie from their view. "I think that was your cue, Lieutenant."

Wyler laughed softly. "Are you kidding? She's still furious with me. If I went out there now, she'd cut out my heart and feed it to the seagulls. No, I think the best thing is to let her cool off."

Meg smiled and said, "Do you mind if I ask you something? How long were you married?"

"Ten years, on and off. Why?"

"Really!" Ten years, and he hadn't learned a thing. "Do you have any sisters?" she added impulsively.

Now it was his turn to look uncomfortable. "If you mean birth sisters, I wouldn't know. I was raised in a series of foster homes," he said, his mouth setting in a grim line. After a pause he added, "My second set of parents, and my fourth, had daughters of their own. Is there a direction this is taking us?'' he asked her coolly.

''I'm sorry,'' Meg said at once. ''I didn't mean to pry.'' Which of course she did. ''Can I be candid? It's just that you don't seem that much in tune, somehow, with how a woman's mind works.''

''I have three women detectives under my command,'' Wyler said testily. ''We get along fine.''

''Oh, sure, detectives. Persons of *logic*. I'm talking about my *sister*.''

He laughed at that, despite himself, and Meg laughed with him.

Feeling vaguely conspiratorial, Meg glanced out at the garden again. She could just catch a glimpse of Allie's yellow shorts. Her sister was sitting on the stone bench under the oak tree at the far end of the property. The stone bench was a stupid place to be if you wanted to read in any kind of comfort; but it was a charming spot to be if you were hoping for a rendezvous. Meg knew that Allie was counting on her to make that happen.

Last night, moved by her sister's pain, Meg would've done just about anything to drag the man back to Allie's feet. Today, with him right there and in no big hurry, she was having second thoughts. She had no business being intrigued by him; but she was.

But a promise was a promise.

''Lieutenant . . . Tom . . . I was just about to put on more coffee for Allie and me. I don't suppose you have time for a cup?''

Wyler had been leaning against the kitchen counter opposite her. Now he walked over to the window through which Meg had a view of her sister. He peered out toward the stone bench. ''Yes,'' he said. ''I'd like that.''

''Great.''

It shouldn't have, but his answer depressed her. Staying for coffee meant his carrying Allie's cup down a stepstone path through sweet-smelling roses and heady viburnums and under a rose-covered arbor, ending up at a stone bench just big enough for two. If you sat close.

The kiss between Allie and him had been bad enough, but this was worse. Allie had goaded him into the kiss, but no one was goading him into staying. He cared for Allie. Dammit, dammit, dammit. He really cared.

Meg made a production of setting up Comfort's prized Bunn coffeemaker. *"So.* How was your séance?" she asked in a stupidly cheerful voice.

She knew damn well he'd thought it was a farce.

"Not 'séance,' " he corrected as he unhooked a happy-face mug from a coffee tree on the counter where she was working. "It's called a 'darkroom session.' "

"Whatever." She flipped the *brew* switch and turned to get the half-and-half from the fridge at the same time that he about-faced, and they bumped into each other. Her breast brushed up against his chest, sending a jolt through her. "How . . . w-was it?" she repeated, faltering.

"Nice," he said instantly. She was half a breath away from him; she could almost hear the gears clunk into place as he rethought her question. "Uh-h . . . you mean the séance," he said, truly embarrassed. He tried to shrug it off. "Yeah . . . well . . . hmm . . . I'm not a big believer in the otherworldly. I tend to put my faith in the here and now."

He was standing very close, close enough for her to see how fair skinned he was, close enough for her to see the faint flush that had begun to darken the surface beneath his skin. It was an immensely endearing trait, this tendency of his to betray his emotions. And yet she knew instinctively that he would never do it on the job. He would never allow himself to be perceived as vulnerable.

"So," she said again, inanely. "How was the séance?"

He looked at her with a puzzled smile and said, "Do I have to keep answering that until I get it right or something?"

"No, no," she said quickly, realizing that she hadn't heard his first answer. "I'm sorry. I was thinking of something else."

She launched into a long and rambling monologue, trying to cover her own embarrassment. "The fact is," she said, "I don't put much stock in that kind of thing myself. I mean, just because there's a millennium coming up, everyone is running around looking for ghosts. You read about it all the time. Groups like Zenobia's are all over Maine. Sometimes they even charge a *fee*," she said indignantly. *"That's* not right. Do you think this mania could've happened in 1950? No. Absolutely not. It's because of the millennium. I'm convinced of it."

"So you think séances are hooey?"

"I didn't say that," Meg said quickly. "I wasn't at yours, of course. On the other hand, I *do* think this Sylvie person had a genuine experience in Thunder Hole. Not that there's anything supernatural about Thunder Hole. You could go anywhere in Acadia and feel what she felt. Clearly she tapped into the . . . the pulse of nature, the flow of energy there. I understand *that* part completely. There's something about the sea . . . something about the awesome, beautiful, uncaring *vastness* of it . . . it's like a starry sky on a moonless night, like—"

He was watching her with a quiet curiosity that brought her up short. "God, listen to me," she said with a nervous laugh. "Can I be any more vague than that? If that was one of Terry's compositions, I'd give it a 'C.' I suppose *you* deal only with hard facts," she added, continuing her babble. "You know, like Jack Webb? 'Just the facts, ma'am'? *Dragnet*?"

The hissing of the coffeemaker, like an audience unimpressed, brought her to a full stop. *"So,"* she said once more, tacking violently off in the other direction. "Read any good books lately?"

From the cosmic to the cliché in one fell swoop. *Naturally*, she told herself, *he will assume I'm insane.*

"Cream? Sugar?" she asked, limping at last to a halt.

That broke the spell; Wyler blinked and tried to sort out the threads of her tangled ramble. "I'm halfway through a pretty good biography of JFK," he said carefully, watching her with a sideways look. "And, ah, no sugar."

"All rightee," she said, seizing the refrigerator door and throwing it nearly off its hinges. She stared unseeing at the contents inside, aware only that her heart was thumping like a pile driver down at the docks. *What is wrong with me*? she asked herself in amazement.

All she could see was a bottle of ketchup. It seemed odd; there used to be more in there than ketchup. She continued to stare blankly at the shelves until Wyler reached in alongside her for the carton of half-and-half.

"You're letting all the cold air out," he scolded gently.

He was so close. She'd never before noticed the slight bump in the bridge of his nose. "This is Maine," she said with a shaky laugh. "No one worries about cold air escaping. Where would it go?"

The phone rang. She felt as if some referee had mercifully ended the round between them. "Excuse me, I have to get that," she said, sprinting out of the kitchen.

The call was from a picky shopper who wanted a description of every room, right down to the number of windows and the directions they faced. After the telephone tour, it turned out that the price was too high and Meg lost the booking anyway. By the time she got back to the kitchen, Wyler was gone and so was Allie's "Allie" mug.

Just as well, Meg decided morosely. One more conversation like that, and he'd be spearheading a drive to have her declared the village idiot. What could've possessed her to open up about her deepest feelings that way? What did an urbanite like him know about nature, anyway? *Zip*.

She craned her neck toward the stone bench at the far end of the garden and saw a patch of khaki pantleg. So Allie hadn't kicked him out. Of course not. Had Eve kicked out Adam?

None of it mattered, anyway, Meg decided with weary resignation. Wyler was a grownup and so was Allie. The only one who didn't seem to want to admit it was Meg, and even she was being forced to come around.

Meg made her way down a side path through the garden and slipped a key into the bright new padlock strung through the hasp on the shed door, then opened it and let herself in. The late-morning sun slanted through newly scrubbed windows and came to rest like a rainbow on the gabled roofs of the miniature Eagle's Nest. The dollhouse was still there, still real, still hers.

She didn't yet believe it, despite her frequent forays out to the shed to pinch herself. The house was so terribly beautiful at every time of day. As the light changed, *it* changed: its aura was alternately gray and mysterious, or twilit and brooding, or sunny and serene. This morning it looked like the summer house that ordinary kids can only dream about; the kind you biked past quickly before the dogs got wind of you and ran to the property's edge, barking furiously, letting the world know you weren't their people.

She walked around the house with the careful, scrutinizing eye of a fussy socialite, checking the rooms she'd already furnished. Yes. Every piece was exactly where it belonged; of that she was certain. She'd rolled out the foot-long Oriental rug in the dining room, placed the Chippendale-style table on it, and set the table for twelve, just the way she'd seen it in Orel Tremblay's house. She'd hung the mauve brocade drapes, set out the silver salvers, used a tweezers to set the candles in the chandelier, all without having to think twice about any of it.

In the library, it was just the same. She knew where the porcelain clock should be on the mantel, and the twin red vases, and the blue-patterned porcelain lamps. She knew that the portrait of the woman went on the right side of the fireplace, the portrait of the man on the left. Knew that the needlework pole screen stood behind the smaller of the kid-covered armchairs. Even the books—maroon and green leather jackets on the upper shelves, tan on the lower—even those, she remembered where to place.

The maids' rooms had taken her two minutes to arrange. The nursery, not much longer. Unpacking the precious furnishings, each piece a new and precious gift, had gone necessarily slowly. But putting each piece in its proper place, as enjoyable as the task was, had taken no time at all.

And that was what frightened her.

How could she possibly have remembered the house in such detail after only a few quick glances into it at Orel Tremblay's place? Granted, some people had photographic memories and were very visual; but Meg wasn't one of them. Meg remembered flower fragrances and birds' songs, not which way a club chair was oriented to a sofa. It wasn't a skill she possessed.

And yet she knew every location of every item at the Eagle's Nest. It didn't seem possible. She reminded herself that the rooms she'd unpacked so far were the rooms that she'd stared at the longest; the furnishings that still lay wrapped in boxes were from rooms she'd barely seen. The house had eighteen rooms. Today would be a real test of her memory—or of something else, she didn't know what. She resumed her unpacking.

One by one the guest bedrooms filled up, each with its own coordinated color scheme. After that she arranged the sleeping and dressing rooms belonging to the mistress of the dollhouse,

done in a classic sunny treatment of green-and-white stripes
and rose chintz. They were cheerful rooms, the rooms of a
gardener. Meg had no doubt that in the original Eagle's Nest,
they looked out on roses and perennials and flowering shrubs.

She opened the next unmarked box and unfolded a bundle
of white tissue. Inside was a massive little headboard, elaborately carved from dark teakwood in a serpentine, Oriental
design: without question, it was from the master bedroom.

Meg held the headboard in her hand for a long time, para-
lyzed by a sense of dread that had absolutely nothing to do
with any fear of dropping it or breaking it. Her hand began to
shake, but still she stood, clutching the headboard, fixed to the
spot. She was overcome by an irrational sense of fear and
revulsion that left her faint. Her heart was hammering out of
control in a wild, uncountable beat. Her chest hurt. She
couldn't breathe. Worse, she couldn't get past the fear,
couldn't make her feet turn and head for the house.

I'm going to die was her only thought. *Right here. Right
now. I'm going to die. I can't believe it.*

"Meg! *Here* you are," came her sister's happy voice from
outside the shed.

Meg wavered and dropped the headboard after all as Allie
rushed through the doorway with a look of radiance on her
face. "Oh, Meggie," she said, encircling her sister in her
arms. "Thank you thank you *thank* you," she gushed.

The embrace of her sister was a restorative to Meg. She
bent over and picked up the headboard, which wasn't dam-
aged. "You're welcome," she said wanly. "What did I do?"

"Brought Tom to his senses! You were right about him; it
turns out that his wife was practically the only woman he'd
ever known well, and they couldn't communicate at *all*. He
thought that when she said no she meant no. It caused endless
confusion. Plus he's so standoffish anyway, which of course is
his great charm, and—Meg! You're white as a sheet," Allie
said suddenly. "What's wrong?"

Meg, still a little shaky, shook off her sister's concern. "Too much caffeine," she lied, placing the headboard carefully against the wall of what she had no doubt was Gordon Camplin's bedroom.

"Caffeine, hell," Allie said. "What's *wrong*?"

"I . . . don't know, Allie. Honest. I'm a little light-headed, that's all. I haven't eaten." She laid one hand casually over her heart—it felt okay—and took the next parcel out of the box and began gingerly unwrapping it. It was the carved footboard to the bed.

"Well, *eat* something, then," Allie commanded. "The doll-house can wait. You're almost done here, anyway, it looks like."

Allie took the footboard from Meg and turned it this way and that. "Pretty," she said admiringly. She nudged her sister with her shoulder. "Doesn't it give you a kick to know that you own this and Gordon Camplin doesn't?"

Meg laughed weakly. "You bet."

"Are you *sure* the dollhouse was Orel Tremblay's to give?"

"I told you, Allie: Gordon Camplin's mother gave it to Mr. Tremblay after he saved one of her dogs from the fire. She didn't want to be reminded of Eagle's Nest, anyway. She assumed he'd sell it, and that would be that. It was a very generous thing to do, even in '47. But it was definitely his, Tremblay's lawyer said. The papers that prove it are part of the probate file."

"Think how galling it would be if Gordon Camplin sent his lawyers after it," Allie said thoughtfully. "God. I'd *burn* it first! Well, gotta go," she said, falling back on a phrase that Meg had heard often in the last ten years.

She headed out the door, then turned back around. "Oh! The most important thing of all," she said. "Tom's moving out."

"What?"

"He just told me. He has a pal in Chicago who owns a log

cabin just outside of town. It's been rented but now the tenants are breaking the lease and moving out. There's no phone; the owner can't even get in touch with the tenants. I guess the owner's completely fed up. He's losing his shirt on it. It was supposed to be such a great investment, but you know how *that* goes. Anyway, he wants Tom to arrange for a realtor to list it, and for any repairs it might need. It all just happened.''

"How long is Tom planning to stay there?" Meg asked, trying to make the question sound offhand.

"It's up in the air," Allie said. "I guess this trip is a combined convalescence and vacation, only Tom says I'm not letting him convalesce, so he's going to have to call it vacation. He has tons of unused vacation time."

Allie added with a roguish smile, "As far as I'm concerned, the real vacation starts the day he moves into that cabin. Bye."

She waltzed out of the shed, leaving Meg with a sudden, fearful sense of emptiness.

A cabin in the woods. Private, quiet, away from the Atwells hullaballoo. A cabin in the woods. A dream place for the right man with the right woman. For one brief, unique second, Meg hated her sister.

Jealousy! The realization took her breath away.

With a shudder, she forced herself to pick up the next tissue-wrapped bundle. She had no heart for it: If the frame of the bed had filled her with such dread, what on earth would the mattress do? But the bundle turned out to be a refectory table, much longer than it was wide, and it belonged in the kitchen. She sighed with relief.

After the table Meg opened a box containing a mother lode of treats: teeny-tiny appliances for a kitchen that was already fifty years old in the 1940s, everything from a coffee grinder to a toaster to a tabletop radio in a cathedral-style case. She placed the utensils in the glass-fronted cabinets, and after she unwrapped the step-back cupboard, she filled it with the set of stoneware dishes and the collection of pewter, copper, and majolica teapots that she'd found. It seemed so obvious to her where everything went, and yet the more she realized it, the more frightened she became.

Meg unwrapped another flat, rectangular piece, an exact miniaturization of a bedspring, made of intricately looped metal coils. The next thing she discovered was the mattress. It was down filled, with a too-bizarre, too-authentic mark that looked like a small bloodstain on it. She shuddered again with a reluctance that bordered on loathing as she covered the mattress with white linens, then spread a little rustic coverlet of dark fur over it. Something about the feel of the soft fur sickened her, physically sickened her. It was almost worse than the runaway heartbeat, this nausea.

I have to get out of here, she told herself, exhausted. Whether it was the coffee, the bed, or the gleam in Allie's eye, Meg's mood had plummeted to a depth of depression she hadn't felt in years.

Suddenly she'd had her fill of the dollhouse. She fled, almost in a panic, not even bothering to lock the shed door behind her.

In the kitchen she ran into Lloyd and Comfort, who were in the middle of an unhappy discussion.

"*Repeat*? Whatd'ya mean, Terry has to repeat?" Lloyd wanted to know.

He was washing up in his wife's spotless kitchen, trying without success to scrub car grease from his hefty forearms. Lloyd hated working on cars, despite the fact that the economics of his life made it unavoidable. Wood was one thing; Lloyd loved shaping it, smoothing it, making it conform to his touch. But dirty, greasy, hostile metal—Lloyd *hated* working on cars. His mood was always foul afterward.

He was furious about Terry's flunking sixth grade. "Terry *can't* repeat, gahdammit. Timmy'll be ahead if Terry repeats.

What the hell, we're not throwing two graduation parties. What does he think, I'm made of money?''

"No, Lloyd, of course not," said Comfort, rushing to hand him a strip of paper towels.

Too late. Lloyd had already grabbed his wife's favorite decorative towel, a linen cloth silk-screened with a red barn and a gaggle of geese, and was rubbing himself clean with it. "If Terry fails, he don't get no party come graduation. No party, no presents. Maybe *that*'ll put the fear o' Gahd in him. Gahdammit.''

"I don't know why he won't study," Comfort said, baffled by her uncooperative son.

Lloyd handed her the ruined towel, took the paper towels she gave him, wiped his sweaty neck with them, and tossed them into the same bag of trash that held Allie's one gray hair. "What'd the boy flunk, anyway?"

"Math. And almost English."

Lloyd gave his wife a dry look. "That about covers it, then, don't it."

"His teacher did tell me he's very good at sports. Although he's not so good at sportsmanship," Comfort felt obliged to add. "He isn't what they consider a team player. Not that he ever was; you know how he likes to go off with only Cough-drop by his side. Why is that? Why is Timmy so much more outgoing, such a better student? How can they be twins?"

"What're you asking *me* for? They're *your* sons," said Lloyd, disassociating himself from the three of them. He tucked his shirt back into his pants and hitched his pants over his belly, then took out his comb and ran it once through his hair. "When do we eat?"

"Right now. Sit," Comfort urged. "Mrs. Blethrow says he'll have to have a tutor."

"Tutor! Forget tutor! We can't afford one. *You* teach the boy."

"Oh, Lloyd . . . I don't understand this new math."

"So teach him old math."

Having settled the matter, Lloyd pulled out a chair from the Formica table and began to leaf through the week's issue of the *Bar Harbor Times*, licking his left thumb carefully before grabbing the lower right-hand corner and swinging the page in an arc to the left. In a hundred such little ways he reminded Meg of their Uncle Billy, the one glaring exception being that Lloyd hadn't come anywhere close to owning his own hardware store.

Meg pulled out a second chair. "Lloyd—*I'll* help Terry with his math."

Her brother didn't bother looking up from the sports page. "No need; Comfort'll take care of it."

"You know how he twists Comfort around his finger."

"He does that," said Comfort ruefully, nodding her head.

"He needs some one-on-one instruction from someone meaner than Comfort. That's me," Meg said with a bright smile. "Besides, you know I was a teacher's aide."

"Meg, you mean well," said Lloyd, favoring his sister with a stiff smile. He went back to his newspaper. "Butt out."

"But why—"

"I *said*—"

"Okay, okay. I heard you. Crabass."

Comfort gave Meg a look of timid apology, then brought out what was left of the day's breakfast bread and began sawing thick, crusty chunks on Lloyd's new work island.

The kitchen is both her refuge and her kingdom, Meg thought, leaning her head against the kitchen wall. She loved to watch her sister-in-law prepare food; Comfort was so obviously happy doing it. Almost nothing interested her more than turning out a really fine meal. It was Comfort's not-so-secret dream to own a home-cooking restaurant, and if the Inn Between ever turned a really, really, *really* big profit, Meg intended to buy her one.

"Gee, that work island turned out well—didn't it, Comfort?"

It was, of course, Meg's blatant attempt to tempt Lloyd back into the conversation. It worked. "Yeah," he said, looking up to admire his handiwork. "It did turn out good."

Meg nodded her head. "It looks *exactly* like the one in the Sears catalog."

"Don't I know it," he agreed. "Right down to the roll-out breadboard."

"I don't know how you do it. Nothing to go on but a picture."

"You scale up, is all."

"Well, it was a wonderful anniversary present. Wasn't it, Comfort."

"Yes. Oh, yes," said Meg's sister-in-law as she scooped clam-filled ladles of liquid into the family's everyday crockery. "Very nice. Especially the roll-out breadboard."

She brought a bowl filled rim-high with chowder to her husband and set it carefully before him.

"Well, someone turns out a chowder good as yours, she deserves a proper place to shuck the clams," Lloyd said gruffly.

Comfort smiled from under downcast eyes and brought her husband the basket of bread and a plate of butter, and Lloyd slipped his arm around her waist in a quick, light squeeze.

It passed, in a house with no privacy, for love play. Meg was gratified to see that despite the years, and their failure to have any more children, and Lloyd's on-again-off-again job situation—despite everything, they still loved each other in the low-key, understated way of Down East men and women.

By the time the meal ended, it was agreed that Meg would tutor the Terrible Twin in math—whatever it took to get Terry to Timmy's graduation party.

CHAPTER 10

Orel Tremblay had left strict instructions that there be no funeral. It was consistent with the lifestyle of a man who'd been known around town as a cranky recluse. But it didn't sit right with Meg. Orel Tremblay had been a good and decent man, and he deserved to have someone mourn his passing—whether he liked it or not. Meg decided to have a memorial service in the shed where his beloved dollhouse sat. Nothing elaborate: no more than an exchange of anecdotes over tea by people who'd known him.

There weren't many. One of the hospice nurses who'd attended him said she'd come, and Allie, of course, and the cleaning woman who'd come once a week to do for him. Allie wanted to bring Tom Wyler; Meg could hardly say no. But when Allie suggested that Zenobia would also be willing to attend, Meg drew the line.

"We're not trying to summon Orel Tremblay back from the dead, Allie," she said dryly. "The man just *got* there."

"Zenobia wouldn't be coming to channel," Allie argued, ignoring her sister's sarcasm. "But she *would* bring a spiritual dimension to the evening. I don't know why you're so afraid of that. We're not getting together to play Trivial Pursuit or something. We're supposed to be memorializing a man's passing."

Chastised, Meg agreed to let Zenobia come too.

Comfort baked an extra pan of apple slices for Meg's gathering and arranged them on a pretty plate for her. After supper, Meg, feeling like a teenager who was hosting her first slumber party, carried the Saran-wrapped pastries out to the shed. The fine weather had turned raw and threatening; the first driving pellets of rain bit into her face as she reached the shed door.

Meg noted the padlock still hanging idly from a nail alongside the door, and decided that the insurance people would *not* be pleased by her casual security. Granted, the dollhouse couldn't easily be carried off; but some of its contents might. Yesterday in an antiques guide she'd seen a miniature bureau that was valued at eight hundred dollars. Of course, the bureau had once belonged to a duchess. But still. She ought to be more careful.

She bumped the door open with her left hip. Almost in answer to Meg's fears, a strange woman hovering over the dollhouse turned sharply around when she entered.

"Oh! You *scared* me!" the woman said angrily.

Meg, also startled, blurted out "Who're *you*?" People had been asking to see the dollhouse all week, and Meg had obliged them. But this one hadn't asked; Meg would've remembered.

"I'm Joyce Fells. Orel Tremblay's *niece*," the woman said, laying vicious emphasis on the last word.

"Ah. I see," said Meg. She'd been half expecting this. "I'm Meg Hazard."

"So I assumed," the woman said through compressed lips. Her gaze shifted from Meg's face to the dollhouse and back.

Joyce Fells was of average height, average weight, average age. Forty-five would be Meg's guess. She was dressed from head to toe in polyester shades of pink and blue. The iridescent necklace she wore sparkled with more pink, more blue. Her bag was pink. Her shoes were blue. She looked like one of the tourists who passed through Mel's Gifte and T-Shirt Shoppe.

Except for her eyes. Her eyes had a kind of fierce blue intensity that seemed, at least to Meg, a little on the nutty side. The fierceness, so at odds with the innocent garishness of her clothes, was eerily intriguing.

"I guess you know about the . . . the disposition of the dollhouse," said Meg, choosing her words carefully. She laid the plate of apple slices on a small card table that she'd covered with one of Comfort's red-checked cloths, and readjusted the fan of napkins as she searched for the right thing to say. "Or else you wouldn't be here," she added lamely.

She turned to face the full brunt of Joyce's blue-eyed anger, fully aware of what Orel Tremblay's whim had cost his niece: at least sixty thousand dollars, and possibly much more. It wasn't a huge inheritance—but for people like them, it was a lot of money.

"Oh, Uncle Orel's lawyer filled me in thoroughly. I know all about the *disposition*," Joyce said, spitting the word out.

The woman sucked in her breath with a pained sound and began circling the house slowly, taking it all in. Meg was reminded of a marsh hawk flying low, searching for prey. Suddenly the woman's hand reached out for the weather vane— Meg thought she was going to snap it from the gable—and then her hand veered away and came down in a sharp, cutting motion as she hissed, "It's *mine*!"

Meg jumped back, shocked by the woman's vehemence.

"But," said the woman darkly, "that's what I get for not minding my own garden. Still . . . *this* treatment! Blood's *supposed* to be thicker than . . . Well! Never mind that now. It's a gorgeous, gorgeous piece. God, I've never seen better. Never. In my life, *never*. Museum quality. No question."

Which was just what Orel Tremblay's attorney had told Meg when he contacted her after Tremblay's death. He'd also implied that Tremblay's own house had been heavily mortgaged and had little value, and that Meg could expect his bequest of the dollhouse to be challenged. Right now, Meg was convinced of it.

Joyce was circling the dollhouse again. Meg was really afraid that this time she'd grab the whole thing in her light blue talons and fly off with it. "You sound knowledgeable about dolls' houses," she ventured, trying to think of something nice to say.

The woman twisted her head toward Meg with that sharp, hawklike look of hers. "Yes," she agreed with a bitter smile. "I collect miniatures. It was Uncle Orel who got me interested, in fact. When I was a teenager my mother brought me out East. I saw *this*, and I fell in love with it. Uncle Orel wouldn't let me touch anything, of course, that—"

She stopped herself mid-insult and took a deep breath, then seemed to calm down a little. "Do you know anything about miniatures?" she said with false brightness.

Meg answered truthfully, "Almost nothing." She realized at once that it was a dumb thing to say; it only rubbed salt into the wounds of this disinherited expert.

"Uncle Orel told me that the original Eagle's Nest was filled with bitterness and tragedy," Joyce said, her mouth twitching in a suppressed smile. "Are you superstitious?"

"No more than the usual amount," Meg hedged.

"Then you don't believe in bad karma," Joyce said coolly.

It seemed ludicrous to have to listen to a middle-aged woman dressed in the worst possible western taste talking about *karma*. "If you mean bad luck—no, I don't believe in it," Meg said, flashing a little Yankee orneriness. "People make their own luck."

"You don't know anything at all," Joyce said, cocking her head at Meg.

Meg had heard enough. "If you don't mind—"

She was interrupted by the sounds of a group hurrying through the rain outside. The mourners—or coffee klatchers,

Meg hardly knew how to regard them—had arrived in a pack. Allie herded them in ahead of her: Tom, lugging a thermal carafe of hot tea; the nurse, all business and dressed for her rounds; the poor shy housekeeper, a mousy thing who seemed in awe of Allie; and Zenobia, grand and warm and undoubtedly in some kind of control.

"Oh! Hello," said Allie to the pink-and-blue intruder standing next to Meg. "Are you a friend of Mr. Tremblay's too?" She stuck out her hand. "I'm Allie Atwells."

Meg gave her sister a be-careful look. "This is Joyce Fells, Allie. Mr. Tremblay's niece."

"Ooh."

There was an excruciating silence, and then Allie rallied and said brightly, "It's really nice of you to come to our memorial service for your uncle. Lots of people in your shoes wouldn't."

Joyce, who hadn't spoken a word, allowed her eyes to open just a little wider, then said grimly, "I have no doubt."

Apparently she intended to stay. Meg conducted a round of awkward introductions. The dollhouse needed no introduction, of course; it simply sat there, all wonderfully lit from within, serene and bright and magical.

As the small group stood around murmuring forced little pleasantries, Meg felt suddenly daunted by the dollhouse. What was the purpose of it, really? It was absolutely useless; a rich man's folly. Too precious to play with, too tiny to sit in— it was simply a pretty thing that you owned for a while and then handed off to someone else before or after you died. She felt utterly crushed. The whole impulse behind tonight was so dumb, so futile. They should've just met in a chapel.

"I think tea would be a good idea, don't you, Meg? Suppose I pour," suggested Zenobia in a wonderfully rich voice.

Immediately everyone relaxed. It was much easier to talk about Orel Tremblay in between bites of an apple slice. Of them all, it was Millie, the shy little housekeeper, who had the most to say about him. She'd been cleaning his house for years, just as her mother, now gone, bless her soul, had done before her.

She knew funny little things about him, like the fact that he used to buy only Idaho potatoes, never Maine (she'd seen the peels) and that he was allergic to shellfish (he once gave her a bag of littlenecks that somebody had brought him). He hadn't thrown his money around, but he'd always remembered Millie's mother at Christmastime—and later on, Millie herself.

"I was sorry to see him go," she said simply. "He never felt sorry for himself, and he never complained."

It was the perfect tribute, potato peelings and all. It was comforting to know that after the fire and before the illness, Orel Tremblay had had a life. Maybe it wasn't filled with adventure or family, but neither was it all emptiness and pain. He had dogs, he took walks, he had a few friends. Meg was glad; her heart became a little more easy about him.

The nurse had begun to look restless, as if it were time for her to be on her way, when Comfort suddenly showed up in search of Allie.

"It's Lisa," Comfort whispered in a voice that tried hard to be discreet but failed. "Her boyfriend's just walked out on her. She's very distraught, Allie. She asked can you come right away?"

"Oh, no . . . Lisa . . . is she still on the phone?"

"She hung up."

"Okay," said Allie. She turned to her sister. "Gotta go. Lisa was real shaky at our last AA meeting. Poor thing; she could see this was coming. I'm sorry, Meggie."

She blew a kiss to Tom Wyler and said, "Be back as quick as I can," and grabbed her windbreaker from the back of a chair. The nurse took the opportunity to leave as well. That left Meg, Tom, Joyce and the no longer shy housekeeper, Millie. And, of course, Zenobia.

"I think," said Zenobia, "that now would be a good time

to all join hands in a moment of reflection. Come. Let's join hands.''

If there was one thing Tom Wyler hated, it was being told to all join hands. He hadn't played that game in kindergarten, and he wasn't interested in playing it now. Not that he objected to the idea of this little get-together. He was quite touched when Allie told him that her sister was rounding up a quorum in memory of Orel Tremblay's passing. Now that he knew Meg more, he could see how typical it was of her. She took care of people in this life—and, apparently, right on through the next.

If he had to hold a hand, he preferred that it be hers. He placed himself between Meg and little Millie, across from Zenobia and the dreadful Joyce Fells. Fells! What a woman! Tacky, self-pitying, jealous, meanspirited—she was one, big, negative vibe, guaranteed to thwart whatever it was Zenobia had in mind.

And what Zenobia had in mind was just a *lit*tle bit hokey.

"Actually, wouldn't it be nice," Zenobia said, "if we made a circle around the dollhouse. It is, after all, our most visible reminder of Orel Tremblay."

Without really seeming to push, she managed to shepherd them into a small circle around the table on which the dollhouse sat. Wyler assumed that Meg would balk at this New Age nonsense, but she didn't. She seemed not so much mesmerized as curious to see where all this was leading. He liked that in her. She'd probably make a pretty fair detective.

What surprised him even more was that Tremblay's niece was tolerating Zenobia's antics. Apparently Joyce Fells was willing to put up with anything to stay close to the dollhouse. She hadn't taken her eyes off it once during the evening.

Which was not good. He'd seen her kind so often. They carried a permanent grudge against those who had something they wanted, and when the grudge got too big, they exploded.

It could be over the most worthless, trivial things: a pair of sneakers, a bag of Chee·tos. He'd seen people murder for sunglasses.

The dollhouse, on the other hand, wasn't simply desirable. It had genuine value.

"Let us take up the circle of joy," said Zenobia.

So now they all were holding hands. He liked the feel of Meg's in his. It had a kind of steadiness that he wasn't aware of when he held Allie's hand. With Allie that could never be for long, anyway; she needed her hands to express herself. But Meg . . . well, her hand felt . . . just about right.

Meg turned, and he turned, and when she gave him a fleeting, tentative smile, he felt something deep inside him shift and move slightly, like the first subtle lurch of a frozen river in spring. It took him by surprise. He rubbed his thumb gently across her knuckles in a gesture as much protective as it was possessive. *Something is happening here*, he realized. It was as disturbing, as intriguing to him as the touch of her flesh against his.

Zenobia began her invocation. "Lord," she said, "we ask you to open your kingdom to Orel Tremblay, a man who by all accounts bore malice toward none."

Maybe just one, Wyler couldn't help thinking. But no one seemed to be counting.

"He loved life, or he would not have lingered so long on earth," said Zenobia. "And yet it's clear that he looked forward to being free of it, because he cared little for its vanities and trinkets—with only this one, wonderful exception," she said, nodding at the dollhouse in their midst. "How beautiful it is," she added, almost involuntarily.

Indeed, in the darkened shed the dollhouse seemed suddenly to glow with an enchanting grace. Light from every one of its rooms, from gable to ground floor, tumbled through dozens of multipaned windows, binding the mourners in a pattern of tiny squares of brightness, blurring the outlines between them. Sparks of light were everywhere, dancing and disorienting. Wyler had the sense that he and the rest were all dissolving into a vague, shadowy presence. He thought of breaking the circle by releasing Meg's hand, but something compelled him to hold on.

This is absurd, he thought. *A trick of light and shadow.* He gathered all his wits and focused on Zenobia's hands, convinced that she'd be rapping out a message on the table next. *Watch her hands*, he told himself. *Keep an eye on her hands.*

''Ohhh . . .''

The sound, somewhere between a moan and a whimper, sent the hair on the back of his neck straight up. The cry was not Zenobia's.

It was Meg's.

''No . . . I won't go in there,'' Meg said in a low wail.

He caught his breath, hardly daring to turn his head and look at her. But when he did he could see, by the light of the dollhouse, that her gaze was vacant and trancelike. She wasn't seeing him. She wasn't seeing the dollhouse. She wasn't seeing anybody in the shed.

''Speak in French—en Française!'' she cried in the same low wail. *''Do you want the children to hear you? Pourquoi ne me vous-laissez pas tranquille? C'est si faux. Je suis une femme mariée. J'ai deux fils. Pourquoi me faites-vous cela? Vous savez qu'il me faut cet emploi. Ne me faites pas cela, s'il vous plaît.''*

The hand he was holding was now cold and limp, in appalling contrast to Millie's warm and trembling hand. He held on to each, completely baffled, unwilling to change a thing until he got more of a handle on the situation. He reminded himself to watch Zenobia, then promptly forgot. All he could think of, all he could focus on, was Meg. Or whoever she was.

In a more frantic voice, now: *''They're waiting for us. We have to go. We haven't much time. It's coming nearer. I can smell it. Oh, God . . . why won't you let me go? Are you insane? Please don't . . . don't . . . don't . . .''*

Meg's voice, bone chilling and exhausted, trailed off into a soft drumbeat of the single syllable. No one else spoke, no one else moved. Wyler could sense, rather than see, that Joyce Fells was weaving in place, like a snake charmed out of its basket, and that Zenobia was holding her breath, mesmerized or mesmerizing, he wasn't sure which. Could she have hypnotized Meg?

Millie, clinging to his hand, was near collapse. He could feel the hummingbird-beat of her heart through the palm of his hand. *It's gone too far*, he thought, and wanted to stop it. But he feared hurting someone in the process.

It was the hostage situation, all over again.

"No!" Meg suddenly shrieked, sending every one of them jumping out of his skin. *"No no no no no no!"*

She lifted both her hands violently, yanking out of his grip on one side and Joyce's on the other, and began pounding against something in midair as she screamed, "Open it! Open it!" And then she fainted.

And then Millie fainted.

When Meg came to, she found herself face-to-face with Joyce Fells, who was gazing at her from under half-lidded eyes, her mouth pursed in something between sympathy and a grimace.

"Are you all right?" Joyce asked, apparently annoyed with her. "You put on quite a show."

Confused, Meg said, "You have me mixed up with my sister; she's the actress." She was breathing with an effort. Her legs were rubbery; her skin felt cold. "How did I get on this chair?" she asked, completely disoriented.

Meg turned to Tom, who was crouched next to her with his finger on her pulse. She lifted her wrist out of his grasp and stared at it, wondering why he'd been holding it that way.

Then she saw Millie sitting in the only other chair, her arms wrapped around herself, her knees literally knocking together. Zenobia was standing over her, trying to comfort her.

"Millie," Meg said, "what happened to *you*?

"I w-want to go home," the young woman said between sobs.

"Well, sure, you can if you want to," Meg said, rising. "I'll give you a lift in my—"

But her knees weren't up to it. She fell back limply, missing the chair and landing in Tom Wyler's arms. "Ooo-ee," she said with a shaky laugh. She turned to him; his breath felt warm on her icy cheek. "The flu?" she suggested with a lopsided, dopey smile.

"Not the flu. I'll tell you after," he said. He eased her back into the chair, an old upholstered thing with wooden arms, and said to the rest of the company, "I think we'll call it an evening. Thank you all for coming. Is there anyone who needs a ride?"

"I d-don't think I can d-drive," said Millie, still shivering.

"I'll take you home, dear," Zenobia offered. "You can get your car tomorrow."

The girl nodded dumbly and Zenobia helped her to her feet.

"Tom? Do let's get together later tonight—" Zenobia began.

"Not tonight," he said, dismissing her.

"At breakfast, then. This is most interesting." Somehow she managed to lean over and give Meg a reassuring hug without letting go of poor Millie. "Good-night, everyone. Joyce? Are you coming?"

It was the nudge Joyce needed. "Nice to've met you," she said to Meg. At the door she turned, hitched her pink handbag under her flabby arm, and said with a bitter smile: "Enjoy it."

Meg was left alone with Tom Wyler. He was leaning against the custom-made table that held the dollhouse, his arms folded across his chest, watching her thoughtfully. "You should be in bed," he said softly.

"God, no," she answered, rubbing her hands together to warm them. "Not until I find out what the heck happened here. I'm fine, I'm fine. Just . . . tea. I'm fine."

Tom took off the light canvas jacket he was wearing and draped it over her shoulders, then brought over an empty cardboard box and turned it upside down in front of her. "Feet up," he commanded.

She did as she was told while he went over to the big thermos dispenser and poured her a mug of tea. He came back to her and put the mug in one hand and wrapped her other hand around it and held his hands over hers for a moment.

Then he pulled up Millie's chair, a battered kitchen reject, and placed it between Meg and the dollhouse. Meg had the insane thought that he was trying to protect her from it, which made no sense; *he* didn't know about her bizarre reaction to the master's bed within it.

"What happened?" she asked simply, lifting the mug to her lips.

"That, dear heart, is the sixty-four-thousand-dollar question. I can tell you what I saw, but not what happened."

She made a wry face at his careful distinction, then said, "I remember holding hands and staring into the dollhouse as Zenobia spoke. After a while it began to seem real—full-size, I mean, like a real house. I could picture myself as one of the inhabitants inside. It was almost like an out-of-body experience. I had such a clear sense of myself—you know—*in there*," she said, pointing into the house. "I was standing in the circle, holding your hand and holding Joyce's. But I was inside the house, too. That's all I remember. Did you feel that way too?" she asked him, without much hope.

He gave her a sigh for an answer, then got up and walked around to the front of the little gabled mansion. He bent over sideways to peek in the windows. "How'd you get all the stuff inside these front rooms, anyway?" he asked.

"The facade of the house comes off in panels. I had to figure it out. The whole thing is very cunningly constructed. I half expect there to be secret corridors inside. You know? The kind where the servants can come and go without sullying the view of their masters?"

"Do I detect an upstairs-downstairs attitude?"

"No, of course not," she said, her chin coming up. "I've always believed that it's not where you are but who you are. But ever since Orel Tremblay told me my grandmother was trapped into working for someone she despised—"

"Are you sure she despised him?" Tom asked, looking back at Meg.

"*Yes*, I'm sure!" Meg said, shocked that he could even speculate. "You know what Orel Tremblay said—how distressed my grandmother was about Gordon Camplin's pursuit of her."

"I'm wondering whether it was a love-hate thing," Wyler admitted.

She simply stared. "God! What a cynic! Is this what happens to homicide detectives? They come to believe that every victim is a willing victim?"

"No, Meg," he said softly, straightening up again and watching her with an expression almost of pain. "That's not what they believe."

"I'm sorry," she said, biting her lip. "That was a stupid thing to say. But whatever gave you the idea that my grandmother was attracted to Gordon Camplin?"

He hesitated, then said, "It was something you said.".

"*I* said? When?"

"When you were in your . . . I guess I'm calling it a trance."

"*Trance!*"

He pulled up the old kitchen chair opposite her, then sat

down and ran through the whole bizarre sequence for her. He repeated every line that she spoke, except for the French, which he admitted to her he hadn't understood.

When he got to the part about how she broke free of his and Joyce's grasp, he took both her hands in his, lifted them up, and mimicked her pounding gesture with them. Then he lowered her hands gently into her lap, like discarded props a magician no longer needs.

Meg didn't believe a word of it, of course; that was her first reaction. But even as she denied it, she was aware from the thumping of her heart that somewhere or other she'd actually experienced the event he was describing—either in her "trance," or on that October day in 1947. Or both.

"Oh, boy," she said, staring down at her folded hands. "Oh, boy," she repeated, overwhelmed.

He laughed under his breath. "My thought exactly," he said.

Neither one of them spoke for a moment. Then Tom leaned forward and cupped his hand under her chin, and lifted her face to his. "Hey. There's an explanation for this. Let's just take our time and work through it."

He seemed unbelievably tender to her just then: gentle, and reassuring, and absolutely confident that there was a rational explanation for her behavior. But she let her chin droop anyway, to hide the tumult she was feeling.

"Meg, listen to me," he said. "You mentioned that you'd been researching Gordon Camplin earlier, didn't you? Besides which, you'd also heard Orel Tremblay's version of those last hours. It wouldn't take a psychic to imagine a scenario like the one you just acted out. Hell, I was halfway there myself. Blame it on the dollhouse. It doesn't mean you're bewitched."

She wanted so desperately to believe him. "You don't understand," she said, her lip trembling. *"I don't speak a word of French."*

"Not . . . a word?"

It was a blow, she could tell, but he only nodded and said, "Okay. Okay, we'll start right there. Does anybody in your family speak French?"

She shook her head, then said, "Maybe my dad, when he was a kid. I could check."

"Do any of your friends? *Their* relations? Did you take French in high school?"

"No to all of it. Oh, Tom . . . this is . . . what'll I? . . . oh, Tom," she said, balancing on the edge of hysteria. "You don't have *any* idea what I actually said when I spoke in French? Is it possible it was just French-sounding gibberish?"

"I don't think so. You spoke very fluently—and with a damn good accent, at least to my ears. But then, I only took a semester of French in college. I caught the words 'two' and 'sons' and that's about it. Maybe Zenobia knows French." He gave Meg a smile that she wrapped around her battered psyche like a thick blanket.

But Meg needed more. Shivering, she said, "M-maybe Zenobia can tell me how *I* happen to know French."

"Unlikely," he said flatly. He lifted a droopy lock of Meg's hair and tucked it behind her ear in a simple gesture that left Meg more weak-kneed than before.

"Meg . . . look, memory is a mysterious and complex thing. Medical and legal experts have their hands full trying to explain it. The issue seems to come up for us all the time, especially in childhood abuse situations. People do funny things with their memories: repress them, alter them, enhance them, distort them. Who knows what your father told you when you were young? What *he* remembered from when *he* was young?"

"I think I would've remembered if my father and I had ever conversed in French," she said testily.

"And I'm telling you I've seen cases where far more sensational facts were repressed for a *lifetime* by all the parties concerned."

"Really?" She took some comfort from the thought. But it was such small, fleeting comfort. She leaned her head on the back of the chair and stared at the cobwebby, open-beamed ceiling of the shed. A tear rolled out the corner of one eye. She let it roll. "My grandmother was raped, wasn't she," she said dully.

"We don't know that."

"And left for dead."

"We don't know that."

"I thought he strangled her or something." She lifted her head. "But this seems so much worse."

"Meg, you're putting yourself through hell for nothing," Tom said, his voice becoming taut. "Don't do this to yourself."

"You track down murderers for a living, Tom," she said, gathering herself together, forcing herself to look straight into his blue-gray eyes. "Do you think we have a case against Gordon Camplin?"

He shook his head.

She wasn't willing to accept that. "It's not just the memory —repressed or whatever," she said eagerly. "There's more. When I was setting up the furnishings in the dollhouse, I knew where *every single item* went. I never once had to stop and think. Piece after piece, room after room . . . it was almost as if—"

She took a deep breath and said, "—as if I'd been haunting the dollhouse for quite some time."

He turned to look at the enchanting toy. "Quaintly put," he allowed himself to say.

"There's nothing quaint about it!" she flashed, impatient with his patience. "Do I look like the type to fly through foot-high rooms? Do you think I enjoy telling you this? I'm just trying to be—"

"I know, brutally honest," he said, standing up. "It's your great charm." He took her by her hands and pulled her to her feet. "Time for bed, m'lady. Do you have something you can take to fall asleep?"

"What, you mean, like pills?" Pills were the same as alcohol in her mind; she had an irrational aversion for both. "I don't take pills just to sleep," she said curtly.

He seemed genuinely surprised. "Really? My wife did. I thought all women did."

Snorting, she shook her head. "Where did you live before you got married, Lieutenant? Under your desk?"

"Funny you should say that," he said amiably. "I got razzed a lot at the office for my workaholic ways. Okay, it's true. Before I married I never dated all that much. It was a pain, making dates and then having to break them. But it's not as if I had a choice: It's on Saturday nights that we do our best business," he said ironically.

"I wouldn't like that," she admitted, frowning. "I wouldn't like you to stand me up all the time."

"No," he said with a look more thoughtful than amused. "You're too committed to the ones you love."

She felt the blood rush to her cheeks. "That doesn't mean I don't sympathize with you," she said quickly. "You must've had to make some agonizing choices when you were married."

"I never did get the balance right," he admitted.

And in the meantime, Meg's hands were still in his. The phrase "circle of joy" popped into her head, but immediately she put the thought aside. Wrong time. Wrong place. Wrong, wrong man.

"*Well*," she said, looking at their joined hands and shrugging guiltily out of his grip. The spell, like all true enchantments, broke at once.

"Meg—"

She looked up into his questioning eyes. "You're right," she whispered. "I *am* ready for bed."

That didn't come out quite right. She thought of the time

she'd teased him with the exact same phrase, and she blushed: for then, for now, for every time she'd seen him in between. She'd been fighting the idea of him from the day she first saw him on her front lawn. And only now was she beginning to understand why: because right from the start, he'd been as irresistibly attractive to her as he was to Allie.

But there were two of them, and there was only one of him.

CHAPTER *11*

"What I mean is . . . I'm dead tired," Meg said, trying to sound as if she'd just got back from a barn raising.

"All right," he said. "I'll walk you to the house."

It killed her to have sent that signal. *If it weren't for Allie . . . always Allie . . .*

"No, truly," Meg said, "please don't bother—"

"I said I'll walk you to the house."

She had no idea whether he was being chivalric, protective, or obstinate. All she knew was that they were ambling down the garden path that hours before he'd walked with Allie. She was intensely aware of him—of his height, and his nearness, and the slight hesitation that still remained in his step. The night was misty, inky, and cold, and if Meg had any sense, she'd be making a beeline for the cozy warmth of her room. Instead, she wrapped his jacket more tightly around herself and made him stop and smell a sweet, wet clump of pale roses drooping from the pergola that Lloyd had built three years earlier as a birthday present for her.

"Smells great," Tom said, his voice low and magical in the darkness. "I'm not much of a gardener," he admitted. "What are they?"

"*Roses*," she said, amazed that he wouldn't know. "A climbing multiflora, to be more exact."

"The only kind I know are the tall red ones they sell by the stem in Dominicks—that's a supermarket chain in Chicago," he explained.

"You never had roses when you were growing up? Of any kind?"

"They're not one of the four basic food groups," he said in that dry way he had.

You never had sisters, either, Meg suddenly remembered. Her life was so much richer than his. It made her want to comfort him twice over. No flowers, no family. How could he bear it?

He might have been reading her mind. "I talked a little with your nephew Terry earlier this evening," he said. "He's a bright kid. I like him."

Meg was glad to hear it. "Really?" she asked, smiling. "What did you two talk about?"

"Pipe bombs, as a matter of fact. Terry wanted to know how they were made."

In a near-choke she said, "My God—you didn't tell him, did you?"

"I didn't give him the recipe, if that's what you mean," Tom said ironically. "But I think his interest was merely academic."

"Ha. Don't be too sure," Meg said, only half kidding. "He's doing rotten in school, and his social skills—well, you see for yourself. He has us all worried. After all, no one wants him to grow up to be a serial killer," she quipped, picking the most horrific career she could think of.

"If he doesn't torture small animals, wet his bed, or set a lot of fires, you have nothing to worry about," Tom answered in a perfectly conversational tone.

It tripped so easily off his tongue, this profile of a serial killer. Meg stopped where she was, shocked that Tom Wyler could know such things about the human psyche. Yes, he dealt with homicide, and yes, he'd been at it a long time. But these were things no normal person knew. Normal persons—normal law enforcement persons—knew how to give Breathalyzer tests and fill out accident reports. Not this stuff.

"I hope one out of three doesn't count," she said, trying to sound lighthearted. "Last fall Terry did start a fire in a locker-room wastebasket."

Tom said, *"Really."*

"Anyway, I'll be sure to watch Coughdrop for cigarette burns," Meg said, trying to match Tom's ironic cynicism. They were standing in the brick path, engulfed by the scent of roses. In this magical place their conversation seemed particularly outrageous.

"I'm sorry," he said, sensing her distress. "You don't think much of gallows humor. We tend to hide behind it a lot in our work. I didn't mean to shock you. Forget it."

"No, no, I'm not shocked," she lied. "Serial killers are an everyday fact of life. Just because I'm from a small town in Maine, that doesn't mean I go around with a bushel basket over my head. *We* have newspapers. *We* have cable."

"You don't have a city morgue," he said bluntly. "And that makes Bar Harbor seem like a little corner of paradise."

Meg heard the wistfulness in his voice. In some indefinable way, her spirits lifted. "You sound like maybe you've had it with homicide," she ventured.

"That's what I came to Maine to find out," he admitted. "There are days that I think I can never go back," he said as they walked up the back steps, "and there are days when I know I will."

"And what kind of day was today?" Meg whispered, unable to resist asking.

He laughed. It was a low and intimate sound, new to her ears. "What do *you* think?"

Meg glanced guiltily through the screen door; the kitchen, thank God, was empty of Atwells. "I . . . I'd say today was the kind of day that would make you jump on the first plane out.''

"How wrong you'd be," he murmured, trailing his finger along the sleeve of her blouse.

"Or maybe you're the type who can never resist a funhouse," she said, faint from the nearness of him.

"Wrong again. I get enough thrills and chills during office hours."

He cupped her chin in his hand, tilting her face to meet his. It was clear to Meg, even in her confusion of emotions, that he was going to kiss her. *Her*. "Wait . . . wait . . ." she whispered, averting her face from his. "There's been a mix-up—"

Meg was saved from having to explain to Tom how mixed up he was by a loud crash of broken glass from inside, followed by Comfort shouting, "I *told* you no roughhousing in the front room! Wait till your father gets home!"

After which Terry came flying through the screen door with Timmy at his heels and Coughdrop in hot pursuit of them both. Comfort stomped out next, looking for the kitchen broom.

"I'm sorry, Comfort. I left it in the shed. I'll get it," Meg said, embarrassed to be caught on the back porch with Tom.

"Never mind," said Comfort grimly. "I'll fetch it. And when I do I'm going to beat that boy from here to Portland with it. That kerosene lamp was in my family for a hundred years. That *wicked* child!" she said, steaming, as she brushed past them both.

Meg turned back to Tom with a sheepish smile. "How's *that* for a mood breaker?"

Tom didn't smile back. "Not as effective as your pushing me away," he said bluntly.

"I'm sorry, I'm sorry," Meg said in a soft wail. "This whole night has been just . . . such a . . . *mess*," she said, fleeing inside and leaving Tom to figure out why.

* * *

The hours that followed were sleepless ones for Meg. Her heart was in a turmoil over Tom, and her soul was in a turmoil over her grandmother. Of the two, it was actually easier to deal with her feelings for Tom: She simply refused to think of them at all. They were too deep, too painful to dwell on, and so she shut them away.

But the weirdness in the shed—*that* made Meg toss and turn. She replayed Tom's account of the channeling—if that was what it was—over and over in her mind until she grew sick of it.

Sick, and yet oddly disengaged from it. She didn't actually remember any of what happened to her, after all. All she remembered were the scary parts around the edges: the eerie, dancing light from the dollhouse before her apparent trance, and her appalling weakness afterward. But the whole middle part, her grandmother's hysterical plea for mercy, that was gone. Lost.

If it hadn't been for Tom's court-reporter recall, Meg might've gone away from the shed with nothing more than a disorienting headache. As it was, she ended up feeling as if she were trying out for the lead in a Stephen King movie— only without a script.

As for Allie, she never did come back that night. She called Meg early the next morning to tell her that she'd found Lisa in pieces, drunk and incoherent, and that she was still putting her friend back together. Allie's voice sounded tired and shaky— and frightened. Meg hadn't heard her sister sound like that in a long time. Very few things frightened Allie. Breakups and divorces—the kind of things that make women put their arms around their mates and hold on tight—those didn't scare her at all. But having a friend fall off the wagon, that terrified her.

"It could've been me, Meg," she whispered over the phone. "I want to believe I'm stronger than that—but it could've been me."

She sounded sixteen again. Meg's maternal instincts kicked

instantly into overdrive. It was as if Allie were once again calling from a party where everyone else was high but her. Meg wanted desperately to scoop up her sister and carry her out of harm's way.

"Come home as soon as you can, Allie-cat," she said, trying to keep the worry out of her voice. "Is there anyone else who can stay with Lisa? Doesn't she have a mentor at AA?"

"Mary's coming over this morning, and then we'll see. How'd it go last night after I left?"

"It was completely bizarre. I'll tell you when you get back."

When Allie finally returned late in the afternoon, Meg had finished wallpapering a tiny guest-room bath and was in the kitchen, rummaging for something to eat.

The first thing Allie did was fall into her older sister's arms.

Allie's hair smelled like stale smoke—Lisa's cigarettes— but her breath was alcohol-free. Meg felt her spirits soar, the way they did in the old days whenever her sister emerged sober through an especially trying time.

"I think Lisa's going to be all right," Allie said after Meg's long and reassuring hug. "Mary talked her into going back to see their high school volleyball coach. They both used to think she was really cool—you know, tuned in to their problems. She may be just the kick in the pants Lisa needs right now."

"That's good news," Meg said, glad that the event wasn't turning out as depressingly as she'd feared.

Allie hiked herself up onto the kitchen counter in a fluid motion that Meg had seen a thousand times before. She gave Meg a thoughtful look, sighed, and said, "You know what I realized? It's not the same between Lisa and me as it is between you and me. On the one hand, Lisa and I share this— let's face it—heavy-duty problem. We should be really close, and in that way we are.

"But on the other hand," she said, "I just can't be there for her the way you are for me. I can do a certain amount, but I just can't give her the same—I don't know—*guarantee*, that you give me. You know?'' she asked plaintively. ''You're just so . . . *there* when I need you. So rock solid. There's no one I could ever trust as much as I trust you. I hope it always stays this way between us.''

She looked so terribly young, kicking her heels absently into the cabinet doors, so terribly open and earnest. Meg had the sense that she was looking through her sister's violet eyes and seeing straight into her soul.

''If you need me to be there, I will be, Allie,'' Meg said, her voice a little unsteady in her throat. ''You know that.''

Allie cocked her head and studied her older sister. ''You've never really screwed up, you know that? I drank, and now I have to go through life looking over my shoulder. But you never gave in to your emotions, you never gave up, even after Paul died.''

''I am woman; hear me roar,'' Meg said lightly. She felt like a complete hypocrite.

''I mean it, Meg. You're just so . . . indominatable.''

Meg shrugged, embarrassed. ''You could argue that it's an obnoxious character flaw.''

Allie laughed. ''Uncle Billy's always said so.''

''I rest my case,'' said Meg, opening the fridge and digging through the fruit drawer for the most bruised apple. ''So what're you up to now?'' she asked casually over her shoulder. Meg hadn't seen Tom's car all day—and she'd been keeping track.

''Nothing much. I think we're going to a movie,'' Allie said, assuming that her sister knew who the ''we'' were. ''What about last night? What happened? You sounded so weird on the phone.''

Meg threw her sister a good apple, then took a paring knife and with surgical precision began cutting out the brown spots in her own. ''Promise not to laugh. And *promise* not to tell. Not that it matters,'' she said, feeling the color rise in her cheeks. "It'll be all over town anyway once Millie recovers from her fainting fit."

"Fit? What fit?" Allie asked, chomping down on the glossy red fruit. "Millie was fine when I left," she said through a mouthful of apple.

Meg turned to her sister and said in a taut, deadly serious voice: *"Promise.* And then don't interrupt. I mean it."

Allie nodded solemnly and took another bite of apple, and Meg told her what had happened with as little drama as possible, trying without success to make it seem like just another gathering over tea. Her sister never once interrupted, which itself was a little scary. Allie was famous for jumping into the middle of other people's sentences, more often than not making them lose their train of thought. It drove their father especially nuts.

But now, not a word. Meg was managing only too well to frighten her sister into silence.

"As soon as I could stand up, Tom escorted me back here," Meg said, wrapping up her tale. "It was so embarrassing; I felt like when the police brought Terry home last fall for skipping school," she said jokingly. She skipped the part about the near-kiss; wild horses couldn't have dragged *that* bit out of her.

"Meggie. Oh, Meggie," said her sister, her face pale with anxiety. "You know what this means, don't you?"

"Yeah. Never eat chili for an afternoon snack."

Allie jumped down from the counter and grabbed her sister by the arm. "Don't *do* that," she said angrily. "Don't make fun. Not now. This isn't about Zenobia and her band of merry men. This is about *you*, Meg. Don't you see? Grandmother is communicating to us through you. She's been trapped in the dollhouse for half a century—"

"Let's say I humor you. Why the dollhouse?"

"How do I know? And now that the house has passed to you, she's . . . she's . . ."

"Moving out?" asked Meg wryly.

"Stop it!" cried Allie, visibly cringing. "Speak with more . . . more . . . *reverence*, for pity's sake. God. I can hear you and Tom now, having a big snicker over this. You're both so strong, aren't you? Two of a kind. The homicide cop and the family boss. I suppose it goes with the territory, not being afraid of—"

"Ghosts?" Meg jumped in with the dread word before her sister could, saying it out loud, doing exactly what Allie claimed she was doing: being a big, brave sister. The truth was, Meg had spent the night in a state of disengaged terror and was doing her best to own up to it.

"Allie, if you think this hasn't affected me, you're nuttier than an airline snack. Trust me, I'm bringing more than enough reverence to this affair. The truth is, I'm frightened. *I* don't know what to do. It's not like Miss Manners has written Rules of Etiquette for being possessed or entranced or whatever I was. I mean, am I supposed to just . . . let Grandmother settle in, and try to make her comfortable? Would it be rude to ask how long she plans to stay? And how exactly would I go about doing that, anyway?"

"You're *still* making fun. You can't *not* make fun," said Allie, slamming her hand on the counter.

Meg lifted the core of Allie's apple and tossed it in the garbage can, then took a sponge and began wiping down everything in sight. She didn't know why; it was something to do.

"What do you want me to do?" she asked, scrubbing furiously. "Get exorcised? *Then* where will she go? *If* she exists. It exists. Whatever. And the worst thing is, I can explain this all rationally. Tom is right, it can all be explained rationally. A couple of visits to Orel Tremblay . . . a little research . . . a little imagination . . . and bingo! I'm a channel!"

She picked up a dirty glass from the sink and plunged her

soapy sponge into it, taking out her frustration on the dried-out milk inside.

The glass broke—exploded, really—in Meg's hand, cutting her and releasing a stream of blood down the side of the porcelain sink.

"*Shit*," she said, dropping the broken glass like a hot coal.

Allie zoomed in on the cut, holding her sister's hand under running water so that they could survey the damage: a triangular tear, not so bad that it needed stitches.

"How did I *do* that?" asked Meg blankly.

Allie ripped off a paper towel and wrapped it around her sister's finger. "Who says *you* did it? Maybe Grandmother didn't like your snotty attitude. Can you blame her?" She reached inside the corner cupboard for the bandages and took out three.

"This is out of control," Meg muttered as Allie peeled away the wrappers.

"Take off the towel. That's the thing about the spirit world," Allie said, wrapping the bandage quickly around the cut. "You can't prove it is. You can't prove it isn't. I say let's play it safe." She wrapped another bandage around Meg's index finger, and then another.

Meg snorted. "The only way to play it safe is to buy stock in a pharmaceutical company," she said, flexing her thoroughly splinted finger. "Too tight," she decided.

"Too bad." Allie scooped up the wrappers and tossed them, then began rinsing down the bloody sink. "Obviously we've got to do something about Gordon Camplin. Anything. Maybe if we just flat-out accuse him—in private; that would be the safest thing—that might be enough to satisfy Grandmother. You think?"

"What're you asking *me* for? *You're* the parapsychologist in the family."

"I thought you wanted to nail Camplin," Allie protested, surprised.

"Because I think he's *guilty*, knucklehead, not because I'm afraid of ghosts. Because no one should be allowed to get away with murder. Because it's the right thing to do!" Meg said passionately.

She threw her arm around her sister and sighed. "And, yes, because of Grandmother. Then or now, she deserves better."

After that, Allie went to her room to crash for a couple of hours and Meg agonized over whether or not to walk next door to see Zenobia. She didn't want to do it. It was like having to go back and ask for directions after you've purposely thrown away the road map. She was still hemming and hawing when she saw a large group of departing guests, all with their bags, making their way to several cars parked behind the Elm Tree Inn. Zenobia was at the head of the pack.

In a panic Meg rushed out the back door and flagged down the spiritualist. "Do you have a minute before you go? It's about last night," she said, arriving at Zenobia's car in a breathless state.

Luckily, Zenobia's passenger was a laggard. "I have at least that long," the older woman explained with a sigh as she dropped her leather bags in the trunk of her BMW. She turned and fastened her clear-eyed stare on Meg and said in her rich, warm voice, "But Tom specifically told me that you didn't want to be bothered about it."

"I didn't. But I do. Or I would. If I only knew. . . . What *happened*, Zenobia?" she burst out. "Were you responsible for my behavior?"

"You mean, did I perform a feat of ventriloquy?" Zenobia said good-naturedly. "Oh, no, dear. What we all heard was a trance voice."

"Which is?"

"Which is when you allow an etheric-world intelligence to use your voice to transmit information."

Meg was scandalized. "*I* didn't allow anyone—thing—to use my voice!"

Zenobia's expression became troubled. "I'm sure you don't mean that, Meg. I'm sure what we saw was not an *involuntary* intervention."

Meg, suddenly cautious, asked, "What if it was?"

The silence that followed was pregnant with foreboding. Zenobia frowned and said, "When a psychic phenomenon occurs to someone who didn't deliberately will it—well, that event is usually blamed on what we call 'lower-quality entities.' "

"Oh? Are they like blue-collar ghosts or something?" Meg quipped. But her knees had begun to go wobbly again.

Zenobia looked sympathetic. "I see you have mixed emotions about what happened to you. You shouldn't have, my dear. It's a gift to be sensitive; most people function on only the most ordinary plane. They hardly tap into the universe at all. Be grateful that you're able to see so much more."

"But what about those lower-quality entities?" Meg persisted.

Zenobia's shrug was no more than a lift of one eyebrow. She fingered the keys on the key ring in her hand and plucked the one for her BMW. "The lower-quality entities are just that: base, inferior entities of the etheric world. It's true, they can be quite dangerous."

Meg felt the blood drain from her body; she wanted to sit down but she didn't dare ask for the time to do it.

"But you must understand," Zenobia said with a reassuring smile, "that mediumship is based on the principle of like attracting like. A lower-quality entity will be attracted only to a medium of low morals and bad lifestyle, and that, my child, is clearly not you.

"By the same token, no superior etheric intelligence would ever impose itself against a medium's free will. Because of that, I deduce that you yourself must have been willing to have your grandmother—it *is* your grandmother?—communicate through you. On some level."

Zenobia's logic seemed irrefutable. But Meg had never been keen on formal logic in high school, so how would she know?

"So you think I'm a sort of natural-born medium; that I in fact willed my grandmother to appear?" Meg said it in a whisper, embarrassed even to be asking such an outrageous question.

"Oh, yes, definitely. As I say, you're clearly not what we call a medium for trivial communications. But you must be very careful of your ability, Meg," Zenobia said seriously. "I'll tell you exactly what I told Tom: You need to practice self-discipline. It would help to develop your psychic abilities in a more formal way. I understand there's a trained medium in the area with whom you can meet regularly."

Meg's jaw fell open. "You're asking *me* that?"

Zenobia sighed, and then she smiled. "Please be careful, dear," she said, laying her hand gently on Meg's forearm. "Be very careful," she repeated. "If you need advice, feel free to call me anytime. Would you like my card?"

"No . . . no, that's all right. I'm sure Julia has your address," Meg added, not to be rude. "There's just one other thing. Did you understand what . . . what was said in French?"

"Oh, yes," answered Zenobia. "The voice said, 'Why won't you leave me alone? This is so wrong; I'm a married woman and I have two sons. How can you do this to me when you know I need this position? Please don't do this to me.' " Zenobia said it with the unshakable calm of a UN translator.

"I see," said Meg unhappily. The statements were all very consistent with what Meg already knew—or guessed. They didn't prove or disprove anything. The facts weren't nearly as much of a problem for Meg as the French.

Zenobia opened the door of her silver sedan and tossed her Gucci handbag in the back, then slid into the driver's seat. "You can learn to use your ability to achieve quite astonishing things, Meg," she said through the open window. "I do mean that."

Meg wanted to know what someone like Zenobia could possibly consider "astonishing." "Well, thanks," she said with a wan smile. "I suppose it could come in handy when the phones go down in winter storms."

It was a shade too irreverent for Zenobia; she gave Meg an impatient look, waved to her passenger who was packed and out of the inn at last, and turned the key. "Good luck, dear," she said. "You surely will need it."

CHAPTER *12*

The evening was wet and foggy, not much good for anything. Wyler, feeling aimless and bored, tossed his book aside and decided to wander over to the Inn Between, for no other reason than to hang out.

Hang out—he despised the very expression. Hanging out was what mall rats did, and street gangs, and bums with no real purpose in life. For the last twenty-five years Wyler had made a point of *always* having a purpose in life, whether it was going to night school or learning to play the sax, mastering the game of chess or becoming a force on the basketball court. Even today, he made himself read a work of nonfiction after every work of fiction.

And yet here he was: hanging out.

What the hell am I doing? he wondered as he knocked on the kitchen door of the Inn Between. *I know this can't go anywhere.*

But he was drawn to the warmth of the Atwells family like a cat to a radiator. They had . . . . something. Something he'd never quite experienced firsthand, although he'd read about it plenty of times in novels. And . . . they had Meg.

But it was Allie who came running to get the door. When she saw him, her face lit up with what he could only call a triumphant smile. ''Tom! *Great*! We're playing Monopoly, but

Comfort would really rather knit. You can take her place. Hey, everybody! Look who I found!'' she called out, dragging him by the hand into the front room.

On their way there, she turned and whispered in his ear, ''I've missed you. Why haven't you come around?''

Simple question; too bad it didn't have a simple answer. ''I've been boning up on a case,'' he said in an easy lie.

''A *case*!'' she said, shocked. ''This doesn't mean you're going *back* soon?''

''Eventually,'' he admitted, greeting the rest of the family with a sweeping ''Howdy, folks.'' His glance settled on Meg, her face flushed with color, sitting opposite Lloyd at a Monopoly board.

For the last several days Wyler's thoughts had drifted back to her constantly. Whatever she'd experienced at that bizarre memorial service had been intense and unforgettable. And yet when he'd called her the next day, she'd acted as if she'd forgotten all about it.

''Oh, that,'' she'd said. ''You were right. It turns out that long ago, my father knew a little French; so who knows what bits and pieces I may have picked up?''

She'd been cool to him on the phone, and he'd chalked it up to embarrassment over that emotional outburst in the shed. This evening, however, cool had turned to cold. Meg looked away from him and said to the others, ''The game's just about played out, anyway. It's obvious that Allie's going to win. Why don't we just call it a night?''

''Not so fast,'' said Allie. ''I want *all* of the Boardwalk. Sit back down, Meg. Comfort, you're excused. Right here, Wyler,'' she added with a sly smile, patting the seat of Comfort's chair.

Lloyd rolled up his sleeves and said, ''Leona, here, is right. It's not over till it's over.''

Wyler, who'd played Monopoly maybe three times in his life, focused on bringing himself up to speed in the game while Allie babbled like a sweet-running brook, and Lloyd rolled the dice as if the fate of the Inn Between depended on it.

Meg, who was on his right, hardly said a word. She seemed completely preoccupied with the mole on her brother's forehead. Wyler made one or two conversational overtures; she ignored them. Annoyed by her indifference, he said, "By the way, I saw Joyce Fells today at the Shop 'n Save."

That got a reaction. Meg's brows twitched sharply and her lips shaped themselves into one of her extra-polite, pissed-off smiles. "Oh, really?" she said, plopping her little metal car six spaces forward.

"Are you *sure*?" asked Allie. She leaned forward over the board, her eyes wide, her voice eager.

"Lotsa pink. Lotsa blue. Yeah, I'm sure," Wyler answered.

"Oh, Meggie, you know what this means," fretted Comfort, her knitting needles clicking a mile a minute. "It means she wants the dollhouse. It means she's going to fight for it."

"We figured that," Meg said, frowning over the exorbitant rent she was having to pay her sister. "So what?"

Lloyd grunted and said, "So you know what a lawyer is gonna cost you per quarter hour?"

Meg glanced at their father, dozing peacefully in his rocker over a fishing magazine. "Nothing's happened yet," she said in a hiss to the rest of them. "It's not today's problem. *End* of discussion."

She saved her most infuriated look for Wyler, who decided that he didn't deserve it—or the cold shoulder she'd been giving him all night. He could understand her feeling a little uncomfortable after her so-called trance in the shed. He himself was feeling anything but comfortable with it, despite the rational explanations he'd offered her.

But this was really about their parting afterward at the screen door. She'd wriggled out of his kiss not because she wasn't interested, but because—well, he didn't know why. Because of Allie, presumably.

But it wasn't because she hadn't wanted to kiss him. Damn it; she'd been sending him signals right up until that moment. The roses that she'd made him smell—what was *that* about, if not about a kiss to come?

The game went on. To an outsider peeking through the bay window, the scene looked as idyllic as could be: an elderly man snoozing in his rocker, a middle-aged woman knitting a sweater contentedly, her husband battling his lively sister for control of the Monopoly board. From the click-click of the knitting needles to the tick-tick of the hall clock, it was just as Wyler had pictured it.

He'd pictured everything except the grim, determined look on the face of the *other* sister, the one drumming her fingers impatiently on the table next to him. It was obvious that Meg Hazard couldn't wait for the game to be done.

And it ruined all the rest of it for him.

Lloyd tipped his chair back and tugged at his wife's housedress. "Comfort, honey, you got any more of that chocolate cheesecake around?" His spirits were soaring; he'd just snapped up another prime piece of Park Avenue, and the rents were flowing in. He was giving little Leona a run for her money.

Comfort took orders all around; Tom shook his head.

"You look as low as a Maine tide," said Allie, puzzled. "Are you all right?"

He glanced at Meg and took a certain satisfaction from the march of color across her cheeks. "Maybe not," he said. "I think I'll call it a day."

"Me, too," said Meg, instantly standing up. She shoved her money toward her brother. "You can have mine; Tom can go to Allie. Good-night, everyone."

Lloyd looked at her, disappointed. "Two's no fun, for cryin' out loud."

"I'm sorry," Meg said coldly, and headed for the door.

Before she got out of the room, a loud bang from outside sent them all jumping. Everett, starting from his doze, said, "Holy bejeezuz, what was *that*?"

"Backfire, probably," said Lloyd, peering through the lace curtain into the darkness outside. "I see a truck at the corner."

Everett settled back in his rocking chair and Meg continued on her way. Allie said to Wyler in a hurt, subdued voice, "Is tomorrow still moving day? Do you still want my help?"

Distracted, Wyler said, "What? Sure. Of course."

He made a hasty exit and took off in the direction of the bang. The sound was too loud for a backfire, but not too loud for a gunshot. Wyler's urban hairs were still standing on his urban skin. If he were on the south side of Chicago right now, he'd have his gun out. But he was in sleepy Bar Harbor, so he was giving the explosion the benefit of the doubt.

He walked soundlessly through the fog, all his senses alert, listening for humans up to no good. He heard quiet voices in the parlors of one or two inns on the street, but all outdoor activity had been suppressed by the thick blanket of Down East fog. At the corner, a couple of darkened houses made him pause and circle; what better place for wreaking havoc?

His hunch panned out. In back of one of the houses he heard two voices that cracked when they giggled. Kids. Only then, when he heard the scratch of a match, did he remember that the Fourth of July was coming up: kids with cherry bombs.

The second explosion rocked his eardrums. Furious, he crept up in the darkness to the bush they were crouched behind, stepped around it, and grabbed two of them by their collars, doing his best to scare the daylights out of them.

One wriggled free and took off; the other gave Wyler a sharp kick in the shins and tried to tough it out.

"Let go of me!" he cried, swinging in the darkness. "Pick on someone your own size!"

"You moron! You could've lost a hand!" Wyler shouted, his bad leg smarting from this latest insult. He sounded more like a parent than a cop, and he knew it.

So did the kid, who didn't show any fear of him at all. "Wait'll my father gets you! Just wait!" he kept crying in a high, shrill voice as Wyler dragged him out to the street for a better look.

Terry. Oh, perfect. The last sour note to the evening's sour symphony. "Was that Timmy who ran off?" Wyler said, automatically yanking the twin in the direction of his house.

Terry, having recognized Wyler under the fog-bleared streetlight, turned surly and indifferent. *"Timmy?* Gimme a break. Timmy's in his room, readin' a book."

"And is there some reason you're not?" Wyler asked, with another yank on the boy's collar.

Terry twisted his head up at Wyler. "Yeah, duh, I can't read," he said in a Beavis-and-Butt-Head voice. "Ain't you heard?"

"Keep this up and you'll have plenty of time to learn—in jail," Wyler answered through gritted teeth.

All the pat phrases came tumbling out as they made their way in lockstep down the street. "What's the matter with you? . . . don't you have any brains? . . . why can't you be more like your brother? . . . do you know what road you're headed down? . . . you'll end up with no money, no future . . . what's the matter with you? . . . don't you have any brains? What would your mother say?"

Terry muttered, "Everything you just said."

Wyler stopped dead in his tracks. It was true. He was basically just foaming at the mouth, in the way of frustrated, well-meaning adults since the beginning of time.

"C'mon," he said abruptly. "We're going for a walk." He about-faced and began heading for town.

"You're not gonna take me to the station, are you?" asked Terry, horrified.

"That depends on how you behave. Can you walk alongside me like a grownup? Or do I have to haul you around by the scruff of your neck?"

"You don't have to do *any*thing," said Terry, falling in step reluctantly. "I don't know why you don't just leave me alone."

"I'm not leaving you alone because—because I care about your aunt," Wyler said, exasperated. "I don't want you going around embarrassing her."

"Oh yeah? Which aunt?"

Good damn question. "*Both* of them," Wyler answered sharply. "I care about your whole family. They deserve better than to have some squirt like you taking them for granted all the time."

"What do you mean?" asked Terry, kicking a stone down the sidewalk. "I don't take 'em for granted. I don't even know what that means."

"It *means*, pal, that you're a lucky little son of a . . . gun, living with your original mother and your original father. A lot of kids don't. A lot of kids have no parents at all, in fact."

Terry plunged his hands into the pockets of his sweatshirt. "So?"

"So let me tell you a little about what it's like to live on the streets. What it's like when your mother and father don't care —or can't care—about you."

"Yeah, yeah, I know: Cops like you round the kids up and throw 'em in jail."

"I'm not talking about this from a cop's point of view, snot. I'm telling you I know what it's like to be a kid on the street."

Terry shot a quick glance up at Wyler. His voice became more respectful. "You were a street kid?"

"Yeah. Before it was fashionable, even."

"No kidding? You ran away from your mom and dad?"

"I hardly knew my mother," Wyler said in a voice suddenly gone hard. "I *never* knew my father. I lived in a series of foster homes."

"So how'd you end up on the street?"

"One of my foster fathers slapped me around a lot. He's the one I ran away from."

"And you lived in, like, refrigerator boxes and stuff? Like on TV?"

"Nah. Mostly in bus stations and subways and parks."

"Did you ever steal?"

"I had to eat; sometimes the Dumpsters didn't pan out."

"Ick. Did you ever kill anyone?"

"No."

"Ever beat anyone up, at least?"

"In self-defense. Lots of times."

"Did you always win?"

"No."

"How old were you?"

"Your age."

"Wow."

The two walked along in thoughtful silence for a while. Wyler had no idea whether he was making the right impression on Terry or not. He had no idea what a child psychologist would recommend that he say. All he knew was that if it weren't for his last set of foster parents, the ones who truly cared, he probably wouldn't be alive to be having *any* conversation with Terry. And that's what he wanted the boy to understand.

It was Terry who broke the silence. "So how come you ended up being a cop instead of a drug addict or—?"

"—or dead?" Bingo. A beautiful opening. Wyler took it. "I got picked up and sent back to the system. By some miracle, I ended up in a foster home with two really good people. My foster mom was—she was really good," said Wyler in a faraway voice. "Your mom reminds me of her. She really loved me. I didn't want to screw up, to disappoint her. You know?"

"Yeah," said Terry in a subdued voice. "They get disappointed so easy."

"That's because they want us to be happy. If we're happy, usually they're happy. It works out pretty well."

"I guess," the boy said uncertainly.

They were in front of Treats, a local ice-cream parlor. Wyler said, "How about a cone?"

The boy shrugged. "I don't have any money."

"This one's on me," Wyler said. "You get it next time."

"Okay," Terry said, satisfied with the grown-up arrangement.

They went inside, ordered double-dip chocolate-Oreo-chunky cones, and headed home, licking like crazy. Sometime after Terry got his dripping cone under control, he said, "So you don't mind being a cop?"

"It's not bad," Wyler agreed. "There's lots of perks."

"Oh yeah? Like what?" the boy asked.

Wyler told him a story he never got tired of telling. "I once got every single member of the Bulls, including Michael Jordan, to autograph a basketball for my son's birthday present."

"*Wow*! Whatta present!"

"Yeah," said Wyler in a rueful voice. "Then I put it in the trunk of my unmarked car, and wouldn'tcha know—the car got ripped off."

"Oh, *jee-e-ez*!" said Terry, wincing melodramatically. He was in real pain. "I saw a Michael Jordan-autographed basketball in a sports catalog once. You know how much they wanted? Two thousand *bucks*! And that was without the rest of the team! Wow," he repeated, thoroughly impressed. "I don't suppose you ever got it back?" he asked hopefully.

Wyler bit into the side of his cone. "Got the guys. Got the car. Never got the ball."

"*Man*, I'd want to pound 'em until they told me where it was. Because that isn't *fair*."

"Yeah. But that doesn't accomplish anything. It only lowers you to their level. Y'know?"

"I have to think about that," Terry decided.

They were nearly home when Wyler tried one last tactic. "By the way, no one else but you knows about what I did when I was a kid. Not even my friends back in Chicago."

That impressed Terry more than anything else so far. With a surprised half smile he said, "*Really*?"

"Yeah. I'm thinking maybe we want to keep the whole evening just between us guys."

"*Yeah*," said Terry thoughtfully. "I'm thinking the same thing."

The next morning Allie rushed into the kitchen with more flour from the supermarket, narrowly averting a mid-breakfast supply crisis.

"You're lucky Tom's tenants need another day, Meg," said her sister as she washed up. "Where would you be without me to do your stepping and fetching?"

"I know. You're wonderful," said Meg, rolling her eyes. She began mixing a second batch of crêpe batter. "All right. Now finish telling me about the Fourth of July dance. Are you sure Gordon Camplin's going to be there?" Meg asked her sister.

Allie took a heated plate and transferred three exquisitely thin crêpes from Meg's stack to it. "Of course he'll be there; the dance is one of the big charity affairs of the summer. No one who's anyone will miss it. And get this: we've even got ourselves a two-fer. Gordon's ex-wife'll be there too; Dorothea Camplin is actually chairing the event."

"*That* must be awkward." Meg ladled runny batter into the sizzling brown butter and twisted the frying pan all around until the crêpe was membrane thin. "Isn't it funny how neither of them would budge from Bar Harbor after they divorced all those years ago? Do you suppose they're still on friendly terms?''

Allie topped the crêpes with a thin slice of orange and a sprig of mint and headed out the door for the guest's breakfast table. ''Probably,'' she said over her shoulder. ''You know these society types.''

Meg didn't have a *clue* about these society types, which was why she was having second thoughts about hiring on to serve them cheese and wine. What if they saw right through her eavesdropping ways? And what could she reasonably expect to overhear, anyway? Gordon Camplin pointing to her and whispering, ''Fine-looking woman. Reminds me of the one I killed that night in '47''?

No doubt about it, she was getting cold feet.

''Let's buy tickets ourselves,'' Meg suggested when Allie came back for the next order. ''It's a charity; anyone can go.''

''Anyone with two hundred dollars *apiece* can go,'' Allie corrected.

''Yowch. Two tickets—or a new washing machine. What d'you think? Are you willing to wash the sheets and towels by hand for the rest of the summer?'' Meg asked, half seriously.

''When hell freezes over,'' her sister said, loading up the next plate of crêpes. ''No. Your original plan's a good one. Not to mention, we'll make a few bucks.''

''You could always try getting Bobby Beaufort to ask you,'' Meg said with a hopeful, almost wistful look. ''I hear he's landed a great new job at Auto Central.''

''Puh-leeze. Bobby is a boy. A local boy at that.''

''Oh, dear! And everybody knows how you feel about *them*!''

''Excuse me. Miss?''

It came from one of their guests, a nicely dressed woman who obviously believed that someone evil had switched the Inn Between for the Elm Tree Inn just before her arrival. This was the third unhappy day she'd spent complaining. About *everything.*

She was holding a plate of Meg's crêpes in her hand. "Excuse me," she repeated. "Have these been fried on hydrogenated fat?"

"Oh, no, ma'am," said Meg blandly. "We only use pure butter."

"Butter! Even worse! I don't see how I can eat this. Will you be serving something less fatty this morning?"

The sisters exchanged a look. Meg said, "We have yogurt . . . home-made granola . . ."

"We can blend you a health drink of brewer's yeast and orange juice," added Allie with no attempt to hide the malice in her voice.

"N-n-no . . . I really was in the mood for cooked food."

Allie, standing behind the guest, made a strangling gesture with her hands, but Meg merely smiled and said, "I can make you some oatmeal with skim milk."

"Oatmeal . . . hmm. No, it's too warm out for hot oatmeal." She waited for more.

"I see," said Meg. "Nothing hot, nothing cold. Something in between. Perhaps you have a suggestion?" she said with a dry smile.

"Yes. I'd love French toast made with egg whites. Or Teflon, of course; no fat. Or maybe with just a wee spray of Pam."

"Certainly," said Meg, taking the plate of crêpes from the fat-fearing guest. "It'll be just a few minutes."

"Oh, good. Because I've a big day planned."

"Hiking?" asked Meg politely. "Bicycling?"

"Antiquing. It can be surprisingly tiring," she said with a straight face. "Ta!"

She went back to the dining room and Allie said, "Yeah, it has to be exhausting, lifting that Visa card in and out of her wallet."

"Now, Allie. Just because the woman *has* a Visa card."

Allie, whose own card had a three-hundred-dollar limit and n interest rate of twenty-three percent, said, "Why do you umor her?"

"Why do I humor *you*?"

Allie snorted and said, "You certainly are in the right trade, Mrs. Hazard."

"True," her sister agreed, dragging out the Teflon griddle. "Maybe we should try returning your degree in hotel adminis- ration for a refund. Or better yet, get it awarded to me. *You* ure as hell aren't going to use it."

"Yes, I am. But I won't waste my time on people like her."

"Allie, that *is* the hospitality business. You have to be able o smile, smile, smile."

"No. People should be honest about how they feel. People hould say what they think. If someone is being impossible, ou should be able to say so to him. People should never be nartyrs to the selfishness of others. The world would be a netter, more honest place."

Meg gave her sister a long, pensive look. *If only that were rue*, she thought, sighing.

She got a loaf of Pepperidge Farm toasting white out of the ridge. "You're beginning to worry me, Allie," she said. "I ust don't think you're cut out for hotel management."

"If this is your idea of hotel management, then you're ight," Allie said, tossing back her mane of black hair. "I nave grander plans."

"Such as what? You showed absolutely no interest in the White Horse Inn during your interview there; I know *that* for a act." She cracked an egg and dropped it back and forth in its hell, separating the yolk from the white.

"The White Horse Inn is not, I repeat not, on my agenda. 've told you before, Meg; I want to work in a big city."

"I don't see you pounding the Boston pavements," Meg aid irritably.

"I don't want Boston." She paused, then said, "I want Chicago. I've decided not to look anywhere else."

Meg whacked the second egg to smithereens, contaminating the first white with yellow yolk. "Chicago! Why Chicago?" she said, without trusting herself to look up. She dumped the egg mess down the drain and started over.

"Why. Why do you *think*?" Allie said impatiently. "Because *Tom* lives there. Because he's not going to relocate his career to some one-horse town on a two-horse island in Maine. Because when you love someone, you don't ask whether it's convenient; you go where he goes. And anyway, it *is* convenient!" she said hotly. "He's established, I'm not. It's the simplest thing in the world for me to pick up and move west."

"What about your ambitions? What about your grand schemes?"

"Chicago has *plenty* of opportunities. And they say the people are open and friendly—"

"You're crazy! You'd hate it! There's nothing there! Flatland! That's *it*!" she said, smashing another egg to a pulp.

"What do *I* care if the land is flat or pointy?" demanded Allie. "The Great Outdoors has always been *your* thing, Meg, not mine."

"What about *us*? What about your *family*?" asked Meg, whirling around on her sister. Her heart was pounding violently in her breast. *When you love someone* . . .

Allie was silent, obviously uncomfortable with the turn in the conversation.

Meg got herself under control and said softly, "What if he doesn't love you?"

"I know he does," her sister answered, just as softly. "That's not the issue."

"He . . . Oh. I didn't know that," Meg said, stunned.

It was as if someone had set off a stick of dynamite on the linoleum beneath her. She watched in slow motion as tables and chairs, pots and pans, the bottle of Joy and the pink Brillo pad all seemed to lift up and away and float back down again, in bits and pieces around her head.

"So it's all settled . . . between you?"

"It's not completely settled," said Allie with a proud lift of her head.

Suddenly it was Meg and not the kitchen furnishings that seemed to be floating upward. "Oh! *Well*—"

"Shhht!" said Allie, glancing out the window above the sink. "Here he comes! I'll die if he catches us at this again!"

CHAPTER *13*

Meg thought Tom looked depressingly cheerful and handsome. Maybe it was the wild Hawaiian shirt he was wearing; it was a charmingly absurd change of pace for him. And his sandy hair was getting truly shaggy, adding to the laid-back look. Homicide cop? He looked more like a volleyball star.

Meg said briskly, "Mornin', Lieutenant," and went back to the fridge for yet another round of eggs.

"Tom Wyler," Allie said, comically shading her eyes with her hand, "where *did* you get that shirt? Not at L. L. Bean's, I can tell you that." She herself was dressed in pure white, her color of choice on hot days.

"This is a gen-yew-ine Acapulco Hawaiian shirt," Tom said with an ironic little tug on its front placket. "The real thing. My sergeant brought it back with him after an R&R trip down there. Acapulco's one of the department's hot spots."

"So why are you in Bar Harbor?" muttered Meg as she dredged through the utensil drawer for the egg separator.

"Why, indeed," she heard him say behind her. It was a question that she knew she'd have to know the answer to, sooner or later.

"I called that realtor you told me about," he said to Allie. "I've had to call a roofer, too. The tenants told me the bedroom ceiling leaks so badly, they've been forced to store the double bed in the garage and put in two singles, with a bucket between them to catch the rain.''

"That's *awful*," said Allie with real feeling.

Meg glanced up at her sister, who was blushing an attractive shade of rosy pink. It didn't seem fair: every emotion that Allie Atwells had ever felt, from anger to embarrassment, only made her look more beautiful. Couldn't she get puffy when she cried, or laugh in shrill tones, or bloat up before her period? Couldn't Allegra Atwells be counted on to do *anything* ugly?

"Meggie!" cried Allie in her damnably enchanting voice. She pointed to the bowl in Meg's hands. "The lady wanted her French toast made with all *whites*, not all *yolks*."

Meg stared into the bowl of creamy yellow yolks she'd been whisking so furiously. "I knew that," she said abruptly, and put the bowl in the refrigerator as if she had a plan.

The reality was, she had no plan—for the yolks, for Allie, or for Tom Wyler. She knew what she *didn't* want: she didn't want Tom and Allie in that cabin alone together. In a single bed *or* in a double. Beyond that, she could not say. "Serve the damn crêpes, Allie," she said with an evil scowl. "The natives surely are getting restless out there."

"Tsk, tsk," her sister mocked in a cheerful voice. "Smile, smile, *smile!*" She scooped up a plate of crêpes and glided theatrically out of the room.

"Are you eating here today, Lieutenant?" Meg asked, flipping the French toast in three vicious slaps.

"Why do I think that's not an invitation?" he answered as he came up behind her.

She forced herself not to turn around; he was far too close. One look into his eyes and she'd be lost. "You know you're always welcome," she made herself say.

"That's not the feeling I got last night—"

Allie glided back into the kitchen with an empty plate in each hand. She whirled around in front of them both and batted her heavily lashed eyes at Tom. "Just practicing my serving technique for the Fourth of July dance," she said in an outrageously sultry voice.

Meg considered breaking the plates over her sister's head and knocking her out altogether to slow her down, but restrained herself.

"The dance is why I'm here, Cinderella," Tom said to Allie. "Guess what I have two of, in the pocket of my shirt?"

"You're *kidding*," Allie said, comprehending at once. She dropped the dishes on the counter and made a mad dash for the tickets sticking out from his shirt pocket.

She plucked out the two invitations with great melodrama—Meg had never before realized how irritating her sister could be—and squealed, "How did you get them? You didn't actually *pay* for them?"

"Connections, child; connections. I knew you wanted to go—"

"With Meg! On business!" cried Allie with a tragic look. "Not with you, for pleasure. Oh, this is too bad—"

"Don't be silly, Allie," said Meg, noticing too late that she'd overbrowned the damn egg whites. Sick to death of the French-toast project, she flopped the ill-fated bread on an unwarmed plate and said grimly, *"I'll* take this out to her. Personally."

On her way out of the kitchen, she turned to Tom. "As for my sister," she said, "of course she'll go with you. I'll fade in with the rest of the help. Between us we ought to be able to come up with *some*thing on Camplin."

"Camplin? What's he got to do with—?"

Allie sucked in her breath and said, "Ayyy . . . haven't quite filled you in on all the details, Tom."

Meg turned to her sister with a ferocious look. "Well, *fill* him, in that case," she said, and stomped away from these people she hated with food she hated for a guest she hated.

When she came back it was to see Tom and Allie with their heads together. Allie said, "We've decided—"

"She's decided."

"—not to do it your way, Meg. Everybody knows that most of the waitressing during high season is done by college kids. You should go with Tom and act, like, well, you're on a date. *I'll* go as the help."

For a moment Meg was speechless. Then she turned to Tom. "You can't possibly have agreed to this," she said.

"Actually, I think that the two of you should take the tickets and leave me out of this," he said amiably.

Allie was scandalized. "How would it look, us walking in arm-in-arm like Bette Davis and Joan Crawford?"

The image popped indelibly into Meg's mind. "Hysterical," she said promptly. "Let's do it."

Both sisters burst into laughter, leaving Tom looking first at one, then the other, in bewilderment.

"This means . . . you two *are* going together?"

"Of course not," Meg said, still smiling. "Allie's absolutely right. We couldn't possibly."

She turned back to her sister. "But I don't have a thing to wear."

"What about that fancy green dress?"

"You've got to be kidding. I haven't worn that in five years." *It hasn't fit me in seven,* she added to herself.

Allie pursed her lips, deep in thought. Then she snapped her fingers and cried, "Wait! That gorgeous silk thing that I bought on sale! I haven't had it altered yet. It'd be *perfect* for you. That lavender shade would look better on you than me, anyway."

"Oh, *that* one," said Meg, her eyes shining. "That *is* pretty."

"We'll try it on right after breakfast," Allie said excitedly. "How much more time here?" She looked at her watch. "Ten more minutes. Oh, the hell with it. Let's close up shop."

*"Al-*lee," her sister warned.

Allie rolled her eyes and took up the coffee carafe. "All right, all right. I'll do the hospitality thing," she said with a jumpy, impatient sigh. "And, Tom?"

He was leaning against the counter, in that ridiculous shirt, with his arms folded across his chest, monitoring their excitement with a bemused look. *"Yo,"* he said, smiling.

"Uncle Billy's Fourth of July picnic is all day Saturday, so you won't be able to run around for a tux then. If there's nothing left to rent in town, you may have to go to Bangor— unless! You happened to bring one with you?"

Tom said, "A tuxedo?"

For some reason he looked at Meg. She remembered the look long, long after that morning in the kitchen. It was a look filled with indulgence, good humor, and plain, sheer amazement.

"No, Allie," he said, his voice filled with a delicious sense of irony. "I meant to pack it but—dadgum—I forgot."

"Too bad," said Allie, completely missing his tone. "Oh, well. The tickets do say black tie's optional. Isn't this *great*? A picnic and then a dance, with my two favorite people," she said, sweeping them both up in a wave of high-powered energy as she waltzed out of the kitchen with the last of the crêpes.

Obviously it made no difference to Allie whether she was going as a guest or as a slave, just so long as she was part of the action.

Tom chuckled and shook his head. He needed a shave; Meg could practically hear the rasp of his chin as he drew his fingers across it and said to her, "How about you? Ready to party?"

Clearly the man was confusing his Cinderellas. Meg was ready for anything *but* partying. The weather forecast for the holiday weekend was perfect; the Inn Between was booked solid. Comfort was flat-out busy with Uncle Billy's annual picnic, so Meg was taking over her chores at the inn. In her spare time, she was trying to research the Bar Harbor Fire. Not to mention, now she'd have to run out and buy a pair of glass slippers.

She shook her head. "Party? I can't remember the last time I went out to anything really fancy," she confessed. "Paul was never very happy on a dance floor. He felt a lot more comfortable at the helm of a boat."

Tom winced and said, "I don't dance *or* sail. God knows where that puts me on the desirability scale."

Right up there, Meg thought with a pained smile.

"What kind of dancing do they *do*, nowadays?" Tom said, still without a trace of ego. "I've read about something called, what is it, hip-hop?"

"Really? They don't do the pony anymore?"

"And what's contradancing, anyway?"

They shrugged, and then they laughed: easy, comfortable, same-age laughter. After he left, Meg wrapped the memory of it around herself like a flannel robe. She knew that they didn't share the same background or lifestyle. She wasn't even sure they shared the same values. But one thing they had in common: a fascination and affection for Allegra Atwells. It was drawing them together—and it was just as surely keeping them apart.

On Thursday, a satisfied couple at the Inn Between pressed fifty extra dollars into Meg's hands. The couple had come to Mount Desert Island expressly to see the grand perennial beds of Thuja Lodge, the wonderful old estate in nearby Northeast Harbor, and when they came back, Meg gave them tea and a tour of the far more humble but still delightful gardens of the Inn Between.

"We had a daughter much like you," the old man, eyes glistening, said before they left. "She's gone now. We thank you very much."

Fifty dollars was fifty dollars. It could've bought curtains or linens or a dried arrangement for the cherry table in the hall. But Meg had no dancing shoes to wear with Allie's lavender dress, and for the first time in a long time, she wanted to indulge herself. With the dress folded carefully in tissue, she drove to Ellsworth to find a pair of shoes to match. She didn't actually plan to *use* the shoes—not for dancing, anyway—but she had a sudden, fierce desire not to look like a bag lady.

The search for shoes turned out to be a lot easier than the search for clues. By now Meg had read every account she could find of the fire of '47: books, newspapers, magazines, even an unpublished manuscript. She'd contacted the few people she knew—relatives of friends, friends of relatives—who had experienced the night of the Great Fire, on the pretext of doing a family history. But many of the people seemed reluctant to dwell on an event that had claimed her grandmother's life.

The most damning clue she could find was in a local newspaper article that alluded to the cuts and scratches that the "courageous Mr. Camplin, bloody but unbowed," had endured on his face while battling on the fire line.

Fire line, my foot, Meg thought as she stared at the crumbling newspaper article in the quiet basement room housing the local historical society. *How come no one else seems to've suffered facial cuts and scratches?* For one brief moment she allowed herself to feel good about the fact that her grandmother had probably managed to inflict some pain, however fleeting, on her tormentor.

But even those minor injuries had been turned to Camplin's advantage: the man had been touted as a hero all around town, a reputation that he enjoyed to this day.

Meg managed to dredge up only one other clue in the hectic days before the picnic. She found it buried in the inside pages of a January 1948 issue of the local paper: a short paragraph, easily missed, stating that Gordon Camplin had donated to a New York public garden some marble statuary that had survived the fire at Eagle's Nest because, according to their owner, "they were associated with memories too painful to be borne."

To the reporter the remark was straightforward enough, but not to Meg. Like everything else in the case—she had come to regard the death of her grandmother as a "case"—Camplin's comment seemed ambiguous. Which memories was he talking about?

Okay. So clue-wise, the findings didn't amount to much. Meg tried not to let it get her down but simply added the information to the copious notes that she was keeping, along with the photo album, in an old bureau that had stood in one corner of the shed for as long as anyone could remember. On the night before the picnic, with everyone off watching the fireworks, Meg took her cup of bergamot tea to the shed and tried to make sense of it all.

The truth was, she'd been hoping for a little help from her grandmother, but Margaret Mary Atwells was clearly keeping her distance from her granddaughter. Since the night of her strange little fit, Meg had felt absolutely nothing that could qualify as a clairvoyant experience—unless she counted knowing where to find Timmy's misplaced book report as a psychic event.

Still, Meg felt duty bound to do what she could to make herself available, as it were. So she hung around the dollhouse and fingered its dolls and furnishings now and then, imagining little scenarios that might have been played out by the inhabitants of the real Eagle's Nest.

Nothing. Not even when she picked up the repulsive little carved-teak bed. No vibrations, no wobbly knees, and no trance—self-induced or otherwise. Someone like Zenobia would no doubt say that Meg was symptom-free.

It was very annoying.

One way or another, Meg had accepted the psychic burden
that had been dropped in her lap. She'd hardly even objected,
because Meg had always believed that there was a world beyond the one she could see and touch and feel. It was nothing
she agonized over very often; the belief was just there, like
breathing, like the beat of her heart.

And now—nothing.

Meg sighed and returned the dreadful little bed to the little
master bedroom. She took one last look through the rooms of
the dollhouse, half hoping to find a miniature note written by
the nursemaid doll laying out the facts of her murder. But
there was nothing on the Sheraton-style desk in the library
except a tiny green leather-bound blotter and an even tinier
gold pen.

Meg had switched off the dollhouse's lights and was about
to pull the string on the overhead bulb in the shed, when her
father came by.

"Just where I thought you'd be, Meggie," he said with an
affectionate shake of his head. "Comfort's looking for you."

"Okay, Dad, I was just going in," Meg said tiredly.

"She wants to know should she make a sheet cake, maybe,
for the picnic tomorrow. In case the kids don't want cobbler."

"Too *bad* if they don't want cobbler," Meg snapped. "Everybody can't have everything he wants," she added. "Comfort can't stay up all night slaving over fifty different desserts.
Enough is enough!"

"Meg!" her father said in mild admonition. "Comfort
don't mind. She's enjoyin' this the way she always does. Your
uncle Bill's payin' for everything just like usual. Why be so
hard on the kids?"

"Because this year things are different, Dad," Meg said
darkly.

"No. This year *you're* different, girl. What's ailin' you,
anyway? In the last few weeks your mood's gone from bad to
worse."

"It has not!" she argued. "I'm just the same. Nothing's changed. I've always been this bitchy."

Everett Atwells looked at his daughter in the bleary light of the uncovered bulb and shook his balding head. "Never like this. Believe me, girl, I'm trying not to notice. You think I want a summer ruint by female emotions? But look at you. You snap, you mope, you sneak out to this shed every chance you get—"

"That's because it's quiet here, Dad," she said petulantly. "I can think. I can't concentrate in my room; it faces the street," she said, whining about it for the first time. She'd rather have had a room that overlooked the garden, but she'd never had the heart to dislodge anyone to get it.

"You weren't at the fireworks tonight."

Meg, who knew that Allie and Tom had gone there with the twins, said, "You've seen one fireworks, you've seen 'em all."

"Terry says you sit here scribblin'. What's that all about?"

"Just collecting my thoughts, that's all. Terry should mind his own business," she added, turning out the light, hoping her father would take her suggestion personally. They stepped outside into the flower-filled night and Meg started on a brisk pace back to the house.

But Everett Atwells, a man rarely stirred to action, was oddly determined tonight. He matched his daughter stride for stride. "And I'll tell you what *else*," he said, saving his best shot for last. "You're beginnin' to embarrass me around town. I was in Jordan's this mornin', havin' a cuppa coffee. First your cousin Mandy, then Pete Ardell came up to me and said, what's with all Meg's questions about Gordon Camplin."

Meg stopped in her tracks. "They *didn't*," she said, appalled.

"Did you think no one'd notice? For goodness' sake, girl, this is Bar Harbor! Rich folk live here, and us poor ones tend to work for 'em. So naturally there's bound to be a good bit of gossip goin' on. Why, it's practically a tradition! And the gossip now is that you're carryin' on a vendetta against Gordon Camplin.''

Oh, shit shit shit was Meg's one thought.

"That's silly," she said carelessly. "I told you, Dad: those accusations were the ravings of an irrational man before he died," Meg said, repeating her previous lie to her father. "No one will take such a claim seriously."

"They are, and it's your fault. So now I have to tell you something I never thought I would. And dammit—your uncle Bill is not gonna take kindly to it."

Everett stopped and waited while his daughter straightened a clump of top-heavy daisies that had flopped onto the narrow brick path. Then he took a deep breath and said, "Listen to me, Meggie: the summer of '48 was real, real hard on the family. Dad was out of work, Ma was gone. We almost lost the house."

Meg looked up from her daisies. "This house? Your house?"

He nodded. "Bank was breathing down our necks like you wouldn't believe. Lots of people got breaks, of course, because they'd lost everything in the fire. Everyone from the federal government to the Hairdressers Association rushed to help. But us, all *we* lost was our mother—our breadwinner," he said with some bitterness. "That didn't qualify us for a federal loan, and we didn't need beds or lumber or a new refrigerator, so the Red Cross and Elks Club and such was no real help for us, either. It was a real predicament.

"We thought things were all up. Then out of the blue comes Gordon Camplin and just like that, pays off three years on the mortgage. He knew our situation and felt sorry for us, y'see. It was an unbelievable kindness. It was all done nice and discreet-like, with lawyers and bankers. That's how their kind do things."

Her father added, "We never even got to thank him in person. Dad—well, he wasn't the type, and we were too young. Anyway, we were able to keep holding up our heads, and eventually Billy began makin' decent money, and then I started chipping in. But without Gordon Camplin's help getting us over the hump, we'd have lost the house for sure.''

Everett stood there with his head still high, but with his chin trembling with emotion.

Meg was absolutely staggered by the news. It was like finding out that the man who broke into your house and assaulted your mother was Santa Claus. "No, that can't . . . how could . . . I can't believe . . . *wait* a minute! Guilt! That's why he helped you out—guilt, not pity!''

Her father's response to that surprised her. "Rich folk don't feel guilt,'' he said firmly.

"They don't feel pity, either,'' she shot back.

"You're wrong. Pity makes them feel richer.''

"This is crazy, Dad,'' she said impatiently. "He probably did it for some other reason altogether.''

There was no answer to that, so Everett Atwells merely said, "I wish you would leave Gordon Camplin alone. And I wish you would stop fooling around with games of . . . magic.''

Coming from him, it was the gravest of reprimands. Meg wondered exactly how much he'd heard about the spontaneous séance in the shed.

"I'm not fooling around, Dad,'' Meg said seriously, which was true, as far as it went.

"Good. Then that's that.'' Everett Atwells sighed with relief; his duty as nominal head of the household was done. "Good night, sweetheart,'' he said, dropping a quick kiss on his daughter's cheek. "I'll see you at the picnic. Not first thing, though; I'll be off for a little fishin' first.''

Comfort got up at four and made the sheet cake after all. Meg got up at six and frosted it for her. Then the sisters-in-law loaded the last of the food into the truck and drove it out to their uncle Billy's. Meg came back alone to the Inn Between to fix breakfast for their guests before handing over the reins to a spinster cousin who absolutely hated picnics, people, and bugs of any kind and was willing to do anything, even babysit an inn, to get away from them.

Allie was off on what amounted to a scavenger hunt for Comfort, and Lloyd was in the cellar, tinkering with the Inn Between's infuriating furnace. Since they were all going in one car—Tom's—to ease the parking crunch at Uncle Billy's, Meg had, for the moment, nothing to do but wait for everyone to assemble.

She was tighter than an overwound clock. It didn't seem possible that now, of all times, the sense of overwhelming dread that she'd felt in the shed would return; but it had, and with a vengeance. Maybe it had something to do with the approaching confrontation with Gordon Camplin. As the dance drew nearer, her resolve was becoming fainter.

She wandered out to her garden, deliberately avoiding the shed and the dollhouse within, and was roused from her anxious reverie by an angry *chick-a-dee-dee-dee* sound issuing from a clump of privet. The bird feeder hanging in its branches was empty, and two hungry chickadees were demanding to know why. Meg smiled at the pair of fearless, tiny birds and went back to the house for a refill of sunflower seeds. When she returned the chickadees were still there, still scolding.

"Me, me, me," she said aloud to them. "You're just like everyone else nowadays—selfish."

Meg decided, on a whim, to make them give her something in return. She scooped a handful of seed from the paper bag and held it out for them in her open palm. She would feed them if they would trust her: that was the trade.

She was standing very near the feeder; the birds could hardly mistake her meaning. They fluttered and darted around her—so close that she could feel the breath of their wings on her cheek—but for all their boldness, they continued to hesitate.

Chick-a-dee-dee-dee! Chick-a-dee-dee-dee!

I'm sorry, she said, communicating with them through the stillness of her pose. *If you want it, you'll have to come get it.*

One of the pair—hungrier or braver or simply more trusting —made a darting pass at her hand, then swerved away at the last minute to the safety of the privet.

Almost, she thought, daring to smile. It occurred to her that her arm should be tired, but the thought—along with her depression, her anxiety, her restlessness—faded away, lost in the simple act of watching a small bird feed.

The chickadee made a decision; she could see it in his eyes. *Here I come*, it said with fine bravado. *Get ready.*

The bird landed lightly on her forefinger, then scooped up the first sunflower seed it saw and flew away with it to the privet. The other bird, somewhat reassured, hopped to a branch a little bit closer to her.

Meg waited.

When Tom couldn't find Meg in the kitchen he turned instinctively to the garden, and that was where he was now, watching her.

It was extraordinary. She was standing as still as a statue, with her open hand extended, while two small black-and-white birds with pale yellow breasts took turns picking seeds from it. He'd never seen anything like it. One of the birds was even ballsy enough to be picking over the seed in her hand—looking for a good one, apparently—and throwing the ones he didn't like over the side. Unbelievable.

Meg looked absolutely beautiful just then, graceful and still and utterly at one with the garden around her. Her T-shirt of camouflage green and her khaki-colored shorts reinforced the illusion; her hair, chestnut brown and shot through with sun streaks of gold, gleamed in the morning light that filtered through a shade tree overhead. Her legs—straight and strong and tanned—suggested an athleticism that struck him as positively erotic. And her face! How had he not noticed her face before? With its straight nose and gently squared chin, her face in profile had the classic balance of Greek statuary.

Diana, he realized at once. A goddess of power and serenity and uncommon fierceness. The Greeks called her the Lady of Wild Things. Oh, yes. The image perfectly matched the woman standing there with her hand outstretched to the birds around her.

He was awed by the sight. And in some way that he didn't understand, intimidated by it.

He made a move to turn and go, and that shattered the moment. Suddenly Meg was aware of him. She threw down the seed, the birds flew away to hide and scold, and Meg became all business, funneling a paper bag into the top of the feeder. He felt like a director who's yelled "Action!"

"Good morning, Lieutenant; all set to go?" she asked in a voice so casually offhand that it was actually irritating. Didn't she understand how overwhelmed he'd been?

"Yeah, sure," he answered, still shaken by the vision of her. "Where is everyone?"

Meg told him and then said, "So we have a little time. I was just topping off the feeders," she explained, clearly self-conscious.

"I've never seen birds so tame," he confessed. "Are they house pets?"

She laughed, and the sound of her laughter was like the sound of water falling from a high place.

"They're chickadees," she said, "and they *are* the tamest things around. Would you like to try feeding these two?"

How could he say no? He felt as if he'd been invited into a secret place. Risking the chance that he'd look like a fool, he let Meg pour a handful of seeds into the palm of his hand, then held it out toward the clump of privet just as he'd seen her do. The curved bench was close by; Meg sat on it without a word and watched him. He didn't dare turn to look at her; he only stood, stone-still, holding out his arm, which ached like hell after twenty seconds.

The chickadees weren't buying it. They flew off to a nearby small tree covered with lilac flowers. *Damn it*, he thought. Rejected by a chickadee. It couldn't get any worse than that. Maybe he was too big. Maybe he was too garishly dressed: He was wearing a yellow Day-Glo T-shirt with big letters that phonetically spelled BA HA BA, just the way the locals said it.

Hell, maybe they just didn't like men. His arm felt as if it was about to fall off.

Damn it, he thought, telepathizing his anger at the ill-bred beasts. *Eat this*.

One of the pair darted not too-too far away from his head—close enough for him to hear its wings flutter. In his life, he'd never heard the flutter of a bird's wings. Instantly his frustration drained away, replaced by—he didn't know what. A feeling that maybe environmentalists weren't all left-wing kooks. A sense that his life so far had been more deprived than he thought. A hunch that in the divine order of living things, chickadees might rank higher than humans.

When the bird came back—after a minute, after an hour, he didn't know or care which—and alighted on his thumb, he felt a sense of piercing bliss. The bird flew off without a seed. It hardly mattered. The bird *would* take a seed. He knew that now.

At that moment he heard Allie cry out, "Tom! I drove by your—"

He turned in time to see Allie approaching them with a look on her face that was entirely new: of being excluded. He greeted her, and so did Meg, with a heartiness that he knew neither of them felt.

Very possibly Allie sensed it, because it was more of a

command than a request when she said, "You're feeding the birds from your hands? Let *me* try."

Meg laughed, but there was an edge to it that Wyler hadn't heard before. "Allie Atwells, you don't have the patience to boil tea. You could never stand still long enough for them to come to you."

"Really? That shows how little you know me, Margaret."

"Okay, fine. If you can last for just five minutes, I'll do up your share of the rooms for a week."

"Okay, fine. Give me some seed."

Meg tipped the feeder upside down into her sister's hand, then sat back on the bench to watch. Wyler himself retreated a little distance away from them both, anxious not to be a distraction in their contest. From his new vantage behind the flowering shrub, he was able to compare Allie to her older sister.

Different breed of cat entirely. Allie was taller, more slender, more exotic, more brightly dressed (in fuschia and purple), more this, more that, more everything. Allie Atwells did not—would never—blend into her surroundings, indoors or out. She was the center, she was the showpiece, and there was nothing she could do about it.

Still, she gave it her best shot. For a good long time she stood stock-still: a more graceful, elegant figure Wyler could never hope to see. The birds, by now thoroughly confused about just exactly who or what the feeder was, continued to hang back. Allie frowned, then began chewing on her lower lip.

And then she turned to her older sister and said, "Does that include the bathroom off the landing?"

Meg jumped up with a victorious whoop. "I *knew* you wouldn't last. Three minutes, thirteen seconds!"

Realizing her faux pas, Allie blushed becomingly and laughed. She was absolutely charming, a great sport. Once he would've found it enchanting.

Now, he hardly noticed.

CHAPTER 14

Wyler had rubbed elbows with Uncle Billy on Chicken Pie Night at the Inn Between, but he hadn't yet seen the man in his traditional role as Lord of the Manor.

He was impressed.

Bill Atwells's house was a solidly built Tudor on an acre of well-sited land overlooking Bar Harbor. The house had a personality more stiff than charming, more proper than whimsical, but from the flat-topped yews to the ball-shaped spruces, it suggested an owner who had the money and the desire to show the summer folk that town boys could be house-proud too.

Wyler and his passengers—Allie, Meg, Lloyd, and the twins —all piled out of his Cutlass and made their way up the curving flagstone path to the front door. Meg was walking ahead of him, riding shotgun on Terry. She had one hand on the boy's shoulder as she issued last-minute instructions in his ear, which Wyler assumed included a warning not to leave the state without permission.

She needs kids of her own. The thought popped into his head from nowhere, but once there, it lingered. Meg was so obviously designed for nurturing: from her strong and capable figure to the way she rushed in whenever anyone was at a loss, everything about Meg Hazard said "parent." He had learned from Allie early on of Meg's two miscarriages. He thought of the zillions of teenage mothers he'd seen in the course of his career. How ironic that this obviously qualified woman had no children of her own.

He thought of his own son, lively and brown-eyed and three thousand miles away, and felt a sudden, aching sense of loss.

"Tom Wyler, if you're not going to listen, I'm not going to talk."

Allie was alongside in her fuschia short shorts and purplish cut-out top. The outfit was wonderfully easy on the eyes—but she had to be freezing. "I heard every word you said," he protested. "You were asking me whether I'd ever gone sailing. The answer is 'never.' " He'd rather sled on hot lava.

"*Good*," said Allie with a mysterious smile.

They passed through the front door and into a breezeway lined with potted palms. Wyler could see why they'd been routed to the picnic this way: the effect of the twin sets of French doors thrown open to the view of the grounds and the harbor beyond was spectacular. The vast lawn, every blade in place, rolled down a gentle slope, ending in what someone said was a right-of-way to the shore. Ornamental trees and evergreens had been planted on the sides of the lawn, framing but not obstructing the view of dozens of yachts moored in the harbor. A cruise ship the size of the *QE2*—maybe it *was* the *QE2*—was approaching with its anchors poised.

Wyler hadn't seen too many backyards like this one.

Two dozen kids and grownups had already assembled, looking much more ordinary than the view: lots of jeans and shirts from Wal-Mart was Wyler's guess. He had the impression that Uncle Billy was *the* success story in this bunch, and that once a year he liked to remind them of it.

Uncle Billy himself was hovering over a mammoth stainless-steel barbecue grill, very definitely not from Wal-Mart. When he saw the new arrivals he waved them over.

"Hey, hey! What's the word?" he said jovially. He pointed

out his new toy with the screwdriver he still held in his hand. "Ain't she a beaut? Not like them slimpsey things you find in your big chains nowadays. This one oughtta go us some. I just hope them steaks is unthawed and ready, that's all."

He hugged Meg with his free arm and said, "Thanks for giving up Comfort all week. This year she's outdone herself; wait'll you see. Lloyd, I'd marry her m'self if I thought she'd leave you. You're one lucky baster. Allie! Yer half nekked. Put something on, for Chrissake. Glad you could come, L'tinnant. How long you aimin' to stay in . . . Ba Ha Ba?" he said in a wry acknowledgment of Wyler's T-shirt.

Without waiting for an answer from any of them, he said, "Beer's in the tub, pop's in the cooler," and rushed off to greet the next incoming guests.

"Well, I guess we've made it through the receiving line," said Meg dryly. "I'd better go help Comfort."

But she didn't run off, and that made Wyler unaccountably pleased.

"Allie?" Meg said at last to her sister. "You planning to pitch in?"

Allie laughed and said, "Look around; do you see any women? They're all in the kitchen with Comfort. There's probably not enough room to swing a cat in there. How about if Tom and I start setting up the chairs and tables out here instead?"

The sisters exchanged a look—Wyler saw the look; he just didn't know what the hell it meant—and then Meg said coldly, "Well, I can't force you."

Meg left and Allie sighed deeply. She was close to tears. Confused, Wyler said, "Is something wrong?"

One tear made it out and down Allie's cheek. "*Some*thing is. Meg and I don't get along at all anymore."

"Don't be silly," he told her. "You two are closer than any two people I know." He took out a handkerchief, which seemed excessive for one teardrop.

"Meg thinks I'm being a princess," Allie said in a low, hurt voice. "I didn't mean to be. It breaks my heart when she's angry with me. I'd better go help in the kitchen."

"Don't be silly," he said again, dabbing awkwardly at her cheek. The one thing he didn't want Allie to do was leave him alone with two dozen standoffish strangers. "Meg agreed with you. And I don't want you to go," he admitted selfishly.

Allie looked away, toward the harbor. "Really?" she asked in a voice as soft as silk.

"Really. C'mon, let's set up some tables," he said, taking her by the hand and walking with her to a small potting shed where half a dozen folding tables were stacked on end. "I'm surprised they're not out already."

"Heavens, no," Allie said with a grin so radiant that it vied with the sun. "Uncle Billy never wants them marring the view until the last possible moment."

They grabbed hold of the first table, and that set off a silent signal that brought all the men running. Reluctant to approach Wyler purely on social grounds, the men seemed much more willing to mingle now that there was work to do.

Introductions were made all around, and things picked up even more when the plates and utensils started coming out. A kind of human utensil-brigade formed spontaneously between the kitchen and the lawn, with baskets of forks and boxes of glasses and napkins by the gross being passed down briskly to the proper tables. Wyler broke out of the line to grab a soda for Allie and a beer for himself. When Meg appeared briefly he offered her a beer as well.

"No, thanks, I'll wait," she said breathlessly, and then she smiled and said, "Maybe just a sip of yours."

He offered her his bottle, and she drank from it, and he felt as if they'd shared something sacred. But then he looked up and saw Allie watching them both, and he felt ashamed to have enjoyed both beer and her sister in front of her.

He wanted to make it up to Allie. He had enough copper-friends in AA to know how hard a social gathering like this could be. He put his beer aside and took a Coke from the cooler, then went up to Allie and said, "It looks like we have a lull while they crank up the grills. Why don't you give me a tour?"

She acquiesced, but her heart obviously wasn't in it. They began strolling down the lawn toward the right-of-way that led to the water while Wyler made small talk about the view. Allie kept answering in monosyllables. Finally he said, "Hey, how come I'm doing all the work? *You're* supposed to be the Energizer Bunny in this relationship."

"What relationship," she murmured, slapping a dandelion listlessly against her thigh.

He had the feeling that "relationship" was maybe a loaded word, but he couldn't think of another, so he said, *"You* know: you, me. Old fart. Young dynamo. Palling around town. Relationship. I think that's what it's called."

"My God, Tom, you don't know anything," she said wearily. "Palling around does not make for a relationship."

He had the sense that he was walking on quicksand now; whether he went forward or backward, it made no difference. So he went forward. "How can you say that? We've been relating like crazy. I know all about you: your favorite song, your favorite movie, your favorite food, your favorite color—"

"Which proves you're a good listener, that's all."

"I've told you all about my ex-wife," he said, much more seriously. "I've never talked to anyone else about the breakup."

"Because it's easier to tell some stranger a thousand miles from home, that's all."

She was right, dammit. "Well, what do *you* call a relationship?" he asked, kicking himself even before the words were out.

"A relationship is when you're only half alive if the other

person's not around,'' Allie murmured, her eyes glistening. "A relationship is when you can't help but do . . . *this*," she added, lifting her arms around his neck.

That was not how Wyler felt about her, but he hated like hell to disappoint her. She was so very, very beautiful . . . and her violet eyes were so very sad . . . and she smelled so terrific . . . and he'd clearly hurt her somehow . . . and now she was closing her eyes and parting her lips . . . so maybe, who knew, maybe he *was* interested in a relationship with her.

He slipped his arms around her waist. He was aware that he was stepping deeper into the bog, but he didn't see how he could *not* kiss her. And then something kicked in, something that had nothing to do with relationships but had everything to do with the image of Meg standing in dappled sunlight.

"Whoa," he said in a shaky voice, suddenly holding Allie at arm's length. "Not such a good idea. I don't want your uncle coming after me with a barbecue fork," he said, offering the first excuse he could think of.

But Allie smiled a dreamy smile and said, "I know where we can hide."

"C'mon, minx," he said, laughing off the moment by sweeping her back up the hill.

They headed back to the house, with Allie's mood only marginally improved. The whole time, Wyler was thinking, *God, I've screwed this thing up*. The whole time, Wyler was wishing that Allie was Meg alongside him.

When they got back, Wyler automatically scanned the crowd, looking for Meg. She had a big stainless bowl of something or other in her arms and was deep in conversation with Comfort, who was holding herself oddly around her waist. Wyler watched with more than passing curiosity as Meg put the bowl down on the nearest folding table, then took Comfort by the shoulders with a look he couldn't begin to fathom: of joy, surprise, dismay, tension . . . but mostly joy, he thought.

She hugged Comfort, then began talking excitedly, then hugged Comfort again. Then Bill Atwells said something to them, and Comfort said something back to him, and Bill Atwells roared out, "Good God! Everybody! Comfort's got a bun in the oven!"

Instantly Allie broke from Wyler's side in a gleeful run for her sister-in-law and got swallowed in the crowd of well-wishers surrounding Comfort. Wyler half expected them to hoist Comfort on their shoulders and carry her down Main Street.

Meg slipped away and came up to him. "This is wonderful news," she said, wiping away tears from her eyes. "Comfort and my brother had given up trying."

Wyler smiled and said, "You know what? I don't think so." He couldn't take his eyes away from Meg's face. She looked so overwhelmed, so emotional. "It's an odd time to announce, no?"

"Oh, she hadn't planned to tell anyone yet. But she's been feeling woozy and I was sure she was coming down with a bug. I was trying to make her leave the picnic, and that's when she told me. We forgot that Uncle Billy has ears like a collie."

"And a voice like a megaphone. How's Lloyd taking the news?" In fact, Wyler was wondering how he himself would take that kind of news nowadays.

"He's ecstatic. But anxious, naturally. Comfort's forty-two, and Lloyd's still trying to find steady work. They have a fierce deductible on their medical insurance. It won't be easy. But I expect we'll manage somehow."

She slipped into that "we" so easily. Their problems were *her* problems. He wondered whether it ever occurred to Meg that she had the means—a valuable dollhouse—to alleviate the whole family's money worries, at least in the near term. But it was hardly his business to say.

Meg had her hands on her hips. "My God. There's the potato salad, on the grass. I'd better get the bowl up and out of the ants' way. Please excuse me." She started off and then turned back to him. "I hope you're having a good time," she said, flushing.

"Just now I was," he answered truthfully.

"I really am glad," she said. "I wanted you to so much."

Two hours later, Wyler, like everyone else, was stuffed with lobster, steak, corn, and fourteen—he counted them—different salads, everything from Caesar's to Szechwan.

He'd made it a point of honor to sample every one, then had gone back for seconds of the crab-stuffed artichokes, the shrimp ring, the lobster mold, and the fisherman's salad. After that he collapsed into an Adirondack chair and chatted amiably with first and second cousins about hunting, fishing, canoeing, and half a dozen other sports he'd never tried in his life.

Someone put an infant in his arms; the smell of baby powder made him feel ridiculously tender and protective. The womenfolk brought out coffee and dessert for the menfolk, which struck Wyler as the way things ought to be. A dozen preteens gobbled cake and ran off to the lower end of the yard to play badminton, while their older counterparts—kissing cousins, presumably—flirted and slipped away to the shore path in couples and small groups.

Everything was perfect until the sisters came and ruined it all.

Allie grabbed his visor from the back of his chair and slapped it back on his head. "Time for my surprise," she said. "I've got us a boat! It belongs to my uncle's neighbor; he said we can take it for a sail. So get up, lazybones. Let's go!"

He stared incredulously at her. She'd come up with the game plan from hell. "No, I don't think so—" he began, quietly locking his elbows around the arms of his chair.

Meg wasn't in on Allie's surprise, either. "Allie, you don't know how to sail," she reminded her.

"You're going to sail the thing, Meg. All I have to do is try to look nautical. C'mon, Wyler. Outta the chair."

"No, really, I'm stuffed," Wyler groaned. "I can't move." Couldn't they do something he merely disliked, like charades? Must they do something he hated?

"Allie, I am *not* going to be your gondolier," Meg said tautly.

Allie, truly baffled, turned from Meg to Wyler. "I can't believe this. I went to all this trouble so that you can see Bar Harbor the way the Norsemen saw it . . . and Samuel de Champlain . . . Henry Hudson . . . Captain John Smith . . . John Winthrop . . . Lafayette . . . Talleyrand . . . Lord Nelson himself, if the legend is true! You're supposed to be the historian; where's your sense of history?"

"I've seen it all by car," Wyler said lamely.

"Cars weren't even allowed here until 1915! Cars aren't historic!"

"Allie, if he doesn't want to, he doesn't want to," said Meg, cutting in. "I have better things to do, anyway," she added.

It dawned a little late on Wyler that Meg was trying to slide out of his grasp again. Normally she was as elusive as a wood nymph, but once or twice today, for whatever reason, she'd lingered near him. He wanted more of her, and if that meant going to sea in a galvanized tub, then that was what he'd do. At least she couldn't slip away.

He got up from his nicely earthbound chair and flopped his visor over Meg's hair. "I'm willing if you are, skipper," he said in a low-key taunt.

Allie clapped her hands. "Awrii-ight!" she cried.

The three of them strolled down the lawn past a badminton game in progress. Once Terry and Timmy got wind of their plan, they begged to come along.

Meg said yes, Allie said no, and the twins fell in behind them, making the outing seem less like a ménage à trois and more like a typical Atwells free-for-all. The group scampered down the right-of-way—an overgrown cut through a neighbor's brush—and emerged on a small, pebbly beach with an upside-down dinghy sitting above the high-water mark.

Wyler didn't like the look of the dinghy, which was wood and undoubtedly leaked, and he didn't like the look of the sailboat—a small, open thing moored a hundred yards away. They flipped the dinghy over and dragged it to the water's edge, and Terry set the oars in their oarlocks.

They went out to the sailboat three and three, with Terry rowing Meg and his twin brother out first, then coming back for Allie and Wyler. Wyler was impressed: the boy knew what he was doing. Allie got into the bow of the dinghy and Wyler, who'd never been in such a cockleshell before, managed to shove off and get in without instantly grounding it. So far, so good.

Goddammit! It does *leak*! "Is there something to bail with?" he asked with tight-lipped offhandedness.

Allie looked around and handed him a plastic cup—a plastic *cup!*—and he began scooping what looked like the better part of the Atlantic out of the stern of the dinghy.

"So, Terry," he said, bailing furiously, "where'd you learn to handle a boat so well?"

"This isn't a boat," said Terry, snorting. "It's just a dinghy."

"His grandfather takes him fishing all the time," Allie translated. "But Meg's the only one who knows how to sail. She learned it from Paul."

"That's nice," Wyler said, flailing with the cup. He'd forgotten just how deep his water phobia went. Somehow, having forced himself through two swimming courses at the Y, he thought he could handle anything that might come up. Obviously the jury was still out on that one.

They came alongside the sailboat and Wyler climbed aboard, counting his one blessing: that he was in water too

deep to have seaweed that could wrap itself around his legs
and drown him.

Allie climbed out next and Terry handed her the painter,
whatever or whoever that was, and then Terry got aboard and
tied the dinghy to the mooring ball. Timmy was unlashing the
tiller and Meg was standing on the bow, already hoisting the
damn sail. Allie, the designated hostess, was popping open a
Coke for him. In the meantime, the boat was rocking like
crazy with every little move. It was like trying to play golf on
a teeter-totter.

The sail was up and flapping like mad over their heads,
whipping the boom viciously and dangerously close to their
skulls. Everyone had to stay ducked down. Meg yelled "Cast
off" to Terry, who threw a line with a float attached off the
bow and into the water. The boat fell away, the sail filled and
quieted, and they were off and running.

Just like that. No team huddle, no prayer. Just your basic
suicide mission. Wyler declined the Coke, declined to talk,
refused to look at the water, and mostly concentrated all the
forces of his being on the single syllable "ohm." Meditation
seemed like the only possible way to get through what was
shaping up to be a genuine phobia-crisis.

At some point he remembered to exhale. It came out in a
long shudder.

Allie said, "Are you prone to seasickness?"

Oh, Christ. He'd never had to consider whether he was
prone or not.

"Anty Meg, can I sail?" asked Terry.

Wyler was scandalized, then relieved, when Meg said, "Not
downwind, Terry. It's a little tricky. Maybe later."

Terry's blue eyes turned squinty and sullen. A minute later,
while Allie was pointing out grand estates, Terry tried again.
"If you hold the helm with me can I sail?"

Wyler could see that Meg didn't want to crush the boy's

fledgling interest in something legal. "Okay," she said, "but you have to let me do most of the steering."

Terry began changing places with Timmy—far too recklessly; did he think they were in a parking lot? In the meantime Timmy noticed a pair of dolphins and cried, "Look! Over to starboard."

Everybody looked, of course, even Meg; and that was when it happened. The boom came crashing from port to starboard with no warning, whacking Terry on the back of the head and knocking him out of the boat.

Wyler saw it all in slow motion: The blue-and-green-striped T-shirt, the blue shorts, the two white legs and two tanned arms, the mop of brown hair—all of it sent flying like a rag doll into space, landing with a tremendous splash and then sinking, disappearing altogether.

Allie screamed and Meg cried out his name. After an eternity Terry popped back up, coughing and spitting and flailing his arms wildly. He was in a complete panic.

Wyler's heart constricted. He was Terry, Terry was him. It was Humboldt Park and the seaweed, all over again.

"I'll save him," Timmy screamed in a high, cracking voice.

"Sit down, Timmy! Sit down! Watch the boom!" Meg cried.

Wyler grabbed him and threw him on the seat. "Stay there! I'll get him."

He hardly recognized his own voice. Someone else, inhabiting his body, was speaking for him. Someone else was pulling off his sneakers while he said quickly to Meg, "Can he swim?"

"Yes, but—"

"Can you get the boat any nearer?"

"Yes . . . alongside. Watch for us. Can *you* swim?"

"Some."

He stared for one brief, eternal second at the deep blue water. Meg said, "Allie! Timmy! Move to the other side!"

To balance my weight as I go over, he realized, admiring Meg's presence of mind.

He slipped into the shockingly, offensively cold waters of the Gulf of Maine. His body seemed to contract into a fetal position. *Drown, hell. I could have a heart attack.* He fought his way back to the surface, blowing air out of his nose, but salt water got in anyway. It was everywhere, different and vile, making him crave a drink of fresh water as he kicked and moved one arm, then the other, in the direction of the panicky twin.

Half a dozen more strokes, and he was there. Terry was croaking "Help, help," in choking gasps, still thrashing hysterically.

"Terry, I've got you," Wyler shouted as he reached him, even though it wasn't quite true. Strictly speaking, Terry had *him*. The boy grabbed onto Wyler and threatened to take them both down.

"Relax, Terry. Calm down. I've got you. It's all right. I've got you. It's all right. It's all right."

The sail back was long, cold, and wet. They had to "beat" back into the wind—perfect word—which meant that the boat stayed over on its ear the whole time, and the air felt twenty degrees colder. Wyler was forced to brace his injured leg, still throbbing from the rescue effort, against the opposite seat as the boat thrashed to windward. Every time they hit a wave, the boat lurched and shuddered, forcing him to brace himself still more, and ice-cold spray came over the bow, making sure his wet clothes stayed wet.

So why was he so happy?

Because a phobia the size of Cadillac Mountain had been lifted from his shoulders. He knew, really for the first time in his life, that he could handle a crisis on the water. It was a great, liberating feeling, but he kept it to himself. Anything else would've been inappropriate right now.

He studied the shaken faces of the others and realized how much he'd come to care for every one of them: for Allie, shivering without the sweatshirt she'd given Terry; Meg, apologizing repeatedly for letting the boat jibe; gentle Timmy, temporarily disillusioned with his tough, clever brother; and especially for Terry himself.

It was Terry that Wyler was concerned about most. The boy was clearly horrified with himself for panicking in front of everyone and had retreated behind a wall of bitter silence. Wyler understood all too well how Terry was feeling. He was determined to reach out to him now—before the boy's fear and embarrassment turned into a full-blown phobia.

After the whole crew was ashore, Wyler told the others, "You go on ahead. Terry and I will stow the dinghy."

Allie said, "Don't be silly! Timmy can—"

"Never mind, Allie," Meg told her quietly. "Let them do it." She gave Wyler a look of complete understanding and hauled her sister and nephew away from the scene.

Wyler and Terry dragged the dinghy onto the pebbly beach and tipped it on its side, spilling out the water that had leaked into it so freely.

"This isn't a dinghy," Wyler said. "It's a colander."

No smile. Obviously the bonding after the cherry-bomb incident hadn't been permanent. Sighing, Wyler decided to tackle the issue head on.

"I understand how you feel, you know," he said quietly.

Terry rolled the dinghy the rest of the way over. "Yeah, right." He lifted up the bow and waited with downcast eyes for Wyler to pick up the stern.

"I mean it. I almost drowned when I was a kid. I'm not even sure the water was over my head. It was in a pond. A nice little pond where the water was warm."

"Yeah, you were probably three years old or something."

"I was almost your age," Wyler said, fudging a bit. He lifted the stern with an exaggerated *oof* and the two of them muscled the dinghy over to some nearby bushes. "I don't really know why I lost it, but I did. I guess it was the feel of seaweed around my ankles. I just started grabbing at it, to get it off, and I swallowed some water and started thrashing around. I just . . . lost it."

Terry took the dinghy painter and knotted it around a branch. "Yeah, but then you prob'ly swam back to shore. Am I right?"

"Nope. I passed out. They told me some guy fished me out and gave me artificial respiration."

"No kidding? *I* didn't pass out."

"You kept your head above water," Wyler agreed. "But this is what I wanted you to know: ever since that day, for most of my life, I've been afraid of water. Until today."

"No *kidding*?"

"I'm telling you. And it was so dumb, because I only *thought* I was afraid. I wasted a lot of good swimming holes."

The boy frowned and said, "You shouldn't be telling me this, admitting that you were—you know—chicken."

Wyler shrugged. "I don't know about that. The way I look at it, it takes a certain amount of courage to admit you were scared."

Terry thought about it a moment. "Yeah. If you're a cop, especially."

The two of them started back toward the house. Terry said, "So you think my brother won't think less of me after today?"

Tom put his hand on the boy's shoulder. "Not if you don't try to fake how you felt out there," he said as they made their way up the right of way.

"Man, I thought I was gonna die."

"Yeah. I know the feeling."

CHAPTER 15

The next day Meg divided her time equally between searching her heart and searching for the right earrings.

Emotionally, she was a basket case. She'd become so jealous of her sister that when Allie was around, she had to look away. It was too painful to compare Allie's sparkling, violet eyes with her own everyday hazel ones; too traumatic to compare Allie's lithe and elegant body with her own distressingly sturdy one. Her sister's laugh had become intolerable; her sister's hug, a bruising encounter. Allie liked to hum, and Meg used to love to hear her do it. Now her sister's hum sounded like the annoying buzz of a mosquito.

It wasn't just because Allie was more beautiful than Meg; after all, Allie'd been that way all of her life. And it wasn't because Tom Wyler was in love with Allie—because Meg was more and more certain that he was not. No, Meg was jealous of her sister because Allie had the luxury of loving a man with all her heart and soul. Meg didn't have that luxury, and she was utterly miserable without it. What woman wouldn't be?

And meanwhile, Meg had fallen into a complete, ridiculous tizzy over earrings. In the morning she'd agreed to wear the ones Allie had offered her, a pair of braided gold hoops. By evening, Meg had changed her mind again. She'd wear the only jewelry her grandmother had left behind, a pair of very ordinary but somehow pleasing pearl teardrops. Allie's gold hoops had been a present from Bobby Beaufort, the leader of the pack of her high school boyfriends. As for the teardrops, no one could remember if they were from Meg's grandfather or from a Cracker Jack box.

"Oh, Meggie, the gold hoops—truly," said Allie as the two sisters stood together in front of the full-length mirror in the hall bathroom. "They're perfect. And they really *are* pretty. I still can't believe that Bobby Beaufort picked them out."

Allie was dressed in her service uniform—perfectly tailored black pants and a white shirt—and was tucking her sister's hair into an old-fashioned roll that lay softly on her neck, an idea that Allie had stolen from a photograph of Margaret Mary Atwells. She'd teased droopy ringlets to fall gracefully in front of Meg's ears and had done her sister's makeup so artfully that Meg was scarcely aware that she wore any. The dress of pale lavender silk that Allie had originally bought for herself —and that looked like a designer parachute on her—fit Meg perfectly, sliding off her hips into a soft, mid-calf flare.

All that was left to decide was the fate of the two pairs of earrings. Meg had a gold hoop in her left ear, a pearl teardrop in her right. She turned her head this way and that, amazed to see that she looked pretty in either one.

"I think, the teardrops," Meg said at last, slipping off the gold hoop and handing it back to her sister.

"I suppose you're right," said Allie through the hairpins clamped between her lips. "They're very old-fashioned, and so are you."

Allie slipped the last hairpin into her sister's hair and stepped back to assess her work. "Yes!" she said, satisfied. "If I squint, you look exactly like Margaret Mary Atwells. What do you think? Will you get a rise out of Gordon Camplin tonight?"

"There'll be a mob and I won't get within fifty feet of

him," said Meg. She wanted to get a rise out of someone, all right; but it wasn't Gordon Camplin.

"I don't know why I'm even going," Meg went on, becoming edgier by the minute. "I *hate* wearing pantyhose in July. This whole thing is pointless. It's too hot in here. Do you feel hot? God, I'm going into premature menopause. I *knew* this would happen. I just knew it. I'll be drenched in sweat . . . I'll ruin your dress . . . or else it's the damned furnace. Lloyd's done something to the furnace. I'd better go see—"

"Meg. *Meg.* You're out of control," said Allie, laughing and giving her sister a shake. "You look completely gorgeous, but out of control. Now calm down. We can't both be emotional at the same time. *Some*one has to have a cool head tonight."

"I'm tired of being the grownup," Meg snapped. *"You* take over for a while."

Allie ignored her. "I do love that color on you," she decided with a dreamy smile. "When I get married, you'll have to dress in lavender." She glanced at her watch and said, "Oh, wow, gotta go. I'll see you there later. You look perfect, Meggie. Nail him."

At the last minute Allie remembered Bobby Beaufort's earrings on the dresser and impulsively put them on, then dashed out, leaving Meg with half an hour in which to pace and brood.

By now their plan to shake up Gordon Camplin seemed truly laughable. It had been conceived out of desperation, because in all their search for clues, they'd found nothing to suggest that Camplin had ever been obsessed with their grandmother. The one bit of gossip that kept surfacing—that he'd had, and still had, a *gambling* obsession—seemed irrelevant. If anything, it suggested that Gordon Camplin would not bluff easily. Not that dressing up like Margaret Mary Atwells was much of a bluff.

And Meg's belief that her grandmother would somehow

point the way for her? Equally laughable. Granted, things had started out like gangbusters with the impromptu séance. But since then, the only truly intense premonition to plague Meg had come yesterday, before the picnic, and nothing even remotely supernatural had happened all day to justify it.

Ah. But Terry had nearly drowned. If that wasn't worth a premonition, what was?

But the boating mishap wasn't a supernatural event. It was about as physical an ordeal as anyone could hope to avoid. So what did this mean? That Meg was turning into some general-practitioner psychic? The village witch?

One thing for sure: her premonitions had nothing to do with eating chili. If anything, her ability to see a threat behind every bush was a direct result of the family's ongoing financial straits. She glanced at a couple of unopened bills she'd tossed on the dresser. Who wouldn't feel edgy when bills arrived twelve months a year, and the high season lasted for only two?

Yes. That must be it. Money. Pure and simple. Everything in life came down to money. If only they had more of it, then everything would be resolved.

Everything, except the mystery of her grandmother's death. And the emotional crisis her sister was hell-bent on provoking. And the steadily rising storm of emotions that was building in Meg's own heart.

Meg caught a glimpse of her made-up image in the dresser mirror and turned away from it, pacing the length of her room the way she would a jail cell. She had no desire to wander around the house waiting for a date who'd had to be arm wrestled into taking her to the dance.

She heard a car door slam and ran to the lace-curtained window that looked out on the street.

"Tom," she whispered, just to hear the word on her lips.

He looked up at her window just then, half convincing her that she'd actually called out his name. She jumped back from view, then ran to check her makeup—Allie's makeup—before the inevitable summons.

A minute later she heard the thumping of sneakers on the carpeted stairs, and Timmy's voice: "Anty Meg! You can come down now. He's finally here!"

Meg groaned; it was all too mortifying. "I'll be there in a minute," she said loudly, as if all she had to do was finish painting a ceiling, and then she'd change and be right with him.

After a decent interval she emerged from her room, heart pounding like a teenager's, head warning her to keep her eyes on the goal. The goal was to get a sense of Gordon Camplin's character; the goal was not to throw herself at Tom Wyler's feet. She stepped gingerly down the stairs, blushing furiously the whole way, trying to seem as if silk and high heels were as normal to wear as shorts and gardener's clogs.

At the bottom landing there was fresh humiliation: her father with his Instamatic, snapping away as she walked past him into the sitting room where Tom Wyler had been ushered in to wait.

"It's not every day my little girl puts on a party dress," said Everett. Snap, snap, snap. "And now, Tom, you stand next to her and pin on the corsage. Oh. No corsage. Well, never mind. Just stand next to her, then." Snap, snap. "And after, we'll get in the whole family. While Meg looks nice. You do look nice, m'dear," he added. "Comfort!" he yelled. "Is Lloyd still down sulla? Timmy, go find your brother, on the double."

"Dad, for heaven's sake, I'm a widow. I was married for ten years. This isn't prom night; give it a rest, will you?" said Meg, ready to slide between the floor planks.

She turned at last to Tom and said, "I'm sorry about this."

Tom's laugh was low and intimate; the sound melted what was left of her resolve not to throw herself at his feet. "Don't be sorry; this is fun," he said. His blue-gray eyes danced with good humor, which somehow made her feel even more embarrassed.

Comfort appeared, wiping her hands in a dishtowel. "Oh, my, Meg. Don't you look nice," she said, instant tears springing to her eyes. "It's been so long. Look, Lloyd," she said to her soot-covered husband when he appeared. "Don't she look nice?"

Lloyd looked at his sister as if she'd been abducted by some cult of makeover artists. "Don't look like our Meg 't all," he said skeptically.

Terry came bouncing in and fetched up hard in front of his aunt. "*That's* not your dress; that's from Anty Allie's closet."

"What were *you* doing in Anty Allie's closet?" demanded Meg, fearing she'd have to add cross-dresser to the boy's criminal profile.

"There's a nest of starlings in the rafters above," he said, taken aback by her vehemence. "You can hear 'em peeping."

"Oh. Well—"

"Everyone squeeze in together," said her father. "Don't worry about your dirty hands, Lloyd; they don't show. Meg, for pity's sake. Move in closer to Tom, will you? He won't bite. Terry, leave your brother alone. And *no* tongues. Now, Comfort; dry your eyes. Okay," he said, setting the camera on top of a tall plant stand he found handy for the purpose. "I'm pressing the remote. Everyone say cheese." He made a mincing dash for the other side of the camera.

Snap.

Meg kept that shot for years and years in a simple wood frame on her dresser. It seemed to her, when she studied it later in her life, that she could see the past and tell the future with it. It was all there, if only she'd thought to look: in Comfort's teary smile, in Lloyd's awkward stiffness, in Terry's poker face and Timmy's earnest one. In her father's pleased and childlike expression. In the way Meg hadn't been able to decide whether to look at the camera or at Tom, to see his reaction. In Tom's hands-in-his-pocket pose, amused and bemused.

But the most telling point of all was that Allie wasn't in the shot. She was off doing Meg's dirty work, trusting Meg completely, happy that she could help carry out her sister's harebrained scheme to trip up a murderer.

"You look very beautiful," Tom said as they walked together through deepening twilight to his car. "I didn't get a chance to say so inside."

"Nobody gets a chance to say anything inside," Meg said lightly, trying to control the happy skipping of her heart. "We all talk at once and cancel each other out."

"I'm glad things worked out this way," he added, glancing at her.

"I'm—" She wanted to say, "I'm glad, too." But she thought of her sister, and the words wouldn't come, so she moved on to other things. "How's your cabin's working out?" she asked.

"Oh—it's okay. A little rustic for a city boy like me."

He got her door and Meg slipped into the front seat and waited for him. "I wanted to thank you again for yesterday," she said after he slid behind the wheel. "For saving Terry."

Tom turned the key and said, "You've thanked me a thousand times already. Allie would've done something if I hadn't."

"She wouldn't have had the strength to handle him. And besides . . . I know you weren't crazy about jumping in," Meg said as delicately as she could.

He laughed ruefully but didn't deny it. "There's a reason for that," he said.

And then he told her the whole traumatic story of his near-drowning as a boy trapped in seaweed in a pond in Humboldt Park, and of his chance rescue.

"It's funny how you picked up on my phobia and Allie didn't," he said in the same musing tone.

"That's Allie all over," she said lightly. "She's always been blinded by—" Meg sucked in the word *love* before she said it.

It hardly mattered. Tom sighed and said, "Yeah. Things have got a little tricky in that area. I think Allie's become, well, fond of me."

Meg thought, *Fond of you! She's picking out her wedding trousseau, you dope!*

"I get that impression, too," Meg said dryly. "Did you know that she's lined up two interviews in Chicago on Tuesday?"

"God, no," he said, startled. "She hasn't said a word to me."

"It must be a surprise, then. Don't tell her I told you."

"Secrets? I'm not good at women's games," he said, irritation creeping into his voice.

"Okay, fine. *Tell* her, then. It really doesn't matter."

"Meg—"

"I'm sorry, I'm sorry," she said, leaning her head back on the headrest. "I've been tense."

"Because?"

Oh hell, we're right back here again. "You *know* why."

He looked at her sharply and said, "No, I *don't* know why. I can think of half a dozen reasons why you might be tense, not the least of which is this little dollhouse drama. But there's only one reason that would excite me, and that's the one, frankly, that I want to hear."

He waited for Meg to speak.

"Because . . . because . . ." She sighed and closed her eyes, frustrated beyond measure that she couldn't just blurt out the truth about her feelings for him and be done with it.

For a minute or so, neither of them spoke. Then, while her eyes were still closed, she felt the featherlight stroke of the back of his fingers on her cheek. It was an overwhelming moment for Meg. At any other time—in any other life—she would have let that stroke lead to something. But not now. Not in this life. She bit her lip, determined not to betray her emotions.

"Just how much *does* Allie mean to you?" he asked.

"Everything," Meg said simply. She opened her eyes and stared ahead, unseeing. "Nothing comes before her."

"It was a stupid question," Tom said, a hard edge creeping into his voice.

But he wasn't willing to let it drop. A moment later, he said, "You're not doing her any favors by creating a dreamworld for her to live in. Sooner or later, Allie's going to have to take a knock on the chin."

"She's had her share of knocks—as you know," Meg said.

"You know what I mean, Meg: I mean the fact that you spend *your* life trying to shape *her* life. She's not a kid anymore."

"Everyone needs someone to lean on once in a while," Meg said defensively.

"You've gone beyond moral support," Tom suggested. "I think *you* need her to need you more than she actually needs you."

"What kind of psychobabble is *that*?" Meg asked, surprised that he'd even tread on such hallowed ground. A bond between *sisters* . . . he had no business tinkering with it.

"I throw it out for what it's worth," he said with careful nonchalance. "At least think about it."

Meg thoroughly resented his attempt to analyze her. *She* wasn't the one with a problem. Maybe *he* had a thing about water; maybe *Allie* had a thing about alcohol. But as far as Meg knew, she was phobia and addiction free.

They were outside of town now, nearly at the granite pillars that marked the entrance to the winding drive that led to the Fairlawn estate. Meg had absolutely no enthusiasm for the

evening before her. She glanced at Tom, whose handsome
chiseled profile seemed etched from the same granite as Fairlawn's pillars, and looked away. Three hours of torture: that
was all that lay ahead.

Tom turned into the drive, lined with trees threaded with
thousands of sparkling white lights, and rolled to a stop in the
portico of the grand shingle-style mansion. A valet opened
Meg's door and helped her out, then accepted the keys from
Tom and drove off to park his Cutlass. Tom offered his arm
with barely a hint of irony to Meg and escorted her past potted
corkscrew topiaries through the double oak doors, where they
handed their tickets over to a sweet old lady sitting at a card
table and marched up to the receiving line of Meg's first—and
probably only—fling with Bar Harbor's Four Hundred.

The reception committee consisted of Camplin's ex-wife
Dorothea, chairwoman of the event; a couple of officials of the
Children's Charity; and the owners of Fairlawn. Meg introduced herself and shook hands down the line, exchanging
pleasantries: delighted to come; a wonderful place; *such a*
good cause; enchantingly done. Tom was right behind her,
presumably offering variations on her themes.

They'd arrived at the height of the crush, which was a blessing; Meg had half expected Dorothea Camplin to buttonhole
her and demand to know what the *hell* she was doing mucking
up the family name. But Dorothea was far too much of a
socialite to give Meg more than a cursory smile as she
scanned the guests behind her for more familiar faces. A guest
or two later, Meg heard her say, "Helen! Come see my garden
before the Japanese Iris are done!"

Meg and Tom were bumped out into a drawing room of
dark-paneled and chandeliered elegance, where large round
tables covered in damask offered a tempting array of hors
d'oeuvres.

Allie showed up thirty seconds later balancing a tray of her own. *"Madame?"* she said to her sister, prodding her with the tray. *"Voulez-vous du saumon fumé?"*

"Allie, what *are* you talking about?" Meg said in a low mutter. "And where's Gordon Camplin? I don't want him seeing me first."

Allie giggled and said, "One of the girls from Quebec is going around *voulez-vous*-ing everybody, so I thought I'd try it. She says I have a terrific accent. I *really* should be on the stage. As for old Gordy, don't worry about him. I saw him go into the library with the owner a minute ago."

Allie turned to Tom and lowered her gaze in that semi-shy way she had that made men want to ravish her. *"You* look awfully dapper tonight, Mr. Gatsby," she said.

Allie's spirits were as high as Meg's were low. "Okay, give me one of these things," Meg said abruptly. "And then *circulate*, for goodness' sake, or people will notice."

"Meg!" her sister murmured, stricken. "Let me have *some* fun."

Chastened, Meg said, "I'm sorry. I just want to get this over with. I'd give anything to be home right now."

"And I," her sister said softly, "would give anything to be you right now."

She left them together, leaving Meg more wretched than before.

The buzz of polite talk around them had become a clamor as the room filled with hungry guests who went straight for the table with the shrimp. From a huge tent that had been set up next to the house, Meg heard a band strike up a tune—no dancing, obviously, would take place on the beautiful parquet floors of the mansion.

Echoing her thoughts, Tom said softly, "I hear music. Will you dance with me?"

He might as well have said, "Will you make wild, abandoned love with me right now, on the floor?"

Meg was truly scandalized. She couldn't dance with him—

couldn't. If she let herself be taken in his arms . . . if she let herself breathe in the scent of him . . . if she let herself come one millimeter closer to him than she was right now . . .

"Don't ask me that," she said in agony. "I *can't*—"

She turned away from him and found herself face-to-face with Gordon Camplin.

If Meg was hoping for something dramatic in the way of a reaction from Camplin, she got her wish. When he saw her, Camplin gasped and put his hand to his breast in oh-dear-God fashion, stopping dead in his tracks.

Guilty! Meg decided on the spot. For a minute she thought she'd given him a heart attack, which would've been the simplest thing; but no, he recovered and, still not taking his eyes off her, he walked up to her uncertainly.

"Please . . . excuse me . . . don't I know you?" he asked in an utterly baffled, distressingly gentle voice. The Archbishop of Canterbury might have used that tone with her. Incredible.

"We've never met, Mr. Camplin," she said grimly. "I'm Margaret Mary Atwells Hazard," she said, deliberately echoing her grandmother's name. Her eyes glittered with pride and cool fury. So this was the man. Normally Meg's handshake was firm, but she was so filled with loathing at the thought that his well-kept hand had worked with evil design on her grandmother's body that she let her own hand lie limp in his, and then withdrew it.

"Ah. Atwells. Yes . . . of course. I should've made the connection. Your—I suppose she would be, grandmother?—worked at Eagle's Nest one season."

"The season," Meg said, refusing to let him get away with polite vagaries.

"Yes, in '47. A terrible time. Tragic . . . utterly tragic. I have nightmares still. We all do, the old-timers in town."

Whatever else he was, Gordon Camplin was not an old-timer. He might have passed his seventh decade, but he'd done it at a brisk jog, as Meg knew well. He had the kind of body that scientists predict may someday last to a hundred and thirty: spare, wiry, not too tall, without an unnecessary ounce of body fat. And he still had all his hair. She hated him for not being fat and gouty and in chronic pain. She thought of Orel Tremblay: only the good died hurting.

Camplin looked expectantly at Tom, waiting for an introduction. Tom stuck out his hand and said, "Tom Wyler. Nice to meet you."

"How do you do. Summer visitor?" Camplin asked.

Tom nodded and said, "Half the summer, anyway."

Camplin turned his attention back to Meg. Even she could see that he was trying hard not to stare, but without success. Good. Let him squirm.

"I was just commenting on Bar Harbor's famous 'cottages,'" Tom said smoothly to Camplin. "Were you aware that there's a replica of the Eagle's Nest at the Inn Between?"

"The Inn Between?" Camplin repeated with a blank frown. Apparently bed-and-breakfasts were not a subject for polite conversation among his set.

"My father's house," Meg explained, well aware that Gordon Camplin had paid for a chunk of it. "We're running it as a bed-and-breakfast nowadays."

"I see," Camplin said politely. "Yes," he said, addressing Tom's question. "Word around town is that the Atwells family were given a gift of the thing. By a carpenter who once worked for us, apparently. I don't remember the man at all, except that he saved my mother's dog on the day of the fire. I suppose my mother gave him the dollhouse out of gratitude. More likely, she didn't want the reminder of Eagle's Nest around her anymore. I can't remember. Frankly, I would've expected Tremblay to've sold the thing long ago. I can't imagine what good it was to him."

It was a nice little speech, coherent and plausible and just a little too well prepared for Meg's taste. She glanced at Tom, hoping to read his expression. But he was doing his cop thing: his face had that bland, impassive look, as if he were waiting for a bus that wasn't due for half an hour.

"My grandmother and Orel Tremblay became very close friends when they worked at Eagle's Nest," Meg said, hoping to provoke a reaction from Camplin. "Very close."

"Perhaps that's why he left the dollhouse to you, then," Camplin said with a distracted smile.

Clearly his interest in the dollhouse was running a distant second to Meg herself. He seemed not to be able to take his eyes away from her face. He'd look away, almost with a frown, but then he'd look back.

"I hope you'll come by to see the dollhouse, Mr. Camplin. It's in museum condition," she added, appealing to his avarice.

"Yes, I'll have to do that," he answered, staring.

To Meg his fascination seemed practically morbid. She began to feel the same sense of revulsion that she'd felt when she'd unpacked the little teakwood bed. She began to tremble; her heart took off on a wild run for oblivion.

Oh, God. It wasn't the most convenient time for one of her little premonitions. It was leaving her tongue-tied.

Camplin had begun to excuse himself when Tom said in an offhand way, "What I'd like to know is, were there always rumors about the dollhouse being haunted?"

"What?" asked Camplin sharply. Immediately he brought himself under control. "No, of course not. Absurd. What rumors?"

Tom smiled blandly and said, "Oh, the usual thing. An unfortunate death . . . the spirit roams the house . . . except that in this case the house has burned to the ground . . . so what's a poor soul to do? The next best thing, of course: haunt the replica."

"That's preposterous," Camplin said angrily. "There were

no 'unfortunate deaths' in the Eagle's Nest—not until Margaret Atwells's. As for haunted replicas, I wouldn't know. I haven't seen the dollhouse since 1947." His eyes glittered with outrage as he said, "If you'll excuse me . . ." and walked away abruptly.

Meg stared with loathing at his retreating figure. The depth of her hatred amazed her; it was as if she were hating him with someone else's emotion.

Still shaking from the experience, she turned to Tom and said, "Nice goin', Lieutenant. Just when I had him hooked."

"You were losing him," Tom said flatly. "I wanted to shake him up."

"Which you did," Meg admitted. "He seemed to take the ghost rumor personally—as if you were accusing him of dumping raw sewage into the harbor or something. Do you think he's afraid of ghosts?"

"I think he's afraid of gossip."

"Yes," she said, all too aware of the risk she was running of being sued. "So what do we do now?" she asked, relieved that Tom was on the case at last.

But apparently he wasn't. He said, "Now, you wait and you watch."

"Wait? Watch? For what?"

"For him to do something stupid."

"And how long will *that* take? You'll be *leaving* soon—"

Exasperated, Tom said, "So I'll be leaving soon. Who knows when soon is? I'm here *now*, dammit. Suppose we talk about *now*," he said, wrenching the subject back to him and her.

"Yes . . . all right," Meg said.

It was obvious that *he* didn't want to talk about either the past or the future, and *she* didn't want to talk about the present.

Clearly they had a problem. Meg murmured something

about the powder room and excused herself. The truth was, she wanted time to regroup.

Instead of a powder room, she found Dorothea Camplin. She was with two other silver-haired women on a balcony, where they were admiring a white clematis that had been trained up a trellis.

Completely on impulse, Meg joined them. *If the husband won't talk, maybe the ex-wife will*, she decided.

She admired the vine, then asked Dorothea Camplin an innocent question about pruning. That led the conversation from one clematis to another until Meg was able to say, without being too obnoxious, "I'm Meg Hazard, by the way. Of course I know of you and your legendary garden, Mrs. Camplin. And I wonder—would you be interested in being interviewed for a gardening piece I'm writing for *Country Living*?"

Pay dirt. Mrs. Camplin preened and fluffed her feathers and did everything but offer money for the privilege of being interviewed for so prestigious a magazine. Meg wasn't quite being candid—she had no connection with the magazine and in fact had never written anything for publication besides the Inn Between's brochure—but that was tomorrow's problem.

Eventually Meg excused herself and left the company. In the hall she found her sister, who grabbed her by her sleeve and said, "Where have you *been*? Camplin's getting *away*. I just saw him ask for his car to be brought around."

"What am *I* supposed to do?" Meg asked. "Carjack it?"

"Very funny. You talked with him for two minutes! That's two hundred dollars a minute. Even lawyers don't get that much," Allie said in a hiss.

"I talked with him long enough to know with certainty that he did it."

"Oh, yeah—like he confessed, I suppose."

"He didn't have to. I could see it in the way he . . . he looked at me," Meg said, blushing at the remembrance.

Allie cocked her head and looked at her sister thoughtfully. "Oh? You got that look?"

"I don't know how you get through life," Meg said softly. For the first time she felt real sympathy for her sister's gift, or curse, or whatever it was, of seductiveness.

Meg looked back—Mrs. Camplin and her friends were returning from the balcony—and whispered to Allie, "Later." She began heading back to the drawing room, wondering what she could possibly allow herself to say to Tom.

"Meg!" came a voice, deep and male and urgent, from behind her. She knew who it was before he asked the next question: *"Where's Allie?"*

Meg turned and beheld him: tall, dark, and handsome, the bad boy of Bar Harbor.

Bobby Beaufort.

CHAPTER *16*

"What're you *doing* here, Bobby?" Meg asked, horrified. The man was a loose cannon; he'd wreck everything.

"I've got to talk to Allie," Bobby said, scowling. "Now."

"She's working, Bobby. This is a *bad* time to visit."

Meg spoke plainly because subtlety was lost on Bobby; he heard what he wanted to hear and did what he wanted to do. She remembered the day Allie sent him packing. The two were in high school. Allie had screamed—loud enough for everyone in Bar Harbor to hear—"I *don't* love you! I will *never* love you! Go *away*!" and Bobby had replied, "What're you trying to say?"

The only reason he'd left the house at all was because Allie had thrown a plate at him and Comfort had come running into the room and promptly burst into tears, because her dishes weren't open stock.

After that Bobby dropped out of high school and went west to make his fortune. If he made one, he must've spent it all, because six months ago he came back to Bar Harbor broke and angry and—people said—with a prison record.

Right now he looked like a hungry tomcat on the prowl.

"How on earth did you get in here?" Meg demanded.

"How d'you think?" he said, looking around for Allie. "I charmed my way in." He turned back to Meg and flashed her a quick, devilish grin. No question about it, he looked like a hoodlum. But with his black hair, green eyes, and cleft chin, he was the best-looking hoodlum in town.

"Bobby, for crying out loud. What's so urgent that you have to see my sister right here, this minute?"

"I just got back from my cousin's," he said in a dangerous voice. "Lisa tells me Allie's about to do a very dumb thing: get married to a Chicago cop."

"Lisa is jumping the gun," Meg said sharply. "There's not going to be any marriage. Now, *please*. Go home and—"

"Hey." Bobby lifted his chin, addressing the laconic greeting to someone behind Meg.

Meg turned around and winced. Allie was standing there with a look of outrage on her face. Why the outrage, Meg wasn't quite sure; there were too many possibilities.

"The earrings look nice on you, Al," Bobby said. His jaw was set, the muscles working.

Instantly Allie snatched the earrings off and held them out to him. "I don't want them. Here. Take them."

"Don't be a jerk, Al. Put 'em back on."

She dropped them in a cloisonné tray that sat on a windowsill. "I don't want you here, Bobby. I thought we agreed."

"I want to know about the cop."

"He's none of your business."

"Every man you meet is my business. That's how it's always been."

"Not this time. Bobby, grow *up*. We're not kids anymore. Look around you. Does this look like our tree house? Can't you tell the difference? I'm a *woman* now."

"And I'm still all the man you need," he said in a voice that was barely more than a primal growl.

Allie looked him straight in the eye. "No. You're not," she said calmly. "Don't ever make that claim."

Alarmed that things were careening out of control, Meg stepped between the childhood friends. She'd never considered Bobby Beaufort dangerous before. But Allie had never been in love before. "This is crazy, you two. Come *on* . . ."

"Stop fussing, Meg," Allie said without taking her eyes from Bobby's. "I can take care of myself."

With B-movie timing, Tom Wyler chose that moment to saunter onto the set. Meg saw him approaching and shook her head at him warningly, which of course set Bobby Beaufort off.

"This is the one?" he demanded as Tom strode up.

Meg stepped in and slipped her arm around Tom's. "This is *my* date," she said with a majestic lift of her eyebrows.

"Oh. Sorry," Bobby mumbled.

Allie said, "Don't be dumb, Meg," and unhooked her sister's arm from Tom's. "Yes, Bobby. This *is* the one."

Tom looked from Bobby to Allie to Meg. "Am I missing part of this conversation?"

"Just the boring part," Allie said with a toss of her head. "In any case, Bobby and I are done talking." She turned to go.

Bobby grabbed Allie's forearm. "We're nowhere near done."

Instantly Tom wrapped his hand around Bobby's wrist.

Meg was sure Tom was going to say, "You heard the lady, pardner. Vamoose." She waited, mesmerized, to see who would throw the first punch.

But the kitchen manager appeared just then, arms akimbo, and said briskly, "If you're going to stand around and socialize, Allegra, please just hand in your bowtie *right* now!"

Allie laughed out loud, then shook her arm free of Bobby's grip and walked away with a look of icy fury on her face.

Bobby gave Tom a bitter, mocking look and stalked off toward the main entrance.

That left Tom and Meg. "Well, that worked out pretty well," Tom remarked in his dry way.

Meg felt obliged to explain. "Bobby's loved my sister from

day one. He's not the only one in town, of course; but he's hung in there the longest. He truly believes they were born for each other.''

"Then he's deluded," Tom said. He made no effort to hide his dislike for the man.

"Deluded or not, he won't go away. She's treated him—well, not like dirt; Allie doesn't treat anyone like dirt, but—with a certain amount of arrogance, you know? Because Allie has always wanted to get out of Maine, and Bobby is a Maine boy through and through. He went west for a while, but that was just to show Allie that he could be ambitious, too. All he did was get in trouble. And thrown in jail."

"Surprise, surprise," said Tom wryly.

Meg shrugged. "He wasn't true to himself. Maine is in his blood. This is where he should be. I've heard he's working as a mechanic again, that he wants his own business. I hope it works out for him."

"Is there *any*body you don't wish well?"

Meg smiled apologetically. "Bobby used to live downstreet. I knew him when his feet couldn't reach the ground from our rope swing. It's hard to think of someone like that growing up to be psychotic. But his father split when he was still a kid, and his mother wasn't much of a role model either. She drank. She ran around. I guess Bobby couldn't have turned out any other way."

"That's not necessarily true," Tom said coolly.

Meg looked at Tom and realized at once what a stupid thing she'd said. His cheeks were flushed; his lips were set in a thin line of self-control. Tom Wyler had been shunted through a series of foster homes and had turned out pretty damn well, as far as Meg could see. Commanding officer of a homicide division in one of the biggest cities in the world, with a future that was bright with promise . . .

"Every rule has an exception," Meg said, embarrassed. "I'm sorry."

"You have traditional notions. It's what makes you Meg Hazard."

She tried to get the subject away from him, away from her. She asked humbly, "Do you really think he's a threat?"

"Hard to say. What I saw just now wasn't exactly reassuring. How did Allie get here? Alone, or with someone?"

"Alone," Meg said. "On her bike. I think she expected to ride home with us."

"All right. Then that's our plan," he said with stoic resignation.

Meg hesitated. "Except that I . . . I don't want to stay any longer," she confessed.

"Fine. We'll drag Allie out of here right now."

"That wouldn't be right," Meg said quickly. "She gave her word. *You* stay and wait for her. I'll catch a ride."

Tom looked at her, amazed, and then his patience exploded. "Are you *nuts*? What is it with you? Why do you keep throwing me in her company? Can't you see that I'm not interested?"

"I *wasn't* throwing you together," Meg said, backpedaling. "It's just that there's nothing more for me to do here. Gordon Camplin's already left, and I've managed to set up a gardening interview with his ex-wife," she said, bringing Tom up to speed on her latest scheme to learn something about the man.

"There's nothing left for me to do here," she repeated miserably, numb from her effort to avoid intimacy with Tom.

He shook his head, obviously exasperated by Meg's evasions. *"You* may have met your goals for the evening, lady, but I haven't." He took her by the wrist and started leading her toward the tent. "We're going dancing."

She hung back. "I *can't*, Tom. Really."

"You can. You will," he said grimly. "If I can stand around on my bad leg for you all night, you *damn* well can waltz around on two good ones for me."

He marched her into the tent, transformed into a fairyland

of ferns and white flowers, and walked her onto the floor to the strains of "I've Got You Under My Skin."

The selection pleased him: he gave her a quirky smile that blended equal parts of sophistication, street smarts, sexiness, and naïveté. And she thought, *How could anyone have let this man go?*

"One dance," Meg said weakly. "A fair trade." But she knew that one dance would be all it took.

He took her in his arms.

After weeks of having to settle for stolen glances and glancing touches, Meg felt overwhelmed by the intimacy of actual contact. This was it, her one moment of pure, permitted ecstasy. In a trance she swayed with him to the delicious, sensuous strains of the Cole Porter tune, played in a slow and sultry tempo. They moved a little in this direction, a little in that; there was no particular rhyme or reason to what they were doing, only a kind of seamless flow.

I tried so . . . hard to resist . . .

The line hung in the air after the lyric moved on. No one was trying harder to resist than Meg, no one. But it was a hopeless struggle. She felt his cheek against her hair and his heart beating against hers, and she thought, *How can this be wrong when it feels so right?*

He didn't say a word, and neither did she. Speech had become as irrelevant as the rain that had begun drumming softly on the tent over their heads. None of it—the flowers, the lights, the other dancers—mattered at all. There was only Tom, and her, and the insinuating, implicating strains of the music. She didn't even feel the need, any longer, to confess to him that she loved him: her body was saying it for her, in the way it pressed so willingly against his.

When the dance was done, he tilted her face toward his and claimed the kiss that she had managed to deny him on the porch of the Inn Between. His mouth on hers felt shockingly intimate; he knew exactly what he wanted and took it, ignoring the fact that they were standing in the middle of a dance floor.

It's not really a kiss, she insisted to herself, despite the fact that he was deepening it. *It's because of the night, and the music, and my thin silk dress. It's not a kiss*, she insisted, answering the electrifying strokes of his tongue on hers. *It's only a token, a gesture, of what can't be.*

But she had become liquid, all hot and sliding, and when he finally released her from the kiss that wasn't really a kiss, she had to steady herself with her hands on his chest.

He lowered his mouth to hers for one, last, glancing caress, as if he'd missed some tiny crumb of desire that she'd left there.

"I'm . . . afraid to look," she murmured, tracing the pattern on his tie. "Is there anyone else on this dance floor?"

"Ah-h-h. No." He slipped his arm back around her waist and said, "The band's taking a break. Do you think if I signed my pension over to them, they'd keep on playing?"

"Please . . . we can't just stand here," she wailed, edging him off the floor.

"You dance beautifully," he said as they wandered back into the crush of guests.

"We hardly moved," she said, distracted. She was looking for her sister.

"You dance beautifully," he said again. "Almost as well as you kiss."

She looked up at him in an agony of remorse and put her hand over his mouth. "That never happened," she said. "None of it. Please. For me."

He took her hand away and shook his head. "I can't act that charade, Meg. Not for all the kingdoms on earth."

"Don't do it for kingdoms!" she said in a low and urgent voice. "Do it for me."

"Meg!" he said, obviously frustrated with her cat-and-mouse antics. "You can't deny what's happening."

"Oh, yes, I *can*," she said, wrenching away from him and fleeing from the tent.

"Thanks for the lift, Mr. Markstrom. I don't know what I would've done if you hadn't been leaving just then." Not that she'd let the poor guy have a choice. "I guess it was the wine that gave me this horrible headache," she said, following up on her original lie. "How lucky that I saw you on your way out."

Her rumply ex-principal said, "Good to talk to you again, Meggie. And I want you to think seriously about those extension courses. You always were a real fine student."

"I will," she said as she slammed the door on his vintage Skylark.

She stood on the sidewalk in front of the Inn Between, reluctant to go inside. A reading light burned bright in the sitting room. Her father, dozing in front of the television, would want to know all about the good time his little girl had enjoyed after years of going without a real date.

But Meg was in no mood to share. Cradling the memory of the kiss the way she would a newly cut rose, she strolled over rain-washed bricks to the back shed, with every wistful intention of reliving the dance at least six times before she went to bed.

But it was not to be.

When she reached the shed she saw at once that something was wrong. The hasp that held the lock, a chintzy piece of hardware, had been pried loose; the lock, useless, still hung from it. Inside, she could see that the overhead light was on and that, more importantly, so were the interior lights of the dollhouse. This was no case of some curious stranger strolling into an unlocked barn to peek at the toy he'd heard about in town. This was breaking, and this was entering.

Meg hung back, ready to run. But there were no sounds from the shed. No movements. Just bright light, spilling onto the glistening brick path that led to the shed. Meg stepped off the path and into the untamed privet that towered over one side of the structure. The branches shook rain all over her nonwashable silk dress. She winced—from the wet, and from the thought of the cleaning bill—and crept as near as she could to the window for a peek inside.

Nobody. Feeling bolder now but more fearful, Meg ran around to the door and entered. *It's the desk*, she was convinced. *That little desk is worth the most, maybe thousands. That's what they wanted.*

She went directly to the dollhouse. What she saw shocked her: tornado-like upheaval of the entire contents, everything in every room, tossed and tumbled and in a heap. She staggered back; it was like being slammed across the chest with a two-by-four. The act was so viciously thorough, so thoroughly vicious, that she had to beat back a sense of nausea.

With shaking hands Meg began at once to right the little pieces. She was convinced that vital evidence had been destroyed or stolen and she was desperate to put things back the way they were so that she could assess the damage.

Very quickly she discovered that there wasn't any. Pieces had been moved around and knocked about, yes; but nothing was missing, and virtually nothing had been broken. It seemed miraculous that such delicate and fragile furnishings could come through such a ransacking intact.

She tried to make sense of it all as she righted the chairs and reset the table. Two aspects of the incident seemed clear. Whoever did this valued the dollhouse and its contents too much to destroy them. Whoever did this was sending a message.

There was Joyce Fells. Clearly Joyce felt the dollhouse was hers by right. She'd done her best to suggest to Meg that the tiny replica of Eagle's Nest carried some awful curse. Was

Joyce hanging around town to carry it out? Maybe the ransacking was her crude attempt to spook Meg into selling the dollhouse at a rock-bottom price. Well, Meg didn't believe in curses—despite Terry's knock overboard—and she was not *about* to betray a deathbed promise by handing the dollhouse over to some badly dressed off-islander who'd think nothing of selling off the contents one by one. Joyce Fells could just take a hike.

Gordon Camplin? Absurd. He'd have taken a godawful chance, sneaking into the shed to wreak this havoc. On the other hand, he knew where the dollhouse was—and more importantly, where Meg was. He *had* left the dance early, and in a hurry. So the opportunity was there. But why would he do this?

Because he was searching for something, stupid. Something he did or did not find. Meg had no idea where *that* conclusion had leapt out from; but it seemed to make a bizarre kind of sense.

Meg sighed and looked around for the hour hand of the grandfather clock and found it—hardly bigger than an eyelash —on the bottom step to the second floor. She wet her finger with the tip of her tongue and pressed it to the hour hand, then stood there without an idea in the world where to lay it down for safekeeping.

It's the minuscule scale, she decided, frustrated. *A person would have to be Alice in Wonderland—after the mushroom— to adequately search the dollhouse for clues.* If, indeed, there were any clues.

Meg felt with all her heart that something in that tiny house was worth discovering. But whether it was her grandmother's ghost or a clue to the killing, that she didn't know.

She slid the hour hand carefully off the tip of her finger and onto a tiny silver tray designed to hold visitors' cards that would never be placed on it. It was all so sad, so unused, so . . . fanciful. If only she could make it all *bigger*. She tugged idly at one of her grandmother's earrings and sat back in her chair, too tired to finish putting everything right, too wired to leave what was left until the next day.

"Tell me what to do."

Lately she'd tried to commune out loud with her grandmother. It seemed like the most direct approach. Never mind reading tarot cards or the innards of a chicken; Meg's personality was too straightforward for that. *Tell me what to do*, she begged.

Her gaze drifted to the master bedroom. The carved teakwood bed was still upside-down, its mattress and linens caught in disarray underneath it. That room, of all the rooms, Meg simply had no heart to set right. How she hated that bed. She stared at it with loathing. Her reaction was irrational and visceral. That carved footboard . . . the gargoyle's head was so badly placed . . . it hit you right in the small of the back when you were pressed against it. . . .

"Mr. Camplin, please don't offer them to me. I can't accept them—"

"Of course you can, my dear. They're the merest trinkets, but they're rather pretty. I thought of you at once when I saw them in town. Let me put them on you."

"No . . . I shouldn't even be here, in your rooms. You shouldn't have summoned me."

"Of course I should have. Who else? I bought these for you, not for the cook. Because you've been so good with the children."

"Oh . . . the children . . . yes . . . I'm very fond . . . of them."

"As they are of you. Now, come. Has a man never slipped a jewel through your ear before? Why do you keep backing away? I have only the simplest design, and that's to see you adorned in the way you ought to be. Really, you're too skittish by half. Ah, very well. Here, then. Open your hand. Take these. They're for you. And when you're in the privacy of your bedroom, slip them through your ears and think of me, and of how unfair you're being."

"Yes . . . may I go now?"

"Yes, yes you may, Miss All-Innocence. But I warn you not to bedevil me with those complex looks tomorrow during the children's tea. And when you push young James on the swing, let me caution you: don't laugh your merry laugh, and don't—for God's sake, the one thing you must *not* do in front of me is —hold him close and whisper in his ear. Or you will send me over the edge, I promise you. These weeks . . . since your arrival here . . . have been absolute . . . hell. You cannot expect me to endure much more . . . than I have already."

"Yes, sir. No, sir."

Meg blinked, and then she blinked again.

My God. What was it? A vision? A dream too vividly imagined? No, she decided; not a dream. It was right there, in front of her, the whole scene, life-size, in three dimensions and Technicolor. She'd seen it all with crystal clarity, right down to the brass buttons on Gordon Camplin's double-breasted blazer and the sapphire ring on his middle finger—the same ring that he wore tonight, in fact.

A vision, then. Either the dollhouse had got big, or Meg had got small. One way or another she'd been there, watching a man who looked very much like the society photos Meg had unearthed in her research: suave, dapper, with slicked brown hair and a pencil-thin moustache. A man not at all used to hearing the word *no*.

But in the vision—if that was what it was—Margaret Atwells had appeared wearing a ho-hum dress in dark gray, with her hair pulled back severely in a bun. A nun would dress that way, or a librarian. For the life of her, Meg could not understand how her grandmother could ever have become an obsession of Gordon Camplin. Couldn't he have found a sexier servant to seduce? What was it about Margaret Atwells that had driven him "to the edge," as he claimed, in a few short weeks? The woman in Meg's vision had seemed so modest, so bewildered, so determined to avoid eye contact.

Ah. But what about the *other* Margaret Atwells—the one who apparently shot complex looks at Gordon Camplin during the children's tea, and laughed at young James's antics, and held him close and whispered in his ear? *That* Margaret Atwells was another woman altogether: alive, spontaneous, loving, playful.

Was she also seducible? Meg buried her face in her hands, trying to recapture the vision in her mind. Obviously Gordon Camplin had seen something in Margaret Atwells's face that Orel Tremblay—and now Meg—had not. *Could* her grandmother have been attracted to Camplin? Or at least intrigued by his attention? Could she even have been sending him signals without being aware of it?

Meg tried to recapture the expression on her grandmother's face, but all she could imagine was her own face, sending signals to Tom Wyler.

The issue of Camplin's guilt had been a cut-and-dried one for Meg. Was she being fair to him? Was she taking into account a woman's emotions, which were rarely cut-and-dried? Meg herself was her own best example. She loved Allie as fiercely, as tenderly, as any mother could. But now—she was able to admit it freely—she also loved Tom Wyler. Any fool could see that those were incompatible loyalties.

It was too confusing. First the dance, and now this . . . Meg had made a hopeless tangle of history and current events, and she was way too tired to try sorting it out tonight. She turned off the lights of the dollhouse and stood up to go. The shed could not be locked; she'd have to take a chance that whoever it was who'd ransacked the furnishings would not be back.

Call it a premonition, she thought grimly.

Meg was in her slip, hanging up the wrinkly remains of her silk dress, when her sister stomped into the bedroom in a fine rage.

"All I can say is, I hope your night went better than mine," Allie said angrily. She was like a tulip closed up tight on a cold, wet day.

"Bobby made another scene?" asked Meg, alarmed.

"I *wish*," said Allie, throwing herself on Meg's bed. "Tom would've taken him out and been my hero. No. What Tom did was offer a *ride* to two of the *help*. *Why* is he so damn chivalrous?"

"Don't be mean, Allie," said Meg, secretly elated. "It's not like we have a transit system."

"They live in *Ellsworth*, for God's sake. 'Oh, no problem,' he tells them. 'That's out my way.' So *I* get dropped off *first*. I hate midwesterners. They're too . . . too . . . *nice*."

"Allie, come on. The night could've ended in outright bloodshed," Meg said flatly. "All's well that ends well."

"Which reminds me. Do you have my earrings?"

Meg picked up the gold hoops from her dresser and dropped them in her sister's hand. "That wasn't very nice, what you did."

"Thanks." Allie fingered them thoughtfully and said, "I don't know what to do about Bobby. I thought we finally had an understanding. I thought he'd be way too embarrassed to show his face around me after the way he screwed up out west. Dammit! Lisa and her big mouth."

"How's Lisa doing, by the way?" Meg asked as she slipped the pearl teardrops from her ears. She'd forgotten completely that they were there; now she looked at them with a mix of fear and fascination. They were the ones, all right: the "trinkets" that Gordon Camplin had given their grandmother. No wonder he hadn't been able to take his eyes off Meg earlier.

"Oh, Lisa's doing all right. Better than I am," Allie said with a glum look.

Meg looked up sharply from her reverie. "Meaning?"

"Meaning nothing special," Allie said tiredly. "I have *not* had a drink—even though everyone around me seems to be awash in alcohol. But . . . I'm getting discouraged, Meg," Allie said, lowering her head in complete dejection. "Tom and I should be so much further along than we are. I love him so much more than he loves me. I wish he'd just . . . catch up. We have such a great thing going. . . ."

Meg put down the teardrops and looked at her sister. When she was four years old, Allie had drooped her head in just that way and said, "I wish Mommy would stop being dead. I wish she would come back and be with us, and then we could take care of her heart so it would keep working."

And Meg had been forced to tell her, "Mommy can't stop being dead, Allie. It's too late to fix her heart." Allie had cried on Meg's breast in wrenching, forlorn sobs, until Meg thought both their hearts would break, hers and Allie's.

Meg couldn't go through that again; couldn't say, "It's too late to fix Tom's heart." So she went up to her sister and rubbed her back in broad, reassuring circles and said, "You're too impatient."

Allie said nothing at first. And then, in a voice as even as steady rain, she said, "You meant what you said to Bobby, didn't you. That there's not going to be any marriage."

"That isn't what I meant at all," said Meg quickly. "I meant . . . I *had* to say something like that . . . Bobby was in a dangerous mood—"

"Oh, *please*. Bobby?" Allie said, dismissing the idea. She shook her head. "That couldn't have been the reason. You know something that I don't, Meg. And I deserve to hear it. Tom's told you he doesn't care for me; is that it?"

"No! No, he's never said that! He's told me that he thinks you're fond of *him*. That's all he's told me."

"You're kidding!" Allie said, her eyes lighting up with sudden hope. "That's as far as he's figured things out? He *thinks* I'm merely *fond* of him? Meg, I've done everything but rip off my underwear and say 'Take me, I'm yours.' Fond? Is he kidding?"

Meg shrugged unhappily.

Allie laughed, relieved. "I guess I haven't been aggressive enough. I *thought* I was. Well, okay—I *will* rip off my underwear the next time I see him."

"Now that would be really dumb," Meg said quickly. "You never want to seem too eager with a man."

"In general, yes. But if I played hard to get with Tom Wyler I'd have as much chance of landing him as . . . as Comfort —or you! No; we're in a relationship—he said so himself. All it needs is a little shove."

"Allie, y'know . . . relationships . . . I read somewhere that sixty-one percent of U.S. women think they're in a steady relationship, but only twenty-eight percent of men do. Doesn't this tell you something?"

"Yeah—that men are masters of denial," said Allie, scrambling from her sister's bed with a new spring in her step. "Thanks, Meg," she added, giving her a quick squeeze on the way out. She stopped and turned at the door. "When I get back from Chicago, I'm hitting Tom Wyler with everything I've got."

Meg, dismayed, began pulling her slip over her head, mostly to hide her emotions. When she heard Allie cry out her name she yanked the slip the rest of the way off in one sharp pull. "What?" she asked, startled, as Allie ran back to her.

Allie took Meg by the hips and turned her toward the light. She touched a spot in the small of Meg's back. "How'd you *do* this to yourself?"

Puzzled, Meg twisted around to look, then turned to the dresser mirror for help. There she saw a black-and-blue mark, dark and ugly and the size of a fist, in the middle of her back.

At gargoyle height.

CHAPTER 17

By Tuesday Allie was in Chicago, gathering job offers like strawberries in June, happily rearranging her life to fit smoothly around Tom's.

In the meantime, Meg's own well-ordered universe seemed to be coming apart at the seams. Besides the visions, besides the ransacking, besides the constant bills and the crumbling inn, there was this: Meg wanted the love of her sister's life for herself.

She sat at the kitchen table on Tuesday morning beside a hamper full of dirty laundry and a counter stacked with breakfast dishes, willing Tom Wyler to come to her. She thought of Allie, then plucked out the thought the way she would a thorn in her thumb, and went back to thoughts of Tom, willing him to come. She lowered her head into her folded arms: *Come to me.*

She wanted him near. She wanted to have him take her in his arms again, to feel his shaved cheek, to taste his mouth on hers. He was all she could think of. A day without him—she'd just gone through one—was like a day without water. She was restless with the fever of him, aching for the sight of him, utterly smitten by his smile, his voice, the irony in his sense of humor. She loved everything about him, from the way he said her name to the way he stroked Coughdrop's ears and the coon cat's throat.

And he was good with kids. It would all be easier, if only he weren't so good with kids. Timmy had adored him from day one. Even Terry was sliding under his spell. (On the night of the so-called backfire she'd seen Tom slip down the street and return with Terry, covered in chocolate ice cream.)

Then, too, the picnic: She could hardly help noticing that Mandy's baby, a hopelessly colicky thing, had quieted at once when Mandy laid the infant in his arms: some men had that touch. There was a stillness about Tom, an inner strength, that Meg felt sure he didn't know he possessed. He was everything she never knew she was looking for. She loved him.

And Allie too.

The sound of a car pulling up in front of the Inn Between made Meg wipe her eyes hurriedly. She knew the pitch of the engine, the slam of the door. Tom had come to her, as somehow she knew he must.

She yanked a pillowcase from the laundry basket and blew her nose in it, and raked her hands through her tangled hair. But then she thought, *What does it matter*? and slumped back in her chair, her heart bound tight in barbed wire, her head strangely free to measure the pain.

Tom came round to the back door and walked into the kitchen without knocking. She thought he looked haggard: his khakis looked slept in, and he had bags under his eyes. But his manner was deliberately cheerful as he said, "I'm feeling frisky today. How do you feel about attacking the trails of Acadia? I've commandeered two mountain bikes."

He was leaning into the counter, casual and offhand; but his eyes were burning bright, and there was an edge in his voice.

She matched the forced lightness in his tone. "In July? That's like asking Santa to leave his shop in late November. You go ahead. Once the fog burns off it'll be a beautiful day for a bike ride."

"You don't want me to go back without seeing Acadia up close and personal, do you? Your beloved Acadia?"

There was a taunt in his voice that she decided to ignore. "You can see it up close on your own," she said evenly, folding her arms on the table.

"But what about the flora? What about the fauna? How will I learn their names?"

"You won't need to know them in Chicago," she said, trying to keep the bitterness out.

He dropped his bantering tone. "This isn't about Chicago, Meg. This is about *now*."

Meg let out a sigh of utter frustration and dropped her head onto her arms again. She couldn't play this game with him. She could scarcely bear to hear the sound of his voice. When she lifted her head, he was still there, which surprised her; she was convinced that she'd summoned him in a vision.

"Why have you come?" she whispered, near despair.

He leaned across from her, his hands splayed on the table. In a voice ripped by emotion, he said, "I couldn't *not* come. *God*. Don't you see? I had no choice."

It was true. "I know," she said miserably. "I know." She stood up, almost in a trance, and said, "I'll tell Comfort."

She found her in the bathroom, woozy from morning sickness. "I'm going out for a while," Meg said, nearly oblivious to her sister-in-law's state.

Dismayed, Comfort said, "You are?"

"Let the machine take the calls," Meg said, and she left her.

The new chambermaid, a bouncy college girl, intercepted Meg in the hall. "The people in room four just checked out, and, like, they took the *key*. Can I have the spare to get in?"

"They *had* the spare. I'll see to it later."

"But what about the new arriv—"

Meg brushed past the girl as if she were a drunken panhandler and went outside.

Lloyd was climbing into the cab of his truck. "Tell Comfort I'm goin' to Ellsworth to pick up some drywall," he said.

"Tell her yourself, Lloyd," Meg answered. She stepped around her openmouthed brother and went out to the front.

A blue bike was mounted on the car rack of Tom's Cutlass. A red one was parked on the street.

"So this is my getaway vehicle?" Meg asked in a light but shaky voice, trying the bike for size. The seat was adjusted perfectly.

"Think of it as your magic carpet," Tom said, lifting the bike onto the rack. "We have food. We have drink. We have the whole day before us."

"Only the morning," she said bleakly. "It can't possibly be more."

He took her by her arm and led her to the car. "The morning, then. I'll take what I can get."

They made a quick trip downtown to the police station, then wove their way through the town's one-way streets—past the fire station with its Forest Fire Danger dial sitting squarely on *medium;* past the gray stone post office from which Meg had sent so many Care packages to her sister during her college years; past the old Rodick House, crisp and white and with its black shutters set off by boxes of red geraniums; past good old, just-folks Jordan's, one of the few restaurants to stay open in winter for the locals; past the odd mix of shops, stores, and sweetly shabby houses that Meg knew like the back of her hand—and finally past the street where she'd lived her whole life.

Five minutes, to cruise from one end of her world to the other.

Meg directed Tom over the Park Loop Road to the Jordan Pond House where they parked the car, then unloaded the bikes and walked them the short distance to the start of the trail. They paused before an exquisite stone gatehouse, commissioned—like the fifty miles of carriage roads that criss-crossed the park—by John D. Rockefeller early in the century.

"He's one of our local heroes," Meg explained. "You have to give the guy credit: he took one look into the future and decided to ban automobiles from the carriage trails. It makes all the difference. You can pedal all day and hardly run into another soul—if you know where to go."

Tom leaned over the handlebars of her bike, slipped his hand behind her head, and kissed her. "Take me there," he said with an urgency that thrilled her. "Where no one else is. Show me your Acadia."

"There isn't time," she answered, averting her lips from his.

She meant it in the most profound way. Acadia did not reveal its secrets to the hit-and-run tourist. It had taken Meg a lifetime to learn them. Tom would have to come back at dusk for the nighthawks, at dawn for the beavers. He'd have to come in spring for the mayflowers, in fall for the witch hazel. He'd have to meander the swamps to see the purple loose-strife, and strike out along the rocky coast to glimpse the blue harebell. For him to see a harbor seal or a breaching whale this morning would be pure, blind luck.

To see Meg's Acadia, he'd have to make a commitment to stay; there was no other way.

Meg was never able afterward to recall anything between Tom's electric demand and their steep meander along the wooded descent of the stream to the Cobblestone Bridge. About all she remembered was that magic carpets came in twenty-one speeds.

When they reached the picturesque bridge, they got off their bikes and leaned over the stone wall, lingering over the loveli-ness of the burbling stream below.

"This bridge is the only one in the Park that's built with cobbled stones," Meg said dreamily, dropping a pebble into the rushing water.

When she looked up at Tom she could see that he didn't care if the bridge was made of cobblestones or quicksand. He was watching her with a look so . . . intense, that she had to look away.

Meg herself rarely carried a camera, but today she would've given anything to have one. She couldn't trust her memory to be able to recreate the look in his eyes in years to come. Without a photo, how could she possibly remember that he had a tiny scar that ran along the edge of his left eyebrow? Tiny scars were so easy to forget. And the two or three freckles, barely visible through his tan; you didn't expect freckles on a homicide lieutenant's nose. Those, too, would fade with the memory of him.

"Should we keep going?" she asked in a voice faint with emotion.

"As long and as far as we can," Tom answered.

He couldn't take his eyes off Meg. He wanted her more than ever. She knew it—it was written all over her beautiful, flushed face—and what was more, he knew she felt the same way about him. But they needed a place where they could make their feelings clear, and so he'd hit on the idea of Acadia. It was hardly neutral territory, but it was a hell of a lot more neutral than the kitchen of the Inn Between.

Neutral or not, Acadia was magical; he was staggered by the beauty and solitude of the place. Wyler had never had any great fondness for the outdoors; his tastes ran to books and basketball, perfect escapes from blood and chaos.

But *this* . . . the silence was awesome. No cars, no sirens, no boom boxes or gunshots; only the soft sound of the bike tires on the path, and the muted, majestic swish of fir trees swaying high over their heads. This was true enchantment. He was reluctant to speak, even to her, and break the spell.

The piney smell of balsam filled his nostrils, filled his lungs. He took great, deep breaths of it as they rode side by side in dappled sunlight; it was a balm to his frazzled nerves after a night of tossing and turning—two nights, really. Ever since the dance; ever since he'd taken her in his arms and kissed her . . .

Three nights. He'd forgotten the night of the picnic. No, wait, for more than that. The plain fact was, he hadn't slept well in a week. He'd been blaming the lumpy mattress in his cabin, and the bizarre woodland sounds he'd had to listen to all night. But the reason he wasn't sleeping well, the reason he might never sleep well again, was pedaling alongside him, and he wanted desperately to reach out and touch her hair.

She was so quiet. He wondered whether he'd said something to offend her; but then she glanced over at him, and he knew that he had not. His heart swelled with emotion: he felt positively medieval, a knight on a horse, escorting his ladylove through ancient woods filled with unknown perils.

Except—dope—she was escorting *him*. Without her he'd be lost on the zigzagging trails in no time. He had no map, no sense of direction, no idea where all of this was going. He shook his head, half bemused, half besotted by his situation. He hadn't been on a bike in twenty-five years, hadn't been under a tree in nearly as long.

He and Lydia had lived in his condo, and even though she'd begged for a house with a yard, he wouldn't have any of it. Tools and grass were not his thing. In general, he believed that animals belonged outside and people inside. The condo association hadn't allowed pets, and his son, like Wyler himself, had spent his early years without them. It had taken up until now for Wyler to feel sorry for them both.

His reverie was interrupted when Meg said, "Let's walk the bikes for a while."

They walked their bikes at a leisurely pace while Meg pointed out various ferns, and clumps of bead lily, and little evergreens with pairs of pink bells called twinflowers. He saw a flash of yellow in the trees overhead: a magnolia warbler,

Meg said at once, and then went on to lament the decline in migratory birds and wildflowers on the island in the last few years. Wyler paid more attention than ever, fearing that whatever it was she was showing him might be gone forever the next time he passed through.

And that was when it hit him with the full force of a blow to the gut: there probably wouldn't be a next time.

He was due, overdue, at his career. The faxes and phone messages from the department had steadily increased—there were three of them at the Bar Harbor station just now—and he didn't know how much longer he could keep his captain at bay.

Convalescence from a gunshot was one thing; trying to use up, all at once, the years of vacation that he'd piled up was another scenario altogether. If he didn't go back soon, they'd be convinced he was having reentry problems after the shootout—the kiss of death to his career.

"Problems at the office?" she asked him out of the blue.

How did she know that? Had she been intercepting his faxes in town? No, he realized; she was merely being her psychic self.

"My boss thinks I'm stalling; that I'm a burnout case," he said, surprising himself with his candor.

She looked taken aback. "I was just being facetious," she said. "Anyway, aren't you on vacation?" she added.

"They don't like you to take too much of it," he said dryly.

"Because?"

"A good cop's not supposed to need it. You get out of the rhythm, out of the flow. And your case load goes all to hell." He added laconically, "It shows a lack of dedication."

She'd been listening intently to his answer. "It does make sense," she admitted with a rueful shrug.

If only Lydia had been so understanding.

He said, "You got home all right the other night?" It was a

fairly dumb question, but he wanted to bring the subject around to the dance, to the kiss.

He was watching her for a reaction and he got a surprising one: her face clouded over into a dark frown.

"Yes," she said, clearly troubled. "I went into the shed when I got back." She hesitated, then said, "Someone had broken into it. The dollhouse was ransacked."

"*What*?"

He made her tell him everything. It was like pulling teeth; she was as reluctant a witness as he'd ever interrogated. Exasperated, he finally said, "You didn't report this to the police. You didn't tell me. How do you expect us to know about this, for God's sake? By reading tea leaves?"

She rounded on him and said, "Well, I've told you *now*, haven't I—and look what's happened. We've brought the outside world *here*, into Acadia. Who cares about ransacked toys? Who cares about police politics, for that matter? We *can't* care, because there's nothing either of us can do about the other's problems. All we can do is enjoy what we have. Here. Now."

She climbed back on her bike and rode off angrily.

She was right. God help them both, she was right. Wyler's days in Bar Harbor *were* numbered; they'd known that from the start. It was absurd to think that he could just up and forget about the ransacking, but he could set it aside. For here. For now. Just as Meg could set his career—and her sister—aside. For here. For now.

They resumed their journey south, riding in silence. The plaintive sound of the swaying balsams gradually resumed its hypnotic hold on Wyler, and his spirit became serene once more. They saw no one else. He began to think that she'd led him to some enchanted, primeval place where only they existed.

They passed a couple of sailboats moored in a picturesque cove, then headed north alongside an open meadow surrounding a quiet, picture-perfect pond. Meg pointed to a small boat-house hanging over the water.

"We can stop here for an early lunch, if you like," she said.

He did like. He wanted to put things right again between them, and that wasn't possible when they were riding along-side each other.

They walked their bikes through the meadow, scaring up crickets in their path, and laid them against the wraparound deck of the little shingled building.

The boathouse, still privately owned, was in perfect repair. They peeked through multipaned windows and discovered a small rowboat floating inside the locked doors, ready to save lives or to carry away guests who were lucky enough to have access to it.

Wyler whistled softly in admiration. Who had this kind of money? Okay, the answer was easy enough—the Rockefellers —but really; who *had* this kind of money?

They sat down in the shade of the freshly painted deck. With an ironic flourish, Wyler opened Meg's box lunch for her: roast-beef sub, brownie, carton of lemonade.

"I have a feeling that caviar's a more common snack on this deck," he said, hating Mr. Rockefeller and all his kin, despite their generosity to the public.

"This is perfect," Meg said with a smile that left him beg-ging for more.

She sat back against the building and took an appreciative bite out of her sub. He did too, while they gazed in lazy con-tentment at the scene before them: a field of golden grass rolling gently down to a pond of clear water dotted with white lilies and—yes, he had to admit—charmingly picturesque patches of seaweed.

To the south and west was the enchanted forest they'd just ridden through, and beyond that, the sea. To the north, a trio of mountaintops reminded him, if he needed reminding, that this was not Illinois. It was an unbelievably lovely sight. If some hack painter had decided to put one of everything scenic into a single painting, this was what he'd come up with.

"You're not *really* envious of the owners, are you?" she asked him suddenly.

Amazed by the question, he said, "Of course I am. I'll admit it; I'm not proud: It bugs the hell out of me." He added, "Doesn't all the wealth bother *you*?"

She laughed. "You're kidding. Who would I be jealous of? Some poor guy in a sealed-in office in Manhattan who's trying to do right by the family fortune? *We're* the ones with the view. *We're* the ones with the picnic lunch."

"We're the ones with each other," he said, reaching out to caress her cheek. He had to do it; she was completely irresistible to him.

Meg's cheek flushed a deep rose, as if his touch had burned her; it gave him an absurd amount of pleasure to see it. They went on eating in companionable silence.

One of Meg's bigger speeches came when she pointed to a water-lily leaf and said simply, "Frog."

He was struck anew with the difference between Meg and her sister. Allie would've jumped up and said, "Oh, look, a little green frog, isn't it cute, let's try to catch it, we'll take off our shoes and wade in after it, come on, are you game?"

Yep. Allie made him feel young, all right. But *Meg*—he glanced at the woman enjoying the scene so contentedly— Meg made him feel whole.

It was a nice old frog, sitting in the sun and minding its own business. Wyler was happy to leave it that way.

They finished their sandwiches and Wyler was careful to pick up every last crumb. It was the least he could do for the poor joker in Manhattan.

After that they ate their brownies and drank their lemonade and—somehow or other—Wyler ended up telling Meg about the shoot-out in Chicago that had cost him a piece of his thighbone and a chunk of his confidence.

It was a violation of her Acadia rules; he knew that. But he had to let her know that he wasn't going back merely to be captain, or superintendent, or ambassador to Rome for that matter. He was going back to Chicago to prove that he *could* go back.

He had to. Everything he was, everything he'd ever struggled to be, was in Chicago. He felt honor bound to explain that to her. Here. Now. In this magic place where silence was golden, and words, if they were to be spoken at all, had to mean something.

Oddly enough, Meg didn't turn away from the subject the way she did when he'd talked about his ambitions on the force. Maybe it was because the outcome of the shoot-out—a little girl murdered, her stepfather killed, a copper wounded—touched her maternal instincts. Whatever the reason, Meg seemed to want to hear him out.

"But why are you blaming yourself?" she asked when he was done. "From what you say, these hostage, or barricade, situations are extremely unpredictable. You couldn't have known that the man had another gun besides the one he threw out."

"You have to assume it," he said in a grim voice.

"But what difference could you have made?" Meg argued gently. "The little girl was already dead when you got there."

"Her stepfather wasn't. The negotiators were right," he insisted doggedly, "and I was wrong. I never should've gone anywhere near the kill zone. The guy was clearly suicidal. I was his hand-picked audience. I've racked my brain, trying to remember him. But sixth grade was a long time ago. I don't know how the hell he remembered me, or why I was important to him.

"All I know is, he was waiting for me. He expected to be taken out, and he wasn't disappointed. I don't even think he wanted to hurt me. He only wanted to die. Suicide by cop: it's a modern phenomenon. And I played right into it."

"You're a homicide detective, not a hostage expert."

"Right," he said bleakly. "Good detective, lousy cop."

Meg wrapped her arms around her knees and stared at her ankles. "The girl was only four?"

"Yeah," he said morosely.

"Do you know why he shot her?"

Wyler shrugged. "He'd just got fired. His girlfriend was leaving him. A double whammy. He'd planned to take her out, too, but she managed to get away."

Wyler closed his eyes. The event washed over him with a pain more searing than the rip of the bullet through his thigh. He'd done everything he knew how to put that saga behind him. Nothing had worked. Thinking about it, not thinking about it; talking about it, not talking about it—nothing had worked.

He stared at the frog, so close that you could have thrown a potato at it, and began being sucked back into a depression. *Christ*, he thought. *Not here. Not now.*

"Tom," she said softly. "Let it go. It's over."

He opened his eyes and turned to her, and she put her hand on his shoulder and kissed him. Her lips were warm, her skin petal soft from their exertions on the trails. Her hair clung to her neck in dark, damp strands and she smelled, not of designer perfume like her sister, but of something more elemental and infinitely more appealing: the warm, seductive scent of a woman.

He shuddered and returned the kiss, turning it into something more, his tongue deep inside her mouth, his hands sliding restlessly across her back. Meg moaned softly, sending his arousal to a new, more fervent pitch. He kissed her with wet, random caresses, ending at the hollow of her throat, chanting her name again and again, lost in the wonder of his hunger for her.

She was wearing a sleeveless blouse the color of gold wildflowers. He unbuttoned the top buttons, sliding his mouth to the top of her breast, cupping her breast in his hand, some primitive part of him relishing its weight. *Earth goddess*, he thought, not for the first time. He wanted to come to her, into her, to encircle her and have her legs surround him.

He slipped her bra away from her breast and kissed the nipple, teasing and tasting until it was swollen and erect. Meg gasped and arched herself into his kiss; the slow, shuddering intake of her breath reminded him of the sound the swaying balsams had made high over their heads in the woods.

She was silent, not protesting with pretty words, not even uttering his name; nothing. The effect on him was profoundly erotic; he felt as if he was making love to some mythic creature, half goddess, half woman.

He lifted his head from Meg's breast and watched her face, her closed eyes, her partly opened mouth, as he slid open the zipper of her cutoffs and slipped his hand inside, stroking and petting, making her wet. Her arousal made her more beautiful than ever to him: her high cheekbones, flushed with desire; her soft brown lashes, caught together in tears; her full, unpainted mouth, erotically, invitingly parted.

He was hard in a way he'd never thought it was possible to be, hard enough that he ached. He bent his head over hers and kissed her again, awestruck by the depth of her arousal, wildly frustrated by the depth of his own.

"Meg . . . ah, Meggie . . . let me make love to you," he whispered into her parted lips.

A tear slid from under her eyelid, down her cheek. She put her hands behind his neck and kissed him deeply, her desire rippling through her.

"But not here," she murmured.

Only then did it occur to him that he had Meg half undressed on the deck of a boathouse positioned over a pond by an open meadow.

"Yes, you're right," he said with a shaky laugh. "It'd be an abuse of the Rockefeller hospitality."

Meg put herself back together and he helped her to her feet, his heart light with longing for her. He wanted to make love to her somewhere in the deep grasses of the meadow. He'd never made love in a meadow. He gathered up their lunch boxes and walked alongside her to their bikes, scanning the meadow beyond for a place well hidden.

He stuffed the cardboard boxes into his bike basket, then turned to Meg and put his hands on her waist and looked deeply, almost wistfully, into her hazel eyes, wanting to see desire there.

But he saw only pain.

"We can't do this, Tom," she said, sending his expectations into a nose dive.

"Sure we can," he whispered coaxingly, all too familiar with what was coming next.

"Allie—"

"No," he said, this time putting his hand over *her* mouth. "No Allie. Not in Acadia."

"But she *is* here," Meg said softly. "And here," she added, taking his hand and laying it over her heart. "What can I do?"

He stared at her uncomprehendingly. Automatically he pulled his hand away from between hers and used it to rake through his hair. "What can you *do*? It's obvious, Meg," he said, his voice thick with impatience. "You can let her grow up! *You* can grow up! Jesus!" he said, whacking the rail behind him with a fist.

"We've been all through this, Meg," he said, forcing himself to speak in a slightly calmer voice. "You're not doing her any favors protecting her emotionally all the time. I don't know why in hell Allie has taken such a shine to me; but *I do not want your sister*! Call me crazy—but it's *you* I want, Meg. And you know you want *me*."

"Just because two people want each other doesn't mean—"

"Listen to me! *You're* not married! *I'm* not married. This is *not* immoral!" he said, beside himself with frustration.

Her mouth set in a line of determination he knew well. "I think we have to leave," she said quietly. She untangled her bike from his and swung one leg over the seat.

"I don't think so," he said harshly. "You go ahead. I'll find my own way back." He was hopping mad; testosterone was running amok through his system. He needed time to work it off.

"Are you sure?" Meg asked in a small, apologetic voice.

"Go."

CHAPTER **18**

Hours later, Wyler was in his cabin and still fuming. Who the hell did she think she was? Didn't she have any idea what had happened between them? Of course she did! How could she just turn herself off that way? *Damn* her!

What exactly were you supposed to do when a woman looked and acted . . . oh, God. Like that. He remembered her face when he had her in his arms and fell into a mood so black with hunger that it left him weak-kneed. Filled with self-pity, he lay back on his lumpy mattress and picked up his Grisham novel.

Aagh!

He flung the book across the room and began stalking back and forth again.

So what the hell was he supposed to do now? Sit in this dreary cabin and rot? He'd lied through his teeth when he'd put on a happy face at the picnic and raved about the cabin, about how rustic it was and—what, charming, did he say? Shit. It was nothing like his room at the Elm Tree Inn. *That* was rustic and charming. This was a log cabin with bare furnishings, a balky hot water heater, and no screens, which—considering that flies in Maine were the size of hummingbirds and mosquitoes in Maine were the size of flies—struck him as a pretty dumb oversight.

He had to ask himself again: Why, exactly, was he staying on?

The answer, again, was: He didn't know. He was staying on because he didn't *know* why he was staying on, and he wanted to find out.

It couldn't be for the sex. For one thing, the possibility of making love to Meg Hazard was looking remote. For another, sex was something available anytime, anywhere. Why knock himself out trying with this one woman? There was the obvious reason—a man always wants what he can't have—but somehow Wyler wasn't happy with that answer.

He sat back down on the edge of the bed and dropped his head in his hands. Had he fallen in love with her?

He didn't know. He'd only fallen in love once before in his life, and that hadn't felt anything like the way he was feeling now. With Lydia it had all been so straightforward. They hit it off, he made a move, she welcomed it, they dated for a few months, they got engaged, they got married, they had a baby.

There were no major impediments to overcome—none that they could see at the time, anyway. But with Meg there were all kinds of obstacles. There was Allie. Her grandmother's ghost. An alleged crime. Geography. Family. Loyalty. Duty. A stupid dollhouse, for God's sake.

He heard a knock at the door without having heard a car pull up. His first triumphant thought was, *she's come by bike to say she's sorry.*

Heart pounding maniacally in his breast, he swung open the door to: Allie Atwells.

This he hadn't expected. She was a day early, dressed in a white-and-yellow jumpsuit with an interesting neckline that would've looked hokey on Meg but looked undeniably sensational on her. In general, he decided, Allie looked radiant. He'd forgotten how stunning a woman she was.

Her first words were, "I *love* your toddlin' town!"

"Welcome back," he said, his spirits hauled forcibly out of

the ditch by hers. "Where's your car?" he asked, glancing over her shoulder.

"Back at the road," she answered. "Your drive's too potholed," she added, bouncing past him into the living area. She took a seat on the couch, the only decent piece of furniture in the place, and crossed her legs in a Buddha pose. It was a mystery to him how she could combine such poise and such childish glee in one simple contortion.

She came straight to the point. Or points. "I got an offer!" she said elatedly. "At *least* one, the one as assistant manager at the Castle Inn on Halsted. The manager told me that as soon as he rolled my videotape, he knew that I was the one. He said experience isn't nearly as important as the fact that I'm obviously not afraid to work long hours—"

With a startled laugh he said, "Excuse me?"

"Wait; that's not the best part. In the bigger hotels you'd have to be prepared to move every couple of years, but the Castle Inn is *it;* it's not a chain."

"Isn't that a bit of a dead end for you, then?"

Puzzled, she said, "But it's on *Halsted*. It's close to where *you* work."

"What about the one at the Westin?" he urged. "Wouldn't that be better for your career?"

"My career?" she repeated, as if he'd just spoken to her in Russian. "The Westin is a lower-level job—desk clerk—and it's not at all convenient to where you are. . . ."

"But it's a Westin," he insisted. "You told me yourself that the best hotels promote from within. Shouldn't you have that in mind when you start somewhere?"

Impatiently she said, "Well, you never know. I might get an offer. But I'm really not interested. The Castle Inn is just so . . . *close*," she said enthusiastically.

Her eyes were bright with what he could only call willingness. It was obvious that she was waiting for him to show her just how great he thought the offer was. He wasn't able to do that. So he jumped up from the couch and said, "Coke, cider, seltzer—what'll you have?"

She was surprised by his manic leap, but she answered, "Coke's fine."

She went back to the Castle Inn. "Think how *close* we'd be. We wouldn't even have to fight rush-hour traffic—which I have to admit, is a real horror story out there—to meet at a club or for lunch or dancing or . . . or whatever!"

He filled two glasses with ice and thought, *Too far, it's gone way too far already. How do I jam a stick in her wheel without sending her flying over the handlebars?* "Yeah, well, my screwy hours . . ." he mumbled, trailing off.

"Thomas Wyler," she said in a low voice very close to his ear. "What is the *matter* with you?"

He turned and there she was: ready, willing, and willing. It was so obvious from the flush in her face; from the pouting expression on her lips; from the way she held herself for the embrace she was expecting to come. Dammit, why *wouldn't* she be expecting him to take her in his arms? He'd done it before, hadn't he? Hell, why not? God knows there were no obstacles standing in their way.

Except one.

"There's nothing wrong with me, Allie," he said as he filled the glasses. "There's something wrong with *us*." He took a deep breath, then let it out. Hoo-ee. Give him a patch of seaweed any time. "C'mon, kiddo," he said softly. "Sit down. We've got to talk."

He left the Cokes and took her by her arm and she let herself be led, stiffly, back to the couch. Suddenly the talk seemed superfluous; clearly she knew what was coming. All he could do now was try to let her down easy. He blushed even to think of himself having to do something like that with someone like her.

"Allie," he said, taking her hands in his. "You know I'm nuts about you. You're the prettiest woman I guess I've ever met. You've done more for my ego than any woman I know. You're fun . . . you're fearless . . . you have the energy of an Olympic skater.

"But . . . that's just it. You're *too* pretty. You're *too* energetic. You're so far beyond me that I can't—I'll never be able to—keep up, no matter how hard I try."

Her eyes opened wide. "You're not good enough for me, is that what this is?" she asked in a voice that seesawed between contempt and hope.

He shrugged. "We want different things. You want to set the world on fire, whereas at this point I'm just hoping the whole place doesn't burn down."

" 'At this point'? You're talking like some old guy in a rest home."

"Because I *am* an old guy."

"Forty is not old."

"Forty is relative. I'm an old forty, just like you're a young twenty-five."

"I'm not a child; don't treat me like one. You're just like Meg." She pulled her hands angrily out of his.

She was right, on both counts. Allie Atwells had just grown up in thirty-five seconds, right before his eyes. Nothing aged a person like rejection. He knew the lesson only too well: He'd been forced to learn it when he was four years old, on the day his mother abandoned him in a Sears Roebuck store on the northwest side.

"If you take the job in Chicago, Allie, take it because it's the best job you can find. Don't take it because it's a short commute to my office; that'd be the dumbest thing you could do."

She still didn't seem to—quite—want to accept it. "It's just not there, Allie," he said finally.

What "it" was, he had no idea. But he had an inkling that he'd found it in Acadia.

"Thank you," she said evenly, "for being so honest."

This time she got it. He could see it in her eyes. She'd pulled up the drawbridge, lowered the portcullis, heated the oil, and tossed a few snakes in the moat for good measure. Her invitation, in short, had been withdrawn.

Somewhere he read that no woman ever hates a man for being in love with her, but many a woman hates a man for being a friend to her. Whoever he was, the guy knew his stuff.

Allie stood up with a togetherness that reminded him uncannily of Meg, and then she walked over to the sink where the ice-filled glasses of Coke still stood. The ice was hardly melted; all things considered, his brush-off had been ruthlessly efficient.

She picked up one of the glasses and poured it down the drain. "I won't be needing *that* anymore," she said calmly, and walked out of his cabin.

He wondered exactly how she meant that.

When Allie arrived, dragging her heavy suitcase behind her, Meg was hunched over in the attic with an ice pick. Lloyd and a roofing contractor were there, too, also with ice picks, looking for rot. Their search was turning out to be a blinding success: the initial estimate for replacing some of the sheathing, a few rafters, and a new roof came to nearly ten thousand dollars.

"Ayeh. The day of the patch is over," the contractor was telling her. "Y'got three layers a' roofin' in some spots already. Water's working through 'em all, who knows from where. You try and add a fourth, yer only makin' a bad situation worse. You'll get more a' *this*," he said, plunging the ice pick up to its hilt into a rafter.

I've died and I've gone to hell, Meg thought.

She was hunched alongside her brother, who was still arguing gamely for patch number four. Sweat was streaming down all of their faces, but only Meg seemed fatally miserable. Maybe it had something to do with the fact that she hadn't slept in twenty-four hours. A series of thunderstorms had rolled through in the night, and the worst of the roof leaks had trickled its way to the fire alarm, setting it off and rousting every one of their guests out of bed. Twice.

That, coupled with the sleep-robbing heartbreak she'd felt since Acadia, had left her absolutely punchy. And now this. Ten thousand dollars. *Ten!* She almost couldn't take it in. She staggered over to the small attic window tucked under the peak and tried to suck in air that hadn't been preheated to a hundred and thirty degrees. That's when she saw her sister, home a day early, dragging her suitcase along the front walk.

Immediately Meg knew that something was wrong. "I'll see you when you're finished here, Mr. McLarty," she said abruptly, and scrambled down the access ladder. She found Allie in her room.

"What *happened*, honey?" she asked, her voice filled with concern. She'd never seen Allie look this way.

"I got dumped," her sister said without emotion as she swung the suitcase onto her bed.

"Oh, no," said Meg, misunderstanding her. "Which one? The Hyatt, the Westin? Surely not the Castle Inn!"

"No, no," Allie said tiredly. "The Castle Inn's a done deal. I'll know about the Westin in a week or two," she said, unfolding a smart two-piece suit in cobalt blue. "And the Hyatt obviously wants someone with more experience. No; I mean, dumped by Tom."

There are times in every person's life that are considered defining moments. The heart stops. Breathing stops. Time itself stops. And afterward, when the heart begins beating again and the clock begins ticking, the person remembers something trivial—what he was wearing, or listening to on the radio, or eating at the table. For Meg, the moment was distilled into the two baseball caps, obviously intended for the twins, that Allie took out of her suitcase just then: one from the Chicago Cubs, the other from the White Sox.

Terry will want the Sox cap, flashed through Meg's mind. *Because the Cubs are too cute.*

"I went straight to Tom's cabin," Allie explained in a voice that was completely unlike her own. "You remember how I was going to offer myself officially to him, since he didn't seem to be taking the hint? Well," she said, pulling out a satin nightie that Meg had never seen before, "I never got the chance. He beat me to the punch. He said there was nothing there."

My God. "He didn't."

"Ah, but he did. It took guts, I'll say that," she said as she scrutinized the nightie, then tossed it in the direction of the hamper. "Not many men would risk making me feel like an idiot. In fact, your lieutenant is the first."

Her lieutenant? Why hers? What had Tom told her? Obviously, nothing about Meg and him. Meg tried to distract her sister with humor. "Assuming you hadn't already torn off your clothes, I see no reason why you should've felt like an idiot."

Allie stopped unpacking and gave her sister a look of—Meg didn't know what. Contempt? Was it possibly that?

"Meg, it's over. Skip the spoonful of sugar; the medicine's gone *down*." She took out the last of her things, closed the suitcase, and slid it under her bed.

"But look, *every*one's heart gets broken sooner or later, Allie. You've just led a very charmed life, that's all." Meg didn't know how to comfort her. She didn't have the words; the situation was unique.

"You're right," Allie agreed in a toneless voice. "The first failure's the worst. I'll be much more philosophical about the second one."

Somehow it didn't seem as if they were talking about love anymore. It frightened Meg. She'd spent the whole night rehearsing a confession of her betrayal to Allie; now, wild horses couldn't drag it out of her. Suddenly the rules had changed. She needed time to think them through.

"Allie, you have your whole *life*—"

"If you don't mind, Meg, I'm tired. Do you need me to do anything? If not, I'd like to go to bed."

"At seven fifteen?"

But Allie was practically weaving as she stood, which conjured up other, more painful moments when she could hardly stand. *Was* she simply exhausted? Meg tried to get closer to her, to smell her breath. But Allie averted her head, unwilling to accept her sister's embrace, and Meg was forced to smile and say, "Sleep around the clock, then. It'll help; trust me."

Over the next week the Inn Between, like an old dowager in poor health, endured several further indignities. The refrigerator suffered a nervous breakdown and had to be replaced. Coughdrop managed to get wrapped up in the extension cord of Comfort's beloved Bunn coffeemaker, pulling it to the floor and smashing it to bits. The new chambermaid got a better offer and quit. A small electrical fire—insignificant, really— caused an impromptu electrical inspection and resulted in a list of violations and a deadline for repairs. And—the worst affront of all—one of the guests sneaked in a sadistic dachshund who chewed a hole in the middle of Meg's favorite hooked rug.

And, of course, the roof still leaked. There was only one cure for the Inn Between: money. *We need more of it.* And yet Meg couldn't sell the dollhouse; she couldn't. A deathbed promise and a spiritual connection that Meg still didn't understand made that impossible.

But they *needed* more money. The refrain pounded like a dull headache through Meg's consciousness day after day, mishap after mishap. *Money, money, money* . . .

If she could've shared her troubles with Allie, she might've been able to appreciate the darkly funny side of them. But

Allie was unapproachable. It wasn't that she was angry or pouting or obviously in pain. In fact, she was more courteous than usual, and less complaining, as she went about her chores. But she never laughed, she never yelled, and she never, ever cried. Meg was sure; she listened at the door.

"Whatsa matter with Anty Allie?" Terry had asked. "She's like a zombie."

"A nice one, though," Timmy had added, yanking on the bill of his new Cubs cap.

And in the meantime, no Tom. He was as good as his word —Meg knew he would be—and was leaving Meg, and now Allie, alone. Meg was having her first taste of what life without him would be like: dry and bitter. As for Allie, it was hard to say.

Dorothea Camplin's "camp," as the summer visitors liked to call their seasonal retreats, was smaller than her ex-husband's house but easily as big as the Inn Between. It had a quainter name than most—Tea Kettle Cottage—and was situated on a large parcel of land outside of town with no view of the sea. Mrs. Camplin, it turned out, did not care for the sea.

The stout, elderly woman put it more precisely than that. "It's not the sea I object to; it's the salt that's in it. Salt spray wreaks havoc with my perennials. One should be able to grow something besides thrift and milkweed if one chooses. And of course one wants roses. After the Great Fire I came back to Bar Harbor, and this is what I found. I've spent my summers here quite happily since."

Meg was busy scribbling every word on a steno pad, doing her best to look like a feature writer. She was dressed to please in a cabbage-rose print and a straw hat rimmed in pink ribbon. For whatever reason, at the last minute she threw on the teardrop earrings as well.

"This is absolutely wonderful," she said with genuine pleasure as she glanced around between jottings.

The gardens were rambling, secret, and charmingly spectacular. No one would have guessed it from the road. Each garden "room," as they said in the trade, was more exquisite than the last, from the all-white garden near the towering chestnut trees, to the carefree border of mixed-color perennials, to the island of larkspur, Madonna lilies, and Canterbury bells. There were fountains—one of bronze, one of marble—strategically located, and birdbaths high and low, and feeders where the sunflower seeds could drop discreetly without making a mess. There was a delightful spontaneity about all of it that Meg knew could only come from a completely controlling hand.

Almost in answer to Meg's thoughts, Mrs. Camplin said, "I pride myself on doing all but the very heaviest digging myself. That border over there? I double-dug every cubic inch of it last summer. Manuel—my Cuban gardener, who's been with me for thirty years and is as decrepit as I am—tells me I'm going to give *him* a heart attack one of these days, just from worrying," she said, chuckling.

"Incidentally," she added, "I'm one of the few who employs a gardener full-time; estate gardeners are truly a dying breed. I took Manuel on when I acquired my own house in Palm Beach. Between the two places there's more than enough work. The fact is, gardening can be a full-time hobby . . . it becomes an obsession for so many of us. I suppose it's a personality thing."

Meg scribbled away, nodding furiously. "You have to have many skills, patience among them," she agreed. "You have to have foresight . . . and a love of beauty . . . a fine sense of color and balance—"

"And grim determination, of course," said Mrs. Camplin, laughing. "Don't forget to write *that* down."

Meg agreed completely. "Gardening isn't for the faint-hearted," she said, thinking of how easily Allie became bored with weeding.

"How well you know, dear. You have your own garden, then?"

"It's nothing at all, compared to this," Meg said at once, dismissing the question. She had no desire to have this portly, amiable woman show up at her door for a tour and discover who, exactly, Meg Hazard really was: *Margaret Mary Atwells Hazard, local rumormonger*. Not yet, anyway.

Mrs. Camplin motioned Meg to sit next to her on an old bench that once had graced a churchyard in Wales. From the bench they had a fine view of the house, a rambling, gabled two-story structure with an attached greenhouse that dated to the 1900's, as well as the herb and cutting gardens behind it.

"I'm so inspired," Meg said, sighing. "I want to go back and level my house and turn all the land into a garden."

"And where do you live, dear?" asked Mrs. Camplin.

Mistake. "Oh . . . in town," Meg said vaguely.

Mrs. Camplin looked at her oddly but didn't press. Meg said pleasantly, "I wanted to ask you about your previous summer place . . . Eagle's Nest could not have had such cozy gardens, could it? The site wasn't at all the same."

"Oh, dear me, no. Eagle's Nest was on high ground, wide open to the north. The winters took their toll. It was so discouraging to come back each summer and see how much I'd lost. Not that there was much to lose. Mr. Camplin had little use for a flower garden. Too frivolous," his ex-wife said dryly. "His tastes were more basic than that."

Meg thought she heard acrimony, even after all these years of being divorced—a hopeful sign. She said, "Mr. Camplin seems to know what he likes. His new place—well, hardly new, anymore—is still imposing, still on high ground . . . and, I assume, still without a flower garden?"

"I wouldn't know," Mrs. Camplin said shortly. "I've never been there."

Excellent. "It must have been a grand old place—Eagle's Nest, I mean," said Meg, inching sideways toward her goal.

"I've read where some of the bigger cottages that burned down had thirty rooms. Eagle's Nest had, I believe—?"

"Only eighteen, including the maids' rooms."

So the dollhouse *was* an accurate replica. "Ah. Only eighteen. So it didn't have all the bells and whistles—secret corridors for the servants to come and go, a grand ballroom, that sort of thing?"

"Not at all. One wing had guest accommodations, and the other had our bedrooms and dressing rooms. The living quarters were on the first floor, the nursery and servants' quarters on the third. It was all very straightforward."

Yeah. For a small castle.

Meg knew from the dollhouse that the master bedroom, bound on one side by its own dressing room, led directly into a sitting room for the mistress of the house, which in turn led to her own bedroom. Meg's theory was that after Gordon Camplin raped her grandmother, he locked her in the master bedroom and left her there to die in the fire that was already nibbling at the edges of the estate. Why else would Meg have pounded on empty air and screamed "Open it!" so hysterically during her little séance in the shed? What Meg needed to know now was whether every door into or out of the master's bedroom—there were three—could be locked.

This was not an easy question to camouflage.

"I suppose running a grand house the size of Eagle's Nest was like running a small business," Meg ventured. "All those rooms . . . all those servants . . . I can just imagine what the key ring looked like!"

Nothing.

"Or maybe the house was more modern than that. Maybe the doors to the rooms didn't even have any locks?"

"For heaven's sake," Mrs. Camplin remarked, staring. "What an odd question. Of course they had locks. For security as well as privacy. I myself used to keep my favorite jewelry in my bedroom, in a covered jar."

She shook her head, wondering at the memory. "I'd never *think* of doing that nowadays, of course. Not after what happened to a friend of mine in Newport. Robbed in her own bedroom, while she slept. Twice. These are terrible times. Terrible. No one is safe anymore."

For one brief moment the strong and capable Mrs. Camplin looked like some fragile old lady at a bus stop, clutching her purse more tightly as a pack of teenagers in running shoes approached. But the moment passed as the wealthy socialite remembered who she was and where she was.

"Anyway," she said in a friendly but puzzled voice, "what does this have to do with my gardens at Tea Kettle?"

Not a heck of a lot. Meg had to temporize. "Well, one of the questions our readers like to see addressed is which rooms face the garden—kitchen, breakfast room, master bedroom. . . . I guess I was wondering, not only about Tea Kettle Cottage, but about your previous summer house."

"My bedrooms *always* face the garden; that goes without saying. But at Eagle's Nest the trees overhung the view of the grounds; it was hard to see much. That house was dark; very dark inside," she added, shuddering. "I never cared for it. I prefer a bright, sunny room. Don't you?"

Meg remembered the gay floral print on the walls of the mistress's bedroom in the dollhouse. She smiled and said, "Yes, ma'am, I do."

Mrs. Camplin cocked her head and looked at Meg curiously. "Now whom did you just remind me of?" she wondered aloud, intrigued.

Suddenly self-conscious, Meg made matters worse by nervously fiddling with one of her teardrop earrings. "I look like just about everyone, I've been told," she said, flushing.

"Perhaps," agreed Mrs. Camplin. She stood up, clearly still trying to make the connection, and signaled an end to the interview, "Now: what about the photos?"

Meg explained that she'd be shooting the shade garden today, but that it was too sunny for close-ups of some of the lilies and paler flowers. Those, she'd like to come back and do on an overcast or even a foggy day. Mrs. Camplin agreed, and they strolled back to the house, taking in the sights and scents around them.

"I'm so glad I found this place," confessed Dorothea Camplin contentedly when they reached the house. "I can't imagine living anywhere else in Maine."

Meg seized the opening and said something that she realized too late was truly stupid. She said, "So in a way the Great Fire was a blessing?"

Dorothea Camplin stopped where she was, pushed her bifocals back up her nose, and stared at Meg. "What a perverse way of looking at it! The fire was a great tragedy," she said in a scolding tone. "We lost a member of our staff in that fire. I suppose that this is what happens after time," she said, viciously yanking out a nervy clump of Queen Anne's lace. "Young people become desensitized to the tragedies of the last generation."

"I didn't mean it the way it came out," Meg said quickly. "I only meant to suggest that, well . . . you *did* end up with the house of your dreams," she said lamely.

Mrs. Camplin shook her head mournfully. "But at a price, young lady . . . at a price."

19

Uncle Billy, who was the mover and the shaker in the Atwells clan, decided that Meg needed moving and Allie needed shaking. He'd heard rumors about what he called Allie's little "tiff" with Tom, and he'd got blow-by-blow accounts from Comfort of the latest setbacks at the Inn Between. He decided to kill two birds with one stone by inviting both Tom and an interested collector of dolls' houses—a Mr. Peterson—to the Inn Between for Chicken Pie Night.

Meg was outraged.

"That *pushy* old bastard!" she said to her sister. "He's too damn tight to give us a hand—not that I'd want him to; we can pay our own way—and yet he's too damn meddling to just let us be. He drives me *crazy*. I don't know *why* Dad puts up with his butting in all the time."

Allie laid out the eighth, ninth, and tenth plates on the supper table and said, "That isn't why you're mad, Meg. You're mad because Uncle Billy is playing matchmaker between Tom and me," she said with supreme, unintended irony. "But *I* don't care, and you shouldn't, either."

"And I *don't* understand why Tom is coming." How *dare* he, after all that had happened?

"Don't blame Tom," Allie said in a weary voice. "I suppose he was just trying to help, passing on Mr. Peterson's name to Uncle Billy.''

"Which is another thing. Why pass it on to Uncle Billy? Why not directly to me?" Meg slammed down a knife and then a fork beside each plate. She knew the answer to *that* question, of course, but it felt good to complain.

Allie avoided looking at her sister as she said, "Maybe Tom knew how reluctant you'd be to sell the dollhouse."

"Not true!" Meg cried. "I'm not reluctant. I'm just not . . . ready." It was pointless to try to explain to Allie about the continued presence Meg still felt in and around the dollhouse. Allie had never felt it, and though at first she'd humored Meg, now she was too caught up in her own pain to care one way or the other.

Meg glanced across the table at her sister. Allie seemed to physically droop, like a daisy without water. Granted, they were in the grip of yet another heat wave; but that wasn't it. It broke Meg's heart to see her like this. Somehow she hoped that Allie would be too proud to grieve.

"Allie . . . honey . . . you don't have to stick around for supper."

"Where would I go?" Allie asked, sighing. "Besides, it's Chicken Pie Night."

"Big deal; *every* Wednesday is Chicken Pie Night," Meg said, just itching to rail at something. "That's the whole problem around here! *Everything's* predictable. *Everything's* a habit. No one has any—I don't know—*gumption*. No one has any plain old get-up-and-go. You're right, Allie. We're all just rotting in place here, like the rafters of the Inn Between."

Meg gave her sister a sideways look. "Thank God *you're* not like the rest of us. Thank God *you* have bigger plans. You can go anywhere in the world: New York, Paris, L.A. . . . Some day you'll look back on Chicken Pie Night and laugh."

Allie had finished her task and was on her way out of the

dining room. At the door she turned, eyes glistening, and said, "All lies; but thanks anyway, Meggie."

Meg wanted to lie more, but the arrival of Uncle Billy ended all that.

"Comfort Atwells!" Meg heard him shout in the kitchen. "Look at you: rosy cheeks and big as a barn door! You look *good*, de-ah! Motherhood do agree with you."

Comfort giggled and murmured something and Meg heard Uncle Billy say, "Where's your sister-in-law? I hear she's gunnin' for me."

When he came into the dining room, Meg fired both barrels.

"Uncle Billy," she said without preamble, "When I need help finding a buyer for the dollhouse, I suppose I'll ask for it! Until then I wish you wouldn't treat it like a toaster at a two-family yard sale! I don't have time to listen to insulting offers from every flea-market customer passing through town. When it's time—*if* it's ever time—"

"Whoa, whoa, let up, will you?" he said, ducking to avoid her wrath. "In the first place, I don't know this Peterson jeezer from Adam; it's Tom Wyler who insists he's more'n just a handshaker. Second place: from what I hear, it *is* time, Meggie," he said seriously. "Time to sell."

He was such a big bear of a man. His voice carried such authority. It was hard for Meg to do what she did just then—to stand up to him and say, "No, Uncle Billy. It's not for sale."

William Atwells didn't take kindly to the word *no*. Everyone knew that, from his younger brother Everett to the woman in Bangor who'd refused his hand in marriage thirty-one years earlier.

He scowled his trademark scowl. "I don't want to hear none a' that bilge from you, young lady," he said, hitching his pants over his potbelly. "When I kick the bucket, you and the rest will be well provided for. But until then I expect to see this family stand on its own two feet. Now, Tom knows someone who knows someone who put this Peterson fella on to the dollhouse. Okay. So here's the plan: We're gonna stuff this rube with Comfort's chicken pie, and then we're gonna roll him out to the shed and show him the most gorgeous friggin' dollhouse he ever did see. We're gonna make him beg for it. We're gonna make him cry in pain that he don't have it. And we're gonna make him offer cold, hard cash for it. And then— *only* then—will you decide whether you'll sell or not.''

He thumped three times on the dinner table with his middle finger. ''Because, little Meggie, *everything* in this world is for sale—whether you like it, or whether you don't.''

The front doorbell rang and Terry let out a whoop and ran to answer it. As promised, Tom Wyler was delivering Mr. Peterson, ready for stuffing, to their door.

Meg and her uncle Billy, each with his own agenda, rushed to the front door to intercept their guests. Mr. Peterson was small, thin, meek, bespectacled, and didn't look as if he had two nickels to rub together, much less the cost of a dollhouse that was fit for royalty. Meg gave him one glance and turned to Tom, who was wearing a jacket and tie and looked as if he'd rather be standing on a mat of hot coals than on the threshold of the Inn Between.

Obviously he'd been strong-armed by Uncle Billy into coming. All right, then. The best thing was just to smile and be polite and wait for all three men to go away. She could do that.

Introductions were made and pleasantries exchanged. Uncle Billy sized Mr. Peterson up and down, then smiled at Meg and whispered in her ear, ''Like eatin' pie.''

After that he scooped up Mr. Peterson the way a grizzly would a brook trout and hauled him into the family's sitting room, leaving Tom and Meg to follow in their wake.

''I'm sorry about this,'' Tom murmured. ''I didn't expect to be part of the deal. Your uncle insisted.''

''I believe I've told you I'm not selling,'' Meg said, smiling.

Tom shrugged. ''Okay. Fine.''

"Please don't use that tone of *fine* with me," Meg said, smiling.

"What the hell tone do you *expect* me to—"

"Or that tone, either," Meg said, smiling.

"Damn! Your uncle's right about you!"

"Thank you. It's nice of you to say so," Meg said—still smiling.

They commandeered seats at opposite ends of the sitting room. Uncle Billy took over as host, pouring drinks, chatting amiably about life in a resort town, asking an occasional question of Mr. Peterson, reeling him in slowly.

It turned out that Meg was right: Mr. Peterson did *not* have the necessary nickels. He was in fact an expert on miniatures, commissioned by an investor who'd got it in his head that dollhouses were a hot collectible. Mr. Peterson had taken pains to advise "this particular gentleman" that collectibles ran hot and cold.

"But with real estate depressed, the market stagnant, and interest rates so low, this particular gentleman is hard pressed to turn a profit," Mr. Peterson confessed between nibbles on a Ritz cracker. "He believes that antiques and collectibles may be in the process of bottoming out."

"They're a damn good hedge against inflation," avowed Uncle Billy.

"If we had inflation," responded Mr. Peterson.

"Beats buyin' waterfront on a flood plain," countered Uncle Billy.

"My client lives on high ground," said Mr. Peterson.

And on it went. Mr. Peterson gave as good as he got, to the point that Uncle Billy was becoming a little flustered. He decided, abruptly, to change the subject.

"Say, where's Allie, anyway?" he demanded in a petulant voice. He turned to his guest and gave him a knowing elbow. "My niece is just about the most fetchin' thing in New England. Wait till you see her. Meg? Where is she?"

"Allie will be on display shortly," said Meg, annoyed with her uncle in more ways than she could count.

He gave her an evil look and added, "Whereas her sister, here, is just about the most *aggravatin'*."

Tom Wyler took the opportunity to mutter, "I'll second that."

Lloyd had arrived through the kitchen, clearly in a good mood. Meg heard Comfort yelp the way wives yelp when liberties are being taken, and heard Lloyd's low laugh of amusement. Still smiling, he strolled right into the middle of an awkward lull that was hanging over the sitting room like a big wet cloud.

"Hey, Uncle Billy, whaddya think?" he asked in his usual Down East greeting.

"I think damn, that's what I think!" Uncle Billy answered, sulking.

Because he didn't say it in his usual hearty way, Lloyd became immediately cautious. He looked to his sister for a clue. Meg gave him a tight-lipped smile. Everett Atwells showed up hard on his son's heels, also in a good mood—his usual mood—and was introduced to Mr. Peterson. Right after that Comfort came in to take away the cracker plate and tell them shyly, "Supper's about ready."

It was obvious that Allie didn't have the heart to make an appearance. With a reproachful look at Tom, Meg said, "My sister won't be joining us after all, Mr. Peterson."

"She's been in a decline," Uncle Billy explained in a grave voice.

"Oh . . . I'm so sorry," said Mr. Peterson.

"It's nothing terminal," Meg said icily.

"Her heart's broke," blurted Lloyd.

"Hearts can't break," said Terry caustically.

"Yes they can," said his twin. "That's what happened to Great-Grampa when Great-Gramma burned. Isn't that right, Grampa?"

"Burned?" said Mr. Peterson faintly.

"In the Great Fire," Meg explained. "It's part of the history—the provenance, isn't that what you collectors call it?—of the dollhouse, which is a replica of one of the grand Bar Harbor cottages that burned in 1947. Surely my uncle told you that? Doesn't that add to the value?" she asked in bitterly ironic tones.

"I didn't know someone died. I'm sorry," murmured Mr. Peterson, clearly uncomfortable.

"That doesn't make the dollhouse cursed, though," Timmy said earnestly. "Even though we've had awful things happen to us ever since we got it."

"Not so much awful as unexplainable," his twin brother elaborated. "Like one night everything in the dollhouse got thrown around every which way. As if a poltergeist lived there."

"How did *you* know that?" Meg said, scandalized.

"I saw you putting everything back," Terry said.

"What were *you* doing up at that hour?" his grandfather asked.

"Does that add to the value, a curse?" Lloyd wondered.

"Of course it does," said Uncle Billy. "Notoriety has a *definite* dollar value."

Meg glanced around the sitting room. There was a certain bizarre feel to the conversation that she would've normally shared with Allie. But Allie wasn't there. As for Tom—it was true that he was following the talk with that wry, amused look that set her heart singing, but—as far as Meg was concerned, he was the tenth plate at the table. No more, no less.

She looked away from him and began a friendly conversation with her father, who had absolutely no idea what anyone was talking about.

"We're selling, then?" Everett Atwells said in a whisper to his daughter. "I thought we weren't."

Meg whispered back, "We're not selling, Dad. This is just to humor Uncle Billy."

Just her luck that all the other conversations tailed off at the same time, leaving her remark hanging in midair like a pair of ratty underpants alone on a clothesline. Embarrassed, Meg fell back into hostile silence.

The hell with it, she decided. *I've had it up to here with them.* She let her glance drift around the room, from Uncle Billy's red suspenders to Mr. Peterson's wing-tip shoes to the cross-stitch sampler—Allie's one and only attempt at needlework—that Meg had got tired of waiting for and had hung on the wall unfinished: HOME SWEET HO, it read.

Only once did she risk glancing at Tom. He had taken the overstuffed chair that was tucked in a corner of the sitting room—the gunfighter's chair, her father liked to call it—and was watching Meg with an intensity that seemed to set her on fire. This was nothing like the bland, disinterested detective's look he reserved for group occasions. This was personal. This was white-hot. He was as focused as a laser beam, and he was focused on her. She looked away, in danger of a meltdown.

And so they sat, Meg and all the men in her life, while she waited for Comfort to call people in to eat so that supper could finally be over with and all the men in her life would go away. But it was Allie who showed up first.

"Allie! How's your headache?" Meg said, covering for what she assumed would be her sister's glum mood.

Allie laughed gaily and said, "You know I never get headaches. Uncle Billy! *Comment ça va?*" she asked in her most cosmopolitan tone. "And *this* must be Mr. Peterson. It's an honor to meet you, sir," she said, taking his hand. "I understand you're an expert in your field. You won't be disappointed with the dollhouse, I promise you. It's a treasure."

She turned to Tom with a smile of radiant confidence. "Tom! You were able to come after all! It's good to see you looking so well. Don't let me forget: I still have three novels of yours. Well, everyone? Shall we go in?''

She slipped her arm through Tom's, surprising everyone, especially Tom, and led the company into the dining room. Meg went in behind Terry, who pinched his twin brother's arm and whispered, ''I *told* you hearts can't break.''

But Meg could see into her sister's heart, and it was breaking. The more Allie laughed and joked and entertained them all, the more Meg was convinced of it. Allie was behaving exactly as Meg had wished: too proud to grieve. But once or twice in the course of dinner, Meg caught Allie stealing a glance at Tom. That was when her mask slipped, and Meg could see the pain.

But Meg was the only one who could see it. Allie was a perfect actress and a perfect hostess, an unbeatable combination for hiding her feelings. She had a funny story to tell for every job she'd ever held—from saddling a llama in a children's petting zoo to hypnotizing lobsters before she turned them into seafood salad at a dockside snack bar. Everyone laughed, including Meg, including Tom; Mr. Peterson was in stitches. Uncle Billy looked over at Meg every once in a while as if to say, ''See? If you wanted to be useful, *this* is what you'd be like.''

But Allie was *too* funny. Her laugh was *too* gay. Her dress, for that matter, was too red. Everything about her was right at the edge, maybe a little over the edge, and it frightened Meg.

Eventually Comfort said, as she always did on Wednesday, ''More chicken pie, Uncle Billy?''

That was when something in Allie snapped. In a perfect imitation of her uncle, Allie boomed out, ''Just a whiska, maybe,'' at the same time that he did, much to his chagrin. Then she jumped up and said to Meg, ''You're right, Meggie. It's all so predictable!'' And she rushed out of the room.

That pretty much put a damper on the supper. There was dessert, of course—peach pie and ice cream—but Tom begged off and Mr. Peterson mumbled something about an early flight. Uncle Billy, jumping in to save the sale, said, *"I'll* drive Tom home. Mr. Peterson, you stay and take all the time you need to look over the dollhouse. No hurry now. Meg, take him out to the shed. You got plenty a' light there? Comfort, you just wrap my pie to go. Give me Tom's piece, too, since he don't want it. I'll bring the car round front."

Tom said good-night to the rest of the family. Then, while Mr. Peterson freshened up, he corralled Meg in the hall.

He leaned one arm into the wall, blocking her from slipping past him. "Is this it?" he asked in a voice wound tight from the effort to sound casual. "Good-bye?"

She shrugged and looked away. "You're the one who passed on the pie."

He took her arm. *"Dammit,* Meg. I want a straight answer. For once!"

She forced herself to look in his eyes. "Okay. The straight answer is, *good-bye.* Again!"

"That's not an answer," he shot back. "That's a stall. You know this isn't good-bye. You know this isn't over. Why are you playing the martyr? What're you waiting for? Allie to get married? She's not the marrying kind. Not to me; not to anyone."

"How would you know what kind she is? Or me, for that matter? The only one who's not the marrying kind around here is *you,* Lieutenant. Which makes you a dime a dozen. So pack up your emotions where they'll be safe: in your suitcase. Go back to Chicago, Tom. Go back to your career; go back to your murders. Go back to your hell."

She glanced at her arm where he still held her, then gave him a withering look. "Even *I* know that that constitutes an assault," she said coldly.

Stunned by her fury, he released her.

Meg brushed past him, her eyes glazed over with tears, hating herself for having done that, hating him for having made her do it. She found Mr. Peterson and led him hurriedly out the back, her conversation with him dinned by the sound of the horn on Uncle Billy's Cadillac, hurrying Tom out of the Inn Between.

Right off the bat, Mr. Peterson was displeased to learn that the dollhouse was being stored in a shed that wasn't climate controlled. Once he saw the dollhouse itself, he shook his head and murmured, "This is not good."

Meg said defensively, "The insurance company said it was okay, as long as the shed is secure."

"That window is exposed to—the west? A hot afternoon sun beating down on the dollhouse? Weathering the paint; bleaching the fabrics and wallpaper inside? What were you thinking, Mrs. Hazard? And some of these dolls—oh, dear, oh, my—are *wax*. In a heat wave like this they could easily melt. Well," he said, shaking his head fatalistically. "Let's see what we have here."

He began a preliminary tour of the house, circling it without a word, holding a magnifying lens to it here and there to study its construction. Meg watched anxiously from the sidelines. She'd become as fiercely protective of the dollhouse as Orel Tremblay had been; she'd be crushed if any harm came to it on her watch.

"It was built way back in the Depression," she said, quietly proud.

"The oldest existing dollhouse dates back four and a half centuries," Peterson said, puncturing her boast.

"Yes, but this is an *exact* replica of a significant Bar Harbor cottage," Meg said, unwilling to yield superiority to any other dollhouse.

"The English commonly had dollhouses made of their country estates," Mr. Peterson said matter-of-factly.

"Yes, but this was made by the estate's own carpenters."

"That, too, is an English practice," he said, studying an

alabaster table set for tea in the mistress's bedroom. "Was the original owner of any prominence?"

"The millionaire who commissioned it? He was a New York merchant, I think," Meg answered.

"Oh. Not an ambassador or playwright or newspaper publisher, then. Nothing to do with Campbell Soup? Ivory Soap?"

The man knew his Bar Harbor history. He picked up a tiny cream-colored serving dish and said, "Hmm. Leeds Ware," then put it back. Meg had no idea whether that was good or bad.

"Marie Antoinette had a dollhouse," he remarked, picking up a tiny woven basket from the kitchen. "Frederick, Prince of Wales, actually *built* dollhouses as a hobby. Queen Anne— still a princess at the time—gave a house, now quite famous, to her godchild Ann Sharp."

"I see what you're getting at," said Meg, annoyed by his condescending tone. "But this house has no alluring ownership associated with it." *Far from it*, she thought bitterly.

"Your uncle said it was a gift?" Mr. Peterson inquired with a bland look. "And that the benefactor has since passed away?"

"Yes. My grandmother worked as a nursemaid for a summer at Eagle's Nest, the mansion I spoke of. The owner of the dollhouse, who once worked there as well, gave it to me because of that . . . connection," she said, for lack of a better word.

"Recently?"

"Last month." She hated telling him that. It implied that she was in a hurry to sell, which was playing right into his hands. Meg didn't want to turn down an offer that was insulting; she wanted to turn down an offer that was impressive. For Mr. Tremblay's sake.

"You foresee no problems with probate, then?" he asked mildly.

"No," she said, surprised. "Why should I?"

"Well, good. Now. Let's have a look at these dolls. It's quite an interesting collection," he said in a strangely controlled voice. "Quite interesting."

He picked up the master doll, a mustachioed fellow in late-nineteenth-century dinner dress that Meg had positioned in the billiard room with a soldier doll and another gentleman doll. "Yes . . . the head is of unglazed bisque . . . quite common, really."

Peterson picked up each of the two other man dolls, examined it, and put it back in place. "The soldier doll is different from the other two . . . what we call a blond bisque. The bisque is tinted, you see. Yes . . . hard to find, especially in a man doll. The sword is a nice touch."

The mistress doll was next, plucked from the dining room where she'd been supervising the laying of the dinner table. Mr. Peterson could not suppress a sigh of pleasure as he turned the doll this way and that and examined its green-velvet gown. He returned the doll to her spot on the twelve-inch Oriental rug.

"*Very* fine," he said. "You understand that it's rare to find inset glass eyes in a bisque of this type. Ah, and the pierced ears. A truly fine—although, as I say, unglazed bisques for dollhouses were very common and continued to be made well into the 1920's."

It was obvious to Meg that Peterson was excited about the dolls themselves and was struggling mightily not to show it. When he stumbled in delight on the white-haired lady doll tucked in a four-poster bed and suffering from a doll cold, he said breathlessly, "Tell me . . . does she have a mate?"

"No," said Meg dryly. "She's a widow."

He let out a disappointed groan. "*Tragic.*" He went on to examine every one of the other dolls: the four ladies in the stucco-ceilinged drawing room who were so stunningly dressed in satin and taffeta; the young man doll, dressed like a dandy, who attended them there; the cook in the kitchen and the butler in the pantry (papier mâché, Peterson said, barely interested); the wooden chore-girl doll, which he considered crude but quite charming; the wax-headed maid dolls turning down the beds and cleaning the hearths of the guest bedrooms; the boy bisque, the baby bisque. He loved them all.

"Do you have *any* idea what you have here?" he asked Meg when he was finished. When she looked at him blankly he said impatiently, "You have virtually a complete family of bisques. It's rare to find a doll family intact; if you had the grandfather, the collection would be of even more value. The family itself is probably German. The bodies are excellently made."

"Ah," Meg said politely.

"The lady guests are undoubtedly French. You can see that their faces are nothing much, although a brown-eyed porcelain head is admittedly rare—but look at the clothes. Magnificent! Definitely French. Some of the poured-wax maid dolls are English; they're of excellent quality, but the limbs are almost all replacements, so naturally the value will be low. But of course you knew that," he said in a cutting voice.

"It's obvious that I didn't," Meg admitted. "I haven't had the time to research."

"I suppose not," he said snappishly, "or you'd be taking better care of it all."

He pressed the tips of his fingers together and eyed the dollhouse thoughtfully. The house positively glowed, as if it were doing its best to bring him under its spell. Meg was absurdly, irrationally proud of it, as if *she* were the one who'd carved the staircase and crocheted the mantel cloth and upholstered the chaise longue; as if *she* were the one who'd hand blocked the wallpaper and gilded the mirrors and lacquered the piano.

She wasn't. The simple truth was, she was merely the house's caretaker, and apparently not a very good one at that.

But she was connected to this exquisite toy in a way that Mr. Peterson's particular gentleman could never be. Her soul hummed to a strange, mystical vibration when anyone else got near her dollhouse. It was that simple.

Peterson began one more turn around the outside of the house—like a burglar who's trying to figure out where the silver is, Meg thought—and his eye fell on the one doll that wasn't inside the house. Meg had removed the nursemaid doll —the Margaret Mary Atwells doll—on the night before. She wasn't sure why; she still didn't know. In some strange way, she was probably hoping to give her grandmother's spirit a break from haunting.

He picked the doll up at once, his curiosity piqued. "Another poured-wax doll," he said, "but nothing like the others. How very odd."

Immediately Meg felt something tense inside of her. She said, "How is it different?"

"It's clearly not from the same dollmaker as the English maid dolls. Obviously this doll was done in multiple pourings. Look at the cheeks, the lifelike blush in them. The color was put in before the last pouring of wax. It's a superb finish: no seams, excellent detail, complete realism. This is an example of remarkable skill."

He motioned Meg, who had begun hanging back, to come closer. "But look at the face," he mused, "at all the fine crazing in it. This doll has been played with—or manhandled —much more than the other wax dolls."

Some meaning behind his innocently spoken words made Meg begin to tremble. Her heart took off at a flyaway beat; she shook her head at the doll expert, declining to come near.

But he insisted. "And come—look at this," he said, holding his magnifying glass over the doll's chestnut-colored hair for her to see. "You can see that the original hair, which was laboriously inserted strand by strand and then sealed over— that hair has been cut away. And this hair, human hair, has been inserted in a similar way, probably with a hot instrument as in the original, and then sealed over again. Not as expertly as in the original, but not at all a bad redo. Extraordinary.''

"Your hair is very beautiful, Margaret . . . thick, silky, pleasing to the touch. Don't bundle it up. Let it hang loose . . . like so."

"Mrs. Hazard? Can you see what I mean?"

Meg shuddered and said, "I didn't know that it was human hair."

"Oh, yes. That's not unusual. Perhaps the original hair was black—an unpopular color—or perhaps some little girl donated a lock of her own hair to replace the original. In fact, this hair is very much like yours in texture, although your hair has more highlights to it. Still, it *is* too bad; naturally the alteration devalues the doll."

"Naturally," said Meg faintly.

"The dress is also not original, of course," he said. "Every other doll in this collection is dressed in late-nineteenth-century. This one alone seems to be wearing a dress from the mid-twentieth. What a shame."

"Yes . . . a shame," she said over the thunder of her pounding heart.

"That's a pretty frock you're wearing. Lavender suits you. But you deserve silk. Silk, and fine jewels . . . I lied about the earrings, Margaret Mary. The pearls are real. How could I give you less? Let me touch you. Please . . ."

"Ah, but the good news is that the limbs are original to the doll. They're poured, not dipped. Look at the tinting of the skin; the color matches the head perfectly. Oh, this is excellent." His voice was hoarse with pleasure. *"Excellent.* Wax limbs are so easily broken. Think of some angry child, hurling a wax-limb doll across a bed." Peterson rolled his eyes. "One shudders to imagine."

"Yes," Meg said, tears slipping down her cheeks.

"Let me! Let me touch you. Let me hold you. Please . . . I

won't be long. I can't think of anything else . . . just this once, let me. The fire? What do I care about the fire? I'll burn either way—if you have me or if you don't. Damn you, Margaret!"

"I wonder . . . would you mind if I undressed this doll? I'd like to go over it for a manufacturer's mark. There's little hope I'll find one, but I'm *deathly* curious to know."

"Oh, Mr. Peterson," Meg said in a low voice, "please don't."

"Don't tell me 'don't'! You want me . . . you know it!"

"Well, if you really don't want me to," Peterson said, puzzled. "But I wish you would. Please?"

Dizzy, Meg said, "No . . . I don't know . . ."

"It won't take long. It won't take long. No one will ever know. Let me . . . let me, Margaret. Take off your dress. Take it off."

"Ah, good," said Peterson. "I'll just slip this over . . ."

". . . your head. Ah-h . . . you have a beautiful body, Margaret. I've wanted you . . . God, how I've wanted you . . . Hey! Don't fight me, goddammit, don't! Not now. You bitch, *not now!"*

Peterson held the limp, undressed doll in his hands and went over every inch of it. He lifted its arms, spread apart its legs, turned it over, and then turned it over again. He pulled the chestnut hair up off its neck and studied its face, and pored over the fine white linen of its torso. He ran his fingers up and down every seam. He studied every stitch, every finger, every toe.

And when it was over, he said in a voice thick with satisfaction: "Very good. Thank you." He left the doll, still undressed, on the desk where he had found it.

Meg was sitting in a chair now, unable to move, the tears flowing freely down her face. She made no effort to hide them; she couldn't if she tried. Mr. Peterson, awakened from his daze, was surprised to see her emotional state.

"There were no marks of any kind," he said, looking away awkwardly. "Absolutely no proof who made it."

"I know that," Meg mumbled through her tears, which surprised him still more. *No marks, no proof, nothing at all.*

"Really, Mrs. Hazard—you don't seem ready to sell. Nonetheless, you have a valuable artifact here, and I'll be recommending an offer to my client. As you may have guessed, I'm more knowledgeable about dolls than dolls' houses. I can tell you this, though: if you really care about the fate of the house as well as the dolls in it, you'll do something about these deplorable storage conditions. Because *this*," he said, tapping the chest of the wax nursemaid doll, "cannot go on."

Doing his best to ignore her tears, he bade her a very pleasant good-night. Meg, who could only nod, remained where she was.

After what seemed like the span of two lifetimes, Meg rose shakily to her feet. She was utterly numb, and it showed: she stumbled and fell forward into the dollhouse, jarring it from its custom pedestal and knocking some of the contents over. Horrified that she might just have accomplished what a vandal could not, she slid the house back into place and checked the rooms hastily for damage. Once again she was fortunate; nothing was broken.

But this time, she was twice blessed. Apparently in her effort to keep from falling, her hand had slammed into the staircase between the first and second floors of the dollhouse. The stairs were covered in a two-inch-wide Oriental runner—with little brass retaining rods on each tread—which disguised a secret spring-loaded mechanism. Once it was tripped—by the pressure on the steps from the palm of Meg's hand—a side door on the wall of the stairwell popped open, revealing a secret closet, paneled over to match the rest of the walls in the dollhouse foyer.

Meg's first thought was, *Orel Tremblay never told me about this.* But neither had he told her that he'd replaced the hair on the nursemaid doll with a lock of her grandmother's hair, so she shouldn't have been surprised. She took a mini-flashlight that she kept handy and beamed it into the hidden closet. There, shoved into the farthest corner, she found a folded piece of paper. She reached in for it, scissoring the paper between her forefinger and middle finger, and pulled it out.

The writing was bold and hurried, a man's:

Dearest Margaret,

It's a form of madness that makes me write this, but the moon is full and I am moonstruck. I sit in my library, alone and in the middle of the night, writing to you by the light of the moonbeams that spill over my desk. This is a love letter, dearest. God help me if I am caught writing it, but the night is long, and I am lonely for the nearness of you. Since you will not be persuaded to leave your sons for the summer and become a sleep-in nurse here, I must be content to commune with you in whatever way I can.

I want you so much: all night long, all day long, in the blink of time between sleep and awake. You are all I ever think about. I have never wanted any woman so much as I want you. I have read about men obsessed, and pitied them; I did not think it could happen to me.

Perhaps I shouldn't be surprised that it has. You know I am a gaming man. I am a man who will not—who cannot— leave a roulette table while the wheel still spins. But that ardor, that hunger, is nothing at all compared to how I feel when I am near you. It seems obscene to mention both in the same breath. I have risked everything at the wheel; I'll do at least that much for you.

I wish I could tell you how much I want you. It isn't a matter of choice any more. I have none; and neither, I think, do you. When you returned my kiss under the willow tree, that's when I knew.

I will have you, Margaret; plan on it. I don't know when or where or how. I'll have you, or no man will. Is this madness? Blame it on the moon.

G.C.

CHAPTER **20**

The letter. The smoking gun.

Meg remembered Orel Tremblay's version of the last harrowing moments he'd spent with Margaret Mary Atwells just before the evacuation . . . how she'd begged for his protection; how she'd waved a letter from Gordon Camplin in his face and tried to get him to read it. Why *hadn't* Tremblay read it, that ass? If he'd only taken the time—

But there'd been no time. Camplin had arrived before Tremblay had had the chance. Not only that, but Camplin had been composed and persuasive, whereas Margaret Mary Atwells had not. You didn't have to be a brain surgeon to understand that most people preferred reason to hysteria. Orel Tremblay had deferred to Gordon Camplin, and Meg couldn't —entirely—blame him. But once Tremblay had seen the black-and-blue marks on Margaret Atwells's arm, he should've gone after Camplin, instead of letting her be dragged back to Eagle's Nest.

Damn Tremblay. Fussing over saving the dollhouse from the flames, when all along . . .

Meg shuddered and shook herself free of the scene that had begun to reshape itself in her soul; she couldn't relive it twice in one night. And yet, what *could* she do? Not sleep, certainly. Not now. She snatched up the letter, locked the shed, and ran out to her car, then changed her mind and ran back to the shed.

Meg couldn't leave the nursemaid doll lying there like that, discarded and undressed. She slipped the doll's clothes back over its head and placed the doll gently back in the nursery. Then, on a grim impulse, she took an armoire from a guest bedroom and jammed it up against the little nursery door.

I'm losing it, she decided when once again she was in her car. *If I don't resolve this soon, I'll probably go the rest of the way out of my mind. And then who'll see to it that Terry gets through school, and Dad remembers his blood-pressure pills, and the Inn Between pays its taxes on time?*

She drove to Tom's cabin with the air conditioning on, even though the sun was down. The East Coast heat wave had pushed north all the way to Maine, leaving the residents of Mount Desert gasping for breath. Meg wondered whether the heat wasn't melting her brain. Maybe all she needed was an air-conditioner and she—and the wax dolls—would be fine.

Meg drove much too fast over Tom's potholed drive and pulled up in front of his cabin. His lights were on, which hardly mattered; Meg would've enjoyed dragging him out of bed to show him the letter. He was a cop, he wanted proof, she had the proof. She banged loudly on the cabin door, the kind of pounding that state troopers give a door before they knock it down altogether.

She heard his voice before the door opened. "For God's sake, Meg; waitaminnit . . ."

So he'd checked and knew who it was. Naturally. City cops didn't throw their doors open casually. It was more evidence of the chasm that divided them. *She* would've yelled, "C'mon in; it's open."

When he did open the door, he was shirtless and belting his pants. "Too hot," was his simple explanation. "What's up?" he asked, obviously seeing from her face that it wasn't a social call.

"I've got the proof that he raped her," Meg said flatly. She whipped out the letter from the pocket of her skirt and waved it in front of him. "You remember the letter my grandmother tried to show Orel Tremblay? This is it. I found it, no kidding, in a secret compartment in the dollhouse. Read it, Lieutenant. I'll wait."

She gave it to him, then watched in bitter triumph as he took it over to one of the two dim lamps in the room. He held it under the muslin shade and read through it quickly. The light fell in a soft halo over his torso and she noted, quite without thinking about it, that he was more muscular than a person convalescing from a gunshot had any right to be.

She folded her arms and waited for the shock, the surprise, the sheepish acknowledgment that she'd been right and he'd been wrong.

He handed her the letter, then took up a T-shirt from the back of the couch and put it on. "She kissed him back," he said.

Meg blinked. " 'She kissed him back?' You read the whole letter, and that's what you got out of it? 'She kissed him back'?"

"It's a love letter," Tom said evenly. "Apparently it was written because he'd had some encouragement from your grandmother."

"En*cour*agement!" Meg said, choking on the word. "My grandmother *spurned* him! Repeatedly!"

"Not under the willow tree, she didn't. Unless you think he's lying."

"Of *course* he's lying!" But even Meg didn't believe that. "He was deluded, that's what he was! Deluded and obsessed."

"I agree he was obsessed."

"Then why can't you agree he raped her?" Meg cried. This was incredible. Meg understood—really understood, for the first time in her life—how a woman must feel who staggers into a police station crying rape.

"This letter doesn't prove she was raped."

"It was the next goddamned step!"

"A jury couldn't be sure."

"Damn the jury!" Meg said, furious in her frustration. "This isn't about our system of jurisprudence! This is about my grandmother! She was raped by Gordon Camplin, over and over again! I had a . . . a vision . . . I didn't *want* to have it, I *didn't* . . . He was demonic . . . insane," Meg said, breaking down into jagged, jittery incoherence. "And he . . . he . . . wouldn't . . . stop . . . until . . . she p-passed out . . . oh, God . . . oh, *God* . . . and not even then . . . Because . . . because she woke up, she knew . . . oh, God."

Meg's knees collapsed under her; Tom caught her on the way down and half carried her to the couch while Meg half resisted every step of the way.

"Don't touch me, *don't,*" she cried, trying to push him away, flailing at him. "How could you not believe me? How could you?"

"Meg . . . Meg . . . stop!" he said. He held her tightly by her arms and sat her down, then sat alongside her. "Listen to me. I do believe you."

"You don't! You said she encouraged him!" she said, hot tears of fury springing to her eyes.

"Shh . . . never mind . . . I do believe you," he repeated, gathering her in his arms and pulling her close.

"No!" She gave him a last, wild, futile push and then collapsed on his chest in bitter, wracking sobs that lasted until it hurt too much to sob anymore. The whole time, Tom pressed her cheek close to his heart and buried his face in her hair and rocked her gently, murmuring soothing syllables with no meaning at all except of comfort. And Meg was aware, as she hadn't been for three decades of her life or more, that she

needed those meaningless sounds the way she needed air and sleep and water. She had gone too long without someone's arms around her, someone who wanted nothing more than to soothe and comfort. Paul had never done that. With Paul, tears and fights had always, without fail, ended in sex.

After she calmed down, she lifted her head from Tom's chest and studied him through the last of her tears. She wanted so badly to have him completely on her side. "You called it a *love* letter," she said reproachfully, wiping her eyes.

He drew a long, deep breath and let it out in a haphazard sigh. "In its twisted way, it was," he said, obviously dreading her response.

But Meg had no fury left; only emptiness. "Is that what love is for men?" she asked dully. "Mindless possession?"

His laugh was sharp and bitter. "You're asking *me* that?"

She winced from his answer. There was so much anger and frustration in it. Meg knew that he wanted her; after Acadia, how could she not know? Nonetheless, she said, "Yes. I'm asking you."

He got up from the couch and walked over to the window, opened to the pitch-black dark of a woodlands night. After a long, long pause, he said, "Probably you're asking the wrong guy. I can tell you what love *isn't*," he said without turning around. "Love isn't mindless sex. Mindless *sex* is mindless sex. Love is—"

He shook his head. "You're asking the wrong guy. I lived in a series of foster homes notable for the absence of love— except for my last parents; they loved each other. But my foster father was diabetic and eventually lost both legs, and that's what the marriage became about, you know?

"I mean, they loved each other, but I don't think they had the time or the strength to say so. There were always too many little crises going on. Like the time my dad was weeding tomato plants in his postage stamp of a garden: he tumbled out of the chair headfirst into the plants, and that's where he stayed until my mother got back from the store. She weighed ninety-five pounds; it wasn't easy setting him right again. *That's* what their days were about. They sure weren't about mindless sex.''

"But you were there to help her," Meg said, moved.

"Not exactly," he said wryly. He leaned his hands on the sill and peered into the darkness, listening. "I ran away from them at sixteen out of the goodness of my heart—because I didn't want to be another burden. I figured my mom could always get a neighbor to help fish my dad out of the tomato plants, but no neighbor was going to feed me or clothe me or buy me a car. At sixteen, your brain hasn't really kicked in yet," he added with a rueful laugh.

"By seventeen I'd wised up and came back. It was too late. My dad had died—heart attack. But I stayed on, finished high school, got a job, did the night school bit."

He turned around, sat back on the sill, and looked at Meg with a smile that broke her heart. "I can tell you all about what makes a great nurse and mother," he said softly, "but I'm not such an expert on the him-her thing."

Meg thought of his wife and bit her tongue. Uh-uh. It was none of her business.

"What about Lydia?" she blurted out.

He grimaced. "Ah; now *that* was definitely not mindless sex. Lydia always had my full attention. But I don't think—looking back—that either of us really loved the other, not in the way you mean. Neither of us would sacrifice for the other," he admitted with a shamed look.

"So you've never seen, firsthand, a man in love with a woman?"

He seemed baffled by the question. "Well, *you* have. What about your father? What about Lloyd?"

"This isn't about me," she said gravely. "This is about you, about why you're not shocked by Gordon Camplin's letter."

"Because *nothing* shocks me anymore, Meg," he said tiredly. "Can't you understand that?" He sat back down and took her hands in his. "Look. A lawyer could take that letter and turn it into nothing more than a macho boast, worst case. He could stack the jury with women who'd get a *thrill* out of it, best case. All I'm saying is, it's not enough to convict, Meg. I wish it were."

She believed him. Maybe it was exhaustion, maybe it was a simple desire to be done with the whole thing, but she believed him. The letter would not be enough. She felt completely limp, as if someone had pulled the plug on her lifeblood. She thought of the nursemaid doll, safely barricaded in the upper floors of the dollhouse.

"Can I stay here?" she asked, dropping her head on the back of the couch and fixing her blank gaze on a dustweb above the door. "For a while?"

"Shoo-er," he said in the Down East dialect that seemed to charm him so much. He sat down again and slipped one arm around her. "Sorry I can't offer you five-hundred-channel cable TV," he said. "Will my shoulder do?"

Meg sighed and said, "You bet," and curled up next to him, instantly soothed. She sat in silence, listening to the steady beat of his heart, wondering how it was that he could make her feel so safe from harm. That was *her* job, to reassure people. And yet, when she thought about it, shouldn't there be someone to reassure the reassurer?

Tom was the one.

After a while he murmured, "You know how you told me to let it go, back in Acadia?"

She nodded.

He said, "Well, it's time for you to let this go."

"I want to," Meg admitted. "They won't let me."

"They? Are we dealing with more than your grandmother here?"

"Yeah. I think Orel Tremblay's in on this, somehow. I don't

know . . . sometimes when I stare at the dollhouse I get a sense—not of her, because with her there's always an over-powering sadness—but of Mr. Tremblay, egging me on. A kind of 'May-the-Force-be-with-you' thing. Don't laugh.''

He rubbed his chin on the top of her head. ''Nothing funny about that. Ask any cop.''

''Mmmn. It's all the same, isn't it?'' she said, sighing.

Sometime after that, Meg fell asleep. How long she slept, she had no idea. Her sleep was deep and dreamless, the sleep of someone who's been piling sandbags against a flood all day and night. It was the kind of sleep that would've carried her easily into the next afternoon. But a wail, tremulous and heart-stopping, sent her bolting upright in the middle of the night.

God in heaven! She sat on the couch, alone and completely disoriented, heavy with sleep, listening to the wail: shivery and high-pitched at first, then descending into a kind of blood-curdling whimper.

Oh, God, it's not over. It's still *not over*, she thought, her head sagging with sleep, her body weaving in a kind of drunken fear. She was drenched in sweat. *It can* never *be over*.

The wailing stopped, as if whatever it was had died or been killed. But then it started up again, as a series of soft, eerie trills, almost purring sounds. Meg jumped up from the couch, unable to stand it anymore.

And then she realized what it was. *An owl; it's only an owl*. It wasn't a sound she ever heard in town. She was relieved; but now she was awake. She turned off the small red lamp that Tom had left lit for her and walked up to the window, hoping for a breeze, hoping to draw some comfort from the other, kinder sounds of the woods: the crickets, the frogs, the silky swaying of the trees.

But no night was all gentle out there, and she knew it. Creatures were hunting and being hunted; it was the way of the woods. She lifted her hair from the back of her neck, hot and tense and irrationally depressed by the thought. She wanted someone to tell her that life was fair and the good guys always survived and the bad guys always got caught.

It was the least he could do.

She went into the bedroom, the one other room of the cabin, and walked over to his bed. Her eyes had adjusted to the darkness, and she could see that he was lying on his back with his arms folded behind his head. His clothes were slung over a nearby chair; he had on boxer shorts.

His voice was low and musing. "What the hell is that thing wailing out there? I hear it all the time. A coyote?"

"An owl," she said, looking down at him.

He laughed softly at himself. "Jeez. Wasn't even close."

She loved the sound of that laugh, loved the intimacy of it, and the way he could make fun of his city-slicking ways. She loved him.

She sat down on the edge of the mattress, aware of the danger.

He said tautly, "Not there, Meg. Not a good idea."

"You're right," she said in a voice overflowing with regret. "You're right." She sighed and reached her hand to his face and stroked his cheek. "I'm sorry," she whispered. "Another time, another place . . ."

She could feel the muscles in his jaw working as he said, "Right. You never know."

This was insane; why was she torturing them both? She stood up to leave. He sucked in his breath—whether from relief or disappointment, she couldn't even say.

Go, go, she told herself. He was doing his part; why couldn't she do hers?

But the bed was closer than the door, and the thought of being with him was infinitely more compelling than the thought of walking out of his life. She turned back to him and fell to her knees beside the bed, then buried her face in her arms on the edge of the mattress. In a muffled voice she said,

"I can't be with you. I can't hurt her. Don't hate me for this. I couldn't bear it."

"Stop." He reached for Meg's hair and threaded his fingers through it and rubbed his hand against her skull. His breath came and went in a staccato pattern as he waited for her finally to leave.

She lifted her head. A sound caught in her throat, a stifled moan of deprivation and despair. She got partly to her feet, then leaned over him. One kiss. And then she'd go. Feeling hungry and entitled and resolved, she lowered her mouth to his.

The taste of his warm mouth against hers was electrifying. Something opened between them, some trapdoor that sent them both hurtling through oblivion. Suddenly there was nothing to hold on to, nothing to hide behind. Suddenly she was reeling from the freedom of it all.

"No more fine words," he said hoarsely, pulling her down to him. "No more reasons."

He kissed her hard and long, taking the kiss to deeper depths, higher heights, than she had ever known. She couldn't breathe, didn't want to breathe; she wanted only this headlong free fall into oblivion. More than anything else, she didn't want to know where she was going.

She wanted to say, "Ravish me, make it not my fault." But she was on top, straddling him. It was her fault. She pulled off her shirt; he undid her bra. She undid her shorts; he pulled off her panties. And in all the sliding heat, she leaned over repeatedly to kiss him: wanton, aching kisses, because she had waited so long—all of her life—for here, for now.

His kisses were hot and deep and utterly desperate. She had the sense that he, too, knew that the free fall couldn't go on forever. He called her Margaret and Meg, wrapping the names around her repeatedly like silken threads. But she broke free, and undressed him, and sat on top of him. Something inside of her, something honest and uncompromising, made her say to him, "I want this. Let me do this."

He let her do it all. She dictated the pace, the pauses, the frenzied acceleration to her climax, then his. She was completely selfish about it, taking her pleasure, savoring it, with no apologies, no regrets.

And when she collapsed on his breast, exhausted and sated and wet from heat and exertion, he gently kissed the damp curve of her shoulder and said, with lingering wonder, "You always seemed like such a *nice* girl."

Her laugh was weak and love struck. She buried her face in his shoulder, unwilling to admit to him that she'd never been that way before with a man, afraid that if he knew, he'd realize how deeply she loved him. Better to have him think she was a wildwoman.

She slid off him and lay alongside, wrapped in his arms, drunk with the mere closeness of him.

"Can I stay?" she asked once more.

He gave her a kiss of surpassing tenderness. "If you left now, I think I'd die," he whispered.

His words, even more than his kiss, were a drug in her system. How could she leave him now? She was hooked. She looked at the small lit clock on his nightstand. Two A.M. The Inn Between would be fast asleep by now, and she could stay, at least for a little while longer.

They listened together to the moaning and groaning of the screech owl, which somehow sounded more comical now than scary—like someone who's afraid to jump in the pool because the water's too cold.

"I can't believe I woke up so frightened," she said.

"You? I thought it was a vampire, my first night here."

"City boy."

"Town girl."

He kissed her again, a lingering, interested kiss with none of the fierce, raw urgency of their earlier ones. His hand slid over the dampness of her skin and cupped her breast; he lowered his mouth to it in a fiery tease that left her gasping for air.

In a voice that was low and seductive and altogether new, he said between kisses, *"Now*, Margaret Mary Hazard: Will you let me . . . make love to you properly . . . the way a gentleman should . . . who's wanted you since the day . . . you threw him off your front lawn?"

She was pleased and incredulous. "You wanted me *then*?"

"Basically," he murmured, kissing the hollow between her breasts. "Only I didn't know it then."

"How could you not know it?" she wondered.

He lifted his head. Even in the dark, she could tell that he was confused himself about the answer. "I guess I was too . . . dazzled," he said softly.

All the air that Meg had been sucking in seemed to come back out in one long sigh. "Yes," she said, turning her head aside. "She's dazzling."

He laid his hand on her cheek and turned her face back to his. "Meg," he said. "I *was* blinded. But now—truly—I can see. Let me make love to you. It's all we have."

The image of Allie, bright and beautiful and trusting, hovered in front of Meg like a ghostly presence, and then vanished. It was a last-ditch effort by Meg's conscience to get her to leave him, and it failed completely. Meg lifted her hand behind Tom's head and drew him down to her. "Please . . . more," she said simply.

They made love again, with Tom very much in charge this time. He drove her to new heights of passion and then, when she thought she couldn't stand any more, drove her higher still. It didn't seem possible that a body could absorb so much heat and not melt down completely, but Meg's life was full of impossible things.

After the second time, the night took on a life of its own. The more Meg made love, the more she wanted to make love. And Tom, who laughed at first and said it couldn't be done, not at his age anyway, somehow turned serious and came through for her.

"When do you go back?" she'd asked him.

"Next week," he'd answered.

She'd read of lovers like the two of them, people who were driven to desperate bouts of passion before some great crisis: before their city was overrun by an enemy army; before the foot soldier headed off to fight on the front lines; before the king married, for the good of the kingdom, some duchess he couldn't stand.

But their own tragedy was less melodramatic than all that. The front line for Tom Wyler was on the streets of Chicago, and their enemy army was the dawn. As for the duchess, Meg didn't even want to speculate.

She and Tom made love—wild love, hot love, slow love, exhausted love—until the first birds sang. And then they fell asleep.

She heard her sister calling her name; that was what woke her up. The knocking came immediately after; that was what woke Tom up.

"Oh my God!" Meg said, wide awake. "What time is it? *Nine*? Oh my God."

"Shh," whispered Tom, reaching for his pants. "Just stay here. I'll take care of it."

He slipped into his khakis and grabbed a T-shirt on his way out of the bedroom, closing the door behind him. Meg sat stunned for one full second after that and then grabbed wildly at her clothes, fumbling with the hooks of her bra, pulling her yellow T-shirt over her head in a blind rush, zipping her shorts so hastily that she caught her skin in the zipper and had to suppress a cry of pain. Through it all, she heard every agonizing word in the next room.

"Tom! Good *morning*!" came Allie's voice, as bright as the sunshine pouring through the windows of the cabin. "I brought your books back. Meg's here already? She gets up with the roosters; I swear I've never seen her sleep late. What's she doing here, anyway? Your blueberry bushes don't look ready to pick yet.''

She must know. She can't not know.

"Yeah . . . Meg's here," Tom said quietly. "She came about the dollhouse."

That's right, Meg thought. *I did.* She began to have wild hopes that Tom could pull it off without being despicable.

"Oh, yeah—Mr. Peterson. I don't know why I stormed out of dinner like that. Uncle Billy just gets to me. *Meg?*" Allie yelled. "Where is she?"

"She's not here."

Meg's spirits sank at the bald-faced contradiction. Now, surely, they were doomed.

"Oh," said Allie, blithely accepting the turnaround. "So how'd it go with Peterson? Did he like it?"

"All too well," said Tom.

Meg heard the irony in his voice. In the course of the night she had described everything—everything—that she'd felt when Peterson examined the dolls. And Tom had held her close and told her how bad he felt about her grandmother, and then they'd spent some time whimsically planning the perfect murder of Gordon Camplin, because fair was fair.

"Did Peterson make an offer? I'll feel so bad for Meg if he does. She truly doesn't want to sell. I don't think she should be forced to do it. I hope Uncle Billy doesn't beat her up too much about that. He can be such a nag."

"Peterson said he'd recommend that his client make an offer," Tom said.

"Well, what's Meg doing now?" fretted Allie, obviously not listening to Tom's last answer. "Where is she?"

"She found a pair of binoculars in the cabin and went out to track down some bird or other she heard. You know Meg. I can show you which way she headed."

Meg heard the agony in his voice. He didn't want to lie to Allie; he was doing it for Meg. And Meg was doing it for Allie.

"Oh, I don't know; it's so buggy out there. Things hop on you. And I've seen snakeskins."

This is insane. Meg combed her fingers through her hair, closed her eyes, and took a deep breath. She opened the door of the bedroom and stood face-to-face with her sister.

"There are no binoculars, Allie."

CHAPTER 21

"**M**eg . . . ?"

Allie, dressed in white and with her hair pulled back, stared at her sister. Her beautiful violet eyes were absolutely blank. She began turning to Tom for enlightenment, then swung back to Meg. "Binoculars?" she said, uncomprehending.

Meg had seen the look before: twenty-two years before, when Allie had toddled out to her while she was hanging laundry on a line, and yanked at her skirt and said, "Mommy's sick. She keeps sleeping and sleeping."

And now this. It didn't seem possible. Meg said in a low, broken voice, "I'm sorry, Allie."

But Allie only stared.

"What happened to your mouth?" she asked Meg with the same blank look. "It's all swollen." She took a few steps toward her sister, then stopped. "Did he *hit* you?"

Meg hung her head. "No. He didn't hit me," she whispered.

"Well, then, I don't—"

Meg waited—without breath, without a heartbeat—for the blow to fall on Allie.

When she looked up again, her sister looked even more blank than before. It was sinking in at last.

Allie let out a half sigh, a kind of soft "Huh!" She shook

her head. "No. Uh-uh. Nooo. This isn't happening." She glanced at Tom, didn't seem to see him, looked back at Meg. Her eyes were wide-open now, starting to show panic.

But Meg was seized by panic and denial of her own. "No, Allie, wait! Nothing happened!" she said in a last-ditch effort to fend off catastrophe.

"Nothing?" Allie asked in a childlike voice. "Really?" She went up to Meg and said, "Then what's *this*?" in a poisonous hiss as she grabbed at Meg's T-shirt.

"I . . . I don't know," Meg said, bewildered. She looked down at her shirt and saw seams. It was inside out. She closed her eyes, aware that her free fall from the night before had hit rock bottom.

She tried to claw her way out of the abyss. "Allie, it didn't mean anything!"

Allie was so surprised by that answer that she smiled, as if a butterfly had landed on her arm. "It didn't? You did this to me for nothing?"

"No—that's not what I meant. It *did* mean something! It meant everything! That's why I did it."

"Why are you *telling* me this?" Allie cried, stamping her foot. "How can you stand there, inside out, and *tell* me this?" she asked as tears streamed down her face. "How *could* you? How *could* you?"

Overwhelmed by her sister's reactions, Meg said humbly, "I couldn't help it, Allie. I can't not love him. Even for you."

Allie's face contorted with pain. She closed her eyes and bit her lip so hard that Meg saw blood. "Oh, how I wish you hadn't said that," she whispered.

Meg looked straight at Tom, who was standing behind the couch, leaning his hands on the back of it, watching them with a wary intensity. In some tiny part of her soul, she was wishing that he'd drop dead, or that she herself would. It would make things so much simpler.

"I'm sorry, Allie," she said without taking her eyes away

from Tom. "I'd do anything to change places with you. Believe me."

She wanted Tom to know that. He looked away.

Allie's answer to that was a bitter, despairing laugh. "I *really* don't think so."

She hesitated for a moment, as if she didn't know which of them to turn to first, and then, obviously, it hit her again: her sister and the man she loved were in cahoots. She had no one. She turned and fled from the cabin, a terrified child who'd strayed too deep into the woods.

Meg ran after her and got as far as the door. Tom grabbed her in mid-pursuit and said, "Let her go! There's nothing you can do. She doesn't want you now."

"Are you *crazy*?" Meg cried, wrenching her arm free. "Who else is there?"

Allie's little Escort was already out of sight on the winding drive; Meg rushed to her own car through the cloud of dust that her sister had left behind, determined to force Allie off the road if she had to—whatever it took to make her stop and listen and understand.

Wyler stood on the porch of the cabin, wondering how it was that the house was still standing. He felt as if he'd been to heaven and back with a quick drop to hell and had reentered life through the eye of a hurricane.

Jesus.

He raked his hands through his hair, surprised somehow that he still *had* hair; that it hadn't been singed clean in the heat of their sex.

He felt rotten. How was it possible for him to have experienced so much ecstasy, without chemicals, and still end up feeling rotten?

Because you don't know a damn thing about women, he decided wearily, and turned to go back into the house. He should've known—should've known, when Meg asked him that trick question about love, that this was going to end badly. *What is love*. How the hell should he know?

What was he feeling now? Exhaustion and regret and dismay and confusion; this was—what? It sure couldn't be love. But it sure couldn't be mindless passion. If it were mindless passion, he'd be feeling fantastic right now.

And he felt like shit.

He dropped onto the couch in a sulk, feeling irrelevant and ill-used. First she wanted him, then she didn't; then she did, then she didn't. She'd whipped his desires back and forth like a pony express rider. By the time she leaned over for that kiss he was practically gnawing on the bedpost, trying to keep his hands off her. God, he could taste her right now, taste the melancholy sweetness of her mouth.

She'd been incredible; incredible. He'd never known anything like it. Of course, it had helped that he was going back to Chicago soon. He understood that perfectly well. It gave the night a bittersweet drama of its own. It had helped, too—why not admit it?—that Meg had been holding herself back up until then for her sister's sake. If you pull back the string of a bow the full twenty-eight inches, the arrow will shoot straight and true when it's released.

Straight arrow. The image fit Meg so well. He'd never known anyone with more integrity, more resolve than Meg Hazard. He closed his eyes to shut out the image of her, but it came back: haunting, lovely, sexy, strong. She was everything a man like him could hope for.

Except that she was too responsible by half. There *was* such a thing as being too responsible. When you tried too hard to be everything to everyone, you ended up being nothing to anyone. Meg couldn't be a lover to him and a mother to Allie, not to mention all the other members of the Atwells family: *that* arrow wouldn't fly.

Meg had told Allie she loved him. He took it with a grain of salt, because women loved everything—dresses, recipes, babies, wallpaper patterns. The word had no more value for them than a Russian ruble.

As for Allie, Wyler had no doubt that she was more devastated by Meg's betrayal than by the permanent loss of his company. He wasn't sure Allie knew he was in the damn *cabin*, not once she saw Meg in that bedroom doorway. He'd ended up feeling a little like the ashtray on the kitchen counter: there, but superfluous.

No, this was about being sisters. Those same sisters were at that moment engaged in a car chase all over Mount Desert Island, and there wasn't a damn thing he could do about it. And the hollow, empty feeling in the pit of his stomach? He'd better get used to it, because there wasn't a damn thing he could do about that, either.

He dragged himself over to the stove and poured himself a cup of yesterday's cold coffee, aware that if he were still a smoking man he'd have himself a whole *pack* of cigarettes after last night, and tried not to think about it—the cigarettes or the sex. He was hot and sticky but too tired to shower. He decided that maybe he hated Maine after all, and dozed off, dreaming of owls and ashtrays.

When he woke up it was three hours later and hotter than ever. Wyler cursed the heat wave—he could get one of those in Chicago, anytime—and headed for the shower. He was hosing himself down, wondering whether his equipment would ever work to capacity again, when he heard the distinctive, crackling sounds of a police radio through the high bathroom window. Instantly he snapped out of his sullen lethargy. He grabbed a towel, hardly bothering to use it, and pulled on a pair of khakis, then got the door.

The cop's name was Matt Marsten; Wyler had waved to him a dozen times over the course of the summer as their cars crossed paths.

"Matt. What's up?" he said tersely. He knew what was up; dammit, he *knew*.

"There's been an accident, sir. Chief Dobney sent me out to tell you, seein' you don't have a phone."

"Tell me who."

"Allegra Atwells. Her car rolled over out on Route 3, north of town. The victim wahn't wearin' a belt and sustained head injuries and at least a broken arm, maybe more. It's the head injuries may be bad. She's unconscious. The chief knew that you . . . well, he wanted you to be apprised, that's all."

"Was there anyone else in the car?"

"Nosir."

"Any other cars involved?"

"No evidence of it so far, sir."

"Where'd they take her?"

Officer Marsten blinked. "MDI Hospital, sir."

Stupid question; big-city question. "Thanks, Matt."

Wyler was out the door and in his car before the squad car had had a chance to negotiate the potholed drive. After that he was forced to drive at a reasonable speed by what seemed like an obscene crush of poky tourists. By the time he pulled into the parking lot of the two-story red-brick hospital, one thought had crowded out all others: *it's over.*

He found Meg in the lobby, waiting with her father and Comfort, both of the others looking far more pale and shocked than she did. Meg had her color—too much of it, he thought. She was pacing in front of her father and sister-in-law, the classic drill of someone still waiting for word. His hopes that Allie had recovered consciousness were dashed.

If Meg saw him, she pretended not to. It was her father who looked up and said, "Ah, here's Tom. He'll have news."

Wyler hated that, when people looked to him as if he possessed infinite knowledge of the universe. He knew exactly what any other schmuck who walked up to the desk knew: that Allie was in surgery. He apologized for disappointing them.

Comfort said, "Can't you find out?"

Meg looked up mid-pace at her sister-in-law and snapped, "Leave him alone, Comfort. He can't do anything."

That pretty much set the tone for their conversation.

"What happened?" he dared to ask.

"My sister lost control of her car and rolled it," Meg said tersely, telling him exactly nothing he didn't know.

"Where were you?"

"When I got the news? Doing laundry. Is that any of your business?"

"Meg!" her father said, surprised.

But Wyler was relieved; she'd been nowhere near the scene.

He kicked himself for not having taken the time to check out the police report. He'd dashed straight to the hospital because he thought—God only knew why—that he'd be accepted as family. But Meg was like a snarling bobcat circling her wounded kitten and fending off a turkey vulture. The turkey vulture, that would be him, apparently.

"Meg . . . we have to talk," he implored.

"Fine. Shoot."

She resumed her stride, her arms folded tightly across her chest, as defensive a position as he'd ever seen in a woman. He was scandalized to see faint black-and-blue imprints, obviously his, on her arm from when he'd tried to stop her from chasing after Allie. Clearly she wasn't aware of the marks; she'd never have put on a sleeveless sundress if she were.

"Can't we go somewhere quiet?" he asked.

"Anything you have to say, say it in front of my family," she said in a taunting voice. "We come as a package."

"This is unnecessary," he said in a voice low with warning, but she only glared at him. "I want to know—" He sighed exasperatedly and tried again. "Did you see Allie after I did?" he asked, as obliquely as he knew how.

"Tom! Allie was drinking!" Comfort burst out, and instantly broke down into tears.

"*What*?" Wyler could picture many things, but he couldn't

picture Allegra Atwells, bright and lively as a neighbor's child, falling from her wagon. She had too much energy, too much grace.

"There was an open bottle of gin in the car," Everett explained in a hushed, somber voice. "Not so much was gone," he added with a look of reproof at his daughter-in-law. "Legally I'm sure she was fine."

"Half the bottle was gone!" cried Comfort, contradicting her father. It was a full confession, to be sure. Wyler had the sense that Comfort was trying to nail down absolution for Allie, and then everything would be fine. God would make her all better.

He turned to Meg; her look was as cold and as icy as a distant star. "This is what we do to drown our big-time sorrows, Lieutenant," she said with dark meaning. "We *drink*."

"That's ridiculous, Meg," said Comfort gravely. She reached in her beige handbag and pulled out a big white handkerchief and blew her nose into it, then wiped her nose left to right, right to left. *"You* don't drink. *I* don't. Dad doesn't. Okay, Uncle Billy has a tendency—but he doesn't have any sorrows! And Lloyd has sorrows, but he hardly ever drinks. So why are you saying that?"

Meg plunged her hands into the big front pockets of her dress and took two steps toward her sister-in-law, then leaned over until she was eye to eye with Comfort. "To piss you off, Comfort," she said. "For no other reason."

"Margaret Mary, that is *enough*! What's the *matter* with you!" her father said angrily, jumping up from his chair.

Meg turned on her father. "Oh, for God's sake, Dad! Allie's lying on an operating table with her life in the balance, and we're sitting around measuring alcohol content! Who *cares* how she ended up in surgery! She's *there;* that's all that counts! Are you too blind to see it?"

Everett Atwells recoiled visibly from his daughter's whip

and fell back in his seat, his cheeks red and smarting from her fury.

Meg was flailing at anything that moved because she couldn't flail at herself. Wyler understood that perfectly well, but no one else knew that. He had to do something, and quick.

He took her arm, the black and blue one, to give her an excuse later for the marks, and said, "C'mon. We're going outside for some air."

"Don't you tell me what to do," she said, seething.

"I'm not impressed by these hysterics," he said in her ear. "You pride yourself on being the adult in this family. Act like one."

He'd pushed the right button. She brought herself under control with a deep, shuddering sigh and said to her father, "We're going outside for a minute. If anyone comes out, come and get me. Right away, Dad," she pleaded. "Don't wait one second."

The two of them went outside without exchanging a word. Meg led the way to a bench at a picnic table in the shade on the hospital's east side, and they sat down next to each other, carefully not touching.

Wyler began at the beginning. "What happened after the two of you left the cabin?" he said in a voice deliberately stripped of emotion.

Meg made an effort to match his tone. Without looking at him, she said, "I tried to catch up to her, but she lost me. She drives like a maniac; you know that. I drove around for a while, checking out her old haunts, but couldn't find her. Then I went home. She never came back."

"All right, okay," he said, relieved. "Then you didn't catch her and engage in some confrontation that set her off."

Meg turned and looked at him with amazement, then said, "I'd say we confronted just fine in your cabin."

"Don't start on that, Meg," he warned. "It's absolutely pointless to play the blame game. You were right to tell your family that the only thing that matters right now is Allie. What you have to understand is this: Allie did what she wanted to do, and so did you, and so did I.''

She heard him; but he wasn't sure she understood him.

"She doesn't have car insurance, of course," Meg said dully. "Except for liability. I just found that out."

He winced. "How about separate medical?"

"Nope. She let it lapse the last time they raised the premium. I couldn't talk her out of dropping it. Allie thinks— thought—thinks—she's invincible," Meg said in confusion.

She crossed her arms on the picnic table and bowed her head.

"I remember the day my mother told me she was pregnant with Allie," she said softly. "I was eleven, and we didn't have any money then either. It was the same old struggle with bills every month; there never seemed to be enough money left over to buy me the right toys or the right clothes or for all I know, a pony—whatever it was that was important to have at that age.

"I remember how *angry* I was that there was going to be another drain on the money; how irresponsible my parents seemed to me. I threw this gigantic tantrum . . . I was horrible. And then, after Allie was born, we all just . . . fell in love with her. She was the light of our lives. She would crawl up on your lap and . . . and *squeeze* you . . . and you would squeeze her back. It was the best feeling in the world."

Meg straightened up and, smiling, wrapped her arms around herself. "As soon as Allie was able to stand, she took off. She never walked, always ran. She'd fall and cry and get up again on her little legs and run. She loved to be chased, just loved it. She'd just . . . shriek . . . for joy, for the fun of it. The house was such a happier place after she was born. . . ."

Meg's lip began to quiver; a tear rolled out the corner of one eye. "It's . . . ah . . . just . . . incredible," she said, struggling to keep control. "All those times in high school

. . . when she was driving around with that crowd . . . and she never got a scratch, never got a ticket. And now, because of me . . .''

"You cannot control your sister's behavior," he said softly. "You can't."

She closed her eyes. "Then I'd like to find the package store that sold her the booze, and cut out the owner's heart."

"Meg—you can't control him either. Don't you understand? Your codependency—"

"Oh, please," she snapped. "Spare me your buzzwords."

"Skip the buzzwords, then!" he said impatiently. He jumped up from the bench, too frustrated with her to sit still. "You are not responsible for your sister's thoughts or feelings or destiny. *Understand* that and learn to live with it, dammit!"

She was so blind. How could he make her see? He stopped mid-pace and looked down at her, rubbing the back of his neck with his hand, and said bluntly, "This situation between Allie and you . . . it's not healthy, Meg. It's a common one —more common than people ever guessed—but it's not healthy."

Meg was quiet, dangerously so. "So you're saying, what? That I need counseling?"

"Maybe when things settle down a bit."

Again she seemed to mull it over. He held his breath.

"You're telling me this *now*?"

"I wanted to before. I've wanted to ask, have you ever been to Al-Anon?"

"But it's *Allie* who was rolled over in a car crash. Why do you keep bringing the subject back to *me*?" Meg asked, bewildered.

"Because *you* need help as much as Allie!" he said. *"You* need to break free of her! *Can't you see that*?"

When he thought about it later, he realized that that was the exact moment he knew he loved her. But that came later, after his rage and hurt died down.

Meg got up almost casually from the bench and stood facing him. She slipped her hands into the big square pockets of her sundress of pale pink, a color oddly flattering to the deep flush in her cheeks. He could see, through the fabric of the pockets, that her hands were balled into fists. No doubt about it: Meg Hazard was getting ready to blow up her last bridge.

"If there's anyone who needs counseling, it's got to be you," she said with a calmness that was belied by her high color. "You're the one with the failed marriage. You're the one from a string of loveless homes. After all, when you finally did land in the arms of people who cared, what did you do?"

She was a terrorist, a terrorist in a pink sundress.

"I'd rather not have to listen to this, Meg," he said in a low and dangerous voice.

"You ran away. Doesn't that tell you something?"

"Leave it alone, Meg."

"It tells me everything *I* need to know. It tells me you're incapable of forming—or keeping—a relationship."

"Don't, Meg," he warned, his face flushing with anger. "We'll both regret it."

"It's not your fault," she said pityingly. "You had a horribly screwed-up childhood. I understand that now; now that you've told me about it. I mean, my God—your mother abandoned you in a Sears Roebuck!"

Wyler laughed at his own stupidity: in a moment of intimacy, he'd handed her the ammunition, handed her the fuse, and now she was blowing his life up in his face.

His laugh infuriated her. "So what the hell do *you* know about family love?" she said, exploding at last. "What the hell do *you* know about relationships—good, bad, or indifferent? You've never stuck around long enough to figure one out! If there's anyone around here who could use some counseling, it's *you*!"

She folded her arms across her chest and turned her back on him. *"How* I curse the day I met you!"

He grabbed her by her shoulders and swung her around to face him. He was short of breath, reeling from her attack. "Listen to me, Meg. What I said to you last night I never told anyone—not Lydia, not anyone. But I told you. You're right," he said, his eyes blazing with anger. "I'm *not* quick to trust. And you want to know something, lady? *Now I see why.* So curse all you want, Meg, but get counseling, and get it quick —because your guilt is making you vicious."

She gasped, speechless with rage, and slapped him, hard; there was nothing halfway about it. It was as low a moment as he'd ever experienced with any woman, anywhere. Meg's face was ashen. He hoped she was strong enough to forgo fainting as he turned and walked away to his car.

CHAPTER 22

To Meg, she looked like Snow White. Even with her head wrapped in bandages and an oxygen mask over her mouth, she was extraordinarily beautiful. The creamy purity of her skin, the hint of color in her cheeks that said she was still alive—neither Disney's animators nor German doll makers could possibly do better. Her heart, like Snow White's, was definitely still beating. You could tell by the monitor that it hadn't been broken completely.

The IV bag that was hooked up to Allie's unshattered arm was nearly empty; Meg frowned and left the room on tiptoe to find a nurse to fill it before the signal beeper went off.

When the phone rang later at the Inn Between, Meg was on her way out the door with two slices of bread in one hand, two slices of honey loaf in the other. She let Comfort answer it and waited to find out if it was the hospital. It was not.

Comfort put her hand over the phone and whispered, "He wants to know how Allie is."

Meg glowered and murmured, *"You* update him," and kept on going out the door. But she paused, with the screen door propped open on her hip, intending to censor Comfort if necessary.

"Tom? Yes, well, there's good news. Allie's regained consciousness. She hasn't actually talked to any of us yet, but someone is always there. It was lucky a neurosurgeon was vacationing here, else she'd be in Bangor now. Anyway, Dr. Aller said the worst is past. She had a depressing skull fracture —what? Oh, that must be what he said, a *depressed* skull fracture. They had to escalate—''

''*Elevate*,'' Meg hissed.

''—*elevate* the pieces of her skull . . . well, I can't talk about that anymore, it's too horrible,'' Comfort said, beginning to weep. ''And her arm is in a temporary cast,'' she said, ripping off a paper towel to wipe her nose on. ''And that's all I know.''

Tom asked a question at the other end of the line and Comfort answered, ''A couple of days. And then she'll go into the regular ward for a few days more. Maybe a week and a half, altogether. We're hoping it's less. We want her home with us and also, well, the *cost*—''

Meg shook her head fiercely at her sister-in-law and Comfort shut up instantly.

Meg heard the faint echo of Tom's voice again—she was surprised at how dispassionate she was being about him—and then saw Comfort glance at her with a guilty look.

Comfort turned away from Meg and lowered her voice. ''Oh . . . pretty well, all things considered,'' she murmured, cupping her hand over the phone. ''She's been at the hospital almost nonstop—''

A poke from Meg stopped Comfort mid-sentence. Tom said something and Comfort, with a defiant look at Meg, said, ''You're not a pest at all, Tom. How else will you know anything? Call as often as you want. Someone is always here . . . well, no,'' she said, turning away and lowering her voice again. ''She hardly *ever* is. I doubt *she'll* come home until Allie does.''

* * *

As it turned out, Meg got to come home well before that. The first time that Allie actually opened her eyes and spoke to anyone, it was to Lloyd. (Meg was in a bathroom nearby, splashing cold water on her face.) Allie's first words were, "I don't want to see her."

Lloyd had no idea how to coat that message with sugar, so when Meg returned, he took her aside and repeated it word for bitter word.

"I'm sorry, Meggie," he said, rubbing his sleeve nervously with a rough hand. He glanced out the window, then turned to her with a baffled look. "What happened between you two? *She* won't tell. And *you*—you been actin' all along as if you ran over her by accident. What's goin' on? We have to know."

He tucked the back of his plaid shirt in his pants and said, "It's got to do with Tom, don't it? You mize well say. Comfort saw you with him outside the hospital," Lloyd explained, his cheeks turning ruddy. "She said you two ain't exactly on formal terms."

In his own roundabout way, Lloyd was asking Meg if she and Tom were lovers. Meg, completely devastated by her sister's command, hardly heard her brother's question.

"She can't mean that, Lloyd. You must've misunderstood her," she said faintly.

"No, she was pretty clear about it," he said unhappily. "Meggie—is there some real feelin' between you and Tom? We have to know," he repeated.

Dazed, Meg only said, "Why, Lloyd? Why do you have to know? Can't I have one little part of my life that I call my own?" She peeked around the corner at her sister, half expecting Allie to be sitting up in bed, ready to shoo her away. But Allie was lying on her back with her eyes closed, exactly as Meg had left her.

Shaking and dazed, Meg began to walk away. In her mind one thought overwhelmed all others: *Whatever Allie wants.*

After a few steps Meg turned and said to her brother,

"Since you seem to have to know: there will never be feeling between Tom and me again."

She left the car at the hospital and walked home in a state of shock. The last week had been a series of nonstop shocks, but this one was leaving her numbest of all. For Allie to reject her so publicly . . . for her to do it so *quickly*, in her first lucid moment . . . it was devastating. If Allie had waited until she'd actually seen Meg; or if she'd got to talking with Lloyd, and Meg's name had come up . . . But to do it first thing . . . It was crushing, and a measure of how deeply Meg had hurt her sister.

Meg turned onto Main Street and walked in a straight line, oblivious of the crowds of tourists and shoppers that bumped around her, and didn't stop until she more or less hit water. She was at the town pier. She walked out to the end of it— aware, vaguely, that she was in the company of hundreds of happy day-trippers—and looked over the edge. It was high tide: the water was dark and murky and stirred up by the wakes of passing boats. She stayed leaning over the dock railing for a long time, convinced she was going to be sick, not daring to risk walking the rest of the way to the Inn Between.

Eventually a fog rolled in and it got clammy, and Meg turned reluctantly in the direction of the house where she'd been born and raised, the house that no longer seemed her home.

She stepped into a different kitchen from the one she'd left. Comfort was there, cooking supper. She'd obviously heard about Meg's banishment, because she made a big, busy production of straining the spaghetti and didn't ask Meg where she'd been. Her father was in the sitting room, looking haggard and watching network news with limp attention; he looked up and with a forced smile said, "I just got back. She's coming around all right."

Meg asked humbly, "Did she say I could see her?"

The smile faded. "I'm sorry, Meggie." Everett Atwells

looked suddenly too old and frail to witness such a gaping rift in his close-knit family. "I'll tell you what. You go with Comfort after dinner. Maybe when she sees you . . ." His voice trailed off, unconvinced.

Obviously they'd all figured out what had happened and had no idea what to do about it. Plan A would've been to go to Meg and ask her. There was no Plan B.

The phone rang. Terry jumped up from his baseball cards to answer it. He dragged the phone to Meg and said, disappointed, "Don't worry, it isn't Tom."

So the twins knew, too. It was the story of Meg's life: that she had no life. Not of her own, anyway. She sighed and said hello.

"Meg? It's Dorothea."

"Who?"

"My dear, Dorothea Camplin. Why didn't you *tell* me you were a granddaughter of my nursemaid?" she said in her no-nonsense way. "I had no idea. It explains your curious interest in Eagle's Nest. I don't blame you a bit for asking, dear. Of *course* you'd want to know. You should have come straight out about it."

The interview seemed so long ago, Meg could hardly remember it. "I'm sorry, Mrs. Camplin. I know I said I'd be back to photograph the garden. But my sister was in an accident—"

Mrs. Camplin gasped. "Oh! Wait. Allison? No, Allegra, it was—Allegra Atwells! I read about it in the *Times* and never made the connection. How stupid of me! I'm so sorry to be bothering you at a time like this—"

"Not at all. In fact, the news today was . . . was very good. My sister's going to be all right. It was a little touch-and-go at first. Anyway, now that she won't be needing me as . . . um . . . much . . ." Meg said, her lip beginning to quiver, "I'll be . . ."

She paused to regroup. "Well! I'll be over tomorrow if it

stays overcast, and if that's all right with you. Otherwise, the next gray day.''

They agreed to that plan and Meg rang off. Dinner came and went in excrutiating silence, and after that Meg packed up her pride in a basket of flowers and went with Comfort to try to see Allie again.

When they got to the hospital, Lloyd didn't look hopeful, and Meg didn't hope. She let Comfort go in ahead to intercede for her, but Comfort came out of Allie's room shortly afterward looking downcast.

"Gosh," Meg said with bravado cheerfulness, "I feel like a skunk at a garden party."

The worst of it was, Lloyd and Comfort seemed to feel that way, too. They didn't say so, of course. Comfort even put her arms around Meg and said, "Give her time." But no one said that Allie was being outrageous, because she wasn't. For the second time that day, Meg was being forced to walk away from everything she held dear and into a twilight zone as disorienting as the thick fog that lay in wait outside.

Oddly, she felt less traumatized after this visit than the last one. Earlier, she'd had to endure the initial shock of rejection as well as the uncertainty of whether Allie was really lucid. Now Meg could be sure: Allie was not going to forgive the betrayal anytime soon.

So where do I go from here? she wondered as she made her way back through the brooding fog. Not to Tom. He was the only one she wanted to see, the only one who understood. But it would be the death knell to her relationship with Allie if Meg went running to him now. Besides, he wasn't exactly beating a path back to her door. She tried not to think about the slap in the face and the cruel words that had preceeded it. *Your guilt is making you vicious*, he'd said, and he was right.

She couldn't think about him now: not with sorrow, not with longing, not at all.

It was all such a mess. With the best intentions in the world,

Meg had managed to screw up royally. She should've been up-front with Allie about her feelings from the start. This was her punishment, and it was about as punishing as life could get.

Meg went straight to bed, slept a sleep of black dread, and didn't wake up until she heard loud knocking on her bedroom door. She jumped out of bed fearing the worst.

It was Lloyd, up to his elbows in soot again.

"That furnace ain't worth a hole in the snow," he said, disgusted. "Inner jacket's rusted out. This is it, Meg; it's over. We got to get new. Either that, or drop dead a' the fumes. Not to mention the guests."

"You can't nurse it along?" she asked sleepily.

He shook his head. "Too dangerous."

"So of course there's no hot water," she said, not bothering to pose it as a question. "All right. Get a new one in here as fast as you can."

"With what? It ain't like we got the money. Or the credit."

"Let me worry about that," she said grimly.

Lloyd shrugged and left, and Meg, still in her nightgown, went straight to the desk in her closet office and dialed the number on the card that Peterson had given her. Enough was enough. No deathbed promise was worth a dozen lives.

"Mr. Peterson? Meg Hazard. I haven't heard from you, so I thought I'd call." She had neither the heart nor the time for chitchat and maneuvering, so she asked him outright, "Is it your sense that your client will be making an offer soon on the dollhouse?"

Peterson hemmed and hawed about the meaning of "soon."

Meg pressed him. "By 'soon,' I mean in the next day or two. I don't mind admitting that I'm in a bit of a cash-flow bind. To that end, I'd be willing to negotiate very handsome terms for your collector."

"Now that's the thing," came Peterson's voice, oozing with sympathy. "These cash-flow binds. Aren't they awkward? My client seems to be in one of them right now. He's gone and made an offer on a wooden sailing yacht, which has been accepted, so for the moment, he's all set.'' Peterson added, ''Apparently he prefers an antique that he can use and enjoy.''

Meg was flabbergasted. ''He couldn't decide between a dollhouse and a *yacht*? Isn't that a little arbitrary?''

Mr. Peterson chuckled. ''To his way of thinking, they're both toys,'' he said pleasantly. ''Toys of the same vintage, in fact.''

''Can you at least tell me what you think the dollhouse is worth, ballpark?''

He didn't like giving Meg information she hadn't paid for; but in the end he took pity on her and gave her a figure that was more than twice the estimated cost of Allie's hospital bill. The roof, the furnace, the repairs—Meg could do them all and still have money left over.

''Be patient,'' he advised her, ''and you'll get that price. It may take a year or two or even three, but you'll get it. Well— it's too bad things didn't work out,'' he said.

Yeah, sure, she thought, hanging up. *What did he care? He got his fee either way. Now what*? She drummed her fingers nervously on her desk. *Now what now what now what*? The dollhouse had been her security blanket. In the back of her mind she'd been assuming she could cash it in any time she wanted, like a winning lottery ticket. Where would she find a buyer overnight?

''It only takes one,'' Peterson had said.

But who had time to wait for him?

Her eye fell on the complimentary calendar, the one with a different lighthouse for every month, that hung above her battered oak desk. Yes! BHS—Bar Harbor Savings. The Inn Between was mortgaged to the hilt, but the dollhouse wasn't. Surely she could secure a loan from a bank with it. It was insured. It was an asset. It had value and *then* some, if you counted the fact that it was haunted. *Yes*!

For the first time in what seemed like a lifetime, Meg's

spirits climbed above her ankles. Emotionally her life was an ongoing disaster, but if she could get a grip on the financial side of it—well, then, she'd have a grip on *something*.

A *bank*. Why hadn't she thought of it before? *Yes*!

"No."

"That's what they said? No?"

"They said it wouldn't be 'valid collateral.' "

Uncle Billy didn't bother hiding his disappointment. He poured himself another whiskey and gestured to Meg with the bottle; she shook her head. Comfort came in to take away the last of the dishes, and then Meg and her uncle were alone across the dining room table. It was time to do business.

Uncle Billy, comfortably stuffed with chicken pie, let out a discreet burp and said, "In a way, it don't surprise me. That Jenny Bowery has acted awful treetoppy since she landed that job in the loan department. Tryin' to prove she can be harder than a man, I expect. Still, it makes it sticky for you."

"Not sticky, Uncle Billy," Meg said quietly. "Desperate."

His eyes glazed over, the way they did whenever the subject directly or indirectly came around to his money. "Now, don't be thinkin' desperate," he said. "There's always hope. I been talkin' up Peterson's visit all around town, hopin' to flush out a competing buyer. Hell, I even spread the word about the secret compartment; everyone loves a secret compartment."

Meg had told the family about the compartment but not about the letter, which Tom had mailed back to her without comment a couple of days after the blowup. "I can't *wait* for a buyer," she told her uncle, linking her hands in a prayerful pose on the oilcloth. "We need the money now. I have less than thirty days to pay for the new furnace. And we're losing business because of the roof: every time it rains, the fire alarm goes off. I had to give one family their money back the other morning."

Bill Atwells grunted and tossed back his whiskey with a

sharp, practiced gesture, just the way Meg had seen him do thousands of times before; it reminded Meg of the way an umpire thumbs a player out of an inning.

He thunked the shot glass on the table a little unsteadily and said, "You wait. One of them summerin' richbitches is bound to come round to the shed and fall in love with the thing."

"I *can't* wait, Uncle Billy," Meg repeated. She took a deep breath and said, "I'd like you to lend me the money. You can keep the dollhouse as collateral until I pay you back. You'll have my permission to sell it whenever you wish."

Bill Atwells's mouth shut tight in a thin line, and the corners dipped down in annoyance. It was the second time in Meg's life that she'd asked him for money. It was the second time in her life that she'd seen that expression on his face.

"I won't do that," he said gruffly. "Don't ask."

"God," she said in disbelief, falling against the back of her chair. "You want to see us lose everything!"

"That ain't true. *I'd* lend if the bank would."

"If the bank would lend, you wouldn't *have* to!"

"You've got thirty days to pay for the furnace," he said petulantly. "What's the rush?"

"Allie gets out of the hospital in a few days. How will we pay?"

"Everybody knows what patients do who can't pay," he said, pouring himself another drink.

Meg's mouth opened slightly. She cocked her head and stared incredulously at him, this blood relation of her father's. "You want us to go on the dole?"

"Public assistance," he corrected. "That's what it's there for. If you can't pay, you can't pay. Why should I throw money down a rathole? Allie's fine. Her head's mendin', her bones are settin'. What're they gonna do? Bash her head in and break her arm again?"

He was fortifying himself with yet another drink. Meg knew the signs well enough to understand that he was getting drunk as fast as he could, to put an end to the discussion. She stood up tiredly and looked at him: old, fat, clever, likable, and tight as a tick. "You should've had children, Uncle Billy," she said softly. "It would've made you a kinder man."

"Kinder!" he said, hiccupping. "Kindness . . . is loving people more than they deserve."

When the fuel oil leaked all over the cellar, that was when Meg pretty much lost it.

Lloyd had been tuning up the new furnace, not paying much attention to his son Terry as he hung around the cellar hoping to wangle money for the movies. Terry didn't get the money, but he did manage to stand on the shutoff valve at the bottom of the oil tank and to break the copper fuel line that led to the furnace. Lloyd left, and his son left, and no one noticed the fuel oil spilling out until it was too late: less than an hour later, the stench had made the Inn Between unlivable.

Meg was the first to have to deal with it. As she stepped out of her car after her return from the post office, several of the guests accosted her, complaining about the horrible smell of oil. They were clustered in the garden, terrified to stay in the house. Meg explained that heating oil was not explosive, but it hardly mattered. When she saw the pool of oil covering much of the cellar floor, she knew at once that the summer season was effectively over for the Inn Between.

She took off her shoes and waded through the mess and turned off the spigot on the tank, and wondered what alignment of the planets was causing this unbelievable streak of bad luck. By the time Lloyd and Terry returned and they all worked backward to an explanation of what had happened, Meg was beside herself with rage.

She grabbed her young nephew by the arm and shouted, "Why? Why were you standing on the fuel line? Wasn't there enough floor for you? Why?"

Terry squirmed and said, "I don't know; it was just something to stand on, that's all." He started to whimper.

"Oh, never mind! Just . . . go! Your father can decide what to do with you later."

Lloyd's mind was on something else. "Comfort can't stay here in her condition, not with these fumes," he said with a worried look.

"No, of course not," Meg said distractedly. "She can stay with Uncle Billy—and what about Allie? She can't stay here either. Dad? The twins? None of them should. You and I will have to do the cleanup alone," she said grimly.

"The insurance—"

"—will not pay for negligence. I've checked. This mess is all ours."

"Oh, Jesus. I'm sorry, Meggie. We're gonna lose a few weeks' business, you know that," he added in an undertone. "That smell's gonna take awhile to get outta the cement."

"I know that very well," she said, rummaging through a kitchen cabinet for the aspirin.

Work on the spill began immediately. Lloyd went out to buy oil-absorbent blankets and Pine Sol while Meg began calling off her bookings. When Everett Atwells got back from the hospital, he was put in charge of making arrangements for the family to stay with his brother, to be joined by Allie later. (Meg couldn't bear to ask her uncle for even that much help.)

By evening the house was cleared and Meg was in her cubbyhole of an office, fighting a splitting headache from the fumes, and Lloyd was in the bowels of hell, pumping out the spilled oil and storing it in containers for proper removal. The cellar was an unbearable place to be, but Lloyd was going at it with a vengeance, hardly stopping to eat. By midnight it was too late for Meg to phone even the West Coast to arrange cancellations. She was exhausted; Lloyd had to be, too. Meg went down to the cellar to drag her brother out of there.

She found three men and a boy mopping down the cellar together, all of them in ragged clothes and gum boots: Uncle Billy, Lloyd and his son, and Tom.

Sometimes—before she could shove the thought away—Meg daydreamed about how or where she and Tom would next cross paths. She pictured the hospital, the post office, the Shop 'n Save, even the church. She never pictured him in her cellar. With a mop.

"C'mon, guys; time to knock off," she said as casually as she could. But her heart was knocking chaotically at her breast as she nodded to Tom and said, "Hello."

He gave her that distinctly Maine greeting, an upward lift of the chin.

She could've handled a snub. She could've handled a snide remark. But that ironic Maine-style nod brought welling tears of sorrow and self-pity to her eyes. She wanted so badly for him to take her in his arms and fix everything.

Uncle Billy straightened up with a groan, more than ready to call it a night. He was drenched in sweat; even his red suspenders were stained with damp patches.

"What a miserable, stinking mess," he said morosely, surveying the cellar. "But by God, we made some progress here tonight, hey, boys? Sulla's almost good as new. You done good, Ter," he said, whacking his nephew on the back.

Terry kept on mopping.

Lloyd pulled off the bandanna wrapped around his brow, and so did Tom. In the bleary light of the overhead bulbs, they looked like escapees from a chain gang, hiding in some unsuspecting widow's cellar.

Lloyd said, "Y'know—I hardly smell it at all," in his downtrodden, hopeful way.

Tom smiled; Uncle Billy laughed out loud. "The fumes have reached your brain, boy," he said. "Let's go. A shower and a good night's sleep, and we'll be ready for another round."

Terry set his mop in a bucket and picked it up. The boy's young face was streaked and filthy and more deeply marked by the tragedy than the others'. He'd done a man's work tonight and had made up for a boy's stupidity. Meg wanted to hug him, but she knew he'd be mortified by the gesture.

She looked at them all—tired, haggard, sweaty, stinking from the fuel oil—and said, "I'm sorry. Everyone, I'm sorry. All of this . . . I've been so . . . I'm sorry."

To a man, they were embarrassed by her display of emotion. Uncle Billy mumbled something to the effect of "Wimmin!" and then led the pack in a shuffling exit up the cellar stairs.

Tom was the last to leave; he hung his bandanna on a nail and gave Meg a look that she didn't want to see: it was filled with far too much sympathy, and far too little burning desire. It told her everything she needed to know. She'd sacrificed one love to protect another, and in the end hadn't saved either. And now, seeing him, her heart just . . . hurt.

Tom was on his way out the cellar door when she took his arm and said in a low voice, "Tom . . . I *am* . . . sorry."

But she didn't say for what.

Half an hour later, Meg was sitting alone out in the shed with a cup of tea. She didn't want to go back into the house, even though the smell in her bedroom, with a fan blowing through, was more endurable than it had been in the afternoon. Probably she should've gone with the rest of her family to Uncle Billy's. But she hated the thought of needing his roof over her head.

Her depression was profound. She felt alone and cut off, and without any options. Over the years she'd convinced her family that she had all the answers, or at least the ability to find the answers. With the exception of Uncle Billy, they'd gradually yielded authority to her until she was undisputed head of the household. Now she was failing them, emotionally

and financially. She could hardly bear to watch the disillusion-
ment in their eyes.

Meg circled the beautifully lit dollhouse with her cup of tea,
wondering how it was that an expert could fail to insist that his
client bid for it. She stopped instinctively in front of the nursery and peered through the lattice-paned casement, which she
always kept tightly shut nowadays.

The nursemaid doll stood on the other side of the window
looking out at Meg, wondering and waiting. The master doll
was still in the billiard room, exchanging risqué jokes with his
gentlemen friends. The lady of the house was still in the dining room, overseeing the setting of the table.

Was the dollhouse just an ordinary object, after all? Meg
shook her head, convinced that it was not. *Lint* was ordinary.
The dollhouse was pure magic. But maybe she couldn't put a
price on magic. Maybe no one could—except the insurance
company.

Was that the key to it all? The insurance? Meg sipped her
tea reflectively and let her mind tiptoe into a place it had never
gone before: the netherworld of fraud and theft. Why not? The
Atwells family had paid insurance premiums all their lives and
had never made a claim—not until the oil-tank leak, for which
they were getting paid zip.

Why not? Allie was insured, but not enough, so what was
she getting after her accident? Zip.

Why not? Comfort would be paying thousands to have her
baby, despite her medical, and God forbid if something went
wrong. She'd get zip.

Why not? The failed roof and furnace were normal wear
and tear, the insurance company said, so they'd be paying zip.

Premiums were always going up, benefits down.

What was the point of insurance, anyway?

In a self-induced trance of indignation, Meg went out to the
yard where spare easy chairs and mattresses—all of them
ruined—had been stacked in a haphazard mountain by Lloyd

and the others. She picked up a couple of plastic milk crates filled with oil-soaked rags and carried them out to the shed, then pulled out some of the rags and scattered them on the table under the dollhouse.

It was the only way. She had to do something. It was the only way. She looked around distractedly for matches, pushing herself into action. *Just do it*.

She needed matches. She ran back to the kitchen for the box that Comfort kept by the stove, then ran back breathlessly with it to the shed. *Do it. Do it. Do it*!

With a pounding heart and a sense of wild resolve she flung open the door to the shed—and found her father, picking up the sodden rags and dropping them back in the milk crates.

If he saw the box of matches in his daughter's hand, he pretended not to. "Meggie, for Pete's sake," Everett said mildly, "these stinky rags are going to ruin the drapes and upholstery in the dollhouse. Don't you know how the smell of heating oil permeates fabric? This is a really foolish thing to do," he said, giving her a look rich with meaning.

"Dad! What're you doing here?" she asked, horrified to be caught in the act. She dropped the matches on her desk. "It's one in the morning!"

"I know, I know; but I couldn't sleep, thinking you were here alone and upset," he said in the same meaningful way. "Don't stay here," he begged. "There's plenty of room at your uncle's house."

"No. Not there," she said tersely. Now what? Her father had obviously witnessed and foiled her plan. She felt she had to explain. "Uncle Billy wouldn't give me a loan," she said bitterly. "Your own brother."

"You knew that before you ever asked him," her father said, lifting the crate of rags as if it were filled with rocks. He paused on his way past her. "The only reason you bothered with him at all was to justify—well, other moves."

He took the crate outside and came back for the second one.

"I don't know about you, girl, but I'll feel a whole lot better with these rags out in the open air. Because you never know. Let's say they—spontaneously—erupted in flames. The insurance company would be all over us like a cheap suit, charging negligence or who knows what. There could be complications —big, legal complications."

He was so tall and thin and stooped and kind, the exact opposite of his brother. He gave Meg a sad little smile and said, "Besides, the dollhouse is all we got left, for better or worse, of your grandmother. You know?"

Meg was so ashamed. Everett Atwells had never cheated anyone in his life. In his quiet way, he'd just given her every reason not to torch the house but one: it was wrong. That, he was letting her figure out for herself.

"I don't know what I was thinking, Dad," she said with downcast eyes.

"You were thinking we could use a change of luck," he said, and turned off the lights to the doll house. "Don't worry," he added, nudging her out of the shed with the milk crate. "It's *bound* to change."

CHAPTER 23

Their luck did change, but not for the better. Incredibly, Meg got a call the next day from the wife of a second cousin who happened to be the mother of a young man engaged to a secretary whose downtown lunch mate's sister-in-law worked for one of Bar Harbor's best-known probate attorneys. The word was that Joyce Fells was planning to challenge Orel Tremblay's bequest of the dollhouse to Meg.

And there wasn't a damn thing Meg could do about it except hire an attorney herself to defend her prize.

"You know, even for a nightmare, this is getting tired," she told Comfort, who had stopped by the Inn Between to check on their progress and feed them lunch. "It's like there's some big wet cloud above my head that won't go away. Sometimes it rains, sometimes it pours, and sometimes it just plain drizzles. But it won't go away."

"Do you think Joyce Fells was right?" asked Comfort with a worried look in the direction of the shed. "That the dollhouse is rightfully hers, and that it carries a curse for anyone else?"

"That's Allie's theory, not Joyce's," Meg said, pushing half of her huge tuna-fish sandwich on her sister-in-law.

Meg added, "I think the dollhouse is *some*thing, though. Not cursed, exactly, but imbedded with some kind of . .

energy. Although, who knows? Lately it just sits there, doing nothing.''

"Oh, it could be dangerous, Meggie, it could be; you don't know," said Comfort. "Come back with me to Uncle Billy's," she pleaded.

How anxious Comfort looked to Meg; how beaten down by events. Her pale green eyes seemed to wash out to a lighter shade after every bout of tears. It was the pregnancy, of course; that was how she was with the twins, too. Meg should never have been so candid with her about the dollhouse just now. That was the kind of thing she could share with Allie, not with poor, misnamed Comfort.

Meg laughed reassuringly and said, "I think everything that *could* happen *has* happened. I'll be fine here, Comfort. I'm still working through the bookings—did I tell you I'm offering a half-price rate?—and now I'm making inquiries everywhere I can to sell the dollhouse."

"Before Joyce Fells can stop you?"

"You bet," Meg said dryly, and changed the subject. "Okay, tell me what this typing assignment is you have for me."

Comfort took a letter typed on heavy stationery out of her bag. "I took this to the hospital because I thought it might cheer Allie up. I knew it was good news because I held the envelope up to the light and saw the words 'very pleased' in it," she admitted, blushing.

Meg scanned through the letter, which was an enthusiastic job offer from the Castle Inn in Chicago—the first, no doubt, of two or three.

"But Allie dictated *this* to me," Comfort said, taking out a note written on the back of the letter's envelope. "I don't know how to type business letters; can you do it? She's turning it down, Meg, I don't know why. She doesn't have to see him. It's a big city. And look, they offered her so much *money*, more than she could ever get around here. Why don't she take it?''

Meg scanned the gracefully worded refusal. ''Because money isn't everything, Comfort,'' she said, sighing. ''Even though it seems that way right now to you and me.''

Comfort left with her newly typed rejection and Meg went back to her phone work. Through her open window she heard Tom's Cutlass pull up; Lloyd had mentioned that Tom would be coming back to help. Meg was careful to stay upstairs for as long as they stayed downstairs. Later in the day she watched from her window as both men loaded the pickup for a dump run, then said good-bye to each other.

Tom had his hand on the door to his car when he looked up suddenly at Meg's lace-covered window. She stepped back quickly, like a nosy neighbor caught in the act. It was wrenching to have him so close. Couldn't he see that? Did he *have* to behave so reasonably—helping just because they needed help? He was supposed to have gone back to Chicago by now. If he was going, then he ought to just—go. Why drag it out?

With a heavy heart she dragged herself back to her list of potential saviors. Meg had thrown her net wide and far, and so far she hadn't caught a thing. It was almost unnatural. She'd left tempting messages on answering machines of miniatures dealers and collectors all over the country; they couldn't *all* be out of town. Still, for the moment there was nothing to do but wait.

That was hard. For one thing, Meg wanted to run out and double-check the shed. She couldn't shake the fear that Joyce Fells was going to steal the dollhouse—lock, stock, dolls, and bedboards. But Meg was a hostage to her phone. So she brewed more tea, and paced from room to room, stopping once in a while to stare through a window into the foggy night, and tried to pretend that the house didn't stink to high heaven.

The silence, inside and out, was unnerving. Meg missed the random shouts of the twins, and the quiet murmurs of the guests, and the bouncy laughter of their latest chambermaid, a college girl from Ireland. She missed Lloyd's gentle grousing, and Comfort's call to supper, and Allie's high-spirited babble.

She felt so alone. Even the pets were gone. The cats had passed through the house and decided, apparently, to stay with friends. Meg would've liked to keep Coughdrop with her, but Terry, convinced that the dog would come down with asthma from the fumes, had talked his great-uncle into taking his pet too. So now Meg was left with the sound of her own silence, broken only by the squeaking of the old oak floors under her bare feet, and the low moan of a foghorn drifting through the open windows.

When the phone rang, she jumped sky-high. Praying for a fairy godmother to be at the other end, she said eagerly, *"Yes?"*

"Mrs. Hazard?" asked a voice that sent shivers through her. "This is Gordon Camplin. We met at the Children's Charity dance at Fairlawn."

Not a fairy godmother. Meg took a deep breath and said, "I remember."

"I'm glad," he said pleasantly. "Do you remember singing the praises of the Eagle's Nest miniature? You invited me to come by and see it. I confess I didn't have much interest at the time; but now I understand that the replica is being offered for sale. Is it?"

The answer was almost impossible to get out: "Y-yes." *Not him! Anyone but him!*

"Have you fixed a price?"

"I . . . I'm open to offers," she forced herself to say. *This can't be happening.*

"The reason I ask is, I'm flying to Nice tomorrow to visit my daughter. We were talking earlier, and I happened to mention the miniature, and she was very curious to know what condition it was in—whether all the pieces were still there, that sort of thing. She seems to remember it quite well, or to think she does. Of course it was never a toy; but a three-year-old sees things differently from an adult. In any case, she was thrilled to know it was being made available.''

"She's welcome to look at it," Meg said faintly. "Naturally."

A daughter. Meg couldn't deny an innocent daughter.

"She's asked *me* to look at it and advise her. "I told her I wouldn't have the time; but as it turns out, I do. It's terribly short notice, I know. But if I could have five minutes—''

"I was just about to go to bed," Meg blurted stupidly. It was eight thirty.

"Oh? Well, maybe someone else is available to show it?''

"There's no—'' But she was loath to admit she was alone in the house. "When . . . when can you be here?" she said, struggling to handle this unexpected twist. Her mind was reeling; the sound of his voice was making her completely irrational.

"I'm just downtown," he said, sounding relieved.

Shuddering, Meg said, "I'll give you directions.''

"No need," he said cheerfully. "I know just where you are.''

Meg hung up in a state of shock. The one thing she hadn't anticipated was the worst thing: that Gordon Camplin might still care enough to pay hard cash for the dollhouse. It was a hideous thought. She didn't think for a minute that he was looking at the house for his daughter's sake. He was coming because he couldn't stand not to, because the rumors and stories had begun to pile up.

Meg knew Bar Harbor. Her uncle had told everyone about the secret compartment, trying to drum up interest in a sale. That, coupled with Tom's remarks at the dance about the dollhouse being haunted, was enough to bring Gordon Camplin scuttling to the Inn Between. Maybe he *was* merely curious;

after all, he was leaving for Nice and couldn't be sure the dollhouse would still be around when he returned.

Maybe he had thoughts of hiding behind his daughter's skirts and buying the dollhouse for himself, now that he knew it was for sale. Maybe he wanted to relive the moment over and over in the privacy of his fantasies. Meg had heard of sicker things.

Maybe he wanted to know if Meg had found his letter. What if he'd figured it all out—where Margaret Atwells had stuffed the letter at the last minute? He might have forgotten all about the secret compartment until Uncle Billy went blabbing around town about it. All these years, he hadn't known the dollhouse even existed; there'd been no cause to worry. But now he had a reason to worry, and an excuse to come.

And she was alone.

She went into a subtle panic, not enough to be considered hysteria, just enough for her to change quickly into a smock with big pockets and drop a small folding knife, with the blade open, into the right one. *This time*, she thought, *I'll be prepared*. And then she realized: there'd *been* no other time.

So her grandmother was still around, after all.

Meg raced through the house, turning on every lamp; the place was as bright as a baseball park for a night game. After that she took up a post in the front room near the window. She remembered Tom's words at the Children's Charity dance: "You watch and you wait."

He hadn't told her it would be in a state of terror.

Get a grip, she told herself. *He's an old man; why should you worry? Old men don't kill. They certainly don't rape.*

Still, at the last minute she dashed into the sitting room and turned on the television, then swung through the kitchen and turned on the radio there. She wanted the Inn Between to look as though it was up and running, a happy place to be. By the time she got back to her post, a dark gray Mercedes had pulled up and Gordon Camplin was walking to the front door. In the golden light of the porch fixture he looked younger and fitter than a man his age was supposed to look, and far more grim than would be expected of a man running a pleasant errand for his daughter.

The effect on Meg was overwhelming. Her stomach constricted as if she'd taken a vicious blow, and her heart began to hammer violently. This was a dreadful form of fear, utterly new to her, more intense even than the fear she'd felt when she was unpacking the little dollhouse bed. She was in danger of fainting on the spot and had to grab the doorknob to steady herself. At the same time, Camplin was lifting the brass knocker on the other side and dropping it in three firm raps.

The result was electric. A current of terror seemed to make a circuit through the door, leaving her limp from the jolt of it. Her head told her there was nothing to fear on the other side, but her spirit—her spirit was making another connection altogether. She rallied herself and swung the door wide, ready for the dread engagement.

"Hello; I see you found me," she said with a lift of her chin.

"There wasn't a doubt in the world," he said amiably. He seemed much less startled by the sight of her than he'd been at the Children's Charity dance. Whatever he'd felt there, he obviously had *that* emotion thoroughly under control. He began to say something, then suddenly stopped and grimaced.

"Oh, my—kerosene, is that it?" he ventured.

The smell. She'd forgotten completely about it. So much for her illusion of a fully booked inn. "It's just a little problem we had with our oil tank," she said quickly. "It's all fixed. Everyone's been *very* understanding. Well, shall we take a look at the dollhouse? It's out back," she said, stepping around him and closing the door behind her. She had an intense aversion to letting him enter her family's house; she'd sooner let in a mangy pit bull.

"Lead the way," he said.

As they walked around the house from front to back, Camplin made small talk about the difference between historically correct miniatures and dollhouses, which he explained were merely children's toys. His manner seemed tense and on guard.

No more than hers. Meg said curtly, "I *like* calling it a dollhouse."

She hated being in front of him, but the fog was thick and parts of the yard were unlit; she had no choice but to go first. She had little reason to assume he meant to harm her; what she was feeling, she decided, was an inherited dread.

Finally they reached the shed. Jittery from the nearness of him, all her senses on hyper-alert, Meg reached into her left pocket for her keys and opened the lock, then stepped inside the shed and turned on, first the dim overhead bulb, and then the dollhouse lights.

"This is it," she said unnecessarily.

She was not prepared for the intensity of Camplin's reaction. He let out a gasp, a kind of "oh-h" sound that had an undercurrent of emotions she couldn't begin to understand. He took a step back, as if he truly had seen a ghost. Suddenly the burden of fear seemed to shift from Meg to him. She watched with increasing fascination as he stood there slightly open-mouthed, staring at the dollhouse. The lattice pattern of light from its windows played on his face and body like the web of a spider, pinning him to the spot. *"Uh-h-h,"* he murmured, stricken.

The light from the dollhouse seemed to pulsate, like the rhythm of a heartbeat: stronger, fainter, stronger, fainter. At the same time, each rhythmic beat became brighter and more penetrating, until the air crackled with energy.

Camplin's face became contorted with fear. "Oh, my God, oh, my God, oh, my God," he kept repeating. He wiped the sweat on his brow backward into his carefully groomed gray hair, then dragged his hands down across his cheeks, pulling his lower lip out in a grotesquely distorted expression of horror. His eyes were wide open, yet unseeing.

The pulsating light became more intense, dazzling Meg completely, preventing her from seeing any more of his reaction.

Fearful suddenly that the dollhouse was about to burst into flame in some ghastly ritual reenactment, Meg reached for its cord and yanked it out of the shed outlet. The dollhouse became dark once more; the crackling air around it became quiescent.

Stunned by the intensity of the event and yet feeling strangely, deeply triumphant, Meg said in a low voice, "I don't think it's lost any of its potency over the years—do you?"

Camplin was breathing heavily, still trying to recover. He looked to Meg like a man who's had one leg caught in hell and somehow managed to escape, leaving his shoe behind. "What?" he said, slack-jawed. "Potency? It's a . . . a dollhouse," he said, almost slurring the words. "That's all."

"Oh, no," she argued gently. "You were quite right. It's a very accurate miniature. Of Eagle's Nest. I'm sure it brings back memories for you? Of the good times, the fun times, the bad times?"

He looked at her with a haggard, sideways glance. Then he seemed to pull himself together and straighten his spine. It was as if he was re-forming himself after being torn apart. She was in awe of that ability in him; of the phenomenal power of his will.

"It brings back nothing at all," he said in an ugly croak.

"How odd," Meg answered, her own spine stiffening in response. "It evokes so many memories for me—and I wasn't even there. But I can see my grandmother rushing around in her lavender dress on the day of the fire: reassuring your children, gathering their things, packing their favorite toys for the evacuation.

"I can see her hurrying through the nursery," Meg went on, "grabbing your daughter's little blanket and wrapping it around her shoulders to keep her snug and warm. It's all so crystal clear to me."

Camplin stood in hostile amazement on the other side of the dollhouse from her, refusing to rise to her bait. But she wasn't finished with him.

Bolder now and more contemptuous of him than ever, she said, "Everyone assumed that my grandmother was overcome by smoke when she supposedly returned to the nursery for something or other, because everyone knew how much she loved your children. What was it you told the press—that she must have been looking for your daughter's teddy bear? How plausible that must've sounded."

"Because it *was* plausible," he said, stepping deliberately away from the dollhouse.

Meg watched him warily. "Plausible, but not true. My grandmother wasn't in the nursery when she died," Meg said. "The nursery wouldn't have had a lock on the door. But *I* know the room she died in was *locked;* she couldn't escape from it. She was trapped in your bedroom."

Meg watched Camplin's jaw clench and a minimal smile form on his lips. "My bedroom? You're suggesting she was a thief as well as a poor nursemaid?"

"I'm suggesting you used her and left her there to die," Meg said, hurling the words at him like sharpened knives.

"Excuse me—why would I do that?" he asked, unflinching.

"That, I can't answer," Meg admitted. "I don't understand that kind of obsession, that kind of evil."

"A dramatic view of a dramatic day," he said, moving closer to her.

"I have your letter," she blurted, stepping back.

He said astutely, "It mustn't be much good to you."

"It's told me everything I need to know about you." She

reached inside her pocket and gripped the knife that lay there. "It's told me you're the lowest form of life."

Even in the dull light of the overhead bulb, she could see that she'd gone too far: his eyes glazed over with hard-edged fury.

He's old, she told herself. *He's old. I can take him.* But she stepped back and around to the other side of the dollhouse, so that their positions were reversed: he was at the open side now, and she was in front. She looked down at the nursemaid doll with a quick, silent plea for help.

Camplin leaned on the edge of the table and glared over the rooftop at her. "Listen to me, you little—young lady. I've been extremely patient up until now. What you've said to me here is reprehensible—but it's not actionable. I warn you, though, if you keep running around town asking leading questions and impugning my name, then I'm going to make sure you and your family are stripped of everything you own and left naked and whimpering in the streets. Do you understand me?"

God, she despised him! "I'm not afraid of you," she snapped, clutching her knife.

"I don't think I'm getting through to you," he said, almost bemused by the fact. He reached into the dollhouse and brought out the hostess doll in her green-velvet drcss. "There's more than one way," he said with a smile that was dreadfully unemotional, "to break someone."

He took the doll by the shoulders and with his right hand yanked the legs from the torso, then tossed the savaged pieces back into the dining room.

Shaking with fear and outrage, Meg said, "You'll pay for that! You *bastard*, you'll pay!"

His eyes narrowed with a look of withering confidence. "It looks like I won't be buying your little toy after all," he remarked, flicking his middle finger against the tiny windvane and sending it into a wild spin. "Some of it is in pieces."

Breathless with fury, she said, "I'd sooner sell to the devil!"

He smiled again, and then he turned and walked out. She watched him until he was swallowed up by the Down East fog —a murkier, darker fog than anywhere else in the world.

Meg's pursuit of justice for her grandmother had run hot and cold ever since her second visit with Orel Tremblay. But now it was running at a white-hot clip. Camplin *would* pay. One way or another, Meg was going to make sure of it. Her mind was in a turmoil as she weighed and balanced strategy and fallout.

One thing she knew: with his deep pockets and sterling reputation, Gordon Camplin would be tough to bring down. Going after his good name would be expensive and futile; her family *would* end up naked in the street.

No; there was another, simpler way to get revenge.

But it was too late to begin tonight. She went around to the open side of the dollhouse, to gather up the broken doll pieces and take them back to the Inn Between. The tiny dining room was a mess. She thought of the earlier ransacking that someone had given the place and realized, suddenly, that it couldn't have been Gordon Camplin; clearly he hadn't seen the dollhouse since 1947.

So it must have been Joyce Fells, after all—crazy Joyce. Well, that was one mystery solved. Meg was grateful for it. In any case, neither Joyce's antics nor her threats to sue bothered Meg a whit. To her, Joyce was nothing more than a colorful footnote in the ongoing saga of the dollhouse.

Meg began righting all the tiny dishes and goblets and then, weary of it, decided to leave it for the next day. She straightened out and stretched, and her eye fell on the tiny knotted floral rug in the sitting room between the master bedroom and the mistress's. It was badly scorched: the fringe was gone, and the pattern of pale and dark pink cabbage roses was almost unrecognizable. Probably the damage had been done when the wiring surged or shorted or did whatever it did when Gordon Camplin was there.

Probably.

Twelve hours later, Meg was sitting with Dorothea Camplin in the bright and sunny country kitchen of Tea Kettle Cottage, presenting her case for blackmailing the woman's ex-husband.

Meg hadn't called to warn Mrs. Camplin that she was coming, which she knew showed dreadful manners, but she didn't want to risk not being admitted. So she'd taken a chance, and the Cuban gardener had brought her directly to Mrs. Camplin, who was in her rose garden "doing battle," as she said, "with millions of aphids."

"This is where live-and-let-live gardening gets you, Manuel," the elderly woman said to her gardener in disgust. "We're going to have to make up a brew to control these nasties, or there'll be no roses for Meg to photograph!"

Meg explained that she was there for another reason, and Mrs. Camplin, sensing the gravity in her manner, asked Meg in for coffee.

As she stirred heavy cream into the coffee Mrs. Camplin had served in charming Quimper pottery, Meg said, "You were very understanding on the phone the other night. Yes, I *am* curious about Eagle's Nest and my grandmother's stay there. But it's not ordinary curiosity. Let me tell you why."

Dressed in baggy pants and a man's dark green T-shirt, Dorothea Camplin looked more like a bag lady than a wealthy socialite as she leaned forward with gossipy eagerness to hear what Meg had to say.

Surely she knew her husband was a beast, Meg thought as she looked into the elderly woman's keen blue eyes. She might have been taken in by his looks, money, and smooth manner, but she did dump him eventually. That gave Meg the confidence to go on.

"It's terrible to bring up the past," she began. "But the

past is too terrible *not* to bring up. Mrs. Camplin, I . . . I don't know why you left your husband so many years ago—no, wait. Please. I *have* to go on. People say he was a compulsive gambler; maybe he still is. But he was also desperately obsessed with my grandmother, and I have proof of it, in a letter from him.''

Mrs. Camplin looked absolutely dumbfounded by Meg's speech. "For God's sake, child. Why are you telling me this now?" She didn't seem angry so much as amazed, a hopeful sign.

"I know. You think it's water under the bridge. Only it's not, Mrs. Camplin. If no harm had come from Gordon Camplin's obsession, then that would be one thing. But he threatened my grandmother, and he went at least part of the way to fulfilling that threat in front of a witness, and it seems obvious, at least to me, that"—Meg lowered her voice—"that my grandmother died because of him," she concluded, staring at the cheerful Quimper cup that she was cradling between her hands.

"My God," the elderly woman whispered, utterly shocked. "Do you have any idea what you're saying?"

Meg nodded silently. No doubt she was about to be booted out the door and down the garden path; but she hung tight, trusting that Mrs. Camplin's sense of fairness would prevail. Meg was entitled to a hearing. And cash for her family, because they were victims, too.

Dorothea Camplin traced the outline of the blue diamond pattern on the yellow tablecloth, in deep, musing silence. At length she looked at Meg with an expression that was one part Solomon, two parts Supreme Court Justice. "All right," she said softly. "I'll listen to what you have to say."

Relieved and elated that the woman had decided to hear her out, Meg told her everything she knew: from Orel Tremblay's story to her discovery of the letter in the secret compartment of the dollhouse. During the whole time, she was careful not to mention Tom's name. Why tell anyone that the law was informed but helpless?

When she was finished, Mrs. Camplin said nothing for a long time. She was shaking her head, but her face said it all: *I thought as much.*

"What can we do?" she asked sorrowfully. "It was so long ago. I don't think he could be—what is it? Indicted? I don't think that would happen."

"I agree with you," Meg said grimly. "But he should be made to pay. I'm not asking him for blackmail money; not really. I'm willing to sign a note for a loan. With a little interest," she added with Yankee reluctance.

"You must be joking! He would never lend it to you!"

"He would if he thought I was going to raise a stink." Meg bounced a fist off the edge of the table, making the little pottery cup jump in its saucer. "I can play hardball too!"

"Oh, I don't think so," Mrs. Camplin said gravely. "Not with him. In any case, where do *I* fit in?" she added, wondering.

"He won't listen to me, not after last night. And there's no way I can bear to look at him—not after last night," Meg said with brutal honesty. "But you're still on speaking terms; you still move in the same set. You could convince him that he wouldn't want his name dragged through the mud and ruined."

A look of reluctance crossed the old woman's face. "It's my name, too, Meg, whether I like it or not."

This was true. "Oh, but no one is going to confuse the both of you!" Meg said quickly. "Mrs. Camplin, I have to do *some*thing; our income's been cut totally off. We need the money now!"

"I know you do, but . . ." The matron sat back in her cane-seated chair, which creaked under her weight. "I have to think about this. Maybe there's another way. Maybe *I* can manage to . . . well, we'll just have to see. Come back to-morrow to photograph the garden,'' she ordered.

She stood up, signaling an end to the visit. ''Come after lunch, say one thirty; I'll have Manuel leave the gates open. That way you won't have to stand there yelling 'yoo-hoo' for half an hour again,'' she said with a wry smile.

''And don't worry,'' she added, squeezing Meg's hand. ''It's always darkest before the dawn.''

CHAPTER *24*

Bobby Beaufort was mounting his Harley—big, black, and full of chrome—when Wyler pulled into the parking lot of the hospital. Wyler got out of his rented Cutlass; the two men exchanged wordless looks. With a James Dean sneer, Beaufort kick-started his motorcycle and revved it into a thunderous roar loud enough to wake the dead.

Not to mention the near dead, Wyler thought with a surge of sympathy for the suffering patients inside. *Jerk*.

Wyler walked through the lobby, stepped into the elevator, and punched 2. His bags were packed, his tickets booked; in two days he'd be on his way home. But it was inconceivable to him that he could leave Meg without seeing her one last time, so after this first and last visit to Allie, he planned to take on the older sister herself.

How ironic that the only way to see Margaret Mary Atwells Hazard, the woman he cared for more than anyone else in the world, was to force himself physically into her presence. He'd tried the phone, he'd tried proximity. The only thing left was to storm the damn inn and force her to see him.

He got off the elevator and went down the hall, then stopped outside the room number he was given at the front desk. Why he'd come to see Allie, he wasn't sure. He had this wild idea that he'd get Allie's blessing before he proceeded with his plan to sack the Inn Between. Besides that, he wished simply to say he was sorry.

Her door was partly open. He knocked twice. "Hey," he said quietly, coming into the room and taking the chair beside her bed.

She was sitting most of the way up, dressed in a white cotton thing with super-wide sleeves, obviously to fit over the cast on her arm. She showed little bruising. Her shaved head was wrapped in bandages, highlighting the superb structure of her face.

She smiled a slow, sad smile, and he knew at once it wasn't an act. Allie Atwells had left her spoiled-darling routine behind forever.

"I'm surprised to see you here," she said in a voice that had no surprise in it at all.

"I'm leaving the day after tomorrow," was all he could think to say.

"Ah. She won't go with you, then?" Allie asked quietly. "I didn't think she would."

"I haven't asked her yet," he said. "That's next."

"She's going to say no," said Allie without triumph.

"We'll see."

Allie bit her lower lip and said, "That time in the cabin? It meant she loved you more than she loved me. And I accept that—now. Meg risked everything for you. She risked *me*. If you don't make her say yes, then what's happened between Meg and me is pointless."

He smiled ironically. "You understand that she won't see me *because* of what happened between the two of you."

"Ignore that. It has nothing to do with how you feel."

"You'd like me to—?"

"Hit her over the head if you have to. You won't hurt her," Allie added wryly. "She's more hardheaded than I am."

"She's not like that."

Allie sat up straight, then looked him in the eye and said,

"Look, Hamlet, this is not an affair of honor anymore; it's an affair of the *heart*. Stop analyzing, will you? Stop being a cop."

She was right. Absolutely right. Wyler grinned, feeling suddenly more lighthearted than he'd felt so far.

He took her hand the way an older brother might and said warmly, "I'm glad you two are making up."

Allie's violet eyes went dark; she shook her head. "Nothing's changed between Meg and me, Tom. It can't possibly."

"What? For God's sake—"

He was about to ask why not, when the door to the room suddenly slammed the rest of the way open with hurricane force. Tom turned on his heel, reaching automatically for a gun he wasn't carrying, and found himself face-to-face with Bobby Beaufort's jealous fury.

"You son of a bitch!" Bobby growled. "One's not enough for you—"

Bobby swung, and Allie screamed, and Tom ended up defending himself with a little more enthusiasm than was strictly necessary, considering they were in a hospital. A passing male aide broke up the fracas, and the head nurse, who knew Bobby, let them leave without actually carrying out her threat to have them both arrested.

"Twenty-six, and what a mess," she said in scathing tones to Beaufort as he skulked past her. "As for *you*," she said to Wyler, "you should be ashamed. Now get out, both of you."

She slammed the emergency exit door closed, leaving both of them in a face-to-face standoff in the parking lot.

"You son of a bitch," Bobby repeated.

"Cool it, ace."

Wyler thought about leveling Beaufort then and there, but somehow he wasn't in the mood any longer. He stuck out his hand impulsively and said, "Look, pal, you've got it all wrong. I'm in love with her sister. With *Meg*."

Bobby glanced at the outstretched hand, then resumed his

staredown. "Yeah, right," he said suspiciously. "So why're you leading *Allie* on?"

"I'm not. Trust me: she couldn't care less. Look, let me buy you a beer," Wyler suggested, inviting the man to a ritual almost as old as the peace pipe. "We can talk about it if you want."

Bobby snorted, which Wyler took as a yes. Forgoing the handshake, he said, "I'll meet you at Sully's," which he knew was where the locals hung out.

Bobby got on his bike and Wyler followed, wondering why he'd let himself get detoured from the business of storming the Inn Between. A wisenheimer voice inside was telling him that he was afraid that Meg might say no—and just as afraid that she might say yes.

Was he ready for another shot at a relationship? Up until a couple of weeks ago he'd have said absolutely, positively not. He'd tried playing that game once, and had come away from it with too many broken bones to want to rush back in. As far as he was concerned, marriage was strictly a spectator sport. If it weren't for his son . . . if it weren't for Mike . . . well, at least there was Mike.

But starting all over?

It was that damn Fourth of July picnic; that was what began it all. All those damn happy families . . . kids, babies, homemade food . . . badminton and blueberry pie. . . . *Naturally* a single guy was going to feel sorry for himself. Since his divorce he'd avoided picnics like the plague. This one had blindsided him. He should've seen it coming, should've been on his guard against baby powder and barbecue grills. But he'd left himself wide open to the experience, from the chickadees to the day sail, and now the day was burned indelibly into his memory.

He wanted another Fourth of July just like that one.

Would she leave Bar Harbor for Chicago? He wasn't sure. God knew he could produce enough picnics and families for her to go to. The area detective division was a particularly close-knit group. But the families weren't his own families. And they sure weren't hers.

One thing, though: the two of them were almost mystically compatible in bed.

With Lydia the sex had been great, then good, then fair— and then, of course, nonexistent. But great or fair, there'd always been these little . . . adjustments. Move it here, move it there, higher, lower, faster, slower, whatever. Always. But with Meg everything just *happened:* pure and spontaneous, full of joy and mind-boggling eroticism. He knew just where she wanted to be, and she knew what to do with him. He wanted another night with her just like that one.

Last but not least, there was Allie. He couldn't begin to guess what the sisters were going to do to mend their rift, but one thing seemed certain: *he* was no longer a factor. He could hang upside down like a bat from Allie's ceiling, and she probably wouldn't notice him. He felt humbled but intensely relieved.

Would Meg leave Bar Harbor for Chicago? He wished he knew.

Bobby was halfway through his first beer by the time Tom slipped onto the plastic-covered stool alongside him. The place was your basic hole-in-the-wall eatery on the side of the road, with no neighbors and plenty of parking. Inside it was dark and generic and smelled of stale beer and half-finished cigarettes. It reminded him of the division's hangout in Chicago, and that reminded him of the last big case they'd cracked, and *that* got him to thinking about serial killers in general. He was sorry, suddenly, that he'd come.

He ordered a double scotch.

"So," he said to Bobby as he slid a couple of bills across the varnished bar at the bartender, "are you having any better luck with Allie than I am with Meg?"

Bobby stared into his beer and shook his head in the time-honored body language of men discussing women. "Obviously I'm not good enough for her," he said. "Well, *I* know that. Anyone can see she could have the King of England if she wanted him. But I swear to God that's not what she wants."

"What *does* she want?" Wyler couldn't help asking.

"Whatever it is she don't have," Bobby said flatly. "Which is why you lasted so long in her fancy, by the way," he added with a wry glance at Wyler.

Bobby slugged down the rest of his beer and signaled the barkeep with a patting gesture in front of the empty glass. "She's been that way ever since she was a kid," he said. "If you had Pepsi and she had Coke, she'd want the Pepsi. But if you offered her a choice, chances are she'd say root beer."

"Yeah," said Wyler, sipping his scotch. "She just hasn't found the right soft drink yet."

"She never will. It's the searching and the sampling that interest her." He shrugged stoically. "So what's with Meg?" he asked Wyler. "Is she still hung up on trying to put Camplin behind bars?"

"You know about that?"

Bobby shrugged again. "Word gets around. She shouldn't mess with them types, y' know. They're all a little wacko—because they're so desperate to hang on to what they've got, y' know? They want things done their way or no way."

Wyler nodded. Despite himself, he was beginning to take a shine to Bobby. He was turning out to be just another kid in need of a shave and a high school diploma. He seemed smarter, more reflective than most: too bad he was hiding those brains under a red bandanna.

"Believe me," Bobby said, still ruminating. "I know. You live in a schizo town like this—rich, poor, hardly no one in between—you learn which ones to avoid. Gordon Camplin's one tough buzzard. Friend of mine was doing some carpentry for him—wahn't even my buddy's gig; he was workin' for someone else—and Camplin went and got him fired.''

"Didn't like the look of him?" Wyler suggested.

"You got it. Wife's the same way. I had this job in Ellsworth before I went out west. Franklin Foreign Auto, you heard of it? They do good work. Anyway, that summer, Dorothea Camplin brings in her Mercedes for a tune-up. Her granddaughter shows up at the same time, in her Lexus, to take the old lady back home. Well, the granddaughter's comin' on to me the way them richbitches do, and I don't mind. We're foolin' around, talkin', no big deal.''

Bobby sipped his beer, smiling at the memory. He was a good-looking hulk; Wyler could understand why richbitches came on to him.

"At some point I look up," Bobby went on, "and there's old Dorothea, givin' me the evil eye. Scared the *shit* out of me. Less than a week later I'm walking along the road at dusk, and I recognize her Mercedes in oncoming traffic. She veers— purposely, I'll bet my life on it—and clips me with her outside mirror. Just about breaks my arm. I'm tellin' you—you don't mess with those people," he repeated, toasting his glass to them.

Wyler hardly heard the moral of the story. His mind was suddenly in overdrive, racing past the useless pieces of information that had littered Meg's case from the start, zeroing in on the one bit that mattered, a line from Gordon Camplin's letter to Margaret Mary Atwells:

God help me if I am caught writing it.

Wyler had slid right over it, focusing where Meg had told him to focus: on Gordon Camplin's threat in the last paragraph. What an *idiot* he'd been.

"I mean, here's a woman once slapped her twenty-one-year-old grandson in front of half the town for using the *F* word in public," Bobby was saying with a wry smile. "Where does that leave *me* on the true-value scale? Somewhere between the grandson and just above a deerfly, I figure."

What had his brain been *doing*, while Meg was waving the letter in front of him? Figuring out whether her bra unhooked in the front or in the back, that was what. God, what an *idiot*.

In a panic, Wyler looked around for a phone: occupied.

"Bobby, look—I gotta go," he said. "Catch you later."

He threw a single on the bar and took off, praying to God that Meg was at the Inn Between.

Dorothea Camplin was in her terraced rose garden, humming a ditty to herself, when her Cuban gardener arrived carrying a galvanized bucket filled with foul-smelling, dark-stained water.

"Here you are, señora. All the butts since we are at Tea Kettle. I am sorry—not so many as other summers. I am trying to cut back. My cousin, in Havana? He has, how you call, the cancer of the throat. Larrin . . . lar . . ."

"Laryngeal cancer, Manuel," Dorothea said, stirring the tobacco-infested mixture with a twig. "Yes. That doesn't surprise me. Tobacco is poison; that's why it does such a good job on our aphids. How many cigars did he smoke a day?"

"His wife say, too many. Eight, ten. *Puros fuertes*," Manuel murmured, shaking his head. "Strong, strong, cigars, the Cubans."

"Ten! Heavens!" Mrs. Camplin said, shocked. "Much too many. I'm glad you're cutting back, Manuel. I want you to live a long life, in good health."

"*Gracias, señora*. You wish something more . . . ?"

"No, no, you go and enjoy yourself. I'll see you back here on Monday. Don't forget to leave the gates open for Mrs. Hazard."

The gardener nodded and left. Mrs. Camplin peered into the bucket and sighed, then went into the house. She came out carrying a plastic kitchen caddy containing a pair of yellow rubber gloves, a small bottle colored ruby red and stoppered with a cork, a fine-mesh tea strainer, a Pyrex glass measuring cup; and a pretty, crystal vial of amber-colored oil.

She put the caddy on the ground next to the galvanized bucket, then knelt in front of them on a gardening pad. She slipped on the rubber gloves, picked up the Pyrex cup, and dipped it gingerly into the galvanized bucket, filling it with the murky, tobacco-shreddy liquid. The ruby-red bottle had a wide base; it stood without tipping on the mulched ground as she held the tea strainer over its neck, then poured the bottle two-thirds full from the measuring cup of tobacco liquid.

After that she untwisted the cap of the amber oil, passed it back and forth under her nose with a dreamy smile, and decanted some of its contents into the little red bottle. She held the red bottle up to her nose and grimaced, then, with a worried frown, poured the rest of the fragrant amber oil into the tobacco mixture. Once again she sniffed the red bottle, thought about it, sniffed one more time, and, with a considering nod—as if she'd finally got the sweet-sour balance for a stir-fry exactly right—popped the cork back in.

After that Mrs. Camplin reloaded the caddy and carried it back to the house. She had a tray of fresh-baked brownies to frost before her guest arrived.

The only vehicle that Tom Wyler found at the Inn Between was Lloyd's rusted pickup. Lloyd himself was in the graveled parking area, which had been turned into a kind of disaster-relief station. There were pans of oil-soaked Speedy-dry that looked not too different from pee-soaked kitty litter; and soaking-wet oil-absorbent pads and blankets; and three twenty-five-gallon drums filled with rescued fuel oil.

"Whatta mess, huh?" Lloyd said as Wyler rolled down the window of his car.

"Where's Meg? Where is she?" Wyler said, not bothering to hide the urgency in his voice.

"Meg? I dunno. She left a little while ago with a camera bag and a tripod over her shoulder."

"*Dammit*! Why'd you let her go?" Wyler said irrationally.

"Go where?"

Wyler threw the Cutlass into reverse and tore out of there, sending gravel flying into the wheelwell of his rented car. This was it, the ultimate nightmare of any cop: rushing to an ambush where the one you love is about to be ambushed.

Dorothea Camplin: old woman, old money, old values. If she could lock a rival in her husband's bedroom and leave her there to burn, if she could crush a peon like Bobby Beaufort for looking at her granddaughter the wrong way . . . then what the *hell* was she capable of doing to an amateur sleuth who was tiptoeing ever closer to a dangerous truth—that Dorothea Camplin was a psycho, a puritanical, possessive, murderous psycho.

If anything happens to Meg . . . if one hair on her head is touched . . .

Meg arrived exactly on time and was met at the open gates by Mrs. Camplin, wielding a pair of pruning shears. The old woman was standing fearlessly on the top step of a folding ladder, slashing through thick English ivy that had overgrown the wrought-iron lamp fixtures that served as finials atop the brick pillars that supported the heavy iron gates. A heap of long, cut-back ivy tendrils lay on the ground at the foot of the stepladder.

She waved cheerfully to Meg and said, "Go right on up to the house. I'm going to close the gates behind you; a couple of dogs have been just itching to get past me for the last little while. I'm blessed if I'll have them digging up my garden. Not before it's photographed, anyway," she said, laughing.

Meg waved an acknowledgment and drove slowly down the

landscaped drive, enjoying the smells and sights of the superbly tended grounds. Huge clumps of pink cleome, unseasonably early, and tall stands of purple coneflower filled the sunny patches between the towering trees that lined the path to the house. Black-eyed Susan and bee balm and phlox—everything was at peak. The summer sweet, too, was in full bloom, filling the air with its delightfully cloying fragrance. How had she missed it all the day before?

Because I was upset then, and today I'm not, Meg told herself. She'd replayed that last moment of yesterday's interview over and over and over in her mind, and she was convinced: Dorothea Camplin was about to lend Meg the money herself. The woman's exact words had been, "Maybe *I* can manage"—something or other. What else, if not a loan?

Okay, so the money wasn't coming from Gordon Camplin, and okay, so it looked a little like a blackmail payment, even to Meg. Too bad. Desperate times called for desperate measures. Besides, Meg was going to pay off every cent, with interest. With any luck, she might even be able to hold on to the dollhouse—although she wasn't sure why that was important any longer. She had a profound feeling that the little house had done its work and that Gordon Camplin, despite his evil bravado, would never sleep soundly again. It was probably the best that Meg could hope for.

In the meantime, she had to keep on with this silly charade about a magazine piece on Dorothea Camplin's gardens. Maybe she'd actually write the thing and submit it. There were worse careers in life than doing articles on gardening.

With a sense that she was making progress at least on the financial front, Meg pulled up in front of the charming facade of Tea Kettle Cottage and began unloading her equipment. Mrs. Camplin joined her and they walked together to the rose garden, the first and obvious "room" to be photographed.

"Your roses are so healthy," Meg said admiringly.

"Because I don't tolerate the ones that give me trouble,"

Mrs. Camplin said bluntly. "Over the years I've winnowed out all the prima donnas. You'll notice there are no red roses, for example; I've yet to find a fragrant one that'll stand up to the moods and rigors of Maine."

"That's all right," said Meg. "The pale ones will show better in this gray light. We could use a breeze, though," she added, swatting at a mosquito on her shoulder. "The bugs are *fierce* today."

"They nearly always are. Do you want something for them?"

"No, no, I'm fine. I try to avoid chemical repellants." Meg swatted her calf, and then the back of her knee. This was going to be misery; why hadn't she thought to rub herself with lemon balm before she came?

And why wasn't Dorothea Camplin talking *money*? She was acting as if yesterday had never happened. It was very disconcerting. Meg swatted again at her leg, irritated; this one had drawn blood.

"My dear, you'll be eaten alive. Let me give you what *I* use; it's my own brew, completely organic." She held up her forearm under Meg's nose. "Smell," she commanded.

"Nice. Lily of the valley?"

"For fragrance. You set up and get started. I'll bring some of this out for you. And meanwhile, I'll brew us a pot of tea to wash down the brownies I made. We can have tea out here while we chat."

Chat. Good. They were going to chat. She *hadn't* forgotten, then. Meg grinned enthusiastically and began walking around the raised beds, looking for the best vantage point to begin shooting. She settled on a trio of pink-and-ivory multiflora roses just breaking into bloom. In the far background was the greenhouse attached to the silver-shingled cottage, an irresistible scene that was sure to excite the fancy of any gardener who saw it. *Yes.* Definitely, she'd do the article, and hopefully more.

She was shooting and swatting away when Mrs. Camplin returned with a gorgeous red bottle and handed it to her. "Use as much as you like; I can easily make more."

Meg pulled out the cork and laid it on a stone bench tucked in a little bend of the perennial border filled with clouds of baby's breath in fading bloom. Everywhere she looked, everything she touched, was beautiful, including the blown-glass, ruby-red bottle. She poured some of the golden liquid into the palm of her hand and rubbed it over her left arm and her legs, then switched and did her remaining arm.

The brew seemed a bit fishy under the lily-of-the-valley smell; but then, it *was* organic.

Mrs. Camplin smiled and said, "The water's boiling by now. I'll pour the tea and bring out a tray. You keep on working."

"Sure," Meg said, assuming they'd be nailing down an interest rate during teatime. She returned happily to the task and thought, *People get paid for this*?

Ten minutes later, her eyes were tearing and she had the beginnings of a pounding headache. She was allergic to something in the garden, apparently: mold spores or pollen, maybe. She thought about returning to the house, but Mrs. Camplin seemed so intent on having tea in the garden; Meg hated to disappoint her. Still, the damn tea was taking forever to brew.

She became restless and jumpy, swatting at the mosquitoes that seemed more interested in her than ever, and still—still! —no tea. This was stupid. If she was promised tea, then she should have the damned tea. And a brownie—what about that brownie?

No, no. No brownie. The mere thought of it made her suddenly nauseous. She fought back a rising tide of vomit, looking around frantically for somewhere discreet to puke. But there was no place; everything was planted, tended, flowering. She couldn't defile the site. Oh, but she was becoming deathly ll. She had to find a place. She turned and ran to one corner, then another, dizzy from her frantic maneuvers.

There was one little spot without flowers; she ran toward it and found it was filled by a big stone frog. *Two* stone frogs; or else she was seeing double. One frog or two, she couldn't wait. She was sick all over it or them, and then she fell to her knees, breathing rapidly, her heart still pounding furiously, struggling to stand and make her way back to the house for help.

She couldn't get up. She lay there awhile, and it seemed to her that she must be getting better, because her heartbeat began to slow down, and then it slowed down some more . . . and then . . . some more . . .

And then it seemed to her, in her lethargic but not unpleasant stupor, that help did come. Mrs. Camplin did come. And Meg had been sweating, she knew she was still dripping wet, and Mrs. Camplin must have felt sorry for her, because through a haze Meg watched her pick up a galvanized bucket from somewhere and pour water all over her. It was very cool . . . it felt very refreshing . . . but it smelled awfully fishy.

CHAPTER **25**

The gates were locked, but that didn't stop Wyler. By stepping on the iron scrollwork of the bottom gate rail, he was able —just—to get a footing mid-picket and haul himself over the gate without—quite—impaling himself on the spear points. Cursing himself for not taking his physical therapy more seriously, he dropped to his feet, then to his knees, before he recovered and went charging down the drive.

He didn't think about guard dogs, he didn't think about alarms; he only thought, *She's here, and if she's here, she's in danger*. It seemed incomprehensible to him that with all she had on her plate, Meg was still pursuing this sham photography scheme of hers. Didn't she have enough to worry about? When he found her, he was going to take her in his arms and kill her.

The driveway seemed to go on forever; the grounds were vast, ringed by thick woods. His cop's eye noted that there were plenty of places to hide the results of a crime. His heart, pounding hard, turned away from the thought. At the head of the drive and in front of a flower-covered house too picture-perfect to be true, he saw Meg's old Chevy parked alongside a Mercedes. He should've felt relieved but didn't; Bobby's words were too fresh in his mind: *They're so desperate to hang on to what they've got*.

He found Meg almost by instinct, lying unconscious on a mulched path near a big stone frog. Her shorts were wet; a knocked-over galvanized bucket lay next to her. The bucket was filled with soggy, half-shredded cigar butts; why, he didn't know. All he knew was that nicotine was one of the most toxic natural substances in existence. Panicking that he might be too late, he dragged a nearby hose over to Meg and rinsed her off quickly, then made a beeline for the house and phone. Two things were on his mind: Get an ambulance. Get the gate open.

He was in the front hall when Dorothea Camplin emerged carrying a large brass tray laden with a yellow teapot, two matching cups in their saucers, and a yellow plate of frosted brownies cut into two-inch squares. She looked absolutely shocked to see him there, but she didn't drop the tray or act hysterical, and he didn't wait for her to say something first, a fact that later he regretted.

"Where's your goddamned phone?" he demanded. "I've got to call an ambulance."

"An *ambulance*? What's happened? A car accident? Who are you? I've seen you before. How did you get on the grounds?"

He saw a phone on a small butler's table in front of a chintz-covered sofa and ran to it, then dialed an ambulance. The call was brief; he had another to make, still in a state of anguish, to the poison control center. All the while, Dorothea Camplin was watching him with a look of horror on her face.

When he hung up the second time, she said, "What should we do? What can I get?"

He ignored her and looked around, then ripped a soft cashmere throw from an arm of the overstuffed sofa and ran out with it, with Dorothea Camplin hard on his heels, saying, "I know what happened. I know just what happened. I had a bucket of cigar-water sitting on an old stump; I was painting my rosebushes with the solution, to kill the aphids. She must have knocked it over on herself.''

Wyler didn't know an aphid from an apricot, but he had no doubt that Dorothea had set up a perfectly reasonable scenario. He didn't care; he didn't care about anything else in the world just then except the woman lying unconscious in the rose garden. When he got back to Meg he stripped away her shorts and rinsed her off still more, rubbing her limbs clean with his handkerchief. He had no idea whether he was doing anything right; his hands were shaking with apprehension.

But he knew how to treat a victim in shock. He wrapped Meg in the cashmere throw, then carried her back into the house and laid her on the thick knotted rug with her legs elevated, and monitored her breathing and pulse, ready to give her CPR, until the ambulance arrived through the iron gates that Dorothea Camplin had been commanded to open.

"You again?"

Wyler lifted his head from his hands and looked up.

It was the curmudgeon nurse, standing above him, only this time she had a look of compassion on her face. "I just heard about Mrs. Hazard. What a bizarre accident. I don't know . . . sometimes fate is so ridiculously cruel . . .''

She put her hand on his shoulder, then pressed her lips together in a hapless smile and continued on her way.

Wyler dropped his head back in his hands, unwilling and unable to change from that position. He'd been like that, numb with anticipation, since Meg was admitted. In his entire life he'd never shut down as completely as he had now. The only part of his consciousness that wasn't focused on Meg's recovery was, every once in a while, saying things like, *Have them bring the old woman in, stupid. Don't let her fool with the scene.*

He didn't care about that; he had no room to care about that. If Meg lived—of course she would live, she *had* to live—

she would be furious with him for not being on top of her case. But he couldn't move. He was in a state of suspended animation. His soul was somewhere outside of his body, moving restlessly between Meg's body and his, trying to reassure her, trying to reassure himself. She *would* live. She *had* to live.

One eternity rolled into the next, and finally, someone came out to see him.

"Her vital signs have stabilized," the physician said, cutting straight to the chase. He knew who Wyler was; he didn't mince words. "She definitely dodged a bullet out there. We're going to keep her here for a couple of days, make sure we've flushed out her system. She'll be on medication to strengthen her heartbeat. I understand her sister's being treated here too? That would be—you?" he asked, shifting his attention away from Wyler.

"Yes, Doctor. That's me. I'm her sister, Allegra Atwells."

Wyler swung around and was stunned to see Allie, wrapped in a yellow robe with one sleeve cut away, standing behind him and hanging as anxiously as he was on every word. Everett Atwells was there, too, materialized out of thin air.

The physician smiled reassuringly. "She's going to be fine."

"Can we see her?" her father asked humbly, rotating his cap in his hand like a peasant seeking an audience with royals.

The physician scrunched his face good-naturedly. "Actually, no. I'd give her a little while. She's been through hell. What she needs now is uninterrupted rest." He repeated, "She's going to be fine," then excused himself and left.

Wyler said to Allie and her father, "I'm sorry. I hadn't noticed either of you."

Allie and her father exchanged looks. Allie said, "We've been waiting here with you for the last half hour."

"Oh, I knew *that*," he said, although he couldn't remember

a moment of it. "I meant, naturally he should've addressed himself to you two, not to me."

Allie drummed the fingers of her right hand nervously on her cast, then closed her eyes and let out a sigh of jittery relief. "I can hardly let myself think about this. If you hadn't gone looking for her when you did . . ."

She shook her head and opened her eyes. "What did you say Dorothea was doing? Bringing out tea to the garden?"

Wyler nodded. At the same time, a red flag went up in the back of his mind.

Allie said, "She would've found Meg, I guess. But who knows what her reaction would've been . . . she might've gone into useless hysterics . . . Some people are like that."

"Not, I think, Dorothea Camplin," Wyler said with tightly controlled understatement. Suddenly he was back in focus. He smiled a private, wry smile, knowing that Meg would be pleased that he was on the case.

Everett Atwells, exhausted and adrift without his daughter to boss him around, said, "Should I stay? Should I go? What would she want?"

"Go back to Uncle Billy's, Dad, and get some rest," Allie said gently. "I'll be here for her."

Allie looked at Wyler as she said it, answering the question that had been hovering in the air between them for the last few minutes. Wyler put his arm around her and kissed her on her cheek.

"You're doing the right thing, kiddo," he said softly.

"I'm not, Tom; things are still the same," she repeated frowning. "But this is different."

Wyler left her there, convinced that if he lived to be a hundred and two, he'd never understand what made sisters tick. All he could do was cross his fingers and hope that love ran deeper than pride. In the meantime, he had a stop to make downtown.

* * *

He was at Meg's hospital room early the next morning, before visiting hours. Strictly speaking, his visit was an official one; but his heart was beating like a schoolboy's as he waited for the nurse to give him permission to enter the room.

Meg looked better than he thought possible after what she'd been through. She smiled weakly when he came in. "Hi. You're the first one they've let me see," she said.

He sat next to her and took her hand in his, just to make sure she was real; the sense that spirits had been coming and going and doing some hard bargaining was with him still.

She was real. Her hand felt warm and solid. He bent over and kissed it in simple homage to the fact that she was alive. He was not a praying man, but he'd prayed plenty on the day before. His prayers had been answered, and now, as he bent over her hand, he mustered one more prayer, a prayer of profound and humble thanks.

She said, "I remember telling you . . . back in your cabin . . . that you were the right man at the wrong place at the wrong time." She smiled and said, "I take it all back."

He laughed softly. "I remember telling *you*—back in my cabin—that you were the most headstrong woman I'd ever met. I stand convinced."

"Okay, okay," she said, blushing a wonderful, healthy shade of pink. "So I've suffered a minor setback. But I think she's going to lend me the money—out of guilt, if for no other reason."

Wyler stared at Meg, amazed. She'd marched in and out of the lion's den without ever realizing there was an animal lurking there. "You have no idea what happened?" he asked, disappointed.

Her face became pale. "I guess not. My recollection and reality don't seem to match. What did Mrs. Camplin say?"

"Never mind her," Wyler answered. "Tell me, from start to finish, what you think happened. Every little thing."

She was reluctant to live through it again, but with some

coaxing, she obliged him. He was hard pressed to keep a calm demeanor when she described the little red bottle, even harder pressed when she described the onset of symptoms shortly afterward. He wanted to jump up and get a search warrant going, but he had to hear her through. It was worth the wait.

"You *saw* her throw the bucket of water on you?"

"Yes. No. No, that part I dreamed. I think I was delirious. I felt so thirsty, I wanted a drink . . . I think she was like a mirage, you know? Everything was so blurry, almost hallucinatory. No. I must've dreamed that part. I must've staggered and pulled the bucket over me, and that's what you found. I mean, what else?"

"All right," he said calmly. "I want you to think about it some more. Someone will be by later to take a statement from you, Meg. Tell them what you remember as accurately as you can. Don't try to make sense of it. Just tell him what you remember."

He leaned over and kissed her on her lips, which brought more delicious color to her cheeks. He backed out of the room nonchalantly, then raced like hell to the nearest phone and dialed the Bar Harbor police. The red bottle was great news; the so-called hallucinatory recollection not so great news. But all the little pieces fit. What pleased Wyler particularly was Meg's recollection that she'd got tired of waiting for her tea.

Because he remembered, in his slow-motion replay of the event, that no steam was coming out of the little yellow teapot; that Mrs. Camplin had decided, finally and suddenly, to haul out to the garden.

Meg had just completed her statement to the police when Allie knocked on the open door and came in. She was dressed in a white sleeveless sundress and a big white baseball cap that she was wearing backward over her shaved head, an odd but whimsical combination that made her look like a street fighting angel.

"I like the look," Meg said when her sister sat down silently next to her. She thumped lightly on Allie's cast. "You always did know how to accessorize."

Meg was being as light and flippant as she knew how, to make her sister feel at ease. But there was a hard lump in her throat, and when Allie didn't say anything, the lump got harder.

"You could have died," Allie whispered reproachfully, a tear rolling down her cheek.

"You could have died," Meg shot back, unable to keep the reproach out of her voice, either.

Allie shook her head in warning. "Don't start, Meg. I know it was a stupid, dumb slip. Do you think I don't regret it? But it forced me to lie still for a while and . . . reconsider."

Reconsider. The word had a joyous ring to it. Meg had hoped for nothing else since Allie's accident: that she would reconsider, and forgive, and someday forget.

Allie took a deep breath and went on. "This sounds so selfish, but—for the first time in my life, I had to ask myself, what would I do without you? Who would I go to for advice? Who would approve my decisions, or even make them outright for me?"

"I don't do that anymore," Meg said lamely. But it was a lie, and both of them knew it.

Allie said, "You've been the mother I got cheated out of, and I've been the daughter you never had. And it worked out well, for a pretty long time. But you have other . . . needs, and I have other wants."

Meg winced. Eventually it had to come around to this, to Tom; it was bound to. "Everybody makes mistakes," she said. "You have to be able to let *me* make them too." She added wryly, "God knows I'm good at it."

"I'm not talking about the cabin," Allie said impatiently. She jumped up and began to pace, the way she always did when she was working something through. "I *have* to come out from behind your skirts, Meg. It's way past the time for it. There are kids out there half my age with twice my experience—''

"But you don't *live* in the Bronx," Meg argued. "You live in a nice, old-fashioned town." And yet she knew that Allie was right: she was amazingly innocent. To Meg, it was part of her great charm, to be twenty-five and naïve.

"I don't want to live in a nice, old-fashioned town, Meg. I don't want to go into the hospitality industry. I've been saying that for a long time; you just haven't wanted to hear it."

"We don't have to talk about that now—do we?" Meg pleaded. The subject was pure, dry tinder. Anything Meg said would put a torch to it.

"We do, because I want you to know that what happened between you and Tom has nothing to do with the decision I've made."

"What happened between Tom and me will never happen again!" Meg said, interrupting her. "I've wanted to tell you that ever since . . . that day."

" 'That day'? You make it sound like it'll live on in infamy, like the Salem witch trials or something. Meg, you're in love with him—and he's definitely in love with you. He's not married, you're not married. You *get* to make love with one another; it's one of the perks of being born after the Inquisition."

"Right," Meg said dully, letting her head fall back on the pillow.

Allie sighed and came back to her seat. "Look. That whole triangle was my fault. There shouldn't have *been* a triangle; Tom was sending me steady signals to butt out all along. I just didn't want to recognize them. He was my first love, Meg," she said in poignant apology. "First loves are pure magic— because we have no idea that they'll ever end."

It was such a sad, disillusioned thing for Allie to say. Meg couldn't agree less; she herself would never stop loving Tom. "Sometimes they *don't* end," she confessed.

Allie leaned over and kissed her sister on the forehead. "All the more reason not to be a jerk."

Allie walked over to the window, past the other, empty bed, and stared outside. "I'm going to Greece, Meg," she murmured. "Next week."

Crease? Geese? Meg didn't quite catch what her sister said. "What's at the end of the week?" she asked.

Allie turned around. "You remember Dmitri Kronos? He spent a weekend here last summer? His parents have a place on Crete. I'm going there to finish out the season, and after that, he and I will go to his parents' winter place in St. Moritz."

"*Why?*"

Allie shrugged. "He asked."

"That's no reason, Allie! Besides, you don't have any money!"

"I won't need it with Dmitri," Allie said dryly. "And I *don't* think you've been listening."

"Oh, no . . . Allie . . . don't," Meg pleaded. "Don't ever put yourself in that position."

"You mean, of a hanger-on with the jet set? Why not? It's a tough job, but *somebody's* got to do it."

"We don't know anything about him! Who are his people?"

Allie burst into a merry, genuinely amused laugh. "His people are filthily rich, is who his people are. Shipping, I think. I expect his mother is asking him the same thing, right about now. Who are her people?"

She added sardonically, "I can just *imagine* what he's telling her: that my family is doubled up with a relative because the roof leaks and the basement stinks and they can't afford to fix any of it. Oh, and we rent rooms—on dry, windy days. That ought to impress his mum."

"But it's *our* leaky roof, and it's *our* stinky basement! Don't you see the difference?"

"Meg, you know something? I *don't*. There are so many generations at the Inn Between that it seems like communism anyway, so what's the difference if I'm a non-owner here or a non-owner there? For that matter, what's the difference between being a charming ornament at one of their soirées, or being a charming hostess at a company Christmas party at a Marriott? It's not like I own either the villa or the hotel."

"Oh, excuse me—you don't want to work for a living, *ever*?"

"Why should I, if I can manage not to? Why would anyone?"

"Because—because you have a *degree*!" Meg said, as if the word had magical powers to restore her sister's sanity.

"I got that for *you*, dammit!" Allie cried. "I wish I could give it back to you! I don't want it! I've wasted my life getting it!"

"Stop. Please. Let's both stop," Meg said dizzily. "I can't go around this ride again."

Allie ran back to her sister's side and squeezed her hand. "I didn't mean to say all that, Meggie, really I didn't. All I wanted was to tell you my plans. Not to ask you about them—to tell you."

She glanced at her watch. "Comfort will have a fit. She's waiting outside with Dad to see you. Lloyd's out there, too, waiting to take me back to the Inn Between. He says the smell's not too bad for family, just not good enough for guests."

"You've checked out of here, then?" Meg asked, her spirits sinking steadily.

"Yeah. I guess you get thrown out tomorrow. I'll see you back home." Allie leaned over and kissed Meg on her forehead again, and left.

Three seconds later, she popped her head back in the doorway. "By the way, in case Uncle Billy asks? The ninety-minute call to Greece that was charged to his phone—that was me."

CHAPTER 26

There was no way the story wasn't going to end up on the front pages of the tabloids.

Meg's adventure made its media debut quietly enough, in a no-nonsense piece by the local paper headlined, *Summer Resident Arraigned in Homicide Attempt*. Then the Portland paper picked up on the local piece. Then the Associated Press picked up on the Portland piece.

And then the tabloids moved in. The family came under siege. The dining room table was turned into Command Central, with Uncle Billy, self-appointed publicist, handling the media. The table began to disappear under a slew of sensationalist coverage.

Every member of the family had his favorite headline.

Allie liked the one that read *Crazed Dowager Breaks Girl's Arm, Forces Her to Swallow Pure Nicotine*.

Meg thought *Two Sisters Chained in Greenhouse by Bitter Heiress* had a poetic ring to it.

Comfort was leaning toward *Vacationing Cop Saves Island Town from Mad Gardener*. It sounded heroic.

Terry and Timmy, showing a genetic bias, voted hands down for *Woman Dipped in Nicotine Grows Second Head*.

"Laugh all you want," said Uncle Billy, punching in a call

to a Boston television station. "This story is gonna make us rich."

Hard Copy, Current Events, Top Cops, Geraldo, Larry, Barbara, Oprah—Uncle Billy was going after them all. He had a vested interest in the family now, having agreed to lend Meg the money she needed at a not-very-nice interest rate that, however, he was willing to waive if Allie got to Europe and ended up marrying either money or nobility.

"A little incentive, Allie-cat," he told his niece, pinching her cheek. "I want you to go over there and show 'em what yer made of."

Meg watched the whole thing with a sense of bemusement that bordered on despair. Her life had become surreal, and she had little hope that it would ever be normal again. If there were some way to roll back the clock to June, she felt sure she'd never have answered Orel Tremblay's initial summons.

Her father, among others, didn't believe that. "You know you'd do everything the same all over again. Everything," he repeated with a meaningful look. "So don't even try to second-guess yourself, Meggie. Just look to the future."

It was the one direction Meg didn't want to look, because she couldn't see anything beyond a big, black hole where hope and joy should be. So she was taking one bizarre day at a time, crying some days, laughing others, trying hard not to think or plan.

Today was a crying day.

Allie was packed and in the sitting room, waiting out that awkward interval that precedes a trip to the airport. Meg had done all she could, from getting full descriptions (including everything but dental records) of Dmitri's family, to presenting her sister with a Care package that included a list of every English-speaking doctor in Europe, a collapsible cup, a box of Handi Wipes, and a pound of hard candies to suck on during takeoff and landing. ("You could burst an eardrum otherwise," she'd insisted.)

Comfort had thought it would be nice if Allie took a jar of her blueberry chutney to Dmitri's mother, and made the mistake of suggesting that Allie leave half the candy behind to make room for it. Meg had burst into tears. The chutney stayed behind.

"I'm sorry, everyone, oh, God, I'm being such a jerk," Meg had said, and retreated to the same rocking chair in which she used to hold Allie and tell her bedtime stories.

That was where Meg was now as Allie explained to their Aunt Nella—not an aunt, really, but an older third or fourth cousin—the story of Dorothea Camplin's diabolical scheme.

Meg had long since tired of telling it, preferring to let the family do the honors. With typical melodrama, Allie explained how Dorothea had planned more or less to stun Meg with the mixture from the ruby-red bottle, then go back for the kill with the contents of the galvanized bucket. How she must have used an ordinary insect repellant on herself, then overlaid it with lily-of-the-valley oil to throw Meg off the scent, so to speak. How she really did set out a tray for tea, which she no doubt would have dropped dramatically at the scene when she discovered the . . . well, the body.

Aunt Nella tsked repeatedly at every pause and said, "I never; well, I *never*. What a brazen old hussy! But I don't understand why she didn't get rid of the red bottle?"

"Once it became clear that Meg was going to recover, she didn't dare take that risk," Allie explained. "But she cleaned the bottle thoroughly; there was no trace of nicotine in it. That was the bad news. The good news is, the *cork* had traces. We figure she put the bottle through the dishwasher, but not the cork; ordinarily you wouldn't, of course."

"She was flustered," Aunt Nella said, nodding sagely. "Now what's this about a haunted dollhouse? It's in all the papers."

Allie rolled her eyes. "That's Uncle Billy's doing. The house isn't *really* haunted," she said, glancing at Meg. "But

Uncle Billy's still trying to get top dollar for it. He thinks a haunted dollhouse has a more 'alluring provenance.' "

Uncle Billy looked up from his phone conversation with Maury Povich and mouthed the words, "Damn right."

"So, he's telling everyone that the lights go on and off by themselves. Really, the press will print *any*thing."

"But why did Dorothea do it?" asked Aunt Nella. "I still don't understand why she went after Meg. And what did it all have to do with the dollhouse, anyway?"

"We're not at liberty to say. *That* matter is under investigation; it goes to motive," said Allie in an official voice, hinting at dark developments to come.

Meg closed her eyes and concentrated on the gentle creak of the rocker, determined not to be drawn into the speculation. Tom had already warned her that the motive in this case was going to be considered iffy, if not downright unbelievable, to a jury. He felt reasonably sure they could prove *what* Dorothea did; but *why* she did it, that was something else again.

And yet the motive—trying to keep Meg from backing Gordon Camplin into a corner and having him implicate his ex-wife—seemed so obvious now. Late that October afternoon in 1947, Dorothea Camplin had rushed back to Eagle's Nest, possibly to retrieve the jewelry that she told Meg she used to keep in a covered jar in her bedroom. From her sitting room she was able to hear and see everything that was going on in her husband's bedroom. Shocked—or maybe not—she simply turned the key and locked both of them inside.

She couldn't be sure they wouldn't escape, of course; but it was worth a shot. As it turned out, Gordon Camplin, fit and athletic, did escape, probably by climbing out his window and dropping safely to the ground, leaving Meg's grandmother behind to die in the fire. Tom had speculated to Meg that her grandmother might have been mercifully dead by then. But Meg knew better; Meg had her vision.

Could they prove any of it? Everything depended on

Gordon Camplin. The police had questioned him, but of course he'd stonewalled them. The only evidence they possessed was his letter to Meg's grandmother. The prosecutor's office had the matter under consideration, but whether the case would go to a grand jury, and whether an indictment for Margaret Atwells's murder would come out of *that* . . .

"Probably not," was Tom's opinion.

So all they had, after all this, was a pretty good shot at Dorothea for attempted murder. The rape and murder that actually succeeded, those would go unpunished. It was outrageously unfair.

And Aunt Nella, warning Allie just then about "pinchy Mediterranean men," had no idea. . . .

Meg opened her eyes when she heard her brother's voice. If Lloyd was here, then it was time. Feeling like a minister at an execution, she took Allie aside and said, "I'll get your carry-on bag and walk you to the truck."

"Meg," said Allie in a heart-wrenching undertone. "We *agreed.* Good-byes in the parlor. No farther than that. Do you want us both to fall apart completely?"

"Okay," Meg said, deflated. She sighed deeply and held her arms open wide to her sister. Allie let herself be engulfed, cast and all, in Meg's embrace.

"Be *care*ful, honey," Meg whispered in her sister's ear. "That kind of crowd is even more bored than the kids you ran around with in high school. And the stakes nowadays are so much higher."

"I know, I know," Allie said, holding Meg tight.

"And call me when you get there."

"I will, I will," she said, tears beginning to roll.

"No, better yet, call me from Heathrow—"

"Meg."

"If you need money, ask. And don't feel obliged to go topless just because everyone else does. Don't give in to group pressure, *ever*. Go with your instincts, Allie. I love you. Bye-bye.'' Meg squeezed her tight, one last time.

"I love you, too, Meggie," Allie said in a desolate voice.

She broke away from Meg and was instantly set upon by well-wishing, farewelling relations who all but carried her out to the truck on their shoulders. The last ones out of the room were the twins, bickering and slapping because Terry grabbed the big suitcase first.

Meg went back to the Windsor rocking chair and sat in it, rocking gently. She heard the truck pull away, taking with it her sister, daughter, and best friend. Eventually it would ease, this pain, but right now it was sharp and throbbing, almost unbearable.

The family filed back in more quietly than they left. There was a sense, felt by all, that life for the foreseeable future would be just a little more ho-hum. Timmy went up to the window and stared out at the impenetrable, melancholy fog.

"Crete doesn't need Anty Allie," he said to no one in particular. "It has plenty of sunshine already." No one argued with him.

Terry said sullenly, "It sure stinks." But whether he meant the lingering smell of heating oil, or life in general, was hard to say.

The house seemed oppressive to Meg. She stood up and said, "I'm going for a walk," then grabbed a yellow nylon windbreaker to ward off the damp and chilly air.

Outside, she turned her steps automatically toward the shore. The fog was thick and chill. It was one in the afternoon, but it looked like eight at night. She should've worn an oil-skin, but it seemed easier to keep on going than to return to the house, change, and start all over. Maine was in a mood today, and so was Meg; she didn't mind the wet at all.

Wyler stumbled onto her by accident as he drove down Mount Desert Street, headed for the Inn Between. Her hands were jammed in the pockets of her windbreaker and her head was bowed in concentration. No matter. His heart leapt up at the sight of her.

His first thought was, *I am hopelessly in love with this woman.*

His second thought was, *If she walks around a big city with her head down like that, she'll be mugged in two minutes.*

He slowed the Cutlass to a stop alongside her and called out her name. She looked up and broke into a surprised but heartbroken smile that made him want to give her candy, money, flowers, anything to lift her spirits.

A diamond ring. He wished like hell he had a diamond ring in his shirt pocket. But he didn't, because the last few days had been so intensely chaotic. If anyone had told him that Bar Harbor—sleepy, touristy Bar Harbor—would be a hotbed of murder, intrigue, ghosts, and passion, he would've laughed and said yeah, right.

In any case, things were on the way to getting straightened out—except that he couldn't wait any longer to see them through, not at the rate the wheels of justice generally turned. Tomorrow he was going back, whether he liked it or not, to Chicago. He had only this one, last chance to persuade Meg to get on that plane with him.

If he had a diamond ring, he told himself, it'd be so much simpler.

"Stay right there," he commanded.

He pulled the Cutlass into a parking spot that was freeing up—a sign from God, surely—and jogged the hundred yards that separated him from her. He had absolutely no idea what he was going to say, how he was going to start. She looked so tentative, as if she was teetering on some edge. And so profoundly beautiful: the fog had settled in tiny crystal droplets on her hair, on her eyebrows, even on her eyelashes. He was struck anew by how much a part of her surroundings she was.

It reminded him of the morning with the chickadees, and the afternoon in Acadia, and the night in the woodland cabin.

But he wanted her with him in his city condo, not left behind in Maine.

"Hello."

"Hello."

Although he'd scarcely touched her since their incredible night in the cabin, he lowered his mouth to hers and kissed her tenderly, hoping she would understand that it meant, "Please marry me or I will wither and die."

"You missed her," Meg said.

He was programmed for one of two answers: yes, or no. "Missed who?" he asked, confused by her illogical response.

"My *sister*. She's gone."

The sister again; always the sister. "I didn't miss Allie," he said, disheartened that Meg hadn't understood the proposal behind the kiss. "We crossed paths as I was rushing back to town."

"Oh, good," Meg said, relieved. "I didn't want her to think —I don't know—that you were boycotting her departure."

He wanted to say, *Are you kidding? I gave a rousing cheer when I heard the brat was leaving the country.* It was the best thing for both of them—for all three of them—but how could he say so just then?

To comfort Meg, he said, "She seemed excited; I think she's really looking forward to Greece."

"Really?" Meg said in a stricken voice.

Mistake; try again. "Bobby Beaufort told me he's going over there in a month or so. 'To make sure no one's doin' nothin' he shouldn't,' is how he put it."

Meg smiled at that. "Bobby, on the island of Crete?"

"The possibilities are endless," Wyler agreed.

They walked through the fog past the odd mix of exquisite and ticky-tacky shops in the cozy downtown area. The crowds were thick with disappointed beachgoers who seemed not to get it about the Maine coast: he marveled at the number of shoppers wearing bathing suits under their trendy, off-the-shoulder tops.

Once in a while they'd stop in front of an appealing shop display. Wyler was keeping one eye open for engagement rings, because you never knew, but Meg seemed restless, and so they'd press on.

"Do you have all your souvenirs?" she asked at one point.

"Who for?" he responded simply.

She gave him a sorrowful look that he didn't altogether mind; maybe she'd come back with him out of pity.

Whatever it takes, he thought, beginning to feel a little desperate. He couldn't very well propose to her in the middle of a pottery shop or a T-shirt store. He'd already asked her if she was hungry, and she'd said no, so there went the restaurants. What was left?

With Lydia it had been so easy. Red roses; dinner downtown; the presentation of the ring as they lingered over Irish coffee. It was all done by the book. He knew the drill, and Lydia loved it, and that was that. But *Meg*. She was too . . . uncommon, too otherworldly, for the tried-and-true approach.

He wanted to knock her socks off, dammit, and that was why he hadn't got a ring: he couldn't afford a ring from Saturn, and nothing else was good enough.

They were past the shops now, on the waterfront. Meg wanted to keep walking, so they struck out along the Shore Path, a pedestrian walkway that followed the curve of the ocean, compliments of the original rich folk who owned the adjacent shorefront.

"I wonder if her plane will get off," Meg mused. "In this mull, maybe not."

The fog was thick, no doubt about it. They could see the few yards of rocky shore exposed by the low tide, and that was it. Where the sea began, visibility ended. From somewhere in the middle of the soup they heard the pathetic bleat of a hand-held air horn. Some boater new to the game was lost and scared, Wyler figured.

He felt for him. "Boy, the only thing worse than water you can see is water you *can't* see," he murmured.

Meg laughed softly and said, "It's never going to be your thing, is it. The sea, I mean."

He shrugged. "I think I'm a fire sign," he said, and left it at that. He didn't want to think about how well he fit or didn't fit in Maine. That wasn't the issue right now.

They walked along at a leisurely amble, watching the kids skipping stones, laughing, screaming, exploring the tide-bared shore: little kids, middle kids, preteens and teeners, many of them bent over, fannies out, searching for treasure. A dead crab, a bit of driftwood, really icky seaweed—to them, all of it was treasure. He saw the shore, really for the first time, through their eyes.

"I've been here for months and I still can't get over how innocent the kids all seem," he confessed to Meg. "They're a different species from what I know."

"Because you see kids in jail, or on the way to it," Meg said. "And yet . . . I truly believe that if you hauled them out here and dumped them on this beach, they'd have half a chance. Kids will stay kids a little longer if you give them someplace to play."

An old man, huddled under a blanket on his chaise longue on the grassy strip alongside the footpath, looked up from his book at the sound of their voices and smiled a greeting, which they returned.

"Sometimes they stay kids for a *long*, long time," Meg added, still smiling, after they passed him.

Wyler plucked a slender stem of ryegrass and stuck it in his mouth, chewing thoughtfully on it. There was so much going on in his mind, and his heart was so full—and time was so short. What could he say to persuade her to leave this serene and tranquil world?

They were nearing the southeastern end of the rocky beach, approaching an enormous boulder ten feet high and wide that stood balanced on one of its rounded corners. It was a striking sight, looming up as it did from the pebble-strewn shore. At the moment a couple of small kids were trying to scale it, grabbing little niches and footholds wherever they could.

"Their first Everest," Wyler said, wistfully envious. "How did it get here, anyway?"

"Dumped there by a glacier," Meg explained. "It gets nudged around by the sea every blue moon or so, if the storm is furious enough."

"And it stays on edge like that? So precarious?"

"As far as I know. It's a solid little pebble," she said, indulging the Down East penchant for understatement. "It's not going anywhere. That's why it's called Balance Rock."

"Let's climb it," he said suddenly.

Laughing, she said, "You're kidding."

He took her by the hand and dragged her over to it—by now the youngsters had given up—and offered her a foothold in his linked hands. But this was Meg, and she knew the easiest, fastest way up it; all he had to do was follow her. They sat down side by side on the high, unsupported edge of the boulder. Meg was right: it wasn't going anywhere.

Meg pulled her knees up to her chest and wrapped her forearms around her shins, peering into the silver murkiness ahead.

Now? he wondered. *Is now the time*?

She said, "So you leave tomorrow. It hardly seems possible."

It's time.

"You know I can't just walk away from you," he said.

He was watching her closely, the way he watched a defendant when the jury brought back a verdict, the way he watched a crucial witness in an interrogation: if she blinked, if she swallowed, if she winced or smiled or was determined not to react at all—he wanted to know.

She drew in a long, slow breath, and then let it out again: not a yes; not a no. He went on.

"I want you to come back with me, Meg. I want you to be my wife."

She said nothing.

He thought, *Well, okay, forget the tears-of-happiness-and-arms-around-my-neck response*. But *some* little thing would be nice.

Instead, she turned her face and looked at him almost slyly and said, "If you stay—all this will be yours." Then she made a wide, sweeping gesture at the fog.

A counteroffer was not what he expected. "All what, Meg?" he asked. "I can't make my living from the sea. As we know."

Her smile was sad and anxious and dead earnest as she said, "You know what I mean. You love it here, you said so yourself. The family's taken to you; Terry dotes on you. And don't think you haven't got used to the quiet. You get annoyed if a dog barks too long. How do you think you'll **do** in the middle of the downtown Loop?"

"What am I supposed to do here?" he asked, amazed that she was serious. "How am I supposed to support you? Get a job in a canning factory?"

"No, obviously not," she said, hurt by the sarcasm. "Help me run the Inn Between."

"Oh, just what you need—a guy who thinks a screwdriver is a murder weapon."

"I don't need a handyman; I have Lloyd for that. I need you, Tom," she said, her lip trembling with emotion. "For me."

"Meg . . . I don't want to run an inn."

"You *have* to want to run an inn. Don't you read *Reader's Digest*? It's everyone's *dream* to run an inn."

He let out a small laugh of sinking expectations. "Now, see, that's the thing: I've always had this other dream. In my dream, I have enough money for food and car payments and—fingers crossed—to send my kid or kids to college. Call me crazy."

"*I* know what the problem is," she said, turning on all fours and beginning a nimble scramble down the rock. "This has nothing to do with college!"

He wasn't quick enough to track her exact route. *The hell with it*, he thought, and dropped to the ground from a fairly high point, setting his recovery back—again.

"All right," he said, hands on his hips. "You tell *me*. What's my problem?"

"Your *problem* is, you're a crime snob. Our crimes don't meet your minimum standard for violence. Well, give us time to catch up, mister," she said scathingly. "Everyone knows we're a backward state."

"Hey, don't sell yourself short. Your family has a damn good crime portfolio. Granted, you *are* the exception around here—"

"Go to hell," she said. She turned from him and started marching off.

He grabbed her and swung her around and didn't give a *damn* if she cried assault. "You're not walking away from this, Meg. We stay till we're done."

"Done what? Negotiating?"

"Yeah, okay, call it that!"

She looked at him incredulously. "We're talking about a lifetime commitment, not a trade union contract!"

"Tell me what you want," he said doggedly.

"I've told you! I want *you*! Here!"

"I can't do that," he repeated. "There's no career for me here."

"So you want me to give up everything—my family, my friends, my house, my responsibilities, my *life* . . . what about you?'' she suddenly asked, plunging her hands in the pockets of her yellow windbreaker. ''What are *you* willing to give up?''

''All right,'' he said angrily, because he knew he didn't have much to put on the table. ''How about this? I'll sell the condo. We'll live in a separate house, with a separate yard. We'll get a dog. And a riding mower. And I'll take every minute of my allotted vacation.''

It was starting to rain. In her clinging windbreaker, with her wet ringletted hair, Meg looked like something he'd just fished out of the sea. He didn't care. It was part of her great beauty, that she could lose herself in her concentration on someone else.

He racked his brain thinking of what cops' wives wanted, what Lydia had wanted. ''I can't do squat about the shift rotation,'' he confessed, thinking of the big thing. ''The hours will be screwy. But I *promise* you, Meg, the way I never promised Lydia: I will do my damndest to put you—and ours—first, before the job. Believe me when I say I didn't do that before.''

She was so intent, listening to every word, ignoring the rain that was coming down harder now. Everyone else had cleared out fast. The old man was gone, and all the kids. No one was there but him, her, and the rock.

Instead of answering him, she said with anguish, ''What about Comfort? Who'll be there for her third trimester? What about my dad? He's frail and forgetful. Who'll run the inn? Who'll save the house?''

She rapped off the questions like bullets from an automatic, and she wasn't done yet. ''Who'll stand up to Uncle Billy? Without me here—''

''Hold it, hold it!'' he cried, unwilling to follow her down that road. He took her by her shoulders and yanked her closer to him, resisting the urge to shake some sense into her. *God*, she was a hard sell.

''There will *always* be someone who needs you,'' he said,

at his wits' end. "Can't you see that? You're that kind of woman. It's like there's a sign around your neck: 'Bring me your shy, your needy, your laundry . . .' *I* need you; I'm not denying it. I need you the way—"

He was utterly at a loss for words to describe how he needed her; he made a sound, deep in his throat, of frustration, then bent his face to hers and pulled her into a kiss that left him dizzy with love for her. "Like *that*," he said, his breath ragged. "I need you like that."

So much for the moon and the sun and the stars. All he could give her, all he could lay at her feet, was a kiss.

"Tell me," he demanded hoarsely, "tell me you need *me* like that."

"I *do*," she answered, her eyes red with rimming tears. "But I *can't*. I can't leave everyone and everything behind, any more than that rock can be rolled away from this beach. This is where I belong, Tom. This is who I am."

His gaze followed her outstretched, pointing hand to Balance Rock: there it was, solid and immovable, as much a part of the coastline as the brooding fog that wrapped them both in its embrace. He stared at the rock with loathing; it represented everything about her that he couldn't overcome.

The rain was letting up, but the fog was moving in more closely, gray and misty and somehow magical. He felt empowered by it, and a little crazy.

He swung back to her. "If I move that rock," he asked her suddenly, "will you come with me to Chicago?"

She swept her wet hair away from her tanned face and said, "Are you kidding? It weighs tons."

"Yes or no?"

She laughed in confusion, then said irritatedly, "Yes, Lieutenant. Yes. If you move it, I'll go with you to your godforsaken city."

He nodded, then walked over to the huge, looming boulder and put his shoulder under the overhanging part, ready to roll it back to the damnable sea from which it came. He pushed, straining, until the sweat broke out on his brow, until he could feel the veins in his head and neck popping from the effort, until he felt a hot, searing pain flash through his groin.

And still he pushed at the rock.

"Stop it, stop it!" she screamed, rushing across the pebbly stretch of sand to him. She pulled him away from the boulder, breathless with fury at his antic.

He narrowed his eyes and stared at her from under a glowering brow. "All right . . . It's moved," he said, panting from his exertion. "Now . . . will you come?"

"It hasn't moved," she said, wondering at his claim.

"It has."

"*Prove* it has!" she cried angrily.

"Prove it *hasn't*," he answered, still catching his breath.

"That's impossible. You're impossible!" She threw her hands up in frustration. "This whole thing is impossible!"

He looked at her and shook his head sadly. "But you'll never know that for sure," he said softly. "Will you."

He walked away from her then, ignoring the pain.

CHAPTER 27

In August the Inn Between got a new roof. In September it got two coats of paint. In October most of the guest rooms were refurbished. In November they found a buyer for the dollhouse. And in December, on the stormy night before the new owners were to crate the dollhouse and its tiny furnishings for eventual shipment to the Dallas Doll Museum, Gordon Camplin ran off the side of a mountain in his Mercedes, which exploded on impact in a fiery crash.

The news stunned the residents of Bar Harbor, no one more than Meg Hazard. She'd been in the kitchen, brooding over a cup of bergamot tea and listening to the storm lash out in fury at the quiet, mostly empty house, when the phone rang.

She heard Comfort pick it up in the other room. A few minutes later, Comfort, almost nine months pregnant, waddled into the kitchen as pale as a sheet.

"He's dead," she said in a gasp. "Gordon Camplin's dead!"

Instantly a weight the size of Balance Rock began rolling off Meg. She felt no joy or satisfaction in the news of Camplin's death; she just felt . . . lighter. "Tell me what happened," she said without emotion.

Comfort's facts were sketchy. She'd got them from Lloyd, who'd heard the news on the scanner during his poker game.

One of the guys called the station, and that was how they learned whose car it was. Comfort, clearly upset, went over to the sink and peered through the window at the pounding sleet.

"Why was he back in Bar Harbor, anyway?" she wondered aloud. "Dorothea's trial won't be for months. Do you think this is related to the dollhouse leaving?"

"I don't know, Comfort," Meg said patiently.

"Do you think there was a guiding hand behind this? Do you think it was just a coincidence?"

"I don't know," Meg repeated.

"Yes, you *do*!" Comfort shot back. "You understand what this is about better than anyone!" She lowered her voice to a reverential whisper and added, *"You've seen across the veil."*

"Well, the veil's become a sheet of plywood lately," Meg answered tiredly. "I haven't seen a thing. I haven't felt a thing. Nothing."

"That's not good, to feel nothing," Comfort said, reading new meaning into Meg's words. With her legs planted broadly apart, she lowered herself into the armchair at the table, doing her best to balance the load she bore. She rubbed her hands idly, almost protectively over her belly, as if she was afraid that evil forces were on the loose now.

"I'm fine, Comfort," Meg said, forcing a smile of well-being. "But how about you? Are you okay? That baby is shaping up to be a twenty-pounder, it looks like."

"I know," Comfort said, looking down at herself. "I look too far along, don't I? But so far, so good," she said with a nervous smile.

"Go to bed, honey," Meg coaxed. "The kids are asleep, Dad's asleep. I'll wait for Lloyd. I'm up, anyway."

"Oh, I'm not worried—not *really*," Comfort said. "Lloyd's a good driver. He's a good man," she added softly. "I'm glad he gets to do this once a month." She pulled a chair closer to use as a handrail, then hauled herself to her feet and padded off to bed.

Meg sat awhile with the news of Gordon Camplin's death, wondering what it all meant. Like everything else in her life lately, it seemed to mean nothing. There seemed no point or purpose to it, just as there'd been no point or purpose to rushing to fix up the Inn Between. (At the moment they had two guests. You'd need a crystal castle to lure more than that in December, and that was a fact.)

She went into the sitting room with her mug of tea, to bid the dollhouse good-bye. The sitting room—double parlors joined by an arched entryway—was large enough to hold the dollhouse, which Uncle Billy had insisted be removed from the shed so that it could be properly presented to potential buyers.

And, really, it did look wonderful in the Victorian setting. It was displayed at the far end of the room, flanked by newly slipcovered wing chairs. From there it cast its light down the long double parlor at a fresh-cut Christmas tree that stood, decorated and magical in its own right, in the bay window opposite. Comfort had turned off all the lamps, leaving only the tree and the dollhouse to illuminate the rooms.

It was early in the month to have the tree up, but Comfort—who was following her own inner holiday clock—had wanted to be able to trim it and enjoy it with plenty of time to spare. The baby was due on the twenty-seventh, although everyone except the twins was hoping for Christmas Eve.

Comfort had been knitting in her favorite stuffed chair; her half-a-sweater and needles were on the tufted hassock where she'd left them to answer the phone. Meg put away the knitting in Comfort's needlepoint sewing bag, and thumbtacked a pine garland back in place above the arched entry. She looked around the dimly lit, freshly wallpapered rooms with their old but charming furnishings and thought, *How could he not want to run an inn?*

Then she walked, not without trepidation, to the other end of the sitting rooms and pulled up one of the slipcovered chairs nearer the dollhouse. She'd spent many late nights during the fall in that chair, gazing into the little house, letting her thoughts drift aimlessly. Most of the time she'd been too sad to focus on the crimes, too sad to focus on vengeance. She'd thought only of Tom, and sometimes of Allie. And after a while, she became too sad to think of anything much at all. She would just stare at the little gabled structure and . . . stare.

Just as she was doing now.

It did look pretty. Comfort had insisted that they decorate the dollhouse, too, for the holidays, and had bought a tiny artificial tree for the drawing room that she'd trimmed with red rickrack and decorated with earrings of hers and Meg's. At the top she'd pinned a tiny gold star, snitched from a garland on the real tree. The dollhouse tree was as primitive as could be, and not only that, but it wasn't even to scale. Meg loved it.

She was relieved to see that she felt nothing of Gordon Camplin's presence. It was over, then. A half-century-old injustice had been put to rest, and the dollhouse could do what it was originally intended to do: enchant and delight kids of all generations.

She inhaled the rich, floral aroma of her bergamot tea and thought wistfully, *So why am I not happy?*

Everything was going so well. Comfort was breezing through her pregnancy, and Lloyd had found a temporary job on a low-income housing rehab project. Timmy was doing standout work in school, and Terry was knuckling down to his books at last. Her father had leveled off at a certain degree of forgetfulness, which wasn't too distressing, and Allie was keeping in touch, writing regularly about the lifestyles of the rich and famous. They'd know more when Bobby got back.

And Tom? Although he and Meg had had no contact—obviously they could never be just friends—Meg had read that the Chicago superintendent of police had declared his candidacy for the mayoral race, leaving room for those below him to move up a rung on the ladder. So Tom's career, almost by default, was right on track.

And it's driving you crazy, isn't it?

"What?" Meg broke out of her reverie and sat bolt upright in her chair.

You'd be happier if he fell on his nose and came out east.

Meg swung her head around left and right. She was alone in the sitting room. She took a deep breath and blinked hard.

That way, you could be in complete control. You'd have everything, then: your old life and a new husband. With any luck, Allie might even come back.

Meg jumped up from the chair, upsetting her cup and spilling the dregs of her bergamot tea on the worn Oriental carpet. "Who is this?" she whispered, cocking one ear as she waited for an answer.

She heard nothing; only the ticky-ticky-ticky of the walnut mantel clock and the soft hiss of the radiator. She walked entirely around the dollhouse, peering in each of its windows and scanning the open end, watching and listening for some sign. The dollhouse was charming and pretty, truly delightful. But that was all. She heard no psychic echoes of any kind. She felt sure of it.

She sucked in her breath and let it out, then bit her lip thoughtfully. The nursemaid doll was still in the nursery. Meg reached in and moved the armoire that served as a barricade against the nursery door. There was no need, anymore.

They're all sick of you, you know.

"Who is?" Meg said in a gasp, dropping the armoire and stepping back.

Your family. They're sick of your moping and drooping and pining. You make them feel guilty. They want you to go.

"Go? Where?"

To him. They'd rather have you happy and gone than joyless and here.

"Who are you?" Meg whispered, even though she knew.

Hark your noise and listen to me, child! Do you think men like him grow on every bush?

The voice, a female's, was all around her or inside her; it was hard to tell. But it wasn't coming from the dollhouse. "Is it . . . Margaret Atwells?" Meg said softly, hardly daring to say the name.

You're frustrated as a cut cat. That's what's wrong with you. You've done all you can here, and now you sit, waiting for tourists. Give it up, girl. This place will never pay for itself year-round. Your brother has found outside work. His wife will have to find it, too. And they will, if you let them.

"*I'm* not holding anyone back," Meg said defensively.

You're holding everyone back. Let them be. See what happens.

"Where are you? Tell me where you are." Meg's voice cracked with urgency. When no one answered, she calmed herself back down and whispered, "Are you all right, now that Gordon Camplin . . . now that . . ."

Oh, him. He wasn't worth the powder it took to blow him to hell.

"But what he did to you! He was depraved!"

The voice that answered was serene and amused, and utterly, radiantly joyful. *Do you think that matters to me now? Oh, my dear child, it does not.*

"You're happy, then," Meg murmured, sighing with relief.

As it's in your own power to be.

"Do you think so? Truly?"

Comfort will be fine, but hold Lloyd's hand. He's always been a bit spleeny.

"Lloyd? What does *he* have to do with—"

"Meggie!" It was Comfort's voice, almost giddily shrill.

Comfort was standing in the kitchen doorway with her coat on. Her little tan suitcase was at her side. Her face twisted in pain, then eased into an angelic smile. "Meggie—it looks like I'll be home for Christmas!"

Lloyd was more than spleeny; he was a nervous wreck from start to very near the finish. He worried about the storm outside, that it was a bad omen. He worried about the contractions—that they were too far apart, then that they were too close together. And when Comfort got loud, he panicked and began mumbling "it's a breech, it's a breech" over and over until the nurse took him aside and knocked some sense into him. Meg had to split her hand-holding between patient and partner; she did it with a sense of awe and privilege.

When the baby's head appeared—which it did in pretty short order, despite Lloyd's fears—that was when Lloyd let himself get into the ecstasy and joy of the birth of six pounds, nine ounces of pure, feminine wonder.

Through freely flowing tears, Meg watched as the doctor placed the baby in Comfort's open arms. Lloyd, calm now and proud, whispered, "Little Sally Atwells. It do fit. What do you think, mother?"

Comfort, her face transfigured with a happiness that Meg had never known, said softly, "It's a real good name. Isn't she beautiful?"

"Shoo-er," Lloyd crooned, filling the baby's tiny, tiny hand with his finger. "But then, the apple don't fall far from the tree." He kissed his wife's sweaty brow. "Her ma's a beautiful woman."

Meg left the birthing room not long after that, leaving the new parents to cherish their moment, and went back home where she woke up her father and let him know that all was well. After that she went into Terry and Timmy's room and told them that they had a new little sister to teach how to fish and play ball.

And after that, although it was not quite dawn, she went for a walk. There was no way she was going to fall asleep anytime soon; too much had happened in the last few hours. She felt overwhelmed by events and needed to walk off some of her excess emotion.

She put on a down parka and a wool cap and wrapped herself in the image of little Sally Atwells to keep herself warm as she slipped outside into the piercing December cold. The vicious nor'easter had blown itself out at last, replaced by a frosty, star-studded clearing. The wind still howled, but it was the kind of howl that any fisherman knew would soon die down.

Meg flipped up the hood of her parka and pulled on her mittens, then began walking briskly along deserted streets toward a downtown that would look not much busier at midday. Bar Harbor in December: the best-kept secret in New England. Shops—the ones that stayed open all year—were trimmed in gold and silver, red and green, for the holidays. But the lights inside were kept low, because in winter it was hard to pay the bills.

She thought of her last walk with Tom. It seemed more like four years than four months. What would he think of the place now, she wondered, approaching the shore—so desolate, so wild, so unforgiving. She imagined other islands in other lands, ringed by warm sand and swaying palm trees.

Maine was a hard, hard place.

Inevitably, her steps took her down the Shore Path. She had refused herself the luxury of a walk there ever since August— and ever since August, she had resented Tom for it. He'd ruined the Shore Path for her, ruined Acadia, ruined the little closet-bedroom he slept in his first night in Maine. He'd ruined the corner chair at the dining room table, ruined the bird feeder in her favorite part of the garden, ruined the little metal car in the Monopoly game. The front lawn, the screen door, the back shed—ruined. As for the cabin in the woods, she couldn't *imagine* going back to it, not if it were the last dwelling on earth.

All the ghosts were gone now but one—and he wasn't a ghost at all, despite his presence everywhere she went.

Balance Rock lay ahead, gray and solitary and indomitable. Meg approached it with a heavy heart, unwilling to relive their last exchange there. And yet she felt driven to it, she didn't know why. It had something to do with the last few hours. But so much had happened in the last few hours. How could she begin to sort it out?

I can't leave everyone and everything behind, she'd told him. *Any more than that rock can be rolled away from this beach.*

She stopped on the salt-coated footpath, drinking in the icy, newly cleansed air, and stared at the rock, gray and solitary and—moved.

No way, was her first thought. *It must be the light.* The dawn was pink and blue and compressed, a December dawn. Still, there was plenty of light, if you knew what you were looking for. Meg walked around the boulder, pushing at it from this direction and that, feeling perfectly dumb as she did it. She thought of Tom, and his heroic effort to persuade her. *It hasn't moved*, she'd insisted.

Fool.

Maybe, was her second, heart-thumping thought. But how to be sure? She stuffed her mittens in her pocket and began an awkward, unfamiliar scramble up the rock. *Different.* The handholds weren't in their usual place. When she got to the top and sat there looking out at the whitecapped, roiling sea, that was when she felt it: Balance Rock was still balanced, but on a different edge.

"I was *wrong!*" she cried, throwing her arms out elatedly to the dawn. "You were *right!*"

The blackness of Lake Michigan exploded into a fairyland of twinkling amber as Meg's plane passed over the lake's shore on its way to O'Hare Airport.

Magic: for as far as she could see, for miles and miles and miles, lights shimmered and danced on a blanket of snow. So this was Chicago. It was so much bigger, so much vaster, than anything she'd ever known; how would she ever find him?

Dammit; why couldn't he be listed in the phone book like everyone else? All she had was his business card, the one she'd stolen from the top of Terry's bureau. She took it out of her purse and read it again, for the thousandth time: LIEUTENANT THOMAS WYLER, COMMANDING OFFICER, VIOLENT CRIMES. A station address and the phone number, and that was it.

When she'd called the number, she'd got a sergeant who knew her name, which had pleased her immeasurably. She had been hoping he'd say, "Hey, here's his home phone; call him there." But the sergeant hadn't offered it, and she hadn't quite dared to ask for it. Instead, she'd made up a story about surprising him and would the sergeant please not mention that she'd called?

In the course of that conversation she'd learned that Tom was delivering a guest lecture at De Paul University on Thursday night, and so that became her plan: to surprise him after his talk there. (All in all, she'd rather be embarrassed in front of a bunch of kids than in front of a bunch of cops.)

After her plane landed she stepped into a cab and said, "De Paul University; I'm in a hurry, please." Her life became a nip-and-tuck battle with the clock as the cab alternately crawled and crept toward its destination. The *traffic!* She had no *idea!* It all looked so *close* on the road atlas!

She said this many, many times to the cabdriver. Eventually he said, "Lady, if you want to get out and walk, I'll give you your money back." After that she shut up. If that was how these big-city types were, then *fine.* She knew it. She just knew it.

One little detail she'd forgotten to nail down was the building where Tom was delivering his lecture. She'd assumed that she would have time to find that out. As it turned out, she had seven minutes left before he'd be gone.

Frantic by now, she blurted some incoherent version of her problem to the cabbie, who broke into a broad grin and said, "No kiddin'? He's a copper? My cousin's a copper. Hey, we'll find 'im."

How he managed it, Meg never quite remembered, but it involved a security guard and high-speed runs at three different buildings. Tom was in the last one. Meg and Conrad—good friends by now—peeked through the small square windows in the doors of the packed lecture hall.

"Zat him?"

"Oh, my God, yes," she said, stunned. "He looks so . . . *real*."

"What, real; he looks like he's supposed to look. Like a cop."

"He does, doesn't he," Meg agreed, taking in the gray suit, light shirt, and dark tie. Even from outside the room, she could see that he was in complete command. The class was hanging on his every word. He said something she couldn't hear; his audience broke out in laughter.

She backed away from the window and closed her eyes. What a *stupid* idea, surprising him. What could she say? *Take me back? I've changed my mind?* What if he'd changed *his*? Who knew? And yet, the thought of asking him on the phone had been even stupider.

"I can't do it. I can't go in there," she said flatly.

"Sure you can. What's the big deal?"

"There are too many people around. I have no idea how he's going to react."

"Hey, you don't know them and they don't know you. That's one of the upsides to living in a big city."

"I'll wait 'till they all leave," she decided.

"No good," said Conrad, rubbing his stubby beard. "He

might leave with them. You got to go right up there, show your face, let him clear everyone out.''

"Maybe it'd be better to do this at the station."

Conrad snorted. "Yeah. Right."

Meg took a deep breath. "Okay, here's what I'm willing to do: Go in, stand in back, if he starts to leave with the class I'll raise my hand."

"I can live with that," said the cabbie. "Well—I'm outta here," he said with a fatherly smile. "Good luck. If you have a Polish band, invite me to the wedding. My cab number's one hundred sixty-three."

Impulsively, Meg threw her arms around him and hugged him. "Thanks, Conrad," she said. "Is everyone here like you?"

He laughed. "Whaddya think? We're New York?"

He left. Clutching her carry-on bag and dragging her parka, Meg slipped into the back of the packed room and got swallowed up in the standing-room-only crowd. Tom said into the mike, "One last question; we're running over."

A young woman dressed in a bulky sweater and jeans stood up and said, "You've said that all the police can do is attack the *symptoms* of illness in our society. Can you tell us what you think is the single biggest factor in finding a *cure* for that illness?"

He didn't say anything right away. Meg could see that he was struggling with the answer, that he wanted to get it right for them.

"Parents," he said at last. "If a kid nowadays has two parents who are involved—really involved—with him, then that kid has a jump start on the rest of society. If he has one parent who really cares, he's still in pretty good shape. An older sibling, a relative, a role model on the block—all of them matter, all of them can make a difference.

"Whoever it is, he or she has to love the kid enough to teach him right from wrong. And that takes a lot of work, a lot of one-on-one effort. When you're in the middle of a divorce, looking for a job, fighting an addiction, setting up a new household—who has the time? You've got to *find* the time, *find* the energy. You can't just cross your fingers or leave it to the 'experts.' You can't just leave a child to raise himself.''

He added thoughtfully, ''I used to think that the right kid, with a break or two his way, could still make it on his own. Not anymore. A kid today doesn't have a chance if someone's not right on top of him. You can reform the schools, add new teachers, rate TV for violence, design new national programs; but government can only do so much.

''It all starts at home,'' he said quietly. ''At *home*. Thank you and good night.''

The class applauded warmly, then began filing out. A huddle formed around Tom, a multiracial group made up mostly of women, earnest and concerned.

But where were the ones who needed to hear what he had to say? They were somewhere else, caught up in the very struggles Tom had rattled off. Meg sighed, thinking of her own family, thinking how incredibly lucky she was.

He knew she was there, of course. She'd seen him glance up once in her direction, then flush deeply and turn his attention to the next questioner. Eventually the huddle began to thin and melt away, like fog on a hot summer morning, until there was only her, only him.

As if she'd seen him just hours ago, she said, ''I like what you said at the end. I wish I'd got here earlier to hear the rest.''

He matched her apparent sense of calm, smiling that wry smile of his as he gathered up his notes. ''Heck, I could've faxed these off to you and saved you a bundle.''

Her cheeks turned bright scarlet. ''Oh, that's all right,'' she said lightly. ''We've sold the dollhouse. We're rich. Compared to what we were, anyway.''

He looked up from his briefcase. His eyes glittered with

unfathomable emotion as he said, "That's great. So things are
working out for you. The Inn Between'll be the showpiece of
Bar Harbor."

She'd been standing a few feet from him, assuming or hoping—she didn't know which—that he would gather her in his
arms and kiss her madly and that words wouldn't be necessary. But this wasn't the movies. He was leery of her, she
could see that. She'd jerked him around once too often.

She walked over to a desk and sat at it; it'd been a very long
time. "The Inn Between does look wonderful," she conceded,
smoothing her hands over the Formica, trying the desk on for
size. "We worked like dogs on it all through fall." *At least it
made the time pass.* "But—it's still empty. I doubt that we'll
bother staying open next winter."

"Really," he said, a little sharply. But his next words were
said almost with a shrug. "Maybe you need to advertise."

"Are you *kidding*?" she asked, genuinely incredulous.
"For a while we were on the front page of every tabloid in the
country!"

"I meant something more like *The New York Times*," he
said ironically, picking up an eraser and wiping the black-
board clean.

"Gee, I don't know why. If you planned to stay somewhere,
wouldn't *you* pick the place where the innkeeper had two
heads?"

He laughed, and so did she, remembering the brief insanity
of it all.

"Did your uncle ever nail down that contract for movie of
the week?" he asked, still smiling.

"Oh, that all fell by the wayside. Which was just as well.
Uncle Billy said he didn't want Brian Dennehy playing him,
anyway; too fat. I think he was holding out for Sean Con-
nery."

Tom sat on a corner of the desk behind the lectern. "And
Comfort?" he asked, a little hesitantly.

"Ah! I should've told you!" said Meg, her face lighting up with pleasure. "She had a beautiful, beautiful girl—Sally Mary Atwells."

"Hey, that *is* great news. Did everything go all right?" Tom asked, obviously remembering their fears.

"The baby slipped out smooth as a smelt," Meg said cheerfully. "Comfort brought her home the day before yesterday. Wait—I have a picture here somewhere." Meg lifted her handbag onto the desk and began rummaging through it with both hands. "It's a cute shot: Sally's on their bed, with a flyrod lying alongside her for scale. That was Dad's idea. He—"

"*Meg*," Tom said sharply, grabbing both her wrists. "What the *hell* is going on here?"

Wincing from the blast of his vehemence, Meg said in a small voice, "I just thought you might like to see the photo—"

"Forget the goddamned photo! What are you doing back in my *life*, for God's sake!"

He yanked her up from her desk as if she were an impossibly frustrating student and held her, still by her wrists, close to him. His breath fell hot on her face and his eyes glittered with fury. Meg thought of dragons; she considered retreat.

"W-well, it's Christmas," she said, uttering the first thing that popped into her head.

"Yeah, it's Christmas—and last month it was Thanksgiving and the month before that, Halloween. You missed Columbus Day, Labor Day, and worst of all, my birthday. I turned forty-one and I turned it without you, goddammit. You missed four full moons, one of them a harvest moon that hung over the lake in the most . . . ridiculously heartbreaking way. You missed three great concerts in Grant Park, and you missed waking up in my arms every single morning between August eighth and"—he let go of her wrist and held up his watch—

"today, December fourteenth. So why here, Meg? Why now?"

Reeling from the onslaught of his words and the agony in his voice, she said breathlessly, "I . . . the rock. It moved."

His eyes narrowed an infinitesimal amount. "Balance Rock?"

She nodded. "The morning that Sally was born, I took a walk on the Shore Path. It's definitely moved. Everyone says so. Then, too, there was the . . . voice. It came right before Sally. But after Gordon Camplin. Oh—"

"I know about him," Tom said, dismissing him. "Tell me why you're here, Meg. In plain English. Because I can't stand this much longer," he warned in a voice that was raw with tension.

She leaned her forehead against his chest and spoke into his striped tie as if it were a microphone. "In plain English, then: I love you. I love you more than anyone else in my life. I can live without everyone else—without Allie!—but I can't live without you. I tried, and I made myself miserable, not to mention everyone around me. And before you ask—I can live without Maine. But not," she whispered, vanquished, "without you."

When he said nothing she felt as if she'd taken a headlong dive down a flight of stairs. If he didn't catch her she'd be forced to take her broken bones and her broken heart back to Bar Harbor and finish out her life an emotional cripple.

She lifted her gaze to his. He had a grin on his face that reminded her of a kid who's caught a home run ball that went into the bleachers.

He held her face between his hands. "It took you four full moons to figure that out?"

He lowered his soft, open lips to hers as she closed her eyes for the kiss. She'd waited so long for this. Every night when she closed her eyes, and whenever in the day she closed her eyes, she imagined it: the warm, soft, totally erotic caress of his mouth on hers, of his tongue seeking hers. If it were possible for a kiss to substitute for making love, then this was such a kiss.

"But . . . if I hadn't come?" she asked in a ragged whisper when he freed her at last.

In a voice of quiet triumph he said, "Before I'd taken half a dozen steps away from you that day at Balance Rock, I'd resolved to resign my position and find something closer to you. I lucked out: on the first of the year, I begin a new job in Connecticut."

She laughed and kissed him again and said, "I don't know how to tell you this, but from Connecticut to Maine is *not* a practical commute."

He wrapped his arms around her tight and spun her around. "Witch! I know that," he said, his voice starting to register the joy that she'd felt in his kiss. "I'm signing on with a national pilot program that's aimed at retraining problem dropouts. The kids volunteer; they have to show some interest in turning their lives around. It's a promising program, the best thing I've seen so far."

"A kind of boot camp for delinquents," she mused, thinking how perfectly suited Tom was to inspire lost and troubled kids. "I guess Maine's not in the program?"

"Not yet. Coming soon, I have no doubt. But until then," he said, cupping her chin in his hand, "until Maine . . . will you live with me and be my wife?"

She lifted her head and their eyes met. "Until Maine, during Maine, after Maine, without Maine—*yes*," she said, moved inexpressibly by his old-fashioned proposal. "Yes and always."

"Meggie, Meggie . . . I do love you," he whispered.

Somewhere in the course of the next prolonged and passionate kiss, a security guard appeared and escorted them gently out the door. Exhilarated and unembarrassed, they found themselves standing outside the locked building.

"Downtown!" Tom said suddenly. "I want you to see how the big boys do one before we leave it forever."

He drove her downtown, both of them talking and laughing and reminiscing at a mile a minute, and they checked into a hotel overlooking the lake, the park, and the fountain. There they made wild and completely indiscreet love for several hours without having to worry about paper-thin condo walls. They ordered in room service, because Meg had never had room service, and after that they made love again, and after *that*, Meg, still wired, said, "Let's go walking," because she was afraid to fall asleep, afraid that this was another dream, another vision.

It was the middle of the night, and they were virtually alone in a city of four million. They walked down Michigan Avenue hand in hand, peering at the fabulously upscale wares displayed in the windows there, and then went around to State Street, because Tom wanted her to see the Christmas windows at Marshall Field's.

"I've come here every Christmas since I was eight," he said, unable to keep the anticipation out of his voice as they approached the fabled department store. "I'd take an El down here myself and leave hand and noseprints on the windows from one end of the store to the other. I loved the village scenes, the happy families. I was a scruffy little urchin, and sometimes I'd have to panhandle for my return carfare. But I never missed the Christmas display. It gave my life . . . hmm . . . continuity, I guess."

He leaned over as they walked side by side and kissed her lightly, his frosty breath mingling with hers. "Little did I know," he mused, "that I was gazing at my destiny."

They came upon the first window, a traditional Santa's workshop scene, with Santa's elves sawing and hammering and Mrs. Claus serving up cookies to all the help, even the little guy who kept falling on his keister. The next several windows were village scenes, charming idylls where the inn and shopkeepers obviously never had to worry about paying the bills, and the carolers never got mugged. After that was a beautiful, elegant crêche scene—Italian, Tom was certain.

But it was the last window that held Meg and Tom fast in its spell: a collection of dollhouses, each on its own pedestal, beautifully spotlighted and shimmering with their own sophisticated magic. At eye level above the others was the Eagle's Nest with all its gabled rooms aglow. The open side faced away from State Street; one could only peek through the tiny latticed windows.

Meg let out a cry of amazement and pressed her hands and nose against the store window for a closer look, much as Tom must've done in his urchin days.

Tom said softly behind her, "Wherever she is, I hope she's at peace."

Meg turned and slipped her arm through his. "I think she's even happier than *we* are," she said, absurdly happy herself.

Tom squeezed her close. "Impossible."

"Nothing," Meg insisted with a grin, "is impossible."

Epilogue

Allegra St. John tapped the cabdriver on the shoulder and said, "Stop! Pull into that space!"

The driver said, "Sure, miss; but the Inn Between's another few blocks yet. You won't be wantin' to walk, not with all them packages you got with you."

"Thank you. I don't intend to," she said impatiently. She pointed to the painted sign that hung over blue-and-white-checked café curtains in a small restaurant window: *Comfort's Kitchen*. "Do you know whether that's owned by Comfort Atwells?" she asked.

"Yeah, sure; Lloyd's wife. Now that I think on it, you might be takin' your suppers there. They got some tie-in with the Inn Between. Make sure you ask for a meal voucher when you register. You don't want to miss Comfort's steamed blueberry pudding; her hard sauce is wicked good."

Allie thought about marching into the café then and there, but the place was packed. Besides, she didn't want Comfort calling ahead and ruining the surprise.

So. Comfort got her restaurant after all. Allie smiled and said, "You can keep going."

The driver pulled out of the space and Allie settled back, more nervous now than at any time since the day a month ago when she decided to fly back to the States. In some ways the decision had been made for her: when one has reached the absolute bedrock of boredom; when one's husband has been sighted on a private beach with a nubile thing half one's own age; when one has tried it, spent it, seen it, toured it, swum it, and skied it. . . .

That's when a girl wants to come back home. If for no other reason than to find out how long and how far she's been gone.

Allie closed her eyes, shutting out the last five years. She took a deep breath, then unclasped her Hermès bag and slipped out a gold compact, snapping its lid open with a practiced motion. Deep violet eyes stared back at her, reassuring her that thirty was an age that only other people looked.

Her face was flushed but untanned, despite her Mediterranean lifestyle. She'd used sunblock before sunblock was all the rage, and had worn long, flowing coverups while competing ingenues skipped across the hot sand in little more than dental floss.

She'd driven more than one man wild with curiosity in the bargain.

She retouched her lip gloss and began mentally going over the presents she'd brought with her. Too many? Would it look as if she was trying to buy her way back into the family's affection? She hoped not. The Swiss-made fly reel, the antique gold earrings, the checkers set crafted of ivory and inlaid wood, the funky solid-silver sheriff's badge that she'd found in a Paris flea market—could anyone really object to such small, discreet trifles?

Possibly the French doll with its couturier-filled trunk was a little extravagant—but Sally must be old enough by now to enjoy it. And Terry and Timmy—teenagers; it was so hard to believe—could either use the Gucci wallets or throw them away, but they should be exposed to *something* besides Velcro-clad nylon to keep their money in.

Allie sighed a jittery sigh and looked around. They were turning onto her old street. She regarded it not as a street of smart and pretty bed-and-breakfasts, but as it was in the old, old days, peely and friendly and a real neighborhood. She thought of Bobby Beaufort, who'd made a tree house and let only her in, no one else. The tree, a towering oak, was still there; she had no idea where Bobby was. When he got back from Switzerland after that wild, wild visit, he'd upped and got someone named Cora pregnant, and presumably he was with her still.

That news had come in a letter from Meg, the last one Allie had had the heart to answer, over four years ago. After that, Allie had fallen off the edge of . . . somewhere. Into . . . something. It was all such a blur now.

But Bobby Beaufort wasn't. She smiled as she remembered the week he'd spent with her in St. Moritz, when she'd broken away from Dmitri and holed up with him at The Palace. What a pair they'd made! She in her Milan knock-offs, he in his funeral suit, stepping through the hotel's carved portal and down the seven fabled steps that led to The Restaurant, where princesses and playboys looked up and then down their noses at them.

The sex had been phenomenal, the best she'd ever had, and it lasted until the money Bobby got from selling the Harley ran out. After that he went back to Maine and apparently found Cora. And after Bobby—because of Bobby—Allie met St. John.

The cab pulled up in front of the Inn Between and she was suddenly reminded of Tom Wyler's Cutlass and the way her heart pitter-pattered when she saw it parked in the same spot. Was it possible?

The cabdriver began unloading her things on the curb. Allie raised one eyebrow and said, "Bring everything inside, please." She paid him generously and, without waiting, walked up the porch—the veranda—of the Inn Between.

She stepped into the hall, the hall that had once seemed so wide and spacious to her: new wallpaper, new carpet, an added stick or two not quite old enough to be antique. It was much the same.

No one came out to greet her. *Nothing's changed*, she thought, irrationally pleased. She looked around for the little service bell provided for the guests, the one she used to bang whenever she came in the front door, and found it almost hidden on a linen-draped side cabinet. She took a deep, deep breath, then raised a perfectly manicured hand and brought it down on the bell with a *pain-n-n-ng*.

The next sound she heard was the high shriek of a child, followed by clump-clump footsteps running in her direction from the back rooms.

"Rachel, honey, no, no!" came Meg's voice, gay and laughing. "That's not Daddy. Daddy won't be here until suppertime—"

A two-year-old with a mop of chestnut-brown hair and big hazel eyes stopped short when the tall woman with jet-black hair standing before her turned out not to be her daddy. Stuffing one hand in her mouth, Rachel looked up at Allie appraisingly, then laughed at her silly mistake, turned on her heel abruptly, and clump-clumped back toward the kitchen.

Two seconds later, the tiny innkeeper was back again, pulling her mother by the skirt. *Customer*! was written all over Rachel's fat-cheeked little face.

Allie laughed, then looked past the toddler at her mother, who was holding a carbon copy, only shyer, in her arms.

"Meg—*twins*," she said softly, tears springing to her eyes.

"Allie!"

"I'm home, Meggie," said her younger sister. "I'm home."

Elizabeth Adler

The Rich Shall Inherit
☐ 20639-1 $4.99

Léonie
☐ 14662-3 $4.99

Peach
☐ 20111-X $5.99

The Property Of A Lady
☐ 21014-3 $5.99

Fortune Is A Woman
☐ 21146-8 $5.99

Legacy Of Secrets
☐ 21657-5 $5.99